THE SAPPHIRE ODYSSEY

THE SAPPHIRE ODYSSEY

By Peter Shokeir

First paperback edition March 2024

Book design by CoverKitchen

ISBN 978-1-7386765-2-1 (paperback)

ISBN 978-1-7386765-3-8 (ebook)

www.petershokeir.com

PROLOGUE

Today was perhaps the worst day of Katelyn's life.

Her father had died less than three weeks ago, yet she was already being crowned the new British monarch. Hordes of paparazzi and insincere mourners had been harassing her nonstop. The Western Union was the worst. A monarch would normally be crowned at least several months after the previous had one died, but after King Reginald's passing, the Western Union had insisted on fast-tracking the coronation. The occupation had taken a turn for the worse due to the recent inception of the United Third, so in order to boost morale, Katelyn would immediately be crowned Britain's new queen, another figurehead to promote the cause.

Katelyn wore a flowing white gown with blue gems gleaming around her neck. All her friends had been awed by her dress. She just found it hot and scratchy. It was originally planned that she would wear red velvet, but since red was often considered the color of the Chinese Empire, the Western Union had rejected the idea.

Worst of all, Katelyn would have to carry around her baby boy for the entire coronation. It was definitely a crowd-pleaser to see a queen cradle her adorable heir, but she despised the idea of all those strange eyes on her child. Not only that, but she was expected to keep her fussy baby well-behaved for the entire afternoon, which would be even more difficult than normal amid the flashing cameras and cheering crowds.

The only thing that made it all bearable was her husband, Michael. Looking as handsome as ever, he sat next to her in the horse-drawn coach, bouncing the baby in his lap and making babbling noises. Katelyn smiled, finding new strength. Her marriage had been a major battle that the Western Union had lost in its never-ending war to control her life. The officials didn't want her to marry a Kenyan for fear of appearing too "friendly" with the natives of the Occupied Territories, but she had put her foot down and even alerted the media. When public opinion took her side, the officials relented, one of her few victories, and whenever she looked at her new husband, she felt victorious.

Their coach pulled up to the curb. It took all the police's effort to hold back the spectators. Ten walkers stood around the edges of the crowd. These particular mechas had only nonlethal weapons installed but remained formidable, nonetheless.

Katelyn walked out of the coach, followed by her husband, who handed her the baby and gave her a kiss. The crowd cheered as she cradled the baby in her arms. She did her best to smile and wave with her free hand, but she didn't feel the joy. The Queen's Guard, wearing tall bearskin hats and red uniforms, stood at attention along her path with rifles. The coach had taken her to the Victoria Tower Gardens, near the Palace of Westminster and right on the edge of the River Thames. London had a light rain just yesterday, so the trees were glistening. The grass was a bright green as well, though one couldn't tell, since hundreds of people filled the park to the brim, countless shoes flattening the greenery beneath their soles.

After several minutes of waving and walking, Katelyn stepped onto the stage. The crowd cheered for a full minute before calming down. The soon-to-be queen of the United Kingdom would give a speech, written by the Western Union, before going to Westminster Abbey for the coronation itself. She cleared her throat and began to speak.

"Good day to you, my beloved people," she said into a microphone. "Today is the day of my coronation, a day of—"

But then she stopped, for the crowd had begun to murmur nervously. She saw her security team running to the stage with their firearms drawn. The walkers also raised their weapons. Everyone was on high alert. The baby started to cry, but Katelyn didn't seem to notice. She turned to where the crowd was pointing. It all seemed to happen in slow motion, every detail etched into her mind for all eternity.

A walker stood behind her with a raised fist.

Katelyn found herself incapable of movement or any reaction. She was only conscious of the weight in her arms and her own heartbeat.

Michael ran toward his wife and son and plowed into them just as the fist came down. Katelyn was shoved off the stage. Woodchips flew through the air as the blow demolished the stage and flattened her husband.

"No!" Katelyn wanted to cry, but she hit the ground with the air knocked out of her. The other walkers began to fire tear gas and nets into the crowd. The horses neighed in terror and thrashed about. The mass of people screamed and ran away, impeding the security personnel attempting to get to the queen.

"What are you doing?" a guard yelled at the walkers.

"I don't have control!" one pilot cried as his walker shot more canisters of tear gas.

Feet came down around Katelyn's head. She was unable to move, and her vision was blurry. She could not make out the face of the individual who snatched the wailing baby out of her hands and disappeared into the panicked mass of spectators.

The only ones who could have spotted the perpetrator were the three police unicopters hovering above the Palace of Westminster. But then, without warning, the unicopters powered down. The pilots tried to regain control, but they kept losing altitude. Two of them smashed into the River Thames. The third crashed into Big Ben, causing the tower to cave in. Rubble rained down on the streets. Pedestrians screamed and dove for cover.

Meanwhile, the kidnapper had escaped.

Katelyn came to. Most of the crowd was gone, and security was running around trying to control the situation. She weakly stood up to find her husband dead in a pile of broken wood, himself broken, nearly unrecognizable and most certainly dead. Not only that, but her baby was gone. All she was able to do was let out a sorrowful moan.

Today was truly the worst day of Katelyn's life.

CHAPTER 1

Half a dozen corpses were wrapped in cloth. Weights had been tied to their feet. General Eisenhorn watched from a distance as the bodies were thrown into the sea one by one. The general was getting on in years. His hair had grayed, his skin had sagged, and his eyes had become milky and full of antagonism. The only reminders of his once-proud past were his stain-covered green uniform and peaked cap.

"Why give terrorists such a nice funeral?" Hank Powers asked. "It's a waste of time, if you ask me. Just burn them in a pile or something."

"Moron!" Eisenhorn snapped. "It's our duty to show these cretins how classy we military men are. We aren't savages. Show some integrity."

Powers was an American ex-marine who many considered crass and annoying. He was tall, covered in thick muscles, and sported a shaved head and a black horseshoe mustache. He also sounded a lot like a pro wrestler. Right now, he was teaching cadets on the USS *Liberation*, the ship that Eisenhorn had been staying on for the past six months. The two men seemed to enjoy each other's company, despite their constant arguing. Truth be told, Eisenhorn found that Powers made his situation a bit more bearable. At least he spoke plainly, though perhaps too plainly for others.

"I just don't understand why we can't bury them in the desert," Powers said.

"Burying them is too much effort," Eisenhorn growled. "The ocean is good enough."

"Ha! You're one to talk about class."

"We give terrorists burials at sea to prevent their graves from becoming shrines," a new voice said. "Both of you should know that."

Powers recognized the voice and immediately stood to attention. "Sir, my apologies! I didn't know you were on board the *Liberation*."

"Good to know you still have some humility," Redwood said. The fleet admiral of the Western Union Navy usually didn't announce where he was going so that he could give his men surprise inspections. Adam Redwood, who wore a white uniform, also had a goatee and deep wrinkles on his cheeks. This man was not only the fleet admiral of the navy but also the commandant of the Marines and a senior adviser for the Western Union Governing Council. The only person he was answerable to was the head of the Western Union himself.

"Really sorry, sir," Powers said. "I didn't mean to speak ill of the dead."

"Eisenhorn, you're wanted," Redwood said, ignoring the ex-marine.

"I'm always wanted," Eisenhorn barked. "It comes with the burden of being devilishly handsome. Not that you'd know, Dagwood."

Redwood sighed. "Just come with me."

Eisenhorn shrugged and followed Redwood inside the ship, leaving Powers behind on the flight deck. The USS *Liberation*, an aircraft carrier, was currently floating in the Indian Ocean, a hundred nautical miles away from Chinese Empire waters.

It had been six months since Jeffery Johnson died. Johnson had been Eisenhorn's caretaker and had also unofficially run the Bunker, a cadet training facility for children of influential and important individuals. Those same cadets were then slaughtered by the scum who killed weapons manufacturer Ammar Zaidi, demolished a casino full of people, and almost destroyed a multibillion-dollar tower. After the incident, Eisenhorn was sent to live on the USS *Liberation* and had been in "protective custody" ever since.

But this was no vacation. On the contrary, it was rehabilitation. Eisenhorn was severely unbalanced, displaying signs of dementia and post-traumatic stress disorder. A team of psychiatrists had given him constant supervision and drug treatments. They had even made him talk about his feelings, of all fricking things. It was quite an unpleasant experience for the general, but he didn't want to appear weak, so he took it all in stride. The final result of his treatment was a man only slightly better than before. Eisenhorn didn't find himself as confused or irritable, but there was no cure for being a jerk.

Admiral Redwood led Eisenhorn into a room guarded by a pair of marines. The door closed behind them. Eisenhorn almost yelped when he saw the two men who were waiting for them. Both were only holograms, but their presence was nevertheless startling.

"Why, look who it is," one of the men said. "Never thought I'd get to see the old warhorse out of his stable again."

Harold Powell, a sixty-year-old with a soft gut, was the vice president of the United States. Eisenhorn had never liked the man. Powell was a bureaucrat who only had the nerve to work behind the scenes. The only thing Eisenhorn and Powell had in common was their similar view on how enemies of the Western Union should be handled.

But Powell barely registered on Eisenhorn's radar, for his eyes were glued to the second person in the room, the most powerful man in the Western Union.

"Hello, Eisenhorn," the president said bluntly. "Nice to see you haven't died."

Jacob Hynes was the head of the Western Union and the president of the United States. The president had been in office for nearly two decades due to the special war acts that granted him emergency power to extend his term. When looking at Hynes, one could almost see the authority radiate off him. He was black, with a balding head, short beard, and a large frame barely contained by a blue suit. It was rare to see the president looking even remotely amused. Rather, he almost always wore an unimpressed scowl.

"Hynes, you dog!" Eisenhorn yelled with joy. "I haven't seen you in years. Still looks like you got a rod up your—"

"Be quiet," Hynes said. "I am your superior. You shall address me with respect."

Eisenhorn grunted. "You obviously haven't changed."

"But you have. I hardly recognize you. I've been keeping up with your treatment, and I'm quite concerned about your mental state."

"Yeah ... I know. Wish it didn't have to be like this."

"Yes, I wish you weren't the one to carry this burden, but we have no choice."

Eisenhorn cocked his head. "Burden? What are you talking about?"

Hynes folded his hands. "You know I'm not one to mince words, so I'll just tell you. We're sending you to the Chinese Empire."

"Huh? China! What am I going there for?"

"You're going to be our ambassador," Powell told him.

Eisenhorn nearly fell over. "What! Me, the mental patient?"

Hynes maintained his gaze. "Yes, we need a new ambassador."

"What happened to the old one?"

"He's dead," Powell said. "It was a rather untimely demise."

"Well, that settles it! I ain't going."

"Calm down," Hynes said. "There's no need for dramatics."

"You can't be serious. I'm completely unqualified and an old coot to boot."

"You won't be an ambassador in the traditional sense. If anything, you're a political hostage."

"Great, much better," the general scoffed.

"This is not a request. You will do it for the sake of the Western Union and its citizens. Are you not a patriot?"

"You dare question my loyalty? Fine, I'll do it, if you're dumb enough to hire me. But I won't be racially sensitive or pleasant to deal with."

"Don't worry. I didn't expect much from you. The plane leaves next week. You have until then to sort out your affairs. You'll be briefed in more detail once—"

"Wait a second! I want to talk about Cloak."

The grin left Powell's face. Hynes's scowl deepened.

"That information is highly classified," Redwood told Eisenhorn. "I thought—"

"Very well, Eisenhorn," Hynes said. "I will discuss the matter with you."

"Are you insane?" Powell shouted at the president.

"Hold your tongue," Hynes snapped. He turned his attention back to Eisenhorn. "In exchange for this conversation, you must swear secrecy about the matter and perform your duties as the new ambassador diligently."

"Deal," Eisenhorn said. "First off, why did you make those cretins?"

"I didn't make them. That was the work of the previous administration.

The very idea of creating such monsters repulses me."

"Then how come you lied about them on the news? You blamed Slate and those United Third terrorists for all the no-good deeds Cloak did. Trying to cover your ass, is that it?"

Hynes sighed and turned his back to Eisenhorn. The president's hologram flickered for a moment, making him look like a tired spirit. Then he gave an answer.

"Incognito and the United Third have become a serious threat to world stability. Now the Chinese Empire has begun to stir in the east. Our relationship with the empire has never been good, but we have never been closer to all-out war."

"All the more reason not to send me," Eisenhorn squawked.

Hynes huffed and went on. "These enemies of freedom are waiting for our moment of weakness. Now you want us to announce to the world that we committed numerous human rights abuses and made supersoldiers that are responsible for the deaths of thousands? Not only would the morale of our citizens plummet, but our current administration would also be ripped apart. I have no doubt our enemies would take advantage of the ensuing turmoil."

"I can't believe this," Eisenhorn spat. "My comrade has turned into a politician, worst of all a good one. This is coward's talk. The head of the Western Union shouldn't quiver before a couple of terrorists and Chinamen. You have no honor!"

"At least I'm not a sick old man who has pushed away all his friends." Eisenhorn ground his teeth.

"Any more questions?" Hynes asked. "No? Then be gone."

***

"Eisenhorn, slow down," Redwood said, following the general down a corridor. "That was no way to speak to the president."

"He doesn't care," Eisenhorn said, walking even faster. "He doesn't care about those cadets or Johnson. All he cares about are his damn opinion polls."

"You don't get it, do you? The president made you the Chinese ambassador for a number of reasons. You were once one of our finest military leaders, and as someone who served during the Korean Invasion, you also have experience in that region of the world."

"Barely! I just got off the boat and started shooting. And you're right, I was one of the finest. Now I'm just a sick old man. The president himself said so."

"He's under a lot of stress. And to be frank, you can be frustrating."

"Nah, he's gotten cold. He probably didn't even shed a tear for those cadets."

"I'll have you know he was shaken for days after the Bunker attack. He showed particular concern for you, in case you think otherwise. And he's still thinking about your safety. This appointment will protect you from getting stabbed in your sleep."

Eisenhorn stopped in his tracks. "What are you talking about?"

Redwood stopped as well, sighing. "Lots of people are blaming you for what happened at the Bunker, and they're out for blood. Sending you to the Chinese Empire would get you as far away as possible from the Western Union and your enemies."

"I thought the blame was on Slate and Incognito."

"Listen to me. Many people, even those within the government, think those cadets are dead because of your incompetence, maybe even malevolence."

"How dare you! You think I killed them?"

"No, I don't. But it is true that you had a history of what some might consider 'abusive' behavior toward your cadets. There are also concerns about your mental stability."

"Those are sick rumors. They're nothing but the work of the Chinese Empire trying to discredit me. Great, now I'm gonna be an ambassador to them. Oh, swell. Just—"

Neither one of them noticed a thin man in a suit walking up to Eisenhorn until it was too late. The man grabbed the general by his shirt and slammed him into the wall. This assaulter had almost unnatural strength accompanying his twisted look of anguish.

"Why are you still alive?" the man shouted.

The general took a breath of surprise, his eyes becoming alert and focused. Redwood grabbed the attacker from behind, but the man refused to let go.

"My son is dead because of you!" the man went on. "Don't play innocent. You let those thugs kill my son!"

"Marker, let go of him right now or I'll have you arrested," Redwood said.

The man let go. His rage disappeared. He now looked confused and dull. Then, almost moping, the man walked away. Several tears streamed down his face.

"That was ... the secretary of defense," Eisenhorn said, staring at his retreating attacker.

"Yes, Gerald Marker," Redwood said. "You may have known his son."

"Marker..."

"Like I said, you have enemies."

***

Hank Powers whistled tunelessly as he strolled down the hall with a smirk. He had been requested as a part of a special ops mission. It had been several years since he quit the Marines, but he still occasionally assisted the military with his customized walker whenever he wasn't teaching half-baked lessons to cadets or starring in a recruitment ad. But he had grown tired of retirement, forgetting how boring civilian life could be. A special ops mission of this caliber was just what he needed. It would give him the chance to really show off.

He opened the door and walked into the conference room. "Well, look at this. Nobody here except you. You must be my new boss, then."

A blonde woman in a navy uniform stood at the end of the conference table. She had blue eyes and a well-sculpted body. But most people were put off by her utter lack of emotion. Her face was so blank, it looked almost lifeless. Powers didn't notice this. His observation skills were not something to brag over.

"I am glad you could come," Camilla Ryder said in a vacant voice. "This mission is an essential one that may determine the balance of world power."

"Yeah, whatever," Powers said. "So, why did you find the need to call on yours truly? This better be good, because I don't have time for pansy missions."

"I assure you that this is of the utmost importance. We have been tasked with the capture of the Helmet Man."

CHAPTER 2

osi kept marching on. The men with guns yelled at him and the rest of the captives to move faster. There were about a hundred villagers and only half that number of soldiers, but these soldiers were well fed and heavily armed.

The savannah was covered in never-ending brown grass and the occasional tree. Five trucks followed behind the group of villagers. Soldiers on foot flanked them. Two walkers also drove ahead of the group. These walkers were rusty and grimy, bought at a bargain price. Looking behind him, Mosi saw that the other villagers weren't the only prisoners. Elephants, rhinos, lions, and a giraffe were chained up and being pulled along by the trucks. These animals were covered in scars and fresh cuts, their spirits broken and their moans low.

"Eyes front, boy!" a soldier yelled in Swahili, giving Mosi a swift kick. Mosi was a young African with a shaved head and thin build. He barely managed to get his balance back after being kicked. The soldier chuckled and then ignored him.

All the villagers were exhausted and terrified. They had been marching for hours on end. None of them had drunk any water since this morning, and they hadn't eaten since yesterday. One woman collapsed, unable to take another step. A soldier told the villagers to halt, the trucks and walkers stopping as well. An elephant trumpeted in relief as it and the other animals got a chance to rest.

"Get up, you lazy cow," a soldier told the collapsed woman. "We did not tell you to fall on your face."

"Just shoot her," another soldier said. "We do not want this disgusting village woman weighing us down."

"That is for General Jengo to decide," the first soldier replied. "Go tell him. Hurry, before he decides to shoot you too."

The soldier ran to the back of the convoy. Mosi knew who had fallen. It was his aunt, a mother of four who had lost two of her children when the soldiers captured them. He knew with certainty and dread that she wouldn't live for long.

The soldier who ran away came back a few minutes later and grabbed Mosi's aunt by her arm. He was literally dragging her behind him as he headed to General Jengo's truck. Mosi kept his mouth shut, as did the other villagers.

"Boy, you go too!" a soldier yelled at Mosi. Before Mosi had time to object, he was being pulled away by his arm as well.

Mosi soon found himself facing General Jengo. The warlord sat in the back of his vehicle on a folding chair. Jengo wore baggy green pants and an open vest that showed off his muscular body. Also in the back of the truck was the largest crocodile Mosi had ever seen. It was a scaly beast over fifteen feet in length, its long snout filled with teeth. The creature was curled around Jengo's folded chair. It seemed docile at the moment, but Mosi knew it could be roused quickly, having witnessed it kill a man from his village in less than five seconds flat.

"Boy, how old are you?" Jengo asked.

Mosi gulped. "Twelve."

Jengo laughed. "Yes, nice and young. That gives us time to train you."

"General, do you want me to shoot the woman now?" a soldier asked. Mosi's aunt lay on the ground, only barely conscious and covered in scrapes.

"No, let the boy do it," Jengo said.

Mosi went cold. His heart began to beat like a drum. "Please, no! I never shot a gun before."

Jengo grinned. "Then it is time to start learning."

A soldier laid a pistol in the boy's hand. There was only one bullet in it, but one was enough. The other soldiers chuckled at Mosi's shocked expression, but they kept their eyes on the boy in case he tried to shoot one of them.

"We need to start training new soldiers," Jengo said. "You shall have the privilege of joining our glorious revolution against the Western Union."

In reality, Jengo did not care about liberating his country from the occupation. All he wanted was to take whatever he pleased. Dozens of these warlords were active in Africa, but the military rarely pursued them due to limited resources. The warlords also motivated civilians to go to safe zones, where they could be better monitored. Even so, many in Africa and the Middle East still refused to head to these safe zones, knowing they would be forced into the slums surrounding the zones. In the end, it was a choice between living in poverty and living in fear. Mosi now wished with all his heart that his family had chosen poverty.

Mosi stared at the gun in his hand, frozen in place. Jengo sighed and waved to one of his men. The man pointed his automatic weapon at Mosi.

"I will give you to the count of three," Jengo said. "Pull the trigger and kill this trash. Don't pull the trigger and you get killed. That is how the world works. Kill or be killed. It is the only law of nature. It is *my* law. Now shoot her already. One…"

Shivering despite the heat, Mosi pointed the gun at his aunt.

"Two…" Jengo said eagerly.

Mosi's aunt moaned a little, unaware of what was going on. Mosi closed his eyes and began to pull the trigger.

"Three…"

Lightning struck one of the soldiers, who fell, dead and smoking.

Jengo jumped out of his chair. "What was *that*?"

The soldiers shot at the sky, but more bolts rained down on them. All of them were soon dead. The smell of ozone was overpowering.

A man landed on the ground right in front of Jengo. The warlord gaped at his enemy. Impossible… He never thought he would see this monster.

Mosi gasped and dropped the gun at the sight of the Helmet Man.

Slate wore black boots, a black vest over a black long-sleeved shirt, and black gloves and black pants, his favorite color being black, despite his inability to see color or anything else. But his defining feature was his silver helmet. It was perfectly smooth and impossible for anyone, including Slate himself, to take off. The helmet acted as a perfect insulator that blinded and deafened him. This wasn't a fatal accessory, since he had special sensory abilities and required no food, drink, sleep, or even air. However, this silver prison may have been a contributing factor to his grating personality.

"So, you must be warlord Jenga," he said, sounding constipated.

"That's Jengo!" the warlord screamed, getting his nerves back. Jengo put his fingers in his mouth and whistled. His pet crocodile pounced out of the truck. The scaly beast managed to knock over Slate and clamp its jaws around his silver helmet. Jengo used this opportunity to jump out of the truck and make his escape. Mosi, meanwhile, ran up to his aunt on the ground and tried to shake her awake.

"Crikey!" Slate yelped. He punched the crocodile's head, sending electricity into it. The beast moaned and relaxed its jaw. Slate pushed the crocodile off and got to his feet, muttering obscenities to himself.

A group of soldiers arrived and aimed their guns at Slate. Laughing, the Helmet Man grabbed the tail of the disoriented crocodile and with unnatural strength yanked the reptile off the ground and threw it at his opponents. The soldiers screamed. The crocodile slammed into them. Alert again, the beast began to maul the soldiers on the ground. None of them managed to shoot the creature as they were torn apart.

Slate chuckled. "Whoa, didn't mean to do that."

A walker threw its giant metal fist down from behind. Sensing the attack, Slate rolled out of the way, a loud boom echoing as the walker punched the ground. The walker fired bullets from its other arm. Slate jumped up and began to fly, electricity trailing behind him. He went up about a hundred feet and circled above the walker. Since these weren't tracker bullets, the walker's pilot tried anticipating the Helmet Man's moves, to no avail.

Up in the air, Slate's arm gave off a blue glow. Sparks flew off him. He pointed his glowing arm at the walker and shot back.

But there was no lightning bolt. Instead, a beam of blue energy came out of his palm and hit the walker. It tore through the mecha, making a huge smoking hole right where the pilot had been. The walker, now without a pilot, fell backward with a loud crash, throwing up dust.

The Helmet Man spun around a little from the beam's recoil, but he was still airborne.

"That training of mine really paid off," he said. "These beams come in handy. Who knew you could improve perfection?"

The second of Jengo's walkers fired a shell. Slate dodged the projectile, which exploded in midair. The walker fired another, but it didn't even come close to hitting him this time. Slate sped toward the walker and slammed into the machine. He punched his way into the cockpit and grabbed the pilot's throat. The pilot could only shriek as Slate sent a thousand volts into him.

Slate jumped off the walker, which now stood useless. A dozen armed soldiers ran to where they saw the Helmet Man and pulled their triggers, but Slate ran fast, shooting bolts of lightning. Six men fell to the ground, shocked to death. The others kept firing and screaming, but Slate made his way to them. He punched one of the soldiers and swung his leg at another, his attacks sending energy into his foes.

Taking advantage of the distraction, the villagers began to rebel against their captors. The soldiers shot at the mob with no hesitation, but only four villagers died. The rest of them tackled the soldiers, swarming them. A few village men snatched up the dead soldiers' guns and started shooting. One woman ran up to the captive animals and unlocked their chains with keys that she had found on a dead soldier. The agitated animals were released, and the elephants were the first to charge. They slammed into several trucks and trampled soldiers. The rhinos and lions also attacked their former masters. Even the giraffe got a few kicks in. The animals and villagers soon killed the remaining soldiers who were stupid enough to keep on fighting. Many other soldiers ran away, abandoning their spoils of war.

Meanwhile, Slate had zapped the last of his attackers. His job was almost complete.

"Don't move!" Jengo shouted in English. He held Mosi by an arm and pointed a gun at the boy's head. Mosi kept quiet, but his eyes were wide with fright.

"Give up already," Slate said. "You've obviously lost."

"Fool, the bounty on your head will more than cover my losses," Jengo spat. "Now put your hands up or I shall kill the boy."

"A smart plan, but you made one dangerous assumption."

"And what is that?"

"You assume I care if that kid lives."

Slate shot a bolt of lightning at Mosi, stopping his heart. The boy gave a small yelp before collapsing.

"No!" Jengo screamed, aiming his gun at Slate. "You are mad!"

Slate shrugged. "What? What did I do?"

"This cannot be! You are the hero of the Third World. You do not kill the innocent!"

"Oh, yeah. I forgot."

Jengo fired. The Helmet Man walked toward the warlord as the bullets sped past him. Only one hit Slate and bounced off his helmet without leaving a scratch.

General Jengo was soon out of bullets. His quivering hand dropped the empty gun. Slate was right in front of him now. Jengo tried punching Slate's helmet. Two of his fingers broke on impact. He cried out and cradled his injured hand.

"I was gonna give you an easy death," Slate said. "But you're really starting to get on my nerves, so I've decided to pass on killing you."

Without warning, Slate punched him in the gut. Jengo fell to his knees, coughing. The Helmet Man picked up Mosi's body and began to walk away.

"Boys, he's all yours!" Slate shouted.

Jengo looked up to see scarred and angry lions eyeing him. They had not been fed in three days, much to Jengo's regret.

"Ni–nice kitties…" Jengo said, wetting himself.

General Jengo's screams could be heard for miles as the lions tore into him.

It all lasted for a long, painful minute.

Slate walked a safe distance away from the lions and dropped Mosi on the ground. He pointed his index finger at the boy and sent an electric bolt into his chest. Mosi convulsed and started coughing.

"Don't be a wimp," Slate told him. "All I did was stop your heart."

Mosi opened his eyes to see the Helmet Man. He began to smile.

"You came..." he croaked in Swahili. "I only heard stories..."

"Sorry, kid. I don't speak Mexican."

Loud cheers erupted behind Slate. The villagers were clapping and yelling praises to the Helmet Man. Many patted him on the back. Some even hugged him.

"Hey, don't treat me like a hero," Slate told them. "My head's already huge enough. Well ... to hell with it. Go ahead and cheer, ya lugs. Cheer for this handsome bastard!"

The people were more than happy to oblige. They cheered until their throats were sore.

CHAPTER 3

Gilda was barely able to dodge the punch.

She pulled back her walker just in time as the other walker swung its arm, then commanded her mecha to backhand her opponent. With ease, the other walker blocked the giant metal arm with one of its own. Gilda smiled as she pulled back, her walker's wheels squealing. Her foe tried to pursue her. Instead, the walker tripped and hit the ground with a monstrous thud. Gilda's walker rolled forward and put one of its stubby legs on her opponent's back, victorious.

"The match is over," Nigel said. "Purp, help Jamal up."

After helping the other walker to its feet, Gilda parked her mecha inside a large wooden shed and climbed out of the cockpit. Being a seventeen-year-old American girl with purple hair, she was not the kind of person one would think to find at a terrorist camp.

"Good job," Nigel said. "You used your walker's foot bolts to dig up the ground. Very resourceful. Jamal didn't notice and ended up tripping his walker." He strolled up to Gilda with his hands on his hips. Nigel was a thin African who was responsible for training the United Third's new recruits. These recruits consisted of teenage boys who were reluctant to have a Westerner train with them, but Nigel didn't discriminate, and he gave Gilda the chance to prove herself. She didn't disappoint.

"Sir, I'm glad you think I did well," Gilda said. She wore green pants and a white T-shirt, like all the other recruits who were standing behind Nigel. They looked at her with distrust but also with something that might have resembled respect.

Jamal climbed out of his walker and approached Nigel. He was about the same age as Gilda, yet he had the face of a hardened warrior.

"Time to shake hands, you two," Nigel said.

Jamal stuck out his hand. Gilda shook it, and they nodded to each other. Then Jamal let go and went briskly to join the other recruits.

"Purp, you are wanted in the tunnels," Nigel said.

That made Gilda stiffen a bit. That was the high command of the United Third, a place she had never stepped foot in before. It was rumored that Incognito lived there.

"What for?" she asked.

"I would like to tell you it was nothing," Nigel said. He left it at that.

Minutes later, Gilda was leaving the clearing where she and Jamal had their duel. Noisy jungle surrounded her, a Congolese rainforest, to be exact. The only signs of civilization were the storage sheds and tents that made up the surface of the United Third's main base of operations. She'd bet the Western Union would give anything to find out about this place.

Gilda approached the tunnel entrance, which was guarded by two fierce-looking men. A camera was also hanging off a nearby rock. It zoomed in on her.

"This way," one guard said. He led her into the tunnels. Electric lamps were attached to the walls, giving off a dull yellow glow. The tunnel system was originally a mine that had been abandoned during the Great Choke. Gilda could tell that it went down deep, because they kept encountering wooden stairs that led into the abyss.

They arrived at a door built into one of the tunnel's walls. The guard opened it and gestured for Gilda to enter. She went into the room, but the guard stayed outside, closing the door behind her. The room had rocky walls, a wooden table, and several chairs. In one of those chairs sat Kevin Straper.

"Gilda, haven't seen you in weeks," Straper said. "Can I get a hello kiss?"

"Yeah, not even in your dreams," Gilda scoffed. Straper had severe acne and wore a similar outfit. Almost the same age as Gilda, he was also training at the United Third camp. However, he did his sniper exercises alone. Straper was a cocky American teenager, so it was safe to assume he was not well liked at an anti-Western terrorist camp. Gilda only managed to train with the other recruits because she was female and thus seemed less threatening, although anyone who knew Gilda and Straper would find such a concept amusing.

"What exactly are we doing here?" Straper asked.

"How should I know?" Gilda asked, plopping herself down in one of the chairs. "But I think Slate might be coming back today."

"Great, here comes another headache."

"Do you think—?" Gilda almost asked, but she was unable to finish, for the door had opened again. It closed behind a man holding a scythe.

Straper jolted upright in his chair. Gilda's face wore a mix of shock and recognition.

"I trust you can guess who I am," Incognito said, "though I wouldn't be surprised if you are unable. Constant consumption and Western propaganda have surely dulled your minds. Even this time of seclusion could not possibly undo years of materialism and individualistic thoughts, or should I say selfish thoughts."

Gilda hardly noticed his arrogant words. She could only stare at the terrorist mastermind. Incognito wore a white suit with gold buttons, his gloved hands grasping a scythe that he used as a walking stick. His gray hair was tied in a braided ponytail that went down to the middle of his back. His oval mask was white, covered in Arabic calligraphy that was inky black and almost hypnotic. Black eyes peered out of it, examining his surroundings with skepticism and self-righteousness. This was the most wanted man in the world, the ultimate enemy of Western civilization. Incognito, who had never revealed himself before, whose identity was the most sought-after mystery in the world, stood before them.

Incognito was Gilda's boss. He was the one who had offered her justice. And she had accepted.

"Hey ... thanks," Gilda told him. "You saved my life when Cloak kidnapped Slate and me. We might both be dead if it wasn't for you."

"Spare me your thanks," Incognito said. "All I want is your obedience."

"Geez, brah, you could be a little nicer," Straper said.

Incognito smacked Straper's head with the wooden handle of his scythe.

"Ow! What did I do?"

"Don't speak unless spoken to," Incognito said. "Keep it up, and I'll send you back to America, where you will have your mind pruned, erasing your vulgar memories. Then you can drown your anxieties in peace with a Big Gulp or whatever revolting beverage you Westerners pour down your gullets these days."

Gilda frowned. "It's not in good taste to hit your subordinates."

"Yes, I should have sliced him open," Incognito said, his eyes glancing at the blade of his scythe. "But he is an investment, so I won't kill him unless absolutely necessary."

Gilda got up from her chair. "Did you call us here just to threaten and insult us? You may be our boss, but we won't be treated this way. If we go, you can bet Slate will too."

Incognito squinted at her. "The reason men don't hit women is because it's considered cowardly to hurt something weaker than you. But everything is weaker than me, so I don't hold such a prejudice. Refrain from testing me, girl."

Gilda growled. The only reason she didn't talk back now was because she hated Cloak more than him. Cloak had killed her best friend, Henry Marker, along with over a hundred other cadets. The organization was run by the Gifted, supersoldiers created by the Western Union. One of the Gifted, Houdini, had acted as the mastermind behind the Bunker attack. Gilda, Slate, and several others had stopped Houdini from destroying the Helios Tower, killing the madman in the process. The other Gifted with Houdini were Repulsa and Sandtrap. Gilda remembered that Sandtrap had burned to death, but what happened to that woman? Incognito must have killed Repulsa before taking down their plane with that strange power of his.

"Are you one of the Gifted?" Gilda asked. "Or were you created by the Western Union?"

"I made myself," Incognito said. "Do not mistake me for those abominations of the West. They are not deserving of the precious gift of life. You and I agree on that point. I'm also the only one with power who cares about stopping them. The Western Union only buries its head in the sand and prunes anyone who dares uncover the truth, or worse..."

"Why don't you just tell the world about the Gifted?" Straper asked, rubbing his sore head. "Won't that, like, help your cause?"

Incognito hit him again with his scythe.

"Ouch!" Straper whined.

"Ignorant boy. Not even illiterate Americans and Eurotrash would believe my claims without concrete proof."

"Look, unless this is about Cloak, we have no reason to be here," Gilda said.

"Your insolence is quite irritating. Nevertheless, you are correct. You see, I am planning an operation against Cloak. They are testing new technology that could be used to infiltrate the Western Union and even the United Third. Obviously, I can't allow this, so I'm assigning you brats and Slate with the task of stopping them. The leader of this operation will be here shortly to discuss the mission and share a meal with you."

"Uh, who's the team leader?" Straper asked, covering his head in case Incognito chose to hit him again.

As if on cue, the door opened. A nonchalant woman strolled into the room.

"Whoa," Straper said. "That babe is our boss?"

"You..." Gilda spat. "I thought Incognito killed you."

"Believe me, he wishes he could," the woman said with a sly smile. "Hello, my name is Naomi. You may also know me as Repulsa."

***

Chul stood in place, unable to move. He couldn't breathe. The pressure quickly built in his lungs. The smuggler stood on a wooden dock in Sydney. One could even see the glowing Sydney Opera House from here, but tonight wasn't for sightseeing.

"You should have talked when I gave you the chance," Geppetto said. "All you had to do was tell me where the submarine was headed, but now…"

Chul's face was turning blue. Five Western Union soldiers stood around him, terror in their unmoving eyes. They had been tasked with transferring their prisoner but had been taken captive themselves, their Jeep now abandoned on the side of the road. Now, the soldiers could not move unless commanded by their puppet master.

Geppetto was short, less than three feet tall, with a shaved head and a five o'clock shadow. Next to him was his companion, a man over seven feet tall with red hair. The giant had a square face and was munching on beef jerky. Both of them wore casual suits that looked a thousand times better than the rags Chul wore.

After almost passing out, Chul gasped in a huge breath of air, only to stop breathing once again. Tears streamed from his eyes. He could taste bile.

"I can only control voluntary actions," Geppetto said. "You can't hold your breath till you die. Your breathing reflex eventually takes over. A real shame. That'd be an interesting way to kill people. I guess this is more like waterboarding."

Geppetto loosened his invisible grip. Chul was now able to breathe on his own terms. He took frantic breaths, making sickening coughs.

"What was I asking you about again?" Geppetto grinned. "Oh, right. It's all coming back to me. You're a smuggler who used to be a crewman for the *Eodum* before you accidentally killed a crewmate in a drunken brawl and ran away with your tail between your legs."

Chul stopped gasping, his breathing normal, but he still couldn't move his body.

"Then you took up human trafficking," Geppetto said. "You attempted to take Filipino refugees to Australia, where they would be forced into prostitution, only to have your boat captured by the Western Union Navy. They were going to send you back to the Chinese Empire, but you gave them some useful intel about the submarine you used to work on, the *Eodum*. You told them your ex-captain made a deal with Incognito, a deal that involved transporting the Helmet Man."

Geppetto walked right up to Chul. Not able to do otherwise, Chul got on his knees and leaned forward. Geppetto chuckled and patted his cheek.

"Tell me where and when," Geppetto said.

Chul gulped. His shirt was soaked with sweat.

"To–Tokyo … the fifteenth … this month…" he whispered in shaky English.

Geppetto smirked. "Finally, we're making progress."

The soldiers surrounding them took out their guns and pointed the barrels at their own heads. Gunshots rang throughout the night. The five soldiers collapsed onto the dock. Chul shrieked, sweating buckets now.

"Atlas, take care of this coward," Geppetto said.

The giant swallowed the last of his beef jerky. He moved forward, wrapped his giant hands around Chul's head, and twisted it around three hundred and sixty degrees. Chul only had time to look shocked before his body crumpled.

Geppetto groaned in exhaustion. He was glad that business was over with.

Cloak now knew where to find the Helmet Man.

CHAPTER 4

"Whoa, you know this chick?" Straper asked.

"She's with Cloak," Gilda seethed. "Her name's Repulsa."

"What? No way!"

"Be quiet," Incognito said, smacking Straper with his scythe's handle yet again.

Straper grabbed his head. "Ah! Seriously, brah!"

"I prefer to be called Naomi," the woman said. "It's a much more human name."

"But you're not human," Gilda spat.

"And you're no lady."

"Quit your prattling and be seated," Incognito snapped at Naomi.

"A simple 'please' wouldn't hurt," Naomi said, sitting on the chair across from Gilda. The former agent of Cloak had straight black hair with long bangs covering her forehead. She wore a plaid long-sleeved shirt and blue jeans with black high-heeled boots.

"Hey, do you have a boyfriend?" Straper asked.

"No," Naomi said. "Why?"

Straper chuckled. "Well, you do now."

An invisible slap hit him. He almost fell out of his chair in surprise.

"Where did that come from?" he yelled. There was a red mark on his face.

"I went easy on you," Naomi told him.

"But what was *that*?" Straper asked.

"She's telekinetic," Gilda said.

"Great, more people with superpowers."

Gilda turned to Naomi. "Hey, I have a question for you."

Naomi smiled. "Go ahead, but I might not answer."

Gilda asked anyway. "Why are you working with Incognito? I doubt Cloak is letting you do this. You must have betrayed them."

"I don't think I'll answer that," Naomi said. "Just know that Incognito and I share similar desires. He can make my dream come true, yours as well."

"Do you think we'll work with you?" Gilda asked. "You're the enemy. You helped Houdini kill all those people."

"I've been working for Incognito for over five years now," Naomi said. "Everything I've been doing has been his will, as is everything you have."

"Don't compare me to you. You're a killer."

"To be fair, I was not aware of the Bunker massacre until it was too late."

"You tried to kill Slate at the Pale Pyramid."

"And you think the Helmet Man doesn't deserve to die?" Naomi asked, her smile fading. "He's a murderer, a beast."

"No more bickering," Incognito said. "Wench, you attempted to kill Slate, but I forgave you in light of your past service. Do not make me regret that decision."

"Let's just eat," Naomi said. "We can quarrel later."

A guard entered the room carrying a tray with a steaming dish.

"Pizza!" Straper yelled, beaming and forgetting his situation.

The guard set it down on the table and left the room in a hurry.

"Go on," Incognito said, gagging a little. "Eat this disgusting Western con-coction. Put enough grease on a dung heap and you Americans would prob-ably devour that too."

"That sure does sound appetizing," Naomi jested.

"Dudes, don't we need to cut this pizza?" Straper asked.

Incognito walked up to the table and swung his scythe eight times at light-ning speed, cutting the pizza into sixteen pieces. Not even a drop of sauce stained his blade.

"Wah!" Straper cried, sweating. "Too close for comfort!"

"Thank you for cutting the pizza," Naomi said to Incognito. She picked up a piece and began to eat, smiling and closing her eyes.

The entire meal was awkward. Incognito sat with them while resting the scythe in his lap. He did not eat, only staring at each one of his subordinates for several minutes before moving on to the next unlucky soul. Straper had a hard time eating under this scrutiny. Gilda kept her eyes on Naomi as she munched on her slice. The only one who enjoyed the food was Naomi, who ate half the pizza. She was either famished or just gluttonous.

Naomi wiped her lips in a tender motion with a napkin. "Ah, delicious. Who on earth made such a fine meal?"

"That would be me," Incognito said. "I hate to sully my hands with such filth, but I knew you all were getting weary of dried meat and bread. This is a gift of sorts."

"You're bribing us with pizza?" Naomi asked. "It's surprisingly effective."

Gilda smirked. "Incognito's a cook. Guess everyone needs a hobby."

"Enough," Incognito ordered. He got out of his seat and leaned his scythe against his shoulder. "Slate will be here soon. I sent him on a little errand earlier."

"Killing another warlord?" Naomi asked. "That's the eighth one."

"Warlord Jengo refused my offer of an alliance. Such a mindless Neander-thal cannot be left to his own devices."

"Meanwhile, you turn Slate into some kind of folk hero," Gilda snapped.

"Oh, so he *shouldn't* save those villagers?" Incognito inquired.

"That's not the point. You're using him as a recruiting tool for the United Third. I thought he wasn't going to be your pawn."

"The agreement was that Slate would not fight the Western Union. One must always read the fine print before signing a contract."

"We had a contract?" Straper asked vacantly.

Incognito was about to hit Straper again when they heard a loud yell.

"I brought dinner!" Slate sang. He kicked down the door and marched right into the room. With a loud thud, he dropped a severed crocodile head on the table, ruining the few slices of uneaten pizza.

"What's that supposed to be?" Straper cried.

"A dinosaur!" Slate yelled.

"It smells awful," Gilda said, pinching her nose. "You actually killed an animal?"

"It was attacking villagers," Slate said. "And it's not often I get to kill a dinosaur. Could you have refused?"

"Yeah, I could have, because it's not a fricking dinosaur," Straper said.

"Wait, you'd kill a dinosaur if you got the chance?"

"Never mind. I'm already sick of you."

"Hey, what happened to Incognito?" Gilda asked.

Straper looked around. The world's most wanted man was nowhere to be seen.

"Yeah, how did he disappear so quickly?" he asked. "Does Incognito not want to meet Slate or something? Wonder why?"

"I could offer a few guesses," Gilda huffed.

"The boss keeps avoiding me, but I could care less," Slate said, walking over to Naomi. "What interests me is this cutie pie. Hey, baby!"

"Slate, that's Repulsa!" Gilda yelled. "She tried to kill you."

"What? Oh, yeah ... I forgive her." Slate leaned on the table next to Naomi. "So, you have a boyfriend?"

Naomi looked disinterested, but in truth, she was expertly hiding her rage. She rose from her chair and strolled out of the room, shutting the door behind her.

"Well, you do now!" Slate yelled after her.

"Dude, that's *my* pickup line," Straper objected.

"Yes, but my execution was better."

Gilda shook her head. "This has got to be the worst pizza party I've ever been to."

***

The motor turned off and the boat slowed to a stop. Straper leaned over the rail to vomit.

"Gross!" Gilda yelled. "Don't get it on the deck."

The boat had taken them out to sea. Nobody was thrilled to be on this rickety vessel, which was covered in rust and full of holes. Gilda stood next to Straper. Both of them faced the open sea. The sun was bright and warm, a welcome start to a long ordeal.

None of the terrorists had said goodbye to them as they left. Not even Incognito came to see them off, which suited everyone just fine. But Gilda did see her instructor, Nigel, nod to her. The other recruits merely stared at her as she boarded the truck, which took her and the others out of the jungle and to the seaport.

"Where do you think we're going?" Gilda asked.

"Probably some crappy slum," Straper moaned, wiping his mouth. "Man, I knew I should have taken those seasick pills."

Slate laughed. "Wussy!"

"I ain't the one afraid of standing next to the rail," Straper snapped.

"Hey, I ain't afraid of nothing," the Helmet Man said, standing as far away from the rail as possible. "I'm just not fond of water. My powers don't work well when I'm wet."

Straper smirked. "Wow, so all someone needs to do to beat you is to sprinkle a little water on you? That must suck. You're like the Wicked Witch of the West."

"Except I don't melt," Slate said. "I just get angrier and angrier."

"Good point," Straper said, a little nervous. "Wait a sec. Where's the chick?"

"She has a name, you know," Slate said.

"Really, what is it?" Gilda asked.

"How should I know?"

"I'm right here," Naomi said, coming out from the inside of the boat. She wore an outfit similar to what she had on the day before, except this included a light blue jacket.

"What are we doing out here?" Straper asked, looking like he would hurl again. "I can't take much more of this. We waiting for a bigger ship or what?"

Naomi winked. "That's exactly it. Just be patient."

Straper cleared his throat. "Yes ... uh ... well..."

"She's mine!" Slate yelled, tackling Straper, who barely had a chance to defend himself before throwing up again.

"Ah!" Slate cried. "It's all over me! That's it! I'm tossing you overboard."

A violent wave hit the ship, getting everyone's attention.

"Excellent, the submarine is here," Naomi said.

"Hang on, you mean the sub we escaped on after we were kidnapped from Dubai?" Gilda asked. "I thought that was a one-time thing."

"Originally, it was, but Incognito has since purchased the *Eodum* and its crew. It'll be our personal transport from now on."

Several hundred yards away, a black shape emerged from beneath the surface of the ocean. Gilda hadn't met any of the crew personally six months ago, but she knew it was filled with ex-North Korean soldiers. They had defected when the country fell under the control of the Chinese Empire, a move many considered wise.

"Sweet, our ride's here," Slate said, jumping up and wiping the vomit off his black vest. "Now I can be all alone with..." He turned to Naomi. "Uh, what's your name again?"

Naomi ignored him and went back inside the boat.

"She doesn't like you, man," Straper said, getting off the deck. "Can't blame her."

"That puke all over you isn't very appealing either," Gilda said.

"Hold the phone," Straper said. "Slate, how old are you?"

The Helmet Man tapped his foot. "Hmm ... about thirty-two, I think."

"Yeah, but weren't you buried for twenty years?"

"You got it," Slate said. He had been discovered near the Bunker, buried under six feet of dirt. How he got there was a mystery. Slate had gotten in a big fight with another supersoldier, killing his opponent and getting seriously injured in the process. As a result, Slate went into hibernation for two decades.

Next thing he knew, he was being awakened by Henry Marker, a day before the boy was murdered.

"So, you were thirty-two over twenty years ago?" Straper prodded further.

"Yeah, I don't age," Slate said. "I'm perfect in every way, baby."

"But that makes you fifty. Or fifty-two."

"What's your point?"

"It's a little creepy that you're trying to hit on a chick who's barely half your age."

"Eww, she probably didn't even hit puberty before you were buried," Gilda said.

"If rich old men can do it, why not me?" Slate asked.

"You're not getting through to him," Straper said. "It's totally hopeless."

Their boat soon pulled up to the side of the submarine. A few sailors with the United Third loaded luggage and supplies onto the sub, a handful of Korean submariners helping them. Gilda was the first to climb inside, followed by the others. It took half an hour before the *Eodum* submerged again.

The gang had no time to explore their cramped quarters before assembling in a bare room with plastic chairs. The captain of the submarine was already there to meet with them. Gilda and Straper chose to sit down, but Slate and Naomi stood.

"I welcome you to the *Eodum*," said the captain, a Korean with a small black beard and a mustache. Like his crew, he wore casual clothes but had a professional demeanor. One of his hands was mechanical and gray in color.

"That's a cool hand," Straper said. "But don't they have growth-patch treatment?"

"The procedure is expensive," the captain said, not elaborating any further.

"What's your name?" Gilda asked.

"My name is Captain Young-Bum. I am tasked with taking you to Japan and back. All you have to do is sit in your rooms until we get there."

"We're going to Japan?" Slate asked. "Care to be more specific, pal?"

"We're going to Tokyo. Japan has had a strict isolationist policy ever since the Great Choke. Only a select few outsiders ever make it inside the country these days, which is why you will need this stealth sub to get past their coast guard."

"So, why are we heading to Japan?" Straper asked.

"Because that's where Cloak is hatching its next plan," Naomi told him.

CHAPTER 5

Eisenhorn took his first step into the Chinese Empire.

To be exact, he crossed a yellow line that cut across a road. It was one of the few roads that connected North Korea to South Korea through the Demilitarized Zone. The general was in a clean and crisp uniform, grunting as he waddled toward his fate. Western Union soldiers stood far behind him with their guns at the ready.

Eisenhorn had the sudden urge to run back. What was he doing here? This was insanity. Of all the people to become an ambassador, the president chose the most intolerant, mentally unstable, and overall unpleasant military leader the Western Union had. Not only that, but they made him an ambassador to the Chinese Empire, the most dangerous enemy of the West, even more so than Incognito and the United Third.

But it wasn't a soldier's place to ask questions. Despite his lack of enthusiasm, Eisenhorn would do his best for America, the Union, and freedom itself.

Eisenhorn walked for ten minutes before reaching a dozen trucks and almost seventy armed Chinese soldiers standing in ranks. They wore red uniforms with even redder sashes tied around their arms. On each sash was the symbol of the Chinese Empire, a golden dragon encircling an equally golden star. A horrible tension gripped the general's stomach at the sight of these men. His leg muscles tightened. His eyes darted from face to face. These men looked like those Korean soldiers—too much like them. Gunfire went off in his head. The smell of blood filled his nostrils. Metallic tastes filled his mouth. His trigger finger twitched. A flash—

"General, are you all right?" a silky voice inquired.

Eisenhorn snapped back to reality. He twisted to the source of the silky voice and found himself facing a hairless Chinese youth, no older than twenty.

"Ugh ... who're you?" Eisenhorn garbled.

"My name is Chao Xing," the young man said. "I'm your escort to the capital."

"Xing?" Eisenhorn scoffed. "Isn't that a street sign? You Asians have some weird names. But not as bad as those terrorists, what with all them vowels."

Xing treated him to a polite smile. "I am also one of the five high generals who answer directly to the emperor. My official title is high general of the homeland. I deal with internal security."

"What! You're not even old enough to buy a beer. How are you a general already? Took me till I was forty."

"The position was passed down to me by my deceased father," Xing said. He had no hair, not even any eyebrows. He also wore a black suit with a red sash on his arm. On the back of his head was a tattoo of a black swirling dragon. Its tail descended down Xing's neck and disappeared beneath the collar of his jacket.

"That's a gang tattoo if I ever saw one," Eisenhorn foamed.

Xing laughed. The soldiers didn't look amused. It was a good thing they couldn't speak English. Otherwise, Eisenhorn might have gotten shot.

"That tattoo was from my younger days," Xing told him.

"Younger? Any younger and you'd be in diapers."

Xing laughed again. "I thought the tattoo made me look more menacing."

"Huh ... think it worked?"

Xing shrugged. "I kept it, didn't I?"

***

Half a day later, Eisenhorn found himself sitting inside a small luxury plane. A meek flight attendant gave him a glass of water, but he ignored his beverage and looked out of his window with dull interest.

"What's that?" Eisenhorn barked, pointing out his window.

High General Xing sat across from Eisenhorn, reading a document-filled folder, but he put it down and glanced outside. Far below, there were dozens of skyscrapers covered in holes, worn down by time. The streets were littered with trash and the skeletons of vehicles. Not a soul could be seen.

"An abandoned city," Xing declared.

"I know that," Eisenhorn snapped. "*Why* is it abandoned?"

Xing, with infinite patience, answered, "The Great Choke did this. Seventy years ago, the world descended into chaos when the virus emerged. Over a billion people were killed, many of the victims from mainland Asia. Like you Westerners, us Chinese turned once again to government after the corporations who were running the world failed to act swiftly to the crisis. But unlike the Western Union, the Chinese Empire was formed through violent revolution. Our dear emperor toppled the weak communist regime and gave the people the vaccine for the Choke, winning over the nation and solidifying his grip on the region."

"Yeah, your emperor stole that vaccine from us hardworking Americans. Had him a bunch of spies steal whole shiploads of the stuff."

"I would advise you not to speak ill of the emperor while in Beijing. Such acts result in ... unpleasant punishments. Not even an ambassador would be spared."

"Whatever. Keep telling the story. Never heard this history from the horse's mouth."

"Naturally, many Chinese were angered that the West hoarded the vaccine for themselves, and the embrace of foreign technology and customs was accused of leading our country to ruin, so the emperor began the Cleansing of the East. In order to purify the lands of Western influences, we had to dismantle the economy completely. China has been ruralized for decades. Now, most of our citizens are either farmers or soldiers. Only subservient nations such as India or Myanmar still have factories, and those are mainly for producing weapons."

"You abandoned all your cities to become farmers?"

"There is much poverty and even some starvation, but our emperor proclaims that this is the way to true spiritual cleanliness." Xing said these words with poise, but his hand was clenched. The general didn't notice this. He was too distracted by what he saw out the window.

"What the hell is that?" Eisenhorn shouted.

"That's the eighth battalion," Xing said. "They're returning from suppressing an insurrection in Mongolia."

Three hundred thousand soldiers marched in perfect formation. They all wore red uniforms. The booms of their synchronized footsteps echoed for miles.

Eisenhorn's jaw hit the floor. In all his years of military service, he had never seen such an overwhelming display of military strength.

"This is only a taste of the Chinese Empire's true power," Xing said. "While the Western Union has technology, we have manpower. General Eisenhorn, you're looking at only a fraction of our billion-man army."

***

After the plane landed, they drove for half an hour through a barren wasteland before reaching an endless concrete expanse. The concrete ground was smoother than Xing's head, stretching all the way to the horizon. Eisenhorn looked both left and right, but he couldn't see where the concrete ended. He sat in the back of a roofless Jeep next to Xing. Four other trucks filled with soldiers followed them, but he saw no other living person besides his escorts.

"This some kind of parking lot?" Eisenhorn asked.

"No, this is the expanded Tiananmen Square," Xing said as the trucks drove onto it. "Anyone who sets foot here without the emperor's permission is put to death."

"Sure hope we have reservations."

"At the center of the square is the Forbidden City, home to the emperor and his many guests, including ambassadors and royal family members."

Eisenhorn looked around. "You got some lax security."

"On the contrary. Over fifty snipers are aiming at us right now, not to mention the mines beneath the square and the hundred thousand troops stationed only ten kilometers away. I haven't even covered the protective measures within the palace."

Eisenhorn's eyes became wild and paranoid.

Five minutes of driving later, a dot appeared in the distance. As they drove closer, Eisenhorn began to make out the capital of the Chinese Empire.

A massive moat filled with water surrounded the Forbidden City. Behind it, an imposing gray wall stood with snipers perched on top. Only a retractable bridge connected the palace to the outside world. The trucks reached the moat and stopped in front of the bridge. They dropped Xing and Eisenhorn off before driving away. Xing talked to the soldiers stationed in front of the palace doors. After getting the go-ahead, Eisenhorn and Xing entered the domain of the Chinese emperor.

When Eisenhorn entered the Forbidden City, he literally gasped, something his cynical and rude ways rarely allowed.

It was a paradise. He had never seen such scenery in all his life. The lawns were dark green, the shrubbery was carefully trimmed, the ponds were a deep blue, the air tasted sweet, and birdsong resonated across the garden. The palace itself, a red building with upturned eaves, inspired awe with its majesty. This wooden building housed one of the world's most powerful figures, a deity to his people. There were other buildings inside the Forbidden City besides the palace, but they were small and inconsequential. The original city had been demolished and remodeled to the emperor's liking. This city was smaller than its predecessor yet seemed more imposing and somehow even more ancient.

But then Eisenhorn noticed the most unique features of all.

"What are those creepy things?" he asked. He pointed at a hundred stone statues lined up in ranks before the palace. Each was of a Chinese man in an ancient warrior's attire, every statue having a unique face. However, an ominous air hung over these statues. Many of them emitted a sound like a low wind.

Xing stiffened. "Those are ... this is the Traitors' Garden, modeled after the Terracotta Warriors. All those who have attempted to betray the emperor are entombed here inside these statues. The statues themselves are carved in their likeness."

"They leave corpses here on the front lawn?" Eisenhorn cried. "That's insanity!"

"You are mistaken. These traitors are fed through tubes. Their waste—"

Eisenhorn froze. He stopped breathing. His skin turned white. "They... can't... be still..." he whispered.

Then he was able to place the sound. He wasn't hearing a low wind.

Those were screams.

With that realization, Eisenhorn vomited all over the lawn.

***

The golf cart came to a stop. Cyphrus stepped out, her heels touching down on the soft grass. She saw her host ten feet away, taking a few practice swings with his driver.

"That some nasty rug on your shoulders," a young Chinese woman said in terrible English. She seemed to appear out of nowhere and now stood in front of Cyphrus. Her name was Lily, a delicate name for a not-so-delicate woman. She wore a red pantsuit and had her hair in two buns. A twisted smile was plastered on her face, a perfect match for her snakelike eyes.

"This coat costs more than all your peasant clothes combined," Cyphrus said. "A grunt like yourself couldn't even dream of obtaining such luxury."

"But I bet that coat's not very animal-friendly," Lily said.

"Why should I care about animals when I can barely give a shit about humans?"

"Lily, stand aside," the host said, swinging his golf club again.

"This ain't over, old lady," Lily snapped.

Lily moved out of the way. Cyphrus walked by her, not paying the vicious youth a second thought. Cyphrus wore a leopard-skin coat, a silk dress, and diamond-studded high heels. Her short brown hair was styled with obsessive care, her nails manicured just so. Her one feature that seemed uncouth was her thick makeup. White powder, eyeliner, and black lipstick hid every inch of Cyphrus's face, but it could not hide her calculating demeanor.

"Good morning, Prince Mao," Cyphrus said, stopping in front of her host. She even bowed a little just to sweeten the greeting.

"I prefer 'prime minister,'" Mao told her. "It took much effort to become prime minister. All I had to do to become a prince was be born."

Heir to the imperial throne, Mao Long was in his fifties, wearing casual yet dignified red clothes, with only a few gray streaks in his jet-black hair. His face was relaxed and calm, as though he had been in a hot tub for an hour. There was even a ghost of a smile. He swung his driver again before turning his attention to Cyphrus.

"When will the Japanese prime minister make his announcement?" Mao asked.

"Next week," Cyphrus said. "Operation Rising Sun is a go."

"What of the main mission?"

"*Leviathan* is scheduled to make its first voyage at the beginning of next month. The preparations have been made. All that's left is the execution itself."

"I shall inform the capital. I must say, this partnership with Cloak has yielded extraordinary results. However..."

"Yes?"

"The incident at the Helios Tower has made the empire concerned about Cloak's reliability. Perhaps if I were to speak with your second-in-command..."

"I'm afraid Sebastian doesn't care for business. He's much too busy with his pet projects and vague schemes."

"Then I would like to speak to this Mentor of yours."

"You and me both. The Mentor is ... elusive. As far as I know, only Sebastian has ever had any contact with our leader."

Mao sighed. "Very well, but remember to keep in mind the empire's unofficial motto: 'The Chinese Empire does not forgive.'"

"An interesting motto. May I ask you an unrelated question?"

"As long as it's not idiotic."

"Why do you play golf? It's a Western game, is it not?"

Mao put a golf ball on his tee. "The West, although corrupt, has some good aspects that should be adopted. My father does not feel this way. That is why when I asked for a golf course on my fiftieth birthday, the emperor gave me a choice. I could either get my golf course or keep my wife's head on her shoulders. Needless to say, I made the right decision."

Mao swung his club, which struck the ball. It soared in the wrong direction, however, and landed in the bushes.

"Bring me the man who mowed this tee box," Mao hissed in Mandarin.

Lily grinned with cruel delight. In less than a few minutes, she had a young man by his scruff. The groundskeeper was shaking.

"You mowed this?" Mao questioned in Mandarin, pointing at the grass.

The groundskeeper hesitated but nodded.

"The lines in the grass are crooked," Mao said. "Get down on your knees."

Lily shoved the groundskeeper toward the tee box. The groundskeeper scurried to where Mao stood and fell to the ground so he could properly grovel.

"Do you see your failure?" Mao asked him.

"Forgive me, Prime Minister! I see! I see my failure!"

"Good," Mao said, raising his club. "Let it be your last."

Mao smashed the club into the man's skull. The groundskeeper went limp. Mao raised his driver and brought it down again. And again. And again. Blood spattered across the grass. Lily bit the corner of her mouth in a distorted grin of sadistic pleasure. Blood trickled down her cheek. Cyphrus just stood there, eyes wide.

Mao ceased his assault. There was no hint of emotion on his face, which was covered with spots of blood. In an empty voice, he spoke.

"The Chinese Empire *does not* forgive..."

CHAPTER 6

Gilda walked into the common room, where Straper sat on a moldy couch. They had been traveling in the submarine for eight days now with little to occupy their minds. The Korean crew spoke only broken English and avoided the outsiders altogether. They did get a few English TV channels, a minor luxury. Gilda and Straper had been cut off from the outside world for six months at the United Third's headquarters. It was strange and unnerving to see how much the world had moved on without them.

"What are you watching?" Gilda asked, sitting next to Straper on the couch.

"The news," he groaned. "Ain't no movies on or nothing."

"This is Union network," an anchorman said on the holographic screen. He had the oily appearance of a used car salesman and talked just as fast as one. "I'm Jeff Springer, here to give you the truth and nothing but the truth."

"Why do I have a hard time believing that?" Gilda scoffed.

"Here's the United Third highlights." Ominous music began to play. "Incognito's bounty has gone up another ten million, reaching a total of three hundred million smackaroos!"

"People complain about their bosses being monsters," Straper said. "And we're no different, except we might actually be right."

"Meanwhile, the search for the two missing cadets is still underway," Springer said. Pictures of Gilda and Straper came onto the screen.

Gilda was numb to having her face plastered on television. She hadn't expected anything else. At least they weren't reporting that she had joined up with the United Third.

Straper laughed. "Hey, who's the stud they're showing?"

"Anyone with information regarding these two cadets must contact the authorities immediately," Springer said. "A reward is being offered for their safe return."

The screen switched to a blurry photo of Slate.

"Now to the Helmet Man. He is not only responsible for the attacks on the Helios Tower, the Pale Pyramid, and the Bunker, but he is also thought to have kidnapped both young Gilda Plato and Kevin Straper. Since then, he has been ruthlessly attacking convoys of African civilians on Incognito's orders. His bounty is now a whopping hundred million!"

"Why is my bounty only a third of fricking Incognito's?" Slate whined. He had just entered the room, back from causing trouble somewhere. "Do I have to burn infants alive? Honestly, people wouldn't know good supervillainy if it bit them in the ass."

"In other news, *Leviathan*, now the largest ship in the world, is scheduled for its first launch next month," Springer said. "Reports of a new walker model are also circulating. President Hynes himself will be one of ship's first passengers and plans to tour—"

The holographic screen disappeared. Naomi held the remote and set it down on a small table next to her. While everyone else was wearing their usual boring clothes, she had on a different outfit.

Straper gawked. "Uh, what are you wearing?"

"Oh! So hot! Ugh!" Slate cried.

Naomi was dressed as a geisha. She wore white makeup and bright red lipstick, as well as a blue kimono, her locks pinned back with two long hairpins. The getup magnified her beauty tenfold. Straper had a hard time keeping his cool, while Slate didn't even bother trying.

Slate rubbed his gloved hands together. "Ah, yes... That's what Daddy likes."

Naomi sighed and raised her hand. The Helmet Man flew across the room and slammed into the wall. He slumped to the floor, leaving a sizable dent in the wall.

"Ouch..." Slate moaned. "I ... regret nothing..."

"Anybody else wish to voice their opinions?" Naomi asked.

Straper quickly shook his head. "No, ma'am."

Gilda scowled. "Yeah, I do. What's with you playing dress-up?"

"There is a method to my madness," Naomi said. "Although I must admit, this getup reminds me too much of Cyphrus."

"Who's that?" Gilda snapped.

"Just someone I knew. But enough of that. We have business to attend to."

Naomi grabbed a wooden chair and sat down. Moaning, Slate got on his feet and went over to join them.

"Cloak has begun to act once again," Naomi said. "They are influencing the Japanese prime minister. Our goal is simple: we must uncover how they are doing this."

Straper laughed falsely. "Doesn't sound so simple."

"Let me explain further, then. As you may know, the world is divided between two superpowers, the Western Union and the Chinese Empire. The Western Union's member nations make up most of Europe and North America, while the occupied regions include South America, Africa, and the Middle East. The Chinese Empire, meanwhile, controls most of Asia and various Pacific islands."

"You're giving us a basic geography lesson," Gilda said. "You think we're idiots?"

"Whoa, we control South America!" Straper yelled. "When did that happen?"

Gilda sighed. "About twenty years ago. Maybe we *do* need a geography lesson."

"The Chinese Empire controls most of Asia, many Pacific islands, and a good portion of Oceania," Naomi continued. "The only country not associated with the Chinese Empire or the Western Union is Japan. Right now, the Western Union is trying to convince Japan to abandon its isolationist ways and reopen itself to international trade. The Union also wants an Asian country besides South Korea to help hold back the Chinese Empire's expansion. Now it seems Cloak is manipulating the Japanese prime minister in order to botch this potential alliance between Japan and the Western Union."

Gilda rubbed her chin. "So, is Cloak working for someone or acting on its own?"

"That remains to be seen."

"How do you know all this?"

"I once worked for Cloak, remember?"

"Yeah, I haven't forgotten..."

"Hey, Slate, you're Chinese, right?" Straper asked. "Know anything about them?"

Slate chuckled. "Nah, just some racist jokes."

Naomi cleared her throat. "Now it's time to explain the plan." She gestured to Slate with reluctance. "Slate here will be the backup and patrol for any signs of Cloak. Straper will accompany him to makes sure he behaves himself."

"Hey, I'm always on my best behavior," Slate said. "My best just isn't good enough."

"What makes you think I can control this guy?" Straper exclaimed.

"Slate won't go on a rampage if he knows his friend could get caught in the crossfire," Naomi said. "At least I hope so. A member of the yakuza, the Japanese mafia, will be your guide. He will make sure you don't draw attention to yourselves. Japan is a homogenous country with less than ten thousand permanent Western residents there. You'll have to disguise yourselves while traveling around Tokyo."

"So, what am I doing?" Gilda asked.

Naomi smiled, her eyes suggesting something mischievous.

Gilda's own eyes went wide. "No. No way. Not in a million years."

"I thought you were willing to do anything to avenge your friend, Henry Marker," Naomi said. "Or does your pride mean that much?"

"What are you guys talking about?" Slate asked.

***

"Now that's what I'm talking about," Slate called out.

Like Naomi, Gilda had dressed up as a geisha. Her face was covered in makeup, and a loose-fitting kimono was draped over her. Gilda's most noticeable feature, her purple hair, was covered by a black wig. Unlike Naomi, she looked like a wilted flower in her outfit. Her face was scrunched up with rage. Fingernails dug into her palms as she squeezed her fists.

Straper tried not to laugh. "Looking good, Gilda."

Gilda clenched her teeth. "Shut up…"

"We are almost in Japanese waters," Naomi said. "Both Gilda and I will deal with the prime minister. You two just stay out of trouble unless it manages to find you."

Straper threw up his hands. "But you've barely told us anything."

"Like what?"

"Like about the other Gifted."

"The only Gifted who may attack us are Geppetto and Atlas. One's a dwarf, the other a red-haired giant. Sebastian and Cyphrus mainly work behind the scenes. As for Ember, she doesn't typically take part in these kinds of missions. I doubt you'll encounter her."

"Oh, I met that dwarf guy over twenty years ago," Slate said. "He's a real hoot. I think I also met this Cyphrus you talked about. Talk about your Grade A snob. A real—"

"Why don't you let me finish?" Naomi snapped. She turned back to the others after composing herself. "Geppetto can possess other people's bodies, and Cyphrus is able to control electronics. But I don't know what Atlas is capable of, other than he's freakishly strong."

"How do you not know your own friend's power?" Gilda questioned.

"'Friend' is a strong word, and Sebastian has a habit of treating his subordinates like mushrooms. Keeps us in the dark and feeds us—"

"There are only five Gifted still left in Cloak?" Straper asked.

"Don't underestimate them. Even without their powers, they are brilliant tacticians and ruthless killers. Eight Gifted managed to create the world's most dangerous criminal organization. You've dealt with Houdini. You know Cloak."

Captain Young-Bum walked into the room, not bothering to knock.

"We are surfacing now," he said. "A fishing vessel will be waiting to take you to the mainland. You best hurry. We cannot let the Japanese coast guard see us."

"Good work," Slate told him. "Let's give the man a hand, everyone!"

Young-Bum growled, touching his mechanical hand self-consciously. "Good thing you are about to get off my ship, because I am about ready to throw you overboard."

***

The fishing vessel docked at the harbor. It was night out. Japanese fishermen began to unload the ship, keeping their eyes down as they worked. Naomi led her entourage off the vessel without causing a ruckus. After several minutes of sneaking around, they stopped behind a rundown warehouse filled with old equipment.

"You the guys?" a voice asked from the darkness.

"Yes, come on out," Naomi said.

A Japanese man in his late twenties emerged. He had donned a worn suit and a bored demeanor. Despite his uncouth appearance, he was highly intelligent and an expert English speaker. Five other men in suits stood behind him. They did not speak English.

The young man glanced at Slate. "Whoa, you must be that helmet guy on the news."

"Yay, I'm famous!" Slate yelled.

"You're infamous," Gilda muttered.

The young man sighed. "Whatever. The name's Rikuto. Behind me are my associates."

Naomi bowed her head. "We are grateful for your help."

"All right, all right," Rikuto huffed, raising his hand. "No need for formalities. First things first, you need to disguise yourselves as Japanese." He took out two silver collars from his coat and handed one each to Slate and Straper.

"Here, put these on. They're the latest in spy technology. It's a real hassle to get your hands on these, so try not to break them."

"Sweet, brah," Straper said, putting the collar on his neck. As soon as he did this, a holographic projection surrounded his head. His face was now that of a Japanese teenager. Slate also put his on. A holographic head of a Japanese man concealed the silver helmet.

Straper laughed. "Whoa, real trippy."

"This thing covers up all my good looks," Slate complained.

"Those collars can translate your spoken words into Japanese too," Rikuto said. "I'll also give you earbuds that translate Japanese into English for you."

Straper took the collar off. "Uh, you sure this isn't offensive?"

"What is?" Rikuto asked.

"You know, pretending to be another race."

"You work for a terrorist, and you're worried about being offensive?"

"Just saying."

"Why do they get amazing spy gear, while I'm dressed up in this stupid outfit?" Gilda spat, resisting the urge to rub off her makeup.

"You have the most important job," Naomi said.

"Yeah, what's that?"

"You make me look even better by comparison."

"Shut up!"

"Would you morons be quiet?" Rikuto asked. "Geez, no amount of money is worth this... Okay, you two ladies need to meet the limo in five minutes. From there, both of you will head to the hotel where the prime minister and his guests are staying. As for you two guys, since it's mostly pedestrian walk-ways, we'll have to patrol on foot near the hotel. We shouldn't have to do anything if all goes according to plan, so just keep cool."

"Cool is my middle name," Slate assured him.

"Dude, you don't even have a last name," Straper pointed out.

"Why can't you let me have anything?"

***

Naomi and Gilda sat in the back of the limo. Gilda was unable to look out the tinted windows, much to her annoyance. Not only was she in this ridiculous geisha costume, but she didn't even get to see a smidgen of Japan. This, among other offenses, motivated her to give Naomi the silent treatment as their yakuza chauffer drove them through downtown Tokyo.

Naomi decided to break the ice. "Are you a lesbian?"

Gilda shot her a bewildered scowl. "What kind of question is that?"

"Nothing to be ashamed about," Naomi said, shrugging with a smirk, almost feline in her predatory playfulness. "Just trying to spark conversation."

"Well, try some fricking lead-up next time. And no, I'm not."

"How about boyfriends? Anyone at the United Third camp?"

"I have better things to do right now than date."

"How about that Kevin?"

"Straper? No way!"

"Fine, settle down. We've got only another fifteen minutes before we reach the hotel. I hope you remember your role."

Gilda scoffed but calmed herself. "Yeah, I remember."

They sat there in silence for a couple of minutes before Gilda spoke again. "Why are you doing this?"

"Doing what?" Naomi asked. "You'll have to be more specific."

"I mean why are you working for Incognito? Why did you betray the other Gifted and Cloak? What are you after?"

"You're asking me all these questions as if we were best friends. Funny, I thought you didn't care much for me."

"I *despise* you. You kill people. You worked with those murderers who killed Henry and countless innocent people."

"Can't you just get over that?"

"No, I can't just 'get over that.' I want to know how you could possibly live with yourself. What motivates a psychopath like you?"

"Fine, let me ask you something. What motivates Slate?"

Gilda laughed harshly. "Don't compare yourself to him."

"Answer my question," Naomi said. Her tone made Gilda tense up. It was not a pleasant feeling.

"Slate wants to find his dad," Gilda replied.

"His dad?"

"Yeah, his dad was a Keymaster. They aren't biologically related, but he seems to really matter to Slate."

Naomi closed her eyes for a second. Then she opened them again. "Slate has another goal, doesn't he? What is it?"

Gilda's lips thinned. "Slate said he wanted to kill the leader of Cloak."

Naomi turned her head and stared at her with a cold intensity that Gilda couldn't match but couldn't look away from either.

"No, he won't," Naomi told her. "The Mentor is mine."

CHAPTER 7

Countless skyscrapers obscured the night sky. They were covered in holographic screens that displayed advertisements and public messages from the government, such as curfews and traffic updates, while three-dimensional holograms of soda bottles and wide-eyed cartoon animals hung in midair. The streets, meanwhile, were filled with commuters and shoppers. Even this late at night, Tokyo was a bustling city. It was also strikingly similar to many Western cities in terms of layout and infrastructure.

However, all advertisements in Japan were for homegrown products and entertainment. There was no Coca-Cola, McDonald's, or Hollywood flicks to be found. Isolationist policies had turned the country into a self-contained and self-sustaining civilization. As such, there was little diversity of products, which allowed black markets and smugglers to flourish. The only way for the average Japanese citizen to keep in contact with the rest of the world was through illegal proxy servers. Japan also had a severe overpopulation problem and often suffered various shortages. The pressure was now on the current government to establish better relations with the Western Union, especially since Chinese military vessels had been getting bolder in recent months. Of course, there was still much distrust of the West in Japan.

"Man, we're just walking around in circles," Straper said, the collar around his neck translating his words into Japanese. "Can't we stop?"

"Just another hour," Rikuto said, also in Japanese. He led the way around downtown Tokyo while staying close to the hotel Naomi and Gilda were heading to. Both Slate and Straper wore collars and plain business suits. The other five yakuza members followed at a distance, keeping their eyes peeled for trouble.

"I can't understand a word you're saying," Slate moaned, not able to wear his translator earbuds for obvious helmet-related reasons. "Speak English!"

"Be quiet," Rikuto said under his breath. "You want to get noticed?"

Straper shook his head. He knew the Helmet Man was not acting out just for the fun of it. Slate wasn't the kind of guy that sat around doing nothing, and he especially didn't like how the hologram was obscuring his silver helmet. He was too used to being the center of attention. Plus, he had to wear some crappy business suit, which Straper didn't care much for either.

"Seriously, I'm starving," Straper said. "I almost want to eat that nasty uncooked fish."

"It's not nasty," Rikuto snapped. "Man, I hate being your tour guide."

"Then why agree to it?"

"Because the United Third is the yakuza's biggest supplier of weapons, genius."

"Huh, Incognito supports organized crime?"

"Yeah, how do you think he funds his little terrorist organization?" Rikuto asked. "You don't get that kind of dough from donations alone."

"I'm learning new things about our boss every day." His stomach growled. "Okay, maybe I *will* eat that uncooked fish. Can we stop?"

"This isn't a vacation, kid. You should have eaten before the mission."

Straper sighed. "Yeah, you're right. I shouldn't be such a whiner."

Rikuto returned his own sigh. "Look, I'd offer you a candy bar, but it could disrupt the hologram if you ate, and once your gal pals complete their mission, we'll have to make our escape pretty quickly. We can't afford to sit down for a bite."

"All right, I get it." Straper chuckled. "You know, you're pretty decent for a guy who works for the Japanese mafia."

"I'm half-decent at best, and in these messed-up times, a lot of decent people get involved with questionable enterprises. Look at you. Working for Incognito? Sneaking into a foreign country illegally? If anything, you're a shadier guy than I am."

Straper wanted to jest, but that observation had been too on the nose to joke about. He only sighed again as his disguise allowed him to disappear into the human sea.

***

Atlas ate a box of sushi, sitting behind the wheel of the car. Geppetto sat next to him in the passenger seat, scanning police radio chatter on a small hand-held device. Large crowds of drab businesspeople passed by their car, as well as some weirdly dressed teenagers, but Atlas was primarily focused on the front of the hotel.

"Look who's coming," Atlas said, plopping another piece of sushi into his mouth.

Geppetto glanced out the window and grinned. "Hey, geishas. *Oh là là.* I like the tall one, but the shorter one is kind of dumpy. Seems a bit sad too. No, more like angrily compliant."

"Do you think they work for Incognito?"

"Probably, but Cyphrus told us not to intervene. We're only supposed to look like we're trying to stop Slate and the United Third."

Atlas frowned as he finished the rest of his sushi. "You sure about this?"

Geppetto stopped grinning and turned his attention back to the scanner. "We both decided on this together. Cyphrus is the best bet we have."

***

Naomi and Gilda got off the elevator and were led down the hall by two officers with the Security Police. After they went through the metal detector, the two fake geishas entered a spacious room with straw mats, sliding doors, and a ceiling covered in paintings. A dozen Japanese men sat on the floor in a large circle, sipping sake from small cups. Naomi walked into the center of the room and bowed. The Japanese men bowed in return.

Gilda came in after Naomi. She knew that most of these men had high positions in the Japanese government. One of them was the prime minister, a balding man with bright red cheeks. Gilda bowed but knew she did it wrong when the men began to laugh.

Flustered and annoyed, she sat next to where Naomi stood. Naomi gestured for Gilda to give her two fans. Suppressing a scowl, Gilda handed them to her.

Naomi stood and looked as though she were about to perform a dance routine. The tipsy politicians leaned in. Naomi waved one of her fans.

An invisible force slammed their heads on the floor, knocking them out. The officers standing in the far corner of the room barely had a chance to draw their guns before Naomi waved her other fan multiple times. Unseen strikes slammed into the officers' heads, knocking them out as well. Distant shouts could be heard. Naomi gestured to some furniture and had the items block the doorway. Officers outside banged on the door, but the barrier would hold, at least for the time being.

Gilda was speechless. She knew Naomi could move solid objects with her mind, but she hadn't expected anything this unreal. She also hadn't expected things to escalate so quickly.

"A silly outfit is one thing, but I wasn't about to do a dance for them," Naomi told her.

"What the hell! Talk about covert. You didn't even need me here."

"I did, actually. You have a very trustworthy appearance, which made it so much easier to get in here, and it's tough to be covert with what I'm about to do."

Naomi dropped her fans and went up to the prime minister, who was lying on the floor. She took a plastic syringe from her sleeve and slammed it into his neck.

"What are you doing?" Gilda cried. She could hear officers trying to get into the room.

"I need a sizable blood sample," Naomi said. "Good, now we can—"

The prime minister grabbed Naomi's arm and rose from the floor. His mouth began to open. The veins in his head turned black, his eyes now bloodshot red and rolled back. A cry escaped him. It sounded like a drowning baboon.

On instinct, Gilda ran up and kicked the prime minister in the head. The man let go of Naomi's arm and fell again. Naomi, meanwhile, was frozen in place.

Gilda almost screamed as the prime minister got to his feet. The man let out another scream, which caused his face to stretch out and become twisted. He bolted at her, saliva spewing out of his mouth. Gilda jumped out of the way just in time as he ran right past her. He slammed into the wall and began to punch it, leaving half a dozen holes in the wood. Unable to hold back any longer, Gilda let out a horrified yelp.

"Death to Chinese!" the prime minister shrieked. "Hail Japanese!"

Naomi finally got her wits about her and, using her mind, shoved the prime minister into an outside window. He smashed right through the glass and fell out of sight.

"We have to leave," Naomi said.

Gilda got to her feet. "You don't have to tell me twice."

"Get on my back, quickly."

Without question, Gilda wrapped her arms around Naomi's neck, piggyback style. Then Naomi flew out the window.

***

"Isn't Naomi done already?" Slate complained.

"Be quiet," Rikuto told him. A few passersby shot them looks, but they attracted no more unwanted attention beyond that.

"I'm tired of waiting on this chick," Slate said. "This is taking too long."

"He might be right," Straper told Rikuto. "Shouldn't we have heard something by now?"

"If we don't hear something in the next half hour, we're supposed to scram," Rikuto said. "Until then, you both need to keep your lips zipped."

Around five minutes later, the phone in Rikuto's pocket began to ring. They all kept walking as Rikuto answered it. "Are we done?" he asked the caller.

"No, I'm being pursued," Naomi replied, sounding out of breath. "We need backup."

"Ah, hell. Where are you?"

"Jumping from rooftop to rooftop. A lone enemy is following."

"Are you—?"

"Just get the Helmet Man over here." She rambled off an address. "It's in the alley south of that building. I'd handle this myself, but I've got Plato on my back."

"Okay, we'll be there." Rikuto hung up and spoke to Slate in English. "Your friends are in trouble. You need to follow me."

"Great, let's kick some ass," Slate said.

The three of them dashed to the right with Rikuto leading the way. The five yakuza members jogged after them, knocking aside pedestrians. They didn't have time for stealth anymore. Rikuto took Slate and Straper into an alley. The five goons hung back to prevent pedestrians from interfering. The trio continued until they reached an adjoining alley.

Rikuto skidded to a stop. "This is the spot."

"So, where are they?" Straper asked.

"There!" Slate shouted, pointing at the rooftop in front of them. A silhouette of a geisha could be seen landing on the roof four stories above. A horrible screech sounded as a figure landed right behind her. Both Rikuto and Straper froze at the sight.

"Crap, it's almost caught up with them!" Slate yelled, aiming his glowing hand.

"Wait, no—!" Straper warned, but he was cut off by the sound of a beam. It flew through the air and passed just in front of Naomi's pursuer, who stumbled backward in response. The beam shot straight through a rooftop water tower.

A tsunami fell down from above.

"Holy—!" Rikuto cried as a wave of water knocked Straper and him off their feet. They were swept down the alley until they collided with the yakuza members. All seven of them were washed into the street. Pedestrians squealed as water rushed over their feet, while a takoyaki stand was knocked down. The vendor screamed curses at the sight.

Rikuto was sprawled on the sidewalk, soaked from head to toe. His men were either unconscious or struggling to stand. Straper moaned as he found himself face down in a puddle. He only found the strength to get up when he felt his neck get shocked.

"Shit!" Straper saw his own reflection in the water. His own reflection! His collar must have shorted out. His disguise was now useless. Pedestrians gathered, a few of them pointing at Straper, many of them muttering to one another in Japanese.

But that wasn't the worst part.

Slate landed in front of him, having avoided the water by flying up in the air. "You all right, kiddo? Don't worry about the suit. Incognito can pay for dry cleaning."

Straper yelped. "Slate, your helmet!"

The Helmet Man self-consciously touched his namesake. The hologram no longer concealed his silver prison. He had fried his collar after using his powers. A businessman gasped. Two teenage girls babbled. A bag lady shrieked. More witnesses now began to gather.

Slate shrugged. "Well, blending in ain't my style anyway."

CHAPTER 8

Hank Powers opened another energy drink and chugged it down in a minute flat. He crushed the can and tossed it on the floor before belching.

"This is dull as hell," Powers said. "How long do I have to wait here? My talents are wasted on this kiddie stuff. I thought I'd be shooting terrorists by now."

Powers sat inside his walker, observing the streets of Tokyo from an alley. Nobody noticed the mecha due to its advanced cloaking technology. It caused the surface of the walker to blend in with its surroundings, making it almost invisible. The Western Union had gotten permission to have a limited task force operate within Japan, its purpose to capture the Helmet Man and his associates. But Powers had been on standby for over four hours now, and nothing had happened. What was taking those terrorists so long?

"Pardon me, sir," his walker's autopilot interrupted. "But you're getting a transmission from Ms. Ryder."

Powers laughed. "She can't stop worrying about me, huh? Fine, put her on."

A holographic screen with an image of Camilla Ryder appeared. She wore her usual blank look but seemed attentive.

"Report," she commanded.

"Nothing to report," Powers scoffed. "Just sitting on my ass."

"And there you shall sit. According to our source, the Helmet Man is here in Tokyo. However, our source was recently killed in Sydney, along with his escorts. The target may know about our ambush. Nevertheless, we cannot pass up this opportunity."

"Then why can't I have tracker bullets or any heavy artillery? Don't get me wrong, I can still do the job, but it won't be as fun."

"The Western Union is attempting to establish an alliance with Japan. The last thing we should do is destroy half of downtown Tokyo."

"Whatever. Civilians get in the way all the time. Killing a few ain't a big deal."

"Is that supposed to be a joke?"

"Right, forgot you don't have a sense of humor."

Camilla Ryder glanced sideways. Someone off-screen was talking to her. Ryder nodded and turned her attention back to Powers.

"The Helmet Man has been spotted by police snipers five blocks north of you."

"Finally!" Powers yelled. "Let's kill some terrorists."

"Remember, no civilian casualties."

"Relax, boss! Don't forget who you're talking to."

"Precisely why I feel the need to remind you."

***

Even with the windows rolled up, Atlas could hear the water tower burst a few blocks away. Having heard the noise themselves, the nearby pedestrians on the sidewalk had stopped moving and now focused their attention on the source of the commotion.

Geppetto raised his chin as he listened to the police scanner. He began to chuckle.

"What is it?" Atlas asked.

"Looks like Slate's causing trouble. How about we go help him out?"

***

Dozens of bystanders pointed at the Helmet Man, many taking pictures with their phones. Everyone gave him a wide berth. Despite being an isolationist nation, even Japan knew of the Helmet Man and his supposed atrocities.

"Uh, nothing to see here, folks!" Slate yelled. "Move along! Just a cosplayer here!"

Still dripping, Rikuto stumbled over to him. "You idiot! We gotta get out of here before the cops show up."

Slate turned on his heels, tensing up.

"What is it, dude?" Straper asked, becoming tense himself.

"A walker's coming," Slate said. "A big one. You folks need to skedaddle."

Before they could take his advice, canisters of tear gas flew into the crowd. The white gas was thicker than morning fog. Bystanders began to cough and flee. Straper and Rikuto ran away as well, leaving the Helmet Man behind.

"About time something happened!" Slate shouted. He shot up in the air, flying low above the streets. Some civilians pointed at the Helmet Man, but most were too busy fleeing the gas to pay him any mind. An arrogant voice boomed on a loudspeaker.

"You must be the Helmet Man," Hank Powers declared. "Prepare to meet your ultimate foe. Tremble as I come at you full strength and guns ablaze. Let me show you the true meaning of pain. Let me show you—"

"Shut your piehole!" Slate shouted from above. He sent ten lightning bolts at the walker. Slate sensed objects through an electrical field and vibrations, so the cloaking device the walker used didn't fool him. All the bolts hit Powers' mecha. The cloaking device shorted out, and the machine became visible. It stood twenty feet tall, five feet taller than most walkers. Its torso was massive and looked like it could take several shells to the chest. The walker was painted a bright yellow, one reason for its ironic name, Hornet.

"Weakling, you didn't even dent me," Powers said. He raised his walker's arm and shot a barrage of bullets at the Helmet Man. Slate flew to the side, and the bullets missed. He rocketed down the street, away from Powers' walker.

"You're not going anywhere," Powers spat. The giant walker strode fast down the street. Civilians jumped out of the way as Hornet sped past. Laughing, Powers aimed his cannon arm and shot nets at Slate. One of them hit the Helmet Man's leg, causing Slate to lose control and crash to the ground.

Hornet stopped before Slate and raised its fist. Slate rolled to the side just as the metal fist came down. It hit the concrete, sending cracks throughout the pavement. Enraged, Powers swung the walker's other arm at where Slate was now, but the Helmet Man had gotten untangled from the net and flew up, avoiding the blow.

"Get back here and fight me like a man!" Powers bellowed. "Don't mess with Hank Powers!"

"Incredible," Slate said. "There's somebody more annoying than me."

Just as Slate was about to shoot a beam, a swarm of bullets flew at him from the side. On instinct, he dove out of the way and fired electric bolts at the skyscraper, right where the gunfire was coming from.

"Crap, who is it this time?" Slate asked himself.

***

Geppetto smiled as he controlled the police snipers like the puppets they were. Atlas stood behind him, unwrapping yet another foreign candy bar. The snipers were supposed to be backup for that yellow walker, but now they were just helpless pawns of Cloak. Most of the men were sweating and shivering and tense with terror. They didn't know why they couldn't control their own bodies, but they were helpless to resist.

Lightning bolts shattered the windows. Shards rained on nearby snipers, temporarily blinding them. Geppetto grimaced. He couldn't get these men to aim properly. Granted, he only needed to make it look like they were trying to stop Slate and his friends, but Cloak still needed to put on a show of effort, perhaps inflict a few casualties.

"Atlas, why don't you show them a little muscle?" Geppetto asked.

Gnawing on his candy bar, the red-haired giant picked up a bazooka.

CHAPTER 9

Gilda held on for dear life as Naomi soared through the air. They flew above skyscraper roofs, the wind rushing past them. It was almost like a dream. The very idea of someone flying was ludicrous, yet Gilda was hitching a ride from someone who clearly could.

They heard a scream behind them. The prime minister was jumping from rooftop to rooftop in hot pursuit. Apparently, Slate had only managed to temporarily impede the creature.

"Just great..." Naomi seethed.

"Can't you just fly up higher?" Gilda asked.

"With you on my back? I'll have to drop you off on this rooftop so I can deal with our pursuer myself. Can't have you hanging on me while I fight."

"What is that thing?" Gilda asked.

"Cloak is controlling the prime minister somehow. I had to get a blood sample to see how they managed to do it, but I didn't think he'd be so dangerous."

Naomi landed on a rooftop. Gilda let go, dropping roughly to her feet.

"Stay back," Naomi ordered. "I'll handle this."

The prime minister landed in front of Naomi. Gilda quickly backed away. A lifeless smile appeared on the prime minister's face, his head convulsing and arms curling.

"Death to Chinese! Hail Japanese!"

Just as he was about to attack, a bullet slammed into his torso. A bright light then consumed the prime minister's body, destroying it.

"An incendiary bullet!" Naomi cried. Twisting reflexively, she raised her hands and stopped the other bullets in midair with her mind. She sent them flying backward before they exploded. The bright light almost blinded her, but she was otherwise unharmed. She sped to her right as more bullets slammed into the roof and also exploded, leaving behind giant holes. To make matters worse, she saw a police unicopter heading toward them.

But this inspired an idea.

Naomi flew toward the unicopter. It didn't have time to attack before she punched the air, compressing it into an invisible attack. The invisible blow smashed through the unicopter's windshield before knocking out the pilot. Naomi flew through the broken window and landed inside the aircraft. Two policemen stood frozen inside the unicopter, rendered stupefied by the geisha that had just flown in. Naomi took advantage of their confusion and waved her hands. The policemen's heads were knocked together, putting them out cold.

More incendiary bullets flew at her. Naomi stopped them with her powers and pushed them back. They exploded in a bright flash that violently shook the unicopter. Scanning the skyline, it took her a few seconds to figure out where the sniper was shooting from. He must be perched on Tokyo Tower, east of her. It was the only vantage point that could have allowed the sniper to take all those shots.

Naomi pushed the unconscious pilot out of his seat and took the controls. She aimed the unicopter's mounted machine guns at the sniper's perch and pulled the trigger, sending hundreds of bullets at Tokyo Tower. Nobody was killed, but she saw the sniper jump off the tower's roof, deploying a parachute as he went down. Naomi had to smile. She rarely saw such daring professionals at work. But she was on a tight schedule, so she decided not to go after him. Instead, she swung the unicopter around and landed it on the rooftop Gilda stood on. Using her powers, she dumped the unconscious policemen out of the aircraft.

"Best hurry," she told a bewildered Gilda. "I think we just broke a couple of laws."

***

Rikuto led Straper into a nearby building for cover. It was a vacant pachinko parlor, but they didn't notice much else as they hid behind the counter. Straper took off his uncomfortable collar, which was now useless. He had no idea where the other yakuza members were but guessed they were either still unconscious on the street or had been smart enough to run away.

"It's like the Korean Invasion out there!" Rikuto yelled. "What are we gonna do?"

"Just wait it out," Straper said. "Let Slate handle it. That's why we brought him."

Then Straper noticed a shadow fall on them.

Outside the window, a red-haired giant pointed his bazooka at the shop.

"Run, dude!" Straper yelled.

A rocket flew out of the bazooka. Straper barely had enough time to get out of the parlor before the rocket struck the building. The explosion consumed the parlor, incinerating everything within. Rikuto caught fire while running out of the building. He screamed and danced around the street, unable to put the flames out.

"Rikuto, no!" Straper cried.

Some of the snipers' bullets struck Rikuto, putting him out of his misery. With no time to mourn his new companion, Straper kept running. Atlas followed, reloading his bazooka.

Down the street, Powers growled. Those snipers weren't supposed to act until he gave the order. To top it off, they had just killed someone.

"Ryder, are you there?" he asked. "Did you see those snipers kill that civilian?"

"Yes, I did," Ryder said over the radio. "We are unable to contact the team. We must assume they have been compromised."

"Damn, guess I have to incapacitate them."

Hornet pointed its arm at where the snipers were. A canister of tear gas shot out and went inside the building. A white cloud spewed out of a broken window.

Geppetto began to cough uncontrollably as the tear gas spread. He lost concentration, and the remaining snipers regained control of their voluntary actions, only to start coughing themselves. They did, however, stop shooting.

"Nuts to this!" Geppetto hacked, fleeing the scene.

On the street, Slate stopped sending out lightning bolts, since the gunfire had died down. It seemed the moron in the walker had taken care of them. Slate was about to fight Powers again, but then he sensed a vehicle fast approaching.

Slate groaned. "Come on! I already have enough to do."

A Japanese man in a black jumpsuit drove toward him on a motorcycle. Each side of the bike had a mounted machine gun.

Both of them began to fire.

Slate flew into the air, dodging the attack, and shot some bolts. The motorcycle expertly swerved, avoiding the lightning strikes that hit the concrete. Now the mounted machine guns pointed upward and fired at Slate once again.

The Helmet Man flew toward a skyscraper and pulled up once he got close. Now he was flying upward, parallel to the building. The motorcycle's bullets slammed into the skyscraper, shattering windows. The only civilian injured was a janitor who received a minor scrape.

"Ha!" Slate hooted. "Try following me now."

The motorcycle, not even slowing down, drove right at the skyscraper. Instead of crashing into it, the motorcycle's front wheel went up into the air and touched down on the skyscraper's side. In a feat against physics, the motorcycle, using state-of-the-art gripping technology, began to drive up the face of the skyscraper.

"That's so cool!" Slate cried. "I want one of those."

He sent more bolts at the bike. The motorcycle avoided them, and the bolts struck the building harmlessly. Reaching the top of the skyscraper, Slate landed on the rooftop. His right arm began to give off an aura as he prepared to shoot a beam.

The motorcycle went up into the air, attempting to land on the roof as well. Slate fired a solid blue beam of energy that hit the motorcycle dead-on. It ripped through the vehicle. Chunks of metal and plastic rained down. Hardly anything else remained.

Slate laughed. "Really, that was it? I wanted a real challenge."

But just as Slate was claiming victory, a sword almost cut his right arm clean off. He barely had a chance to move aside, getting a bloody gash in the process.

"Ah!" Slate cried. "My beautiful body is ruined. You'll pay for that!"

The motorcycle driver standing before him had short hair that stood up and a stern demeanor that could only be matched by a scolding father. But the feature that caught Slate's attention was the sword, a katana, in the attacker's hand.

Soundlessly, the man attacked.

***

Atlas fired another rocket.

It sailed over Straper's head and blew up a car. He nearly got blown over and felt like his hair would catch fire. Atlas reloaded as he jogged after his target. Straper looked over his shoulder and yelped. He couldn't keep dodging rockets forever. Maybe he could hide in another store. No, he had to take a stand.

Straper stopped running and pulled a handgun out of his belt.

"Taste lead, brah!" he shouted, firing until his gun was empty. Every one of his bullets met its mark. Seven in the chest. Two in the neck. Three in the arm that held the bazooka. Atlas reeled and toppled over.

Straper let out a sigh. It was good that Naomi had told him to bring the gun. It was also good that the United Third hadn't skimped out on his training. He rewarded himself with a weak smirk. Gilda would be jealous when she heard—

Atlas slowly rose from the ground. His bullet wounds were almost completely healed. The flesh pushed the bullets out, the wounds sealing themselves up immediately afterward. The giant also spat a bullet out of his mouth. It hit the street with a ding.

"He's one of the Gifted," Straper whispered. "Shit, this ain't happening."

Just as Atlas was raising his bazooka, an annoying voice broke the tension.

"You must work for the Helmet Man!" Powers yelled from his walker's loudspeaker. "Prepare to meet the wrath of Hank Powers!"

The walker's fist swung down at Atlas. Instead of hitting its target, the metal fist slammed into the concrete as Atlas hopped to the side.

"A slippery one, huh?" Powers yelled. "No biggie! Soon you'll—"

Atlas grabbed the walker's arm. His arm muscles bulged, the tendons in his neck visible.

With inhuman strength, Atlas threw the walker over his shoulder.

"What the—" Powers cried. His twenty-foot-tall mecha slammed down into the concrete. A giant boom echoed down the street. Atlas let go of the walker and relaxed. Hornet spat sparks as it lay in the middle of the roadway. Its chest looked partially caved in.

"My arm!" Powers screamed from inside his walker. "My arm's crushed! Gah, you'll pay for that! Nobody messes with Hank Powers! I'll hunt you down! I'll—"

Atlas ignored him and looked around. The boy who had shot him was nowhere to be found. Sighing, he took a hot dog out of his pocket and began to eat.

***

Just as the swordsman struck, Slate flew up and sent down a dozen bolts, but the man sliced his sword through the air impossibly fast, blocking all the lightning attacks with it.

"What the ... Are you some kind of lightning rod?" Slate yelled.

The man kicked the roof and shot up into the air. Slate hovered almost twenty feet above, yet the swordsman easily reached his elevation. The man swung his sword, almost cutting Slate in half. The Helmet Man landed on the roof and fired more bolts, but the man kicked the air and flew forward, evading Slate's attacks. The man threw four ninja stars that slammed into the rooftop instead of their intended target.

"Hey, how can you jump in midair like some kind of video game character?" Slate asked. Then he noticed something on the bottom of the man's shoes. They were repulsion pads, similar to the ones on the sides of unicopters. Those pads must give the man the ability to jump unnaturally high and do double jumps in midair to avoid attacks.

The swordsman landed. He didn't even look remotely tired.

"All right, no more Mr. Nice Guy," Slate said. He shot countless lightning bolts, but the swordsman twirled his blade, blocking them. Then he dashed toward Slate.

"Crap, this ain't working!" Slate yelled. He ran up to his opponent and threw a punch, but the swordsman ducked and swung his katana. Slate blocked it with his helmet. The swordsman then tried to cut Slate's leg. However, the Helmet Man jumped up into the air at the last second. Electric arcs formed in between Slate's fingers, and a bright flash erupted from his hands. The swordsman was blinded and closed his eyes tight.

"Got you now!" Slate fired more bolts at the man, but the sword spun once again and blocked all the lightning strikes, despite his blindness.

"What a show-off!" Slate yelled.

The swordsman was about to attack again, but gunfire sounded. Bullets pitted the roof. A unicopter was shooting at the swordsman from above. The man jumped to the next rooftop with his repulsion pads and began his retreat.

"Hey, I wasn't finished!" Slate shouted. "Oh, you men are all alike!"

The unicopter hovered above Slate. It was piloted by a geisha.

"You better get on quickly," Naomi told him from the loudspeakers. "I'm very tempted to leave your annoying ass behind."

CHAPTER 10

Naomi flew the unicopter above Tokyo Bay. She glanced at her three passengers. Straper stared out the back of the unicopter while Gilda tended to Slate's wounded arm.

"Who was that guy?" Slate asked. "He didn't have any superpowers, but he was able to take me on with only a few gadgets and a sword. He's like an Asian Batman."

"That was Keito Kusanagi, an infamous mercenary," Naomi said. "He is supposedly the world's greatest assassin."

"A regular human took on Slate?" Straper cried. "That's someone I don't want to meet. Geez, let's get outta this crazy country. You should have seen what Cloak did to Rikuto. Poor guy didn't deserve to die like that."

"Perhaps he would still be alive if you two had been more subtle."

"Hey, you're the one who needed bailing out," Slate shot back.

"Whatever. I suppose that's what I get for relying on you."

Gilda began to apply red gel to Slate's wound.

"Don't bother," Naomi said. "Growth patches don't work on the Gifted. Our biology is too altered for it to have any real effect. Just use regular bandages on him."

"Growth patches work better than normal bandages, even without the accelerated healing," Gilda said. "Dr. Taylor told me that."

"Geez, wish he were here right now," Straper said.

"Um, how did you meet up with Naomi again?" Slate asked.

"I phoned her like a normal person," Straper told him. He then sharply inhaled and raised a finger. "Son of a ... unicopters are coming our way!"

Six military unicopters of the Japanese Defense Force trailed behind them in the night sky. They were also armed to the teeth.

"I'm not surprised," Naomi said. "We did kill their prime minister."

"You did *what*?" Straper exclaimed.

"It was mostly the sniper's fault, but the Japanese think we're to blame, which is only partially true. Slate, stall them. You need to make up for that water tower nonsense."

Slate stood up, his wound dressed. "Only for you, my lady. Can I get a kiss for good luck? Even a friendly butt pat would do."

"Just go," Gilda hissed. "You can flirt with her later."

Slate jumped out of the unicopter and flew at top speed toward the pursuing aircraft. Bolts left his hands, destroying the missile launchers on a unicopter. It retreated while two others went after Slate.

The three remaining unicopters continued their pursuit. Naomi put their own unicopter on autopilot and left the pilot's seat. The pursuing unicopters fired their machine guns. She raised her hands and stopped the bullets in midair before pushing them back. The bullets slammed into two unicopters, which had to retreat due to serious damage.

"Yeah, they're running away!" Straper yelled.

"No, there's still one tailing us," Gilda told him.

The unicopter fired its missiles.

"Ah!" Straper screamed. "We're gonna die!"

Naomi raised her hands again and focused on the incoming projectiles. Then, with great effort, she twisted her hands.

The missiles exploded in midair. Fire consumed half the sky. The unicopter shook. Behind them, the pursuing unicopter turned sharply to the side to avoid the fiery cloud and gave up the chase. Meanwhile, Slate had taken care of the two remaining unicopters, destroying their weapons and forcing them to flee. He flew back, victorious.

"Hey, did you see me?" Slate asked. "Pretty cool, huh?"

Straper whistled. "That was badass, Naomi. You saved our lives."

"What about me?" Slate whined, waving his arms. "Hey, pay attention to me!"

"I have to admit, that was something," Gilda told Naomi. "Thanks."

"Come on! I'm right here! What am I, chopped liver?"

"How are we going to escape now?" Gilda asked. "I bet a fighter jet is going to show up any minute to finish us off."

"There's your answer," Naomi said, pointing down at the water.

The *Eodum* emerged from the water. The black sub glistened in the moonlight. A metal platform emerged from the back, a landing pad for the unicopter.

"Looks like Captain Young-Bum has come to our rescue," Naomi said.

***

Four hours later, long after the *Eodum* had fled Japanese waters, Naomi entered her private room and washed the geisha makeup off her face. She undid her long hair, letting it fall and hit her shoulders. After getting dressed in a red windbreaker and blue jeans, she got up and activated her hologram transmitter.

Incognito appeared before her. His holographic image shivered. He wore his usual white suit and mask. The intricate pattern on his mask always made Naomi a little dizzy when looking at it. She managed to compose herself, putting on her best smile.

"I heard your mission was a failure," Incognito said. "But tell me, was the mission a complete failure or only a partial one?"

Naomi took out the syringe full of the prime minister's blood and held it for her employer to see.

"You stupid wench," he spat. "Put that blood on ice before it goes bad."

"I *did* have it on ice," Naomi said, her smile thinning. "I only took it out for your benefit. You should be more grateful. I almost died several times over."

"From the looks of it, you didn't. Any injuries I should know about? Your death would make my endeavors far more difficult to undertake."

"No," Naomi said. This was the most concern Incognito had ever shown for her. Although tempted to sigh at that fact, his limited gesture did puzzle her somewhat. Was he merely worried about one of his tools getting damaged?

"The yakuza are quite angry that your guide perished, but I've placated them with a free shipment of firearms," Incognito said. "I also discovered that information was leaked by one of Young-Bum's former crewmates, compromising our mission. Very sloppy indeed. I may have to cut Young-Bum's other hand off as punishment for his incompetence."

"So that's how Cloak was tipped off about our operation."

"But it wasn't just the Gifted who attacked. Who else was there?"

"A sniper shot at me during the mission. He was a trained professional who used incendiary bullets to destroy the prime minister's body, erasing all the evidence."

Incognito's interest seemed piqued. He thought for a moment before responding. "There's only one sniper of that caliber who would work with Cloak. It must be Poppy, an agent of the Black Lotus."

"The Black Lotus... They work directly under the Chinese emperor. This isn't good. If we have to deal with both Cloak and the Chinese Empire, we could be in serious trouble."

"Not to mention Keito Kusanagi and the oaf in the yellow walker. How bothersome. Why must I deal with this rabble?"

"There's also something the prime minister said twice during his little episode: 'Death to Chinese. Hail Japanese.'"

"I have heard rumors that the prime minister was planning to announce the resurrection of the Japanese Empire. Cloak must have been hired by the Chinese to take control of the prime minister's mind. They would make him reject the Western Union and turn Japan into a serious military power."

"Then the Chinese would use that as an excuse to invade Japan," Naomi finished. "They would not only destroy one of their most bitter enemies but also keep the Western Union from gaining control of another Asian country."

"Oh, how the Asians quarrel. My goodness, they're almost as bad as the Western plague that sweeps the planet."

"And who says Incognito's racially insensitive?"

"Silence. I must attend to other matters now. You and the halfwits will stay on standby. I have a feeling your ordeal has only just begun."

***

On a Western Union aircraft carrier floating outside Japanese waters, Camilla Ryder was getting the dressing down of a lifetime.

"You really made a mess this time," Redwood told her. "A real mess."

Admiral Redwood was currently overseeing the final preparations for the first launching of *Leviathan*, so he had to talk to Ryder via hologram transmission. But his authority was not diminished by the lack of his physical presence. Vice President Powell stood next to him, also in holographic form, looking equally ticked.

"Is this how you conduct covert operations?" Powell snapped. "I've been working on this alliance with the Japanese for half a decade. Do you realize how much booze and geishas it's gonna take to placate those Jap politicians?"

Redwood gave Powell an irritated glance.

"My apologies, sirs," Ryder said. Although she was regretful, her face was still an utter blank. Only her dispassionate words held any hint of remorse.

"The Japanese are furious," Redwood said. "They already resent the West for hoarding the Choke vaccine decades ago, but now you turned their biggest city into a battlefield. Their prime minister is dead, dozens of civilians are injured, and there's millions of dollars' worth of damage. You may have single-handedly botched a potential military alliance that would have made the Chinese think twice before going to war with us."

"I did not anticipate that Cloak would be involved," Ryder said. "I take full responsibility for what occurred in Japan. You may punish me in any way you see fit."

Redwood rubbed his eyes. "Ugh, feels like I'm talking to a brick wall." He let out a haggard breath. "Look, you're technically not going to take responsibility. We're going to blame the Helmet Man for this one."

"But I must be disciplined. I must answer for my mistakes."

"To be honest, we could care less if you suffer or not," Powell said. "You think such measly offerings will appease us?"

"Please, punish me. I insist."

"Are you some kind of masochist?" Redwood asked. He sighed. "The president acknowledges that the situation was largely beyond your control. That being said, we cannot tolerate another major incident like this. Deal with the Helmet Man discreetly or we'll find someone who will."

"Sir, that won't be an issue, I can assure you."

***

A few hours later, Ryder swiped her finger across the holographic screen. Another image of Tokyo slid into view. She examined it closely with dead eyes, took a sip of black coffee, and swiped her fingers again. This photo showed the Helmet Man firing a bolt. She leaned in closer. She noticed the fumes coming off his extended finger, the reflection of skyscrapers on his silver helmet, the terrified faces of civilians in the background, the—

Coffee spilled on her lap. Ryder snapped her head downward but remained neutral despite the pain that shot through her leg. Putting the mug down, she stood up from her desk and cleaned her plants with a spare tissue. How unusual... Had she been distracted? By what? The photos? Had they managed to create a ripple? She hadn't anticipated the hunt to be this stimulating. Did it have something to do with her quarry? Ryder would have spent more time reviewing her internal state but checked the clock on the corner of the holographic screen and realized that time was too limited for introspection. She had a meeting to attend.

Ryder soon made her way to the other side of the aircraft carrier and walked into a conference room. Hank Powers sat at a table. He was now missing his left arm and wore a hollow plastic cast filled with red gel over the stump. His limb would grow back in about a week, but Powers still complained, nonetheless.

"This blows hard," he said. "That guy was a dirty cheat. Used some kind of magic trick to flip me over. No way could a human do that. Must be using some fancy robotic exoskeleton. There ain't anyone with superpowers. Just a bunch of conmen."

"Powers, you are relieved of duty until you recover," Ryder said. "Please, no monologues next time you do a covert mission or I shall ensure you never pilot a walker again."

"Hey, gotta keep my image up."

Powers left the room, laughing to himself. Ryder had seriously considered replacing him, but she had to admit that Powers was a gifted walker pilot. He had also helped limit civilian casualties. In fact, the only civilian who died was a member of the yakuza. Ryder would keep Powers for now, even with his personality defects.

Putting Powers out of her mind, she turned her attention to her other subordinate.

"Since we missed our chance in Tokyo, we are now forced to be more pro-active in our mission," Ryder told him. "Intelligence is also lacking, so you will have to use your connections with the criminal underworld to track down our target. Regardless, your mission remains the same. Capture the Helmet Man, dead or alive."

Keito Kusanagi smiled.

***

Cyphrus sat down at the end of the table. She wore a fox fur coat, looking nice and snug in her outfit. Geppetto and Atlas sat down as well, tired and annoyed, but they had done their job well. Everything was going according to her design.

"Excellent, we have all assembled," said Sebastian, sitting at the other end of the table. "Now we can discuss that little incident in Tokyo."

Atlas took out a caramel apple from under the table and took a huge bite.

"Where's Ember?" Geppetto asked. "This is the third meeting in a row she's skipped. Not that I miss that psycho bitch."

"Nothing to be concerned about," Sebastian said. The second-in-command of Cloak wore a blue suit and round sunglasses. His oily hair was combed to the side. An even oilier smile was plastered to his face. Sebastian was also blind, but it seemed to hardly impede him.

"One of the Gifted is missing, and you say that's nothing to be concerned about?" Cyphrus asked. "Pardon me, but I think it is."

Geppetto sighed. "I hope Ember really is dead, but it'd be too good to be true."

"Ember is busy running an errand for me," Sebastian said. "You needn't worry about her safety. She is the strongest of us, after all. Anyway, I plan to send Atlas and Geppetto out again to capture Slate. Houdini failed, so it now falls on you two."

"What? We barely got out of there alive!" Geppetto yelled, slamming his hand on the table. "I want to go back to doing actual work like assassinations and espionage. Hell, I'd rob a convenience store at this point."

Cyphrus nodded. "I agree. There's no point. Why do you want Slate anyway?"

"It is the Mentor's will," Sebastian said. "What other reason do you need?"

"You made his capture our top priority, and you have yet to explain why you are interested in him. One of the main reasons Houdini and Sandtrap were killed was because you told them to do the impossible."

"You forgot about Repulsa. She's dead too, isn't she?"

Geppetto and Atlas looked at each other grimly.

Cyphrus just sighed. "Repulsa is still alive. She is now working with Slate and Incognito. For all we know, she may have been a double agent for years."

Sebastian raised his eyebrows. "How do you know this?"

"I was contacted by Prime Minister Mao Long. The Black Lotus sniper, Poppy, had a run-in with her. She was actively working against us."

A small tear left Atlas's eye as he finished his caramel apple. Geppetto pinched his brow, his face slack. Even Cyphrus seemed distraught at the news of Repulsa's betrayal.

Sebastian, however, was not moved. "Such mundane things are of no concern to the Mentor. Ignore Repulsa but kill her if she gets in the way of Slate's capture. That's all that matters. Ever since he resurfaced, all else has become secondary."

Atlas and Geppetto stared at Sebastian with open mouths.

"What of our partnership with the Chinese and Operation Leviathan?" Cyphrus snapped. "Are those also secondary and mundane?"

Sebastian smiled. "Naturally. It seems you're starting to understand."

"Yes," Cyphrus said. "I think I am."

Geppetto seized control of Sebastian's body. Sebastian tensed up. A bead of sweat ran down his forehead as his grin became strained and malformed.

"We've had enough of you," Cyphrus said. "I sincerely wish it hadn't come to this, but you left us no choice. You are unfit to be our leader. As such, I shall be taking command."

"Yeah, you shouldn't have pissed us off," Geppetto spat.

Cyphrus smirked. "So, Sebastian, what have you got to say?"

Geppetto allowed Sebastian to speak. But when he did, no fear could be found in his voice. His smile even grew wider.

"Yes, I have a question ... What took you so long?"

CHAPTER 11

S hu put a small stone down on the board. "It is your turn."

Eisenhorn crossed his arms. "This game hurts my head. Ain't there anything else to do in this dump? It's all we've been doing for two weeks."

Shu sighed but also smiled. The servant was in her fifties but could have passed for forty. Her hair was tied behind her back, and she wore plain blue robes. Although Shu was mildly beautiful, her kind eyes were what Eisenhorn usually took notice of.

Eisenhorn laughed. "Hey, your name sounds like shoe!"

"You have mentioned that already," Shu said. "Several times, actually."

"Oh … yeah … right…" Eisenhorn said, rubbing his head. He had been confined to his room ever since he came to the Forbidden City. Right now, he was sitting at a table with Shu, his personal caretaker. President Hynes was correct when stating that Eisenhorn would be nothing more than a political hostage. The general had done nothing vaguely official, not even meeting any of the Chinese higher-ups, except for Xing, who occasionally came by. That left Eisenhorn with nothing but free time on his hands. He just slept and ate the strange foreign food. And he couldn't sleep in his uncomfortable bed. Often, the general would curl up in the closet, falling asleep in a nest of sheets and clothes.

Shu alone made his stay in this place bearable. She conversed with him, mostly about different types of food and events occurring within the Forbidden City. However, they soon ran out of conversational subjects. Shu had suggested they go to the courtyard outside the palace, the only other area Eisenhorn was permitted to be. But the general refused, remembering the Traitors' Garden and those statues.

The only activity left was to play Go, a Chinese board game. It hurt his head, but it ate up a lot of time.

With little thought, he put a piece down on the board.

"Ha! Bingo, I win!"

"The game is not over until one of us resigns," Shu said. "But yes, you managed to capture some of my stones. Congratulations."

"Are you sure there ain't anything else to do?" Eisenhorn asked. "How about we smoke some opium? Don't act like you don't have any. The Brits and Chinese got into a whole war over it. How about some alcohol? I haven't had a drink in ages."

Shu giggled. "You are a funny man."

"Ah, yeah…" Eisenhorn said, blushing. "Johnson sometimes told me that."

"Who is he?" Shu asked. "You have mentioned him before."

"He was my subordinate. Like a son, almost. But he kicked the bucket half a year ago."

"I am sorry."

"Not like you killed him. Anyway, I met him during the Korean Invasion. I was one of the leaders of the Western forces. I met Johnson when he was first deployed there. He saved my life, pushed me out of the way of gunfire. Took him under my wing after that. He told me he never had a real dad, just a mom who had to support them both, so I taught him all I knew. This was back before my mind turned to mush."

"You have a beautiful mind," Shu told him.

Eisenhorn scoffed. "But right when the war was ending, I began to act… strangely. My troops had a hard time understanding me … something about surgery…"

"Are you okay?" Shu asked.

The general snapped back to reality. "Yeah, I'm fine. Just a little DJ view."

"You mean déjà vu?"

"Hey, whose first language is English?"

***

Cyphrus was flown to an airport outside Beijing and then driven to the massive Tiananmen Square, at last arriving at the Forbidden City. She walked through the courtyard outside the palace and almost shivered when going through the Traitors' Garden. If she wasn't careful, she might end up there as well.

Before she entered the palace, she was scanned by a metal detector and had to undergo a thorough physical search. No electronics of any kind were permitted inside the palace, nor was any other contraband material such as all forms of Western media. The only electronics allowed in the palace were the equipment in the communications room, technology used by the emperor's personal guard, and anything the emperor himself allowed into his domain.

A couple of searches later, Cyphrus stood in front of the imposing red doors that led to the emperor's throne room. Next to her was a familiar face.

"You gonna get it now," Lily said, her hands clasped behind her back. "Can't wait till emperor string you up and skin you alive, if you lucky."

"I see your English is still wrenched," Cyphrus said.

"You no 'see' me speak, stupid old lady. You 'hear' me speak. Ha! My English better than yours! That so sad, so very sad."

Cyphrus decided she'd already had enough of Lily. She especially hated how that girl kept calling her "old lady" when she was barely in her forties.

"I am shocked to see that you showed up," another familiar face spat. "Instead of fleeing to the ends of the earth, you have stepped right into the dragon's den."

Prime Minister Mao Long strode over to Cyphrus, his eyes filled with loathing. Mao wore a tailored red suit with golden buttons. Draped over him was a crimson cape with golden shoulder pads, each one glinting in the light of the gas lamps mounted on the walls. Cyphrus was also wearing her best. She had on her finest fur coat made from blue Maltese tiger fur, a cat many believed didn't even exist.

"Why, Prime Minister, so good to see you again," Cyphrus said.

"Did I not show you what becomes of failures?" Mao seethed.

"Yes, beating a man to death with a golf club really illustrated the point."

"If not for Poppy, vital technology could have fallen into enemy hands, and our plans would have been foiled."

"I don't recall asking for your help. If anything, you need us."

"Contrary to your belief, we don't require Cloak for Operation Leviathan, and we certainly don't require you."

"The emperor obviously doesn't feel the same way. Otherwise, I wouldn't be here."

Just as Mao was about to spit a reply, the red doors swung open. A man emerged from the throne room, wearing a balaclava, a dark suit, and a conical straw hat. But his most notable feature was his eyes, which had misshapen red irises that looked like petals on his pupils. A large metal sphere rolled beside him. It was black and about four feet in diameter. It had a face carved on its front and a lotus carved on its back.

Cyphrus took a wild guess as to who they were.

"Hello, Mother," Lily said in terrible English, perking up.

"Daughter," the black sphere boomed back.

Lily turned to her brother. "Poppy, long time no see."

"Why are you addressing me in that mongrel language?" Poppy hissed in Mandarin.

Lily giggled. "Somebody woke on bed's wrong side."

"Enough," Mao growled. "Lily, wait for me here."

Both Mao and Cyphrus walked forward, entering the throne room.

"Behave yourself, Mao Long," the black sphere warned.

"Do not lecture me, you sorry excuse for a concubine," Mao snapped back.

The red doors slammed shut behind Mao and Cyphrus. The echo was all too noticeable.

The throne room's ceiling rose high above. Red carpets stretched from the door all the way to the throne itself. Fifty stoic guards were lined up along both sides of the hall. They wore bright red uniforms and sheathed swords that weren't just for show.

An imposing throne decorated in ornamental gold was positioned at the other end of the room. High General Chao Xing stood next to it. He appeared formal and collected, his hairless head gleaming and his black suit impeccable.

The man of the hour himself sat on the throne, Emperor Jin Long, the most politically powerful man in the world besides the head of the Western Union. The emperor was ancient, well over a hundred years old. He was draped in red robes and wore a variety of jewelry. But his rich attire could not obscure his revolting form. His long gray beard was covered in crumbs, his fingernails were almost three inches long, and his stench was so powerful that Cyphrus could smell him from across the throne room. Perhaps the most unnerving trait about the emperor was his demented eyes, dull and insane. They were focused on the floor. A thin line of drool hung from his mouth.

Mao and Cyphrus approached the throne and knelt twenty feet away from it, both trying to look as humble as possible. After a prolonged pause, the emperor made a series of horrid sounds like a cat throwing up a hairball. Xing nodded to his emperor and translated.

"The emperor can understand English, but he does not wish to taint his tongue with the language," Xing said. "As such, I shall translate for our Western guest."

Cyphrus nodded, trying to ignore the foul smell.

The emperor hacked again.

"The emperor is displeased," Xing translated. "He asks why Operation Rising Sun failed. Because of this debacle, he will not be able to subjugate the Japanese dogs."

"Your Highness, the Helmet Man interfered," Cyphrus said. "He was once one of us but chose to join Incognito instead. Both Incognito and the Helmet Man conspire against you and your glorious empire. Not only that, but our former second-in-command, Sebastian, wanted to capture the Helmet Man alive, which is also the major reason for our failure to destroy the Helios Tower. As such, we had to forcibly remove Sebastian from his position. I myself now control Cloak and all its agents."

The emperor coughed before spitting out more words.

"You must deal with the Helmet Man yourself," Xing said. "The emperor also wants Operation Leviathan to continue as planned. After the operation is over, you will hand over your second-in-command and the Mentor to the empire. They must be punished for their failure."

"I have no problem handing Sebastian over to you," Cyphrus said. "But I have no idea where the Mentor is located, nor have I ever met or had any prior contact with our leader. All I can promise Your Highness is that the Mentor shall be hunted down by what remains of Cloak until the end of time."

After a few seconds of thought, the emperor vomited out more sentences.

"The emperor accepts this," Xing said. "He will not punish you, since you are but a feeble-minded woman who was led astray by her imbecilic leaders." What the emperor actually said was far more insulting, but Xing decided to be tactful with his translation. "If that is all you wish to say, you are—"

"Actually, I have a proposal," Cyphrus said, trying to act meek.

Xing would have raised an eyebrow if he had one. "Oh, and what might that be?"

She looked up, staring at the emperor with seductive eyes.

"Marriage," she cooed.

Mao, who knelt next to her, stared at her in utter bewilderment. Xing almost stepped backward, his composure broken. Even the guards were tempted to exchange incredulous looks.

All the emperor did was laugh.

Smiling, Cyphrus kept staring at the emperor. The emperor's haggard laughs turned to a fit of coughing. After recovering from this, Emperor Long went silent. His misshapen grin remained present on his face as he licked his shriveled lips. The emperor barked out something in a hoarse voice.

"If you are serious about wanting to wed our dear emperor, he shall consider it," Xing translated, still looking befuddled.

In a flash, Mao got to his feet. "Father, you cannot mean to wed this Western sow. She is a trickster, an abomination, not even human."

The emperor hissed something unintelligible, pointing a filthy fingernail at his son.

"Be silent, Prime Minister," Xing told Mao. "You of all people should know what happens to those who question the emperor's divine wisdom."

Scowling, Mao went back onto his knees. Cyphrus smirked softly.

"But the emperor currently has thirty wives," Xing told Cyphrus. "He does not need another, especially one so … mature. What do you have to offer that no one else can?"

"Your Highness, I do have something to offer you," Cyphrus said as she kept staring dead-on at the emperor. "Something that will amuse you greatly…"

***

As soon as the giant doors closed behind Cyphrus and Mao, the prime minister turned to her. He was tempted to pounce on Cyphrus like a jungle cat.

"What a wretched little shrew you are," he said. "You failed your mission in Japan on purpose so you could get an audience with my father and make that indecent proposal. Do you take me for a fool?"

Cyphrus thought for a moment before nodding.

"So, you like to play games?" Mao flared. "I can play games too."

"Is that an invitation?"

"Don't flatter yourself. My father's tastes have obviously deteriorated over the years."

"Should you really be saying such things about your emperor?"

A throbbing vein appeared on Mao's forehead. "The Helmet Man may have gotten a blood sample of the Japanese prime minister. If he figures out—"

"If that happens, Cloak will take care of it. You just wait here and twiddle your thumbs. Just think, in a few months, you may have to call me Mommy."

Mao Long said nothing. He just stormed off with his cape fluttering behind him.

Lily approached Cyphrus with an exaggerated smile. "You surprise me, old lady," she said. "But be careful not to bite off more than you able to chew.

You too greedy for own good."

In a casual movement, Cyphrus stroked Lily's side. Lily's limbs twisted behind her. They were beyond her voluntary control. Confusion and anger filled her snakelike eyes.

"What–what you do, old lady?"

"So, the rumors are true," Cyphrus said. "You said I'm too greedy? I have only embraced the true meaning of life."

"You going to die, cow!"

"Yes, life is greed. It's greed for love, greed for youth, greed for wealth, knowledge, power, and anything else worth having. All of us were born with a hole in our hearts, an unquenchable thirst. My thirst is greater than most. I won't stop drinking, no matter what. I'll drain the oceans to quench it. And guess what? I won't stop there. I won't stop until I have it all, until I have consumed everything, because that's what we were meant for ... accumulation."

Cyphrus touched Lily again, releasing her. Lily's arms snapped back into place. She gasped and fell to a knee in relief with her arms limp at her sides. Her murderous rage was only contained by the fact that Cyphrus had the emperor's protection.

Cyphrus took a breath in, looking up toward the heavens.

"I ... will accumulate *all*."

CHAPTER 12

"The Helmet Man strikes again!" Springer yelled on the holographic screen. "Japan has become another victim of the terrorist fiend. The prime minister of Japan assassinated. An entire city block leveled. Oh, what tragedy!"

"Wait a sec..." Slate said. "I didn't do any of that. TV lied to me!"

Gilda and Straper sat in front of the holographic screen while Slate stood next to them with crossed arms. They were back to wearing their usual outfits. Gilda was unfathomably grateful to be out of that geisha getup. She had better get a combat role next time, or she might be inclined to go AWOL. She also wouldn't have minded staying in Japan for a bit. Then again, she didn't join the United Third to go sightseeing.

"Isn't there anything else on?" Straper asked. "We've been watching the news for hours."

"This is the only channel we're getting in English," Gilda said. "Everything else is either Chinese propaganda or cheap Japanese cartoons."

"Nothing wrong with cartoons. Well, at least my parents aren't on the news again begging Slate to release me. I mean, they're total tools, but it's still kind of a bummer."

"Coming up, have you been having any strange dreams lately?" Springer asked. "Surveys show a dramatic increase in stressful dreams, particularly lunar-related ones. A panel of experts discuss possible causes behind this phenomenon."

"Hey, Straper, come over here for a sec," Slate said.

Sighing, Straper got off the couch. Slate led him to the corner of the room so they could speak privately. Gilda tried to ignore them.

"Dude, I was watching that," Straper said.

"Shut your hole!" Slate whispered, crouching next to his confidant. "I need your advice. You're the only one I can turn to."

"Okay ... what is it?"

"You've gone on dates before, right?"

"Yeah, dude, totally, I—wait, haven't you?"

It took a second before Straper had his realization and chuckled.

"Hey, be quiet!" Slate hissed. "Do you want a knuckle sandwich?"

"Brah, for real, you've never had a date?"

"Never had the time. I'm very devoted to my evil work."

"I bet that helmet doesn't score you too many points."

"Babes love the bling!"

"Is this about Naomi? If it is, you can forget it."

"Why not? We have so much in common. We both got superpowers, a great sense of humor, and murderous tendencies. Plus, we're both dead sexy!"

"Well, for one thing, she hates your guts."

"I won you guys over, didn't I?"

"Another thing, she tried to kill you."

"Who hasn't? I'm a popular guy."

"You're also super annoying, selfish, graceless, violent, dumb—"

"All right, don't rub it in!" Slate yelled. Gilda glanced over but went back to watching the news almost immediately.

"Dude, relax, I have a lot of those problems myself," Straper told him. "All you gotta do is be cool and act like a gentleman around her. You know, lure her in."

"Ah, you mean trick her? Why didn't I think of that? I shall manipulate her until she is mine! Yes, good, very good!"

"I can hear you!" Gilda yelled. "Geez, you guys are such creeps."

Slate and Straper's immoral chat was interrupted when Naomi and Captain Young-Bum entered the common room.

"Everyone, gather around," Naomi said.

Gilda turned off the TV without much remorse. The group assembled in front of Naomi to hear what she had to say.

"The main purpose of the last mission was to get a blood sample from the Japanese prime minister," she said. "He was being controlled by Cloak in an attempt to destroy Japanese relations with the Western Union and give the Chinese Empire cause to invade Japan. Our mission was only supposed to confirm this revelation, but it seems we were able to interrupt Cloak's plans, even if it meant exposing ourselves."

"Wait, so we just saved Japan?" Straper exclaimed. "Sweet! I remember when stopping a tower from getting blown up was a big deal."

Gilda smiled. She hadn't thought they would be making a difference so quickly. It helped ease her worries about working for Incognito, at least somewhat. But her good cheer faded fast when she realized the implications of their discovery.

"So, Cloak is working with the Chinese?" Gilda asked.

Naomi sighed. "It appears so."

Straper shook his head. "Okay, it's official. Everyone wants to kill us now."

"What was that thing we fought?" Gilda asked. "That prime minister wasn't normal. His veins were black, and he had freakish strength. There's no way he was human."

"Those were the mind-control nanobots," Naomi said. "They're administered via aerosol. The nanomachines enter through the lungs, into the bloodstream, and then the brain, where they rewire neural connections. It's similar to pruning, except these nanobots are rewiring connections rather than breaking them. They were programmed to rewire the brain of the prime minister so that he would hate the West and attempt to recreate the Japanese Empire. Needless to say, Cloak may try something like this again."

"That doesn't explain how the guy was able to jump from rooftop to rooftop or punch holes through the wall."

"The nanobots can also stimulate the adrenal glands. Whenever the mission is threatened or there is a task that requires unnatural strength, the nanomachines push the victim's body past its normal physical limits. The vessels in the eyes burst due to the suddenly increased heart rate, giving them a red hue. The black veins, meanwhile, are caused by the nanomachines flooding toward the head. They reproduce inside their host, so this mind control lasts indefinitely."

"Any cure?" Straper asked.

"No, there is no hope of recovery once someone inhales the nanomachines. The victim is forever controlled. Even if the nanomachines could be purged from the person's system, it would be virtually impossible to rewire the brain back to its original state."

"Disgusting," Gilda spat. "Nothing worse than taking away someone's free will."

"It's a good thing free will doesn't exist, then," Naomi said, smiling. "Anyway, I managed to get a blood sample from the prime minister before he was incinerated by that sniper. I sent it via courier to one of Incognito's contacts, who analyzed the nanobots within the blood. It seems that the nanobots were made by a group of scientists I personally encountered years ago. I helped transport them to a certain location while I was still working for Cloak. I honestly forgot about the whole affair until the nanomachines were traced back to them. Thankfully, I still remember where I put those pesky scientists."

"And where's that?" Straper asked.

"An abandoned research facility on a deserted Indonesian island. It was set up by the scientists I helped transport. They used to work for the Western Union before their funding got cut due to a lack of results, but then some unknown entity began financing them, and they were able to continue their work on this island."

"Let me guess," Gilda growled. "Cloak was funding them."

"Right on the money. From what satellite photos tell us, the island is uninhabited. It's quite possible the scientists were killed by Cloak when they outlived their usefulness."

"So, why are we headed there if nobody's left?" Straper asked. "Seems like a waste of time, if you ask me."

"Well, I didn't ask you," Naomi said coolly. "There may be some research materials left on the island. From those materials, we might be able to find a countermeasure to this mind-control weapon and maybe even a vaccine. There's just one problem…"

"The Neutral Zone," Gilda finished.

"What's the Neutral Zone?" Slate asked. "Is it like the friend zone? You know, like the one I'm trying to escape right now?"

"Except we're not friends," Naomi hissed with a wide grin.

"Idiot, it's disputed territory," Gilda told Slate. "It's between Australia and the Philippines. The Chinese and the Western Union can't decide who gets it."

"Yes," Naomi agreed, regaining her cool. "It's used as a buffer zone between the two superpowers. As such, there's no real political authority there. It's a lawless zone filled with pirates, smugglers, and other nasty characters. The Choke wiped out most of its population seventy years ago, so there is no permanent civilization there. The research facility was put there by Cloak so neither the West nor the Chinese could get their hands on it."

"Oh, why don't I just write my will now?" Straper cried. "We gotta go to a fricking island surrounded by pirates."

"Relax," Gilda said. "We have a stealth submarine. It shouldn't be too hard to avoid trouble and keep out of harm's way."

"Yes, if we had a submarine," Naomi said.

"What are you talking about?" Gilda asked.

"My crew and I will not take you into the Neutral Zone," Young-Bum said. "I refuse to go near that cursed place."

"Young-Bum is afraid of a few haunted islands," Naomi huffed.

"How do you think I lost this hand?" Young-Bum spat, opening and closing his mechanical appendage. "A sea dragon took it from me there."

Naomi rolled her eyes. "First haunted islands, now sea dragons…"

"Regardless of your disbelief, this sub is not taking you into the Neutral Zone. I do not care if I am reprimanded by Incognito. My fear of him cannot even begin to compare with my fear of the Neutral Zone. It is foul water full of disease and despair."

"Really selling us on this place..." Gilda said.

Straper sighed in relief. "So, this means we aren't going to the island?"

"No, it just means we can't take the *Eodum* there," Naomi said. "I managed to convince Captain Young-Bum to take us to the edge of the Neutral Zone. It will be half a day's boat ride from there to the island. Hopefully, we won't come across any hostile forces."

"Haunted islands, sea dragons, and pirates," Straper said. "Great, what else is there?"

"We may encounter a deadly storm, causing us to capsize," Naomi said. "Slate and I may be able to save ourselves, but the rest of you will surely drown."

"I didn't want you to answer!"

***

A unicopter came to rest on the landing pad of a yacht that served as Cloak's unofficial headquarters. Cyphrus stepped out of the aircraft and smiled as the smell of the ocean overtook her senses. It was now hers, all of it. Cloak. The yacht. The remaining Gifted. And soon she would have the Chinese Empire, maybe even the world.

But first, she needed to take care of that laboratory. Too bad she had no clue where it was.

However, she knew someone who did.

She stepped inside the yacht and opened a nearby door without an invitation. Inside the room, Sebastian sat on his bed, petting a yellow dog that panted happily. On Sebastian's neck was a metal collar, which was set to explode should he leave the room. Two dogs, Cyphrus thought, but only one had a collar.

"Cyphrus, how good of you to grace me with your presence," Sebastian said, his oily smile as wide as ever.

"Spare me. I've come for information. You'd be wise to give it. It's the only reason you're still alive."

"So, how did your meeting with the emperor go? It must have gone well. Otherwise, you'd probably be in the Traitors' Garden right about now."

"That's none of your concern. Tell me about the laboratory."

Sebastian sighed, though still in good spirits. "I hired a team of mercenaries to kill all those scientists five years ago. The facility itself is still intact, should I have ever felt the compulsion to do more weapons research. Yes, such wonderful times."

"Do you know why we betrayed you?" Cyphrus asked.

"I assume because you are greedy," Sebastian said, rubbing behind his dog's ears.

"You think all our struggles are mundane."

"Only because they are."

"You treated your subordinates like crap, ignored your duties, engaged in secretive activities, and were apathetic to anyone's needs except your Mentor's. Now I have to resort to keeping you prisoner while I try to prod secrets out of your demented mind. And yet you sit here, oblivious to all that's around you."

Sebastian chuckled. "Oblivious? I know that you proposed to the emperor so that you can manipulate *his* demented mind. You wish to be an empress, ruling a good fourth of the world. I also knew that you planned to betray me."

"Then why didn't you try to stop me?"

"Because you're clearing away all our enemies, like that pesky Mao Long. You also managed to get an audience with the emperor, paving the way for the Mentor to control the Chinese Empire. And if your plan involving *Leviathan* goes smoothly, the Western Union may soon be in our possession as well. But it takes the Mentor time to act, so until that time does arrive, I might as well sit back and enjoy the show."

Cyphrus said nothing for a while. Then, after calming herself sufficiently, she spoke.

"The Mentor isn't real. This leader of ours never existed. The Mentor is just a figment of your fractured mind. In reality, the only other two people who ever shared your devotion to the Mentor were Houdini and Ember. That's because they needed the dream. They needed a protector and a teacher to keep them going. They were too broken to live without the Mentor, as are you. Now Houdini is dead and Ember is missing. All that's left of the delusion called the Mentor is you, Sebastian."

Sebastian shook his head. "You're the only one who is deluded, Cyphrus. I'm the blind one, yet you cannot see the raw power that is the Mentor. I'll tell you what, because I pity you so, I shall answer your question. The laboratory is located on a small island in the Neutral Zone. I have the exact coordinates for you right here. Be careful, though. Repulsa's been there before, so I'm sure Slate and his young friends will be headed there too."

He handed her a slip of paper. She snatched it out of his hand. The dog next to Sebastian growled, foaming at the mouth. Cyphrus jumped in her skin.

"One day, I'll make a fur coat out of that mutt," she spat.

Sebastian continued to smile. "And one day, the Mentor may do the same to you."

CHAPTER 13

They saw the island in the distance. Naomi turned the boat toward it. It had been a long trip. The gang had done nothing but sleep, watch the news, and prepare for when they landed. They neared their destination by the break of dawn, so they would have the whole day to search the island. Naomi wasn't very hopeful they would find anything, but they had no other realistic options for finding a countermeasure to Cloak's weapon.

"There it is," Naomi told her comrades. They all stood in the wheelhouse of their small vessel. Straper had gotten some medication for his seasickness, so it didn't hammer at him anymore. Everyone, except for Slate in his black attire, wore green combat fatigues. Even Naomi was subject to this dress code, which she took in stride.

"We're going to try spending as little time as possible here," she said. "Straper, you're staying on the ship. Use your sniper rifle and the radar to watch out for any unwelcome guests who might come near the island."

"Fine by me," Straper said. "Glad I don't have to wander around some creepy island."

"The rest of us will be responsible for finding the laboratory," Naomi said. "The exact location of the facility is not known. Satellite imagery couldn't help us due to the dense jungle foliage. Thus, we need to do a ground search of the island, starting with the east shore where we will land. Then we'll work our way to the west shore."

Gilda glanced out the window. "Looks like we're almost at the island."

Straper used binoculars to look at the distant landmass. "I see an empty boatshed where we can put our boat. It's old and ratty-looking, though."

Naomi snatched the binoculars out of his hand and had a look. "It'll be fine," she said, handing back the binoculars. "The shed will conceal our boat better than any other spot on the coast that I can see. Just stay vigilant."

The group could now see the island up close. It was covered in thick jungle, but several wooden structures lined the coast. A dormant volcano poked out of the jungle, brownish in color. Decrepit concrete buildings from the distant past could also be seen, but nothing else was visible through the vegetation.

"What do you think is on that island?" Slate asked. "Maybe there are tiny people, or cannibals, or pirate treasure!"

"Dude, remember, be cool," Straper whispered, glancing discreetly at Naomi.

"Oh, right." Slate leaned against the wall. "Yeah, whatever. Life is meaningless. I'm a rebel without a cause."

Straper smacked his forehead. Gilda and Naomi simply ignored the Helmet Man.

Slate went on for another minute. "Just a stone-cold thug. That's what I am."

The boat reached the coast, and Naomi parked it in the old boatshed. Using her powers, she levitated a sheet of rotting plywood in front of the boatshed to conceal their vessel.

"I left a little opening so you can watch the ocean," Naomi told Straper. "Enjoy the view, but keep your eyes peeled."

"Okay, but what if one of the Gifted shows up, like that Atlas dude?" Straper asked. "I shot twelve bullets into the guy, and he just shook it off."

"Gilda and I will have radios," Naomi said. "Give me a call if you encounter a situation that you're incapable of handling."

"Geez, you're making me sound pretty feeble."

"That was my intention," Naomi teased. "Gilda, it's time to unload your walker."

Gilda nodded and went to the back of the boat. A large tarp was covering a massive piece of equipment. She yanked it off, revealing Magenta.

Her walker was custom-made and unique in design. Its limbs were slim and thin, making it faster and more agile. It could also jump much higher than the average walker. The namesake of the walker came from its unique paint job. Its odd color wasn't good for stealth missions, so Gilda was surprised they hadn't painted it over. Then again, it was a rather pointless endeavor to conceal a fifteen-foot-tall mecha without a cloaking device.

But the most abnormal feature of this walker wasn't its color but its ability to fly. Large dragonfly wings could extend out of its back, levitating the mecha and allowing it to fly at speeds even faster than most fighter jets.

Gilda had stolen Magenta during the terrorist attack at the Helios Tower and fought off agents of Cloak with it. When she and her comrades fled Dubai, they had used Magenta as the getaway vehicle. But Incognito had kept it from her until now. The United Third must be letting her use Magenta as a sign of trust. She was grateful to see it again. It gave her a sense of purpose outside of dressing up like a geisha.

"Stop daydreaming," Naomi snapped. "Get in the walker. We're heading out."

"All right, don't get your panties twisted up."

Not long after, Slate, Gilda, and Naomi began their long trek across the island. Magenta took the lead, its wheels rolling silently. Naomi and Gilda were both going out of their way to be tight-lipped and stealthy. Slate, on the other hand, was singing out loud and marching onward with a cheerful attitude.

"Jungle! Marching in the jungle! Marching in the—!"

"Shut up already!" Gilda shouted from her walker's loudspeaker. "Were you dropped on your head as a baby?"

"You two need to be quiet," Naomi said. "Especially you, Slate. Enemies may be around, and your singing is awful. Those are two excellent reasons for you to keep your trap shut."

Slate shrugged. "Whatever, babe. Just keeping it real, as always. I'm a bad boy who follows nobody's rules."

"I have an idea," Naomi hissed. "Why don't you search the north side of the island while Gilda and I go work through the south side?"

"No way! A man must protect his female companions." Slate proclaimed this with hands on his hips, attempting a heroic pose.

"Please, do this for me," Naomi said, smiling slyly. "Or I'll break your neck."

"Whoa, threatening, flirtatious, and polite," Slate said. "That's the ultimate way to make a man do something."

"Just leave!" Gilda shouted.

"See ya later!" Slate giggled, running away with his hands in the air.

Naomi shook her head, opened her canteen, and took several large gulps. Today was going to be long, and it was already hot out, not to mention humid.

Gilda sank into her walker's seat. Her anger cooled as her thoughts turned to other matters. Something had been eating at her ever since they left Japan. It had to do with Naomi. What was her motivation? Why did she betray Cloak? It must be revenge. Gilda knew how that felt. Her best friend, Henry, had been gunned down by Cloak. Although Gilda still wanted to stop them, she had realized that she couldn't let hate drive her. But if Naomi had been living off the desire for revenge for years on end, who knew what was boiling inside her? It made Gilda worried, even a little scared, thinking about what made Naomi tick.

"Why do you hate Slate?" Gilda asked. "I know he's annoying, but you really got some sort of vendetta against him."

"I'll tell you this much," Naomi said. "Slate only acts righteously when it suits him. Once you and your friends no longer interest him, he'll run off, maybe even discard you all. There's no real logic to his actions, only deranged selfishness."

Naomi looked in the direction where Slate had gone. "His loudness and lack of stealth may be to our advantage. He'll attract any hostiles while we quietly search the island. And if we're really lucky, he might even die."

***

Trudging through the dense growth, Slate trampled bushes and snapped branches with his arm. He wasn't allowed to fly over the island so as not to attract attention. The same applied to Gilda and her walker. Now Slate was trying to avoid clearings and paths in order to be more inconspicuous. It wasn't working out.

"Stupid plants," he growled. "What ever happened to climate change? I thought we would have killed nature by now."

It had been over an hour already, and Slate hadn't found a single thing of importance. If he was going to impress Naomi, getting some intel was the best way to do so. He had to be back on the boat by sundown. That gave him only nine hours.

Slate stumbled into a small clearing, relieved to be out of the thick vegetation. He took a step, but then something snapped near his feet. He hopped backward. A large net fell right where he had been.

"Huh, that's weird," he said. He kept moving forward, undeterred by the failed trap. After five more minutes of walking, he sensed another snap. He flew up into the air. A large log rolled down the hill and passed underneath him before it fell into a ravine.

Slate dropped to the ground. "Something funny's going on. Whatever. Ain't my problem."

A small figure scurried into the bushes. It carried a spear.

"Hang on a sec, it *is* my problem!" Slate exclaimed. "Okay, let's figure this out. Traps don't just set themselves ... unless this is a haunted island. Ah, ghosts!"

The figure approached from the rear, preparing to pounce.

"Nah, it ain't a ghost," Slate said. "Because ghosts don't use spears..."

Before the figure could attack, Slate spun around and shot a bolt of energy. The bolt hit the figure dead-on and knocked it over.

"Ha, you suck at this!" Slate yelled. "Nobody gets the best of—"

Slate tripped on a root and fell flat on his front. After several seconds of scrambling, he got back on his feet and ran to where his attacker lay. It was a young boy, covered in dirt and wearing filthy gray clothes. His face was dark and handsome. Curly black hair covered his head. The bolt had burned a smoking hole in his shirt. His eyes were shut.

Sighing, Slate pointed a finger at the boy's chest. "Better restart his heart. Don't want everyone nagging me."

But that wasn't necessary. The boy jumped back to his feet and pointed his spear right at Slate. His eyes were hostile yet calm.

"Who are you?" the boy asked. "Where did you come from? Are you a monster?"

"Well, I've been called a monster before," Slate said. "But I'm more of a sexy beast."

The boy kept pointing his spear at Slate, but he started to smile. "Heh, what does that mean? Is that a swear word?"

"Yep, and I know lots of others!" Slate began to list them off one by one, even providing some detailed definitions.

The young boy started laughing. Dropping his spear, he fell on the ground, where he rolled in the dirt and held his belly from sheer amusement.

"Sadly, that's all I know," Slate said. "I'm impressed you managed to shake off my attack. I must have gone easy on you or something."

"Ha ... don't worry," the boy said, getting up. "It was just a little scary. I was told by my friends to go limp if something tried to attack me."

"Guess your friends have never heard of double-tapping before."

"What's that?"

"It's when you shoot someone twice to make sure they're dead."

"What's dead?"

"Oh, that's a bit harder to explain. It's like ... hmm ... when you fall asleep forever because your body's been too badly damaged."

The young boy thought about it for a second before nodding. "That's what happened to all those pigs and birds I ate. Didn't know for sure that people could be 'dead' too."

"Those were your traps?"

"You bet. I sometimes catch two birds if I'm lucky."

Slate smacked him upside the head. "Brat, I almost got killed! Do you know how precious my life is?"

"Sorry, but I wanted some meat," the boy said. "Fruits and bugs and roots get really boring after a while. Sometimes I catch a fish, but it's hard."

"All right, quit your whining. They call me Slate. What's your name?"

"Thomas. You got a weird head. Are you a robot?"

"Not since I last checked. I wear this helmet as a fashion accessory. It also helps me restrain my powers."

"You have superpowers? So cool! You got to show me."

Slate chuckled. "At last, I got a fan club."

CHAPTER 14

S late pointed his finger and sent a lightning bolt at his target. The wooden log flew backward with a scorch mark on its surface.

"That's amazing!" Thomas yelled. He was sitting cross-legged on the ground, his wide eyes focused on Slate's performance.

"I'd show you my beam attack, but it'd attract attention," Slate said. "Took me a while to perfect it. My beam's really done wonders against some of my more heavy-duty enemies."

"Geez, I wish I could see it."

"Don't worry. You'll see it later. Do you honestly think I'd pass up an opportunity to show off?" Slate stretched his arms before remembering his whole reason for being on the island. "Hey, kid. Do you know where I can find a lab?"

"What's a lab?" Thomas asked.

"Crap, this is gonna be harder than I thought. Okay, do you know where buildings are? Do you even know what a building is?"

Thomas's stomach rumbled. "I'm hungry. Let's head back to my hideout. I got to show the others what you can do. They'll be so excited."

"Hang on. Others?"

"Yeah, my friends are waiting."

"Are they imaginary or something?"

"They're as real as you and me. Come on! Follow me!"

Dutifully, Slate marched after Thomas, who knew his way expertly around the jungle. He hopped over rocks and crawled under logs like he had been doing it his whole life, which he likely had. Slate almost had a hard time keeping up.

After several minutes of walking, they came upon a small cliff.

"I'll be able to get down by flying," Slate said. "You need to take the long way. I'd carry you, but you'd be shocked to death if I—"

Thomas responded by jumping off the cliff.

"Ah!" Slate cried. "What are you doing?"

The young boy tumbled down the cliff. His body bounced off several rocks.

"Don't die!" Slate yelled. "I'll never get a date if you do!"

Slate jumped after him. He tried to fly, but a loose rock hit his shoulder, and he ended up falling the whole way. A small avalanche of rubble followed him. Slate soon found himself lying at the bottom of the cliff with a large boulder on top of him.

"That's always fun," Thomas said, dusting himself off.

"Ow..." Slate groaned. "My neck ... my back ... my buns..."

Thomas blinked. "You didn't like it?"

"Kid, don't you know what pain is?" Slate asked, moving the boulder off himself. He got to his feet and rubbed his sore shoulder.

"Uh, no ... I just thought it was fun," Thomas replied.

"What, you're telling me you don't feel pain?"

"I guess so," Thomas said, putting his arms behind his head. "What is it exactly?"

Slate shook his head. "Seriously, how could a kid who grew up on a deserted island be so ignorant? Okay, well ... pain happens when you're hurt."

"Like when a lizard can't walk because its leg is broken, or when fish and bugs stop moving when they get damaged or pulled apart?"

"Yeah, when stuff like that happens, your body starts getting ... uh..."

"Sad?"

"Kind of ... Hold the phone. You're saying you can't get hurt?"

"Why would that happen to me?" Thomas asked. "I'm not a bird."

"Huh..." Slate picked up a piece of wood and smashed it upside Thomas's head. The young boy flew backward and landed on his rear.

"That was fun!" Thomas cheered, sitting up. "Do it again!"

Slate laughed. "Whoa, it's true!" He lifted Thomas effortlessly and tossed him at a tree, slamming him into it. Bits of bark flew everywhere. But the boy hopped back onto his feet and smiled even wider.

"Geez, I never get to have this much fun," Thomas said.

"Me neither!" Slate hooted. "I should try this with other children."

"I just got to show you to my friends!" Thomas shouted, running off into the jungle.

Slate jogged after him. They kept pushing their way through the brush and tumbling off the sides of cliffs. After about an hour of this, they finally arrived at a wooden shack with a rust-covered satellite dish on the rooftop. There was also the hum of electricity.

"This is my hideout," Thomas whispered. "Keep it a secret."

"No promises," Slate said.

Thomas opened the door and let Slate in. It was filthy inside, a thick layer of dust and dirt everywhere. The small mattress in the corner was blanketed in leaves and smelled of urine, although Slate couldn't smell and Thomas didn't mind. A bag of fruit and roots rested in the corner. It gave off a sweet smell that slightly covered up the stench. There also appeared to be running water. The faucet dripped incessantly.

A holographic screen floated in the other corner. Its image was shaky and distorted, but one could still make out a couple of cartoon animals jumping up and down. Two figures, meanwhile, sat on the couch before the screen.

"Guys, I'm back," Thomas said. "I brought a friend."

"Someone on the island?" a scholarly voice exclaimed in a Greek accent. "Send him in, quickly! I must examine every inch of him."

"Who are you people?" Slate asked. "I want to know where the laboratory is. I also want some lady advice."

"Can't help with this lab nonsense," a commanding voice told him. "But I do know a thing or two about the enigma that is the opposite sex."

A man rose from the couch. He had messy white hair and wore a suit with a blue outer jacket. His clothes were grimy and torn.

"What's your name?" Slate asked.

"My name? Well, good sir, I'm George Washington."

***

After trekking for two hours, Naomi spotted something of interest.

"Finally, we made a discovery," she said. Before them was moss-covered construction equipment and piles of rotting wood.

"Tim, do you notice anything?" Gilda asked.

"None of the construction equipment looks operational," Tim said. "Judging from that and the decay of the timber, it's safe to say this site is very old."

Tim was her walker's autopilot. Gilda had almost forgotten that he existed, but she was grateful to the computer for helping her during the Helios Tower incident. Hopefully, he would prove to be just as useful in the future.

Naomi noticed a laminated piece of paper on the ground. She picked it up and began to read, her eyes quickly scanning it.

"It's a list of building materials," she said. Naomi had an earpiece on so that Gilda didn't have to use her walker's loudspeaker to communicate, thus attracting less attention. Gilda had only used it before for Slate's benefit, since he couldn't wear an earpiece.

"This place was a building site for a carousel," Naomi went on. "See the horses over there?"

Gilda glanced over at nearby greenery and saw the plastic face of a horse poking out of the palm leaves. Its red smile seemed empty and twisted. She could practically hear the laughter. How could something so innocent give her the creeps like that?

"Here's another piece of paper," Naomi said, picking it up. "It says 'Blast from the Past Island, opening next year.' It has pictures of George Washington, Julius Caesar, and some dinosaurs. It must be a historic amusement park."

"Hang on, this island's a theme park?" Gilda asked. "I thought a laboratory was supposed to be on it. Did we come to the wrong place?"

"This is definitely it," Naomi said, furrowing her brow. "I remember dropping off the scientists, but I never went onto the island itself. This amusement park must have been abandoned before being finished, probably due to the

Great Choke. The Choke spread through Indonesia like wildfire, killing virtually its entire population. It's likely that when the Neutral Zone was established, all hopes of finishing the park were lost."

"How come we didn't know about this until now?"

"Cloak must have paid people off to erase all records of the island. Not only did this island have preexisting utilities, but it was also isolated and free from any government control. It was the perfect place for Cloak to set up a top-secret laboratory."

"Ms. Naomi, there's a pathway to your left leading to an old building," Tim said.

Naomi saw the top of a building rising out of the foliage, but she couldn't see a path through all that thick jungle. She took Tim's word for it and began to move slowly through the foliage. She raised her hand, making a small path with her powers by pushing the branches and grasses to the side.

"Wait here," she told Gilda. "Your walker is too big to follow me."

After a short trek, Naomi found herself in front of a twenty-story building. It was full of holes and covered in vines. The stone façade around the front entrance had numerous cracks. The doors had fallen off their hinges long ago. She lowered her hand, and the foliage shifted back into place behind her. She went cautiously through the front entrance.

The lobby was dimly lit, but sufficient light shined through the broken windows. Water damage had ruined the wallpaper and the carpets, while the front desk had practically rotted away. Three rusted luggage carts sat in the middle of the room. Naomi deduced that this had once been a hotel, presumably for potential guests of Blast from the Past Island. Judging by how everything was falling apart, Cloak likely hadn't set up its laboratory in this building, but she decided to explore the main floor to confirm this suspicion.

She moved slowly through the hotel as if she were underwater and went through a door leading into a conference center. She looked up. The ceiling was high enough to be obscured by a veil of darkness. Water droplets rained down. Naomi let one hit her cheek but used her powers to divert the others.

She glanced around. Clipboards and storage bins rested on tables that lined the walls. Large water containers and cases of medical supplies sat in the corner. Hundreds of flimsy mattresses lay on the floor.

And on each mattress rested a human skeleton.

They had been dead for decades. Over three hundred forgotten souls. They must have been sick with the Choke and were unable to leave the island. Ants crawled in and out of the fleshless skulls, having made nice homes out of the remains of the Choke's victims. Naomi could imagine all those abandoned cities throughout Indonesia, all the skeletons and decaying infrastructure. All she had to do was multiply what she saw before her by a million.

A horrid thought occurred to her. What if the virus was still floating around? They could all be getting infected. But she quickly dismissed such a notion. Even if the Choke could survive this long without a host, Gilda and Straper must have had their shots against the virus. As for Slate and herself, they were perfectly fine, since the Gifted were theoretically immune to all diseases. Theoretically... No, she had to get hold of herself. Young-Bum's paranoia must have rubbed off on her.

There was nothing of worth here. She let another droplet hit her cheek and left.

Naomi soon returned to where Gilda and her mecha were waiting.

"Find anything?" Gilda asked.

"No," Naomi said. "Not a thing."

***

Slate sat down next to Thomas. The young boy was munching happily on some fruit. Across from Slate sat George Washington.

"What was your name again?" Slate asked.

"General George Washington," the man proclaimed.

"Hmm ... Do I know you from somewhere?"

"Uncultured swine!" a scholarly voice exclaimed. "He's the first president of the United States. My word, you youngsters really must read more."

The scholarly voice came from a severed head resting next to Thomas. The head was that of Aristotle, who had a flowing beard and stern eyes. A bundle of wires came out of the bottom of his head. Next to him was a knight in gray armor who was missing an arm. Colorful wires dangled from his stump.

"Okay, I appreciate the history lesson, but I seriously doubt that the fricking king of America himself would be here," Slate said. "Who are you people?"

"We are not people," Aristotle spat. "We are androids, attractions for Blast from the Past Island. I remember being activated just before everyone started to leave. They didn't even bother to turn us off. That's how fast they left. Yes, I also remember that several other humans stayed behind, but they died quickly from some ailment."

"This place is a theme park?" Slate asked. "Then why aren't there any churro stands?"

"It never opened," Washington said. "The owners haven't been back here in decades. We're practically nothing but rust now." To illustrate this point, Washington unbuttoned his shirt, revealing a bunch of old circuit boards and corroded wires, then quickly buttoned it back up again. "The only other humans who have been here since were a group of ruffians. They came over ten years ago but soon perished. The only good that came of them was this boy. He's been nothing but a blessing to us. We fed him and took care of his basic needs for the first couple of years, but he has since been foraging himself."

The knight nodded but kept silent.

"Can this knight guy talk?" Slate asked.

"He used to utter boring phrases," Aristotle said. "But the march of time has damaged his speakers beyond repair."

"Can you show me where these 'ruffians' hung out?" Slate asked. "I'm trying to impress this chick, so I need to trick her—uh, I mean woo her—into dating me by getting some info."

"Why would we help someone with such foul intentions?" Washington questioned.

Aristotle sighed. "Love is composed of a single soul inhabiting two bodies."

Thomas burped. "That was tasty. Hey, Slate! I'll show you the place if you want."

"Finally, we're getting somewhere," Slate said. "I've had it up to here with invulnerable children and robots and haunted islands. Let's just—"

A continuous screech came out of Washington's mouth. Slate jumped to his feet and raised his fists. Thomas yelped and scurried backward.

"What was that?" Slate exclaimed.

"I don't know," Thomas said. "That's never happened before."

"It's the intercom system," Aristotle said. "A signal is being sent to us."

"Then why aren't you doing it too?" Slate asked.

"I don't have a receiver anymore, and the knight's speaker is broken."

After a minute of this, the beeping and screeching stopped. Then, abruptly, a pleasant voice came out of Washington.

"I see you..." the voice cooed. "I'm so glad these androids were just lying around. It makes it that much easier to communicate with you."

"Who are you?" Slate demanded. "And why is your voice so sexy?"

"You said the S-word again!" Thomas exclaimed. He laughed in relief, but he was still plenty tense.

"My apologies," the voice said. "Allow me to introduce myself. My name is Cyphrus, the new leader of Cloak."

CHAPTER 15

Straper stayed in his position all morning, not even going for bathroom breaks. While he was at the United Third camp, Nigel had taught him some of the basics of shooting. One of those basics was how to keep still for long periods of time. Any time Straper moved, Nigel had given him a sharp swat to the neck. It proved to be an effective learning tool.

Straper looked through the scope of his long rifle at the calm ocean before him. The plywood that Naomi had put up provided some cover for their boat, with a small hole allowing him to poke out his rifle barrel, but if any enemy managed to get close up, it wouldn't be a very good disguise. He needed to spot his foes long before that could happen.

So far, nothing of interest had crossed his sights or popped up on the radar. Straper sighed. Was sniping all he had going on for him? Gilda had her skills as a walker pilot and a mechanic. Plus, she knew how to fight pretty well. Slate and Naomi, meanwhile, could do practically anything with those freaky powers.

Of course, Straper didn't mind sticking behind during suicide missions, but guard duty? He sighed again. Was it a smart move to join the United Third? Definitely not. Gilda had been the one with conviction. He just got swept up in the moment. Now he was an enemy of the West and working for a psycho with a scythe. What exactly would the rest of his life look like? Would he die young fighting supervillains? Even if they did defeat Cloak, would the Western Union accept him back? Could he live a normal life again?

But then Straper remembered normal: a boring childhood with two neglectful parents. True, his parents had demanding government jobs, but they had spare time. They just chose to spend it at fancy parties and adult-only vacations. Straper loved them, he supposed, but he didn't miss them much either. Most of his other relationships, including girlfriends, had sucked too. And he would have ended up a soldier, probably get his leg blown off during combat and earn a cheap medal before spending the rest of his life in veteran housing.

He also remembered Gilda and Slate, how much he enjoyed hanging out with them and helping them out, how he had stopped being such a douche, how the massacre at the Bunker had changed him, and how much he wanted to beat Cloak.

"Maybe this is the life for me," Straper whispered.

Then he remembered Rikuto's wails as he burned alive.

"Maybe not…"

A gunshot rang out.

Straper almost swallowed his tongue. He stopped contemplating and peered through this scope. A line of smoke crossed his vision. He followed it to its source and gulped. At least a dozen boats were approaching the island, each one filled with trigger-happy pirates.

He groaned. "Looks like Cloak's showed up."

***

The unicopter landed near the base of the dormant volcano. Atlas, who was devouring a large slice of pizza, was the first to get out. Geppetto exited next, binoculars and a tablet computer in his hands. Two more unicopters landed behind them, each containing a dozen mercenaries equipped with automatic weapons and wearing camo outfits. From this high vantage point, they could see almost the entire island.

"The pirates have just landed," Geppetto said, looking through his binoculars. "Those idiots are supposed to start wreaking havoc when Cyphrus gives the word." He snorted. "Seriously, I thought we'd be done with Slate now that Cyphrus is in charge."

"So, what are we going to do?" Atlas asked, finishing his pizza.

"Why, we have the dubious honor of killing the Helmet Man ourselves."

***

"You're the head of Cloak?" Slate scoffed. "Then what happened to the Mentor?"

"The former leadership has been deposed," Cyphrus said through Washington. "But I don't want to talk about them. I want to talk about you, Slate, and about the future of Cloak."

"Why should I care about Cloak? All you guys do is attack the weak. A real suave villain attacks the strong, like the military or something."

"Perhaps you could make Cloak that way. I'm asking you to join us. Repulsa and your other friends are also welcome. You see, we're in need of some recruits, since only three of the Gifted are still with Cloak, including myself."

"Probably due to bad management. Can't say I blame you for taking out your bosses. They're bad eggs. So, is the Mentor still alive? I really wanted to kill that guy."

"I am afraid you're chasing a phantom. Really, why does everyone always wish to talk about the Mentor? I suppose the air of mystery is appealing, but still..."

"Who's that lady talking?" Thomas asked. "I see ladies sometimes on TV, but I haven't ever met one in real life."

"Is that a friend?" Cyphrus asked. "You keep strange company."

Slate shrugged. "What can I say? I've got a wide circle of friends."

"He who hath many friends hath none," Aristotle said.

"Maybe you should shut up," Slate growled, kicking Aristotle's head.

The severed head pouted. "You're even worse than Alexander."

"I think we're getting off track," Cyphrus said. "You know, Slate, I've always idolized you. Repulsa did too at one time. Do you remember me? We met once. I was young, barely a girl. You were full-grown. But now we're both full-grown, aren't we? Just how handsome are you underneath that helmet?"

"Ooh, a frisky one," Slate teased, caressing George Washington's face.

Thomas and Aristotle exchanged unnerved glances.

"What do you say, Slate?" Cyphrus asked. "Would you consider working with me?"

Snickering, Slate shook his silver head and withdrew his hand. "Working for Incognito ain't a picnic, but I'd rather work for a terrorist than you cretins. Now that Cloak's losing, it wants to become best buds with me? Forget it. You guys are either too weak or too crazy."

"And which one am I?"

Slate laughed. "Actually, you're both!"

Aristotle chuckled. "Oh, what banter!"

Thomas laughed too but was unable to hide his apprehension.

"Fine, spit on my offer," Cyphrus hissed. "Here's another proposal. You and your friends leave the island immediately and never again interfere with Cloak's operations. If you don't comply, we will be forced to slaughter you all."

"Okay, now here are my two offers," Slate said. "The first is to get bent. The second is to eat a turd. Either one is fine with me."

"So, slaughter it is…"

The knight android lunged at Slate, but the Helmet Man roundhouse-kicked the knight's abdomen in retaliation. The android was knocked to the side and fell onto the gross mattress.

"No, don't fight!" Thomas yelled. He ran up and started punching Slate's legs. "You leave my friends alone!"

Slate growled and kicked Thomas back. "Stupid kid! That lady is controlling them somehow. Just stay outta the way."

George Washington and the knight both ran at Slate, but all Slate had to do was fly up in the air. The two androids crashed into each other. Their mechanical limbs got tangled together as Washington made electric screeches.

"Let us leave," Aristotle told Thomas. "We must find that foul woman who's controlling the others and put a stop to her."

"Whoa, this Air-is-throttle guy's pretty smart," Slate said. He grabbed Thomas's hand and Aristotle's severed head and dragged them both out the door before shutting it behind him. He barricaded the entrance with some old logs. Washington and the knight slammed their bodies into the door, attempting to break it down, but their attempts proved futile.

"What's happening to my friends?" Thomas asked, tears in his eyes. "Are they going to be ... ah ... hurt like the bird and its broken leg?"

"Quit crying already," Slate said. "We'll kick that Cyphrus's ass and stop your friends from acting crazy, so be quiet. Men don't cry."

Sniffling, Thomas calmed down a bit and wiped his runny nose. His eyes were red, but life in the jungle had made him tough. He nodded with determination.

"Just save my friends, please."

"Have no fear, my boy," Aristotle said. "If this brute looks good for anything, it's solving matters by force. He will defeat that horrid woman. Just you wait."

***

"Looks like we found the scientists," Naomi said.

A large pit had been dug right in the middle of a clearing. Scorched bones and burnt pieces of clothing littered the bottom of the hole. Naomi jumped in and scrounged through the remains. Magenta remained near the edge of the pit, keeping watch.

"Judging from these bullet casings, my guess is they were shot," Naomi said. "The bodies must have been burned afterward."

"Cloak did this," Gilda spat through her radio.

"It is rather revolting," Naomi said. She picked up a half-melted driver's license with a picture of a jolly man in his fifties. She smiled softly and put the card back on the ground.

"What is it?" Gilda asked.

"I remember this man," Naomi said. "His name was Dominick, a man from Berlin. He always smelled of peppermint."

"You seem a little ... sad. Weren't these scientists bad people? They worked for Cloak and built that horrible mind-control weapon."

"They just wanted to continue their research. Cloak hid their true intentions from these scientists until it was too late. At that point, I have no doubt that these men and women became Cloak's slaves. Then they were disposed of."

Naomi got out of the pit. "Gilda, you asked me how I could live with myself. The truth is I can't. I can't possibly live with my actions or with what Cloak has done. To be honest, I sometimes wonder why I still bother to breathe."

Gilda blinked. "Then ... what keeps you going?"

Naomi took a breath in, looking into the sky. Everything seemed so peaceful up there. "Revenge ... salvation ... I'm not sure. Hope for either one, anyway."

Something rumbled behind them. Gilda spun her walker around. Naomi raised her arms. But they just stared with open mouths when they saw what had made the noise.

A Triceratops emerged from the foliage. One of the dinosaur's three horns had broken off, and a huge chunk of its scaly flesh was missing. Wires and shifting gears could be seen inside the beast. Smoke billowed from its mouth.

"Ms. Gilda, that's no dinosaur!" Tim exclaimed. "It's a machine, like me."

Gilda sighed. "Thanks for stating the obvious."

"Interesting," Naomi said. "It must be one of the attractions. Androids never really caught on, probably because they looked too lifeless and were costly. And human life is far too cheap these days for androids to be utilized as a labor force. Only wealthy enthusiasts and theme parks still have them. What's really intriguing is this one still works after seventy years."

"Excuse me, but that's not the only one," Tim said.

Naomi twisted to see an Ankylosaurus waddling into the clearing behind them. It was covered in a spiky shell and had a large, club-like tail. Half of its face was torn off, revealing a metal skull and its camera eye.

"Any others we should know about?" Naomi asked.

"Actually..." Tim began.

Another mechanical dinosaur came out of the jungle, the biggest of them all. Its arms were small, but its mouth was full of teeth.

"A Tyrannosaurus rex," Naomi observed. "What else did I expect?"

"Naomi, can you hear me?" Straper yelled over the radio. "Get back to the boat! A bunch of pirates are coming. I can't fight them on my own. Naomi, help!"

Naomi ignored him. She had her own problems to deal with. "On the count of three, we fly," she whispered to Gilda. "One—"

Without provocation, the dinosaurs charged.

CHAPTER 16

The Helmet Man dashed through the jungle with Thomas and Aristotle's head on his back. They were on a mission to get Cyphrus, wherever she was hiding. Stopping her was the only way to get the androids back to normal.

There was just one small problem.

"Uh, where are we going?" Slate asked.

"I thought you knew," Thomas said. "We need to hurry. My friends are in trouble."

"Geez, that's all you talk about. Maybe that hag is hiding out somewhere on the island. Naomi told me she could control electronics. I guess the first place to look is somewhere with computers and stuff. Know any places like that?"

"Yes, the lab," Aristotle said. "The building you wanted to go to earlier."

"That must be the place," Thomas said. "I can't think of anywhere else."

"Great, let's go," Slate said.

"Slate, who's this 'Naomi' you mentioned?" Thomas asked.

"She's this hot chick I'm trying to hook up with. What a babe! She's a solid nine out of ten. Solid ten girls are a myth. Don't let anybody tell you otherwise. It's a conspiracy!"

Aristotle made a face. "Vile creature ... ranking women like that."

"Is she on the island?" Thomas asked.

"Yep, along with two of my—"

Slate stopped talking, skidded to a stop, and fired two bolts of lightning. Thomas almost jumped out of his skin. Two pirates stumbled out of the bushes and fell to the ground. One pirate had perished instantly from the shock. The other fired his gun into the bushes a few times before dying. They looked unwashed and uncivilized. Each one wore a bulletproof vest that had done little to protect them. The pirates had been stalking the Helmet Man and Thomas and had almost shot the duo in the back.

"Who are they?" Thomas yelled, not sure what just happened.

"Keep quiet," Slate said. "They must work for Cloak."

"What—what's Cloak?" Thomas asked.

"They're basically jerks with superpowers."

"They have powers like you?"

"Nah, a lot of them are just cream puffs. Stop asking questions, or else you're gonna get shot. Not even your tough hide can take a bullet ... or can it?"

***

Before Naomi and Gilda could fly away from the rampaging mechanical creatures, hundreds of bullets flew at them. Magenta extended its wings and blasted into the air, the bullets ricocheting off its armor. Naomi, however, remained on the ground and raised her hands, stopping the bullets in midair and pushing them back toward the jungle where they came from. She heard panicky screams and foreign babbling. Those must be the hostiles Straper warned her about.

A tail swung at her. She jumped up in the air to avoid the Ankylosaurus's attack. More bullets flew at her, but she redirected them around her with her telekinesis. The Ankylosaurus swung its tail again. To make matters worse, she spotted an Indonesian man wearing dirty clothes step out of the jungle. He also wore a bulletproof vest that looked expensive. Naomi guessed he was a Neutral Zone pirate. They must have been hired by Cloak to stir up trouble.

The pirate lifted a rocket launcher onto his shoulder.

Naomi was so distracted by the new arrival that she was almost hit by the Ankylosaurus's club. She flew up higher, almost twenty feet up now. The pirate fired, and the rocket locked on Naomi. But instead of fleeing, she focused her mind on the rocket and changed its trajectory. It slammed into the side of the Ankylosaurus. The dinosaur gave an electric squeal as it blew up into a hundred pieces.

Meanwhile, Gilda had problems of her own. The T. rex had moved incredibly fast, biting her walker's ankle as she tried to fly away.

"Major structural damage inflicted on left leg!" Tim shouted. "Unable to provide enough lift to break free!"

"Just great," Gilda growled. The T. rex tugged backward. Her flying walker pulled back, trying to resist the mechanical dinosaur. She noticed movement on her periphery. Three more pirates were running out of the jungle. They also had rocket launchers.

"Warning, enemies spotted!" Tim shrieked.

"You're not helping!" Gilda yelled. She aimed her walker's cannon arm at the pirates and fired. A canister of tear gas landed near the pirates. The white gas spewed everywhere, forcing the pirates to disperse. Gilda aimed her cannon arm at the T. rex. It was one ugly piece of work. There were numerous holes in its fake skin that revealed the metal skeleton and electric innards. Seeing the artificiality of the T. rex made it easier for Gilda to fire her shell.

The T. rex's head exploded. Bits of metal and fake skin flew everywhere. Its head had been completely blown away, leaving only a smoking stump. Most of Magenta's left leg had also been destroyed as a result, but at least she was free. With a groan of rusted joints, the T. rex fell onto its side with a thunderous noise.

"Ms. Gilda!" Tim exclaimed. "One of Magenta's wings has been damaged by shrapnel. We need to land immediately!"

Gilda noticed that Magenta was shaking as it tried to stay floating in midair. Gritting her teeth, she had no choice but to land her walker.

Magenta floated down and landed. It had to fall on its hands, almost like it was doing push-ups, because most of its left leg was gone. The pirates had retreated. She saw no signs of any other foes.

"How are you doing?" Naomi asked, strolling to Magenta. It almost made Gilda angry that Naomi could be so cool and collected. Then she realized that Naomi had probably been in many intense situations like this before. Okay, maybe not exactly like this...

"My walker is busted up," Gilda said, feeling stupid. She had let her walker get this badly damaged on her first real mission. Maybe she wasn't ready to pilot such an advanced piece of machinery, if all she was going to do was wreck it.

"I can see that," Naomi said. "Fantastic, I'm going to have to use my powers to tow it away. But don't worry too much. You didn't do *that* bad of a job."

While Naomi was talking to Gilda, a large shape shifted behind her in the bushes. The Triceratops had fallen back when the action began. Now that the pirates and all the other mechanical dinosaurs had failed, it would try taking its targets by surprise.

It dashed out of the jungle, right at Naomi.

Before Naomi could react, Gilda raised her walker's arm and fired a shell. A flaming explosion ripped the Triceratops apart. All that was left of it were chunks of scorched metal and other miscellaneous bits. Naomi covered her face, protecting herself from the heat.

Gilda huffed. "Well, we better leave before a Stegosaurus shows up."

***

Geppetto turned his binoculars to the gunshots. Cyphrus had given the go-ahead to kill the Helmet Man and his friends. Atlas had bought Kobe beef while in Japan. Both he and Geppetto planned to make a fine meal out of it after they killed Slate. Still, Atlas didn't bother to save his appetite, currently devouring a package of licorice. But despite the constant gorging, he was not fat. He had an inhuman metabolism, a necessary evil that came with his accelerated healing abilities. Slate could also heal fast, but not even the Helmet Man could compare with Atlas's rate of regeneration.

After a bit of hard looking, Geppetto at last spotted Slate. The Helmet Man appeared to have something on his back. Geppetto squinted. It was a boy.

"Hey, Atlas," Geppetto asked. "Are there supposed to be any kids with Slate?"

"There were two teenagers," Atlas said, eating another piece of licorice.

"Yeah, you're talking about the purple-haired girl and the pimply blond guy, but I'm talking about a little black kid. He seems to be ten, maybe eleven."

The redhead giant frowned. "There shouldn't be a child that young."

"Whoever he is, he's in the line of fire." Geppetto rubbed his shaved head. "I'm calling Cyphrus. I don't like this one bit. Not one bit at all."

Geppetto put his binoculars down. He turned on his tablet, selected the video-chat function, and clicked his first contact. After a moment of waiting, Cyphrus answered. Her face appeared on-screen. She wore her usual heavy makeup as well as an irritated frown.

"Speak," she ordered.

"I see a kid with Slate, a ten-year-old," Geppetto said. "Who is he?"

"How should I know? It makes no difference. Kill them both."

"Beg your pardon?"

"I said *kill* them."

"I don't *kill* kids. I have a hard enough time sleeping at night as it is. Do you think I'm some kind of psycho like Ember?"

"What other choice do we have? If he's in the way, he's in the way."

"Weren't we going to ignore Slate? Sebastian had us trying to catch that moron for months. Houdini and Sandtrap died because of that stupid crusade. Now you—"

"We can't afford to have him do as he pleases anymore. It's obvious he won't stop until he has destroyed Cloak and killed us all."

"But—"

"End of discussion." Cyphrus hung up, her image vanishing from the touchpad.

Atlas ate the last of his licorice. "I thought things would be different now that Sebastian isn't in charge."

"Ditto," Geppetto said. He clicked an icon on his tablet. A map of the island appeared. Red dots were blinking all over it.

Geppetto sighed and pressed one of the dots.

***

A bomb went off behind Slate and Thomas. The two flew off their feet with a giant bloom of fire behind them. They fell into the bushes as debris rained down.

Aristotle's head rolled into a puddle. "Ah, quickly, get me out before I short out!"

"What was that?" Thomas yelled. "It was loud!"

"Some kind of bomb went off," Slate mumbled, getting back on his feet. He grabbed Thomas by the arm and helped the boy up. Thomas picked Aristotle out of the water but gasped when he saw the destruction that the explosion had left behind. Many bushes had been incinerated. Nearby trees were scorched all over.

"What happened?" Thomas cried. "What—"

Bullets whizzed by. Slate ran for cover, putting Thomas on his back. Judging by the angle, the shooters were firing from higher ground near the dormant volcano.

"You need to tell me where this lab is," Slate snapped as he dashed through the jungle. "The sooner I get off this crazy island, the better."

"It's near the volcano," Thomas said.

"You mean where the gunfire's coming from? Oh, fantastic! In case you can't tell, I'm being sarcastic."

"What does that mean?" Thomas asked.

Aristotle cleared his throat. "Well, my dear boy, it means—"

"Please..." a voice croaked from the bushes. Slate skidded to a stop. A pirate had been caught in the explosion. He still clung to life, covered in burns and soot. He knew only a few English phrases, mainly swears, but he did know the magic word.

"Please..." the man moaned. He was lying on his back. A trickle of blood came from his mouth as he struggled to undo his bulletproof vest.

"Is he ... hurt?" Thomas asked, shaking. He had never seen another human being hurt, since he had only watched children's programming and hung out with machines. This was something new, something that chilled him to the core.

"He's hurt, all right," Slate said. "And now he's begging for his life."

"Please…" the pirate sobbed. "Geppetto…"

The pirate exploded in an instant. Slate jumped backward, avoiding the blast. More bullets flew at them, but Slate managed to flee the area. He stopped running after a minute. Thomas was more shaken up than ever, his eyes the size of dinner plates.

"Did he … die?" Thomas whispered.

"Please, my boy," Aristotle said. "Take a breath."

"Now I get it," Slate said. "Those pirates were given bulletproof vests by Cloak. But what they didn't know is that these were also bomb vests. Now this Geppetto character is using these human bombs to smoke us out, shooting at us whenever we're caught off guard. That pirate we just saw must have figured it out before he—"

"Died…" Thomas whimpered. "He's dead… Dead! He's dead!"

"Calm down!" Slate yelled.

"Yes, please," Aristotle said. "You might—"

More pirates emerged from the bushes, having heard Thomas's cries. They aimed their automatic weapons at Slate and were about to fire when they too exploded.

The Helmet Man flew into the air with Thomas, who clung on to his back. Slate burst from the jungle canopy. The fiery explosion consumed the vegetation behind him. Another barrage of bullets came at them as he floated in midair.

But instead of fleeing, the Helmet Man flew toward the shooters.

Now he was pissed.

CHAPTER 17

Lightning strikes hit the ground, but plenty of them also hit the fleeing mercenaries. Slate was approaching fast. He did not seem merciful.

Geppetto snarled. They were supposed to kill the Helmet Man from a distance, but now he was coming right for them.

"Retreat!" he yelled. "Take cover in the jungle!"

The mercenaries complied. Some of the dumber ones stood their ground and kept firing at the approaching enemy. They soon met their end. Slate was still a speck in the distance, but he continued to send bolts at his enemies.

Atlas was forced to act. He swung a custom-made weapon that looked like a black tube over his shoulder and lifted Geppetto off the ground by his scruff.

"Hey, put me down!" Geppetto shouted.

But Atlas had no time to worry about his comrade's dignity. They had to move.

Half a minute later, Slate landed, surrounded by dead mercenaries. Geppetto, Atlas, and the remaining mercenaries had already fled, but the Helmet Man could tell where they went judging by their tracks. To be thorough, he walked over to the resting unicopters and sent a surge of energy through them, frying their circuits. These unicopters weren't going to be flightworthy anytime soon.

Thomas kept his eyes shut as he continued to whimper.

"I normally can't carry people on my back when I fly," Slate said. "I'd fry those suckers in an instant with my electric personality. But you're made out of tougher stuff, like leather or beef jerky. Good for you!"

"What's with this cheerful attitude?" Aristotle spat, unaffected by Slate's electricity due to being held by Thomas. "You just committed murder. At least have the—"

"I just saved this kid's life, pal. You've got no right to criticize me."

"Slate..." Thomas sniveled. "They're dead."

"Get over it, kid. I did what I had to do."

"But they're dead..."

Slate made a whining sound that could have been mistaken for a dying horse. "Would you shut up? Look, I don't know how to handle kids very well. Just keep your eyes shut if you have to. But be a man for your friends. They need a guy to protect them."

"I ... you mean I'll protect them myself?"

"Exactly! People have things that are precious to them, but most wussies can't even defend themselves. It takes a true man—or woman, whatever—to protect the ones they love."

"But what can I do? I'm just a kid."

"That may be. However, I just came up with a devilish idea..."

***

Straper kept running, not even looking back when he heard the boat explode behind him. It seemed the pirates had found it. He knew he couldn't have fought them on his own. Instead, he had gotten off the boat and ran into the jungle.

But even with pirates nearby, he couldn't keep running like this. He slowed to a stop when he was about a mile inland and gasped, hands on his knees. He was covered in sweat and carried his rifle on his back, not having had a chance to grab anything else besides water. He had to find the others. Naomi and Gilda hadn't responded to his calls, which meant they were probably busy with pirates too.

Loud booms sounded in the distance. Straper jumped at the noise. If this kept up, he would probably get PTSD like that jagoff General Eisenhorn. Despite the situation, he wondered for a moment what the old coot was up to.

The bushes behind him rustled. He spun around to find a dinosaur staring at him, a Velociraptor covered in black feathers. Its deadly claws and rows of sharp teeth made his surprise turn into fear.

In a swift movement, Straper yanked the rifle off his back. The Velociraptor lunged at him from the bushes, teeth bared. He fired, using instinct to aim, and hit his mark. The bullet ripped through the Velociraptor's skull, and it fell flat on its stomach. Sparks came out of its head as it twitched on the ground.

"It's ... a robot?" Straper asked himself. "One of those days..."

Straper heard foreign shouts behind him. The pirates must have heard the gunshot and were coming to investigate. Or, rather, they were coming to kill him.

Knowing better than to stay, he ran away at top speed from the pirates' shouts for five minutes and then slowed down to a steady jog. He tried to get his breathing under control and took a swig of water to ease his raw throat. All this running was getting annoying. He couldn't hear the pirates' yells anymore but was still on guard. He had to—

A bullet whizzed over his shoulder. Straper was already spinning on his heel before he felt the adrenaline hit. His eyes caught sight of a pirate in the bushes. He aimed his rifle and pulled the trigger. The recoil confirmed his bullet had been fired. The pirate let out a shrill cry before falling on his face. Blood spurted from his chest wound.

Straper was frozen, his eyes fixed on the corpse. He was looking at his first kill. Sure, he had shot that Atlas guy, but he had gotten right back up.

The pirate, however, didn't budge an inch.

Shaking, Straper dropped his rifle. A small squeak escaped his lips. He found his hands shaking. Was this...? Was this war ... or murder?

Straper gulped and picked up the rifle. It had been self-defense, he told himself. It wasn't his fault. Slate did this every day, right? This would have happened sooner or later. He needed to get used to it. He needed to stop whimpering and keep running.

Straper did just that for twenty more yards until several trees fell to his right. A massive object was pushing its way through the branches. He tensed up. The snapping of wood was far too audible. The pirates would definitely hear this racket.

But he had nothing to fear from the object itself. Magenta floated in midair with one of its legs missing. Gilda still sat in the cockpit in case she needed to use the walker's cannon again. Naomi had her hands raised as she walked behind the floating walker, levitating it with her mind. Beads of perspiration ran down her forehead. She looked like she was about to bust a vein.

Naomi spotted Straper and lowered the walker to the ground. Panting, she leaned against Magenta and rubbed her temples. Straper let out a breath and approached her.

"You all right?" he asked. "What happened to Gilda's walker?"

"Mechanical dinosaurs attacked us," Naomi said. "You know, the usual. I'm not used to lifting such large objects with my mind. Give me a minute to rest."

She sat down on the ground and chugged her canteen. Straper also sat down and lowered his head. His fingers flexed as his body remained rigid. Gilda and Naomi both noticed this, but business came first. They could console him later if need be.

"Cloak has made its move," Gilda told Naomi. "What now?"

"I wanted to find that laboratory, but we may have to retreat," Naomi said. "Pirates are one thing, but now we also have violent androids to contend with. This must be the work of Cyphrus. She's not supposed to be doing fieldwork anymore. Putting herself in danger like this must mean she's desperate to stop us. My guess is that the Chinese Empire is angry about Cloak's failure in Japan and is now putting pressure on her to fix the situation."

"Sucks for her, but what about us? Our boat's destroyed, and Slate's missing."

"Relax, I doubt that imbecile is dead. We just need to find another boat and get in touch with him. Then we'll leave and reevaluate our situation."

***

The Helmet Man continued to carry Thomas on his back as they approached an old building. It was a single story, covered in vegetation, made of concrete, and had only a few windows, all shattered. The structure appeared abandoned and empty, but it was more modern and less dilapidated than the other buildings on the island. This was the place Slate had been searching for.

Thomas caught a glimpse of the building but squeezed his eyes shut soon after.

"This is the lab," he said. "I think I used to live here, but that was a long time ago. There was something in my arm… Then there was a fire … and loud noises … and screams."

"Can't remember five years ago?" Slate asked.

"No, sorry…"

"I remember that day," Aristotle said. "Very loud. Very upsetting."

"Guess this is the right place, then," Slate murmured.

"Why are you so interested in this ghastly mausoleum?" Aristotle asked.

"Naomi wants intel on that mind-control weapon."

"Mind control?" Thomas asked.

"Yeah, Cloak used it on a guy to justify some invasion. They're probably gonna use it again, so we're looking for a way to counteract it."

"Can we go in already?" Thomas complained. "We need to hurry."

"Fine, no need to get your rags in a bunch."

They entered the building through an empty doorway. The door itself had come off its hinges long ago. It looked like it had been kicked down, but Slate didn't mention that detail.

The hallway they stepped into was covered in bugs and leaves. Large spots of mold grew on the walls. There was also no artificial light; the fluorescent tubes on the ceiling were dark and covered in grime. Some sunlight managed to sneak its way in through the broken windows and holes in the roof, but it did little to brighten up the place. Slate, however, didn't need light to navigate the lab, and Thomas continued to keep his eyes closed.

Bullet holes scarred the walls. Dried blood stained the floor. Thomas shivered. Even though he didn't know what death was, he knew the smell of it on instinct and knew very well to fear it. Aristotle could only comfort him with a hushed lullaby.

Slate stepped into the first room he came upon, full of filth and dust-covered beakers and other lab equipment. He moved on to the next room, which contained an examination table, but found nothing of interest. He also discovered bedrooms, offices, storage closets, and a kitchen, but still nothing that would impress Naomi. Right when he was about to start whining and give up, he found a room filled with computers and file cabinets.

"Jackpot," Slate said. "Hop down, kid. Nothing to see here that'll scar you for life, but I guess it's a little late for that."

Thomas let go of Slate's neck, dropped to the floor, opened his eyes, and glanced around.

"What are we looking for?" he asked.

"Stuff. I don't know. Help me look."

They began to search for anything of value. Slate opened up some cabinets, only to grunt and slam them closed again. Thomas lifted a dead phone from the table and inspected it. He played with the keypad for several minutes before the Helmet Man smacked him.

Neither Slate nor Thomas could read, so they put Aristotle on a desk and got him to read for them. The severed head glanced at the musty lab reports with a sneer.

"How esoteric!" Aristotle cried. "This pseudo-scientific babble is beyond me."

"Thanks for the help," Slate scoffed, but then he stopped pacing the room and tilted his head downward. Sensing a space beneath his feet, he kicked a hole in the floor, which revealed a hidden safe. He ripped off the door with his superhuman strength, making a loud racket. He reached into the safe and took out two small disks.

"Here, kid," Slate said, holding them out. "I might accidentally fry them."

Thomas grabbed the disks and put them in his pocket.

Slate nodded. "Great, now let's—"

Gunshots interrupted him. Bullets hammered right through the already crumbling walls and windows. Sunlight streamed into the room through the bullet holes.

Slate and Thomas didn't even have a chance to dodge.

CHAPTER 18

Naomi led the way as she levitated the walker through the jungle. Making noise was unavoidable, since Magenta clumsily knocked aside tree branches and palm leaves. Straper was on high alert, following close behind. His eyes scanned the jungle, and his rifle was at the ready, but he couldn't brush off killing a man so easily. Only the threat of immediate danger kept his mind from wandering back to that dark place.

"Let's hope one of the pirate boats is anchored nearby," Naomi grunted as she kept Magenta floating. "And I hope that one of the boats will be big enough to put this walker on. I can't keep this up forever."

Gilda sighed as she kept a lookout for pirates or androids. Wow, that sure sounded strange. But even the absurdity of the situation couldn't erase her failure. How could she become such a burden to the group? Granted, she did save Naomi's life and took out her fair share of enemies, but she had also let her walker get damaged. Magenta was too valuable to leave behind, so now Gilda had to watch as Naomi hauled her busted walker through the jungle. It wasn't just embarrassing. It was downright shameful.

"Don't worry, Ms. Gilda," Tim said. "This is only your first—I mean, second—mission. There's always next time."

"Thank you," Gilda said. "But I don't want to talk about it anymore."

"Ms. Gilda, please!" Tim wailed.

"I said I don't want to talk."

"No, I detect enemies!"

Gilda jumped in her seat. "Naomi, pirates!"

Naomi heard her over her earpiece and dropped the walker with a thud. Gilda banged the back of her head but didn't complain. Bullets bounced off Magenta. Straper took cover behind the walker, where Naomi was already crouched down. At least the immobile walker still had some use. Naomi looked relieved at not having to carry Magenta anymore, but she also wore the intense expression of a hawk about to strike.

"Gilda, your walker's cannon still works! Help me!"

Gilda raised Magenta's cannon arm and fired a canister of tear gas into the jungle. It erupted, blinding most of the pirates and causing them to run around like headless chickens. Naomi focused her mind on ten of them and snapped their necks. The pirates fell to the ground with their heads twisted at horrible angles.

"You killed them!" Straper cried. He had never seen such an efficient mass killing before, except perhaps by Slate. It shouldn't be so easy to kill that many people. Just what kind of monsters were Slate and Naomi?

"Gilda, why didn't you fire a shell?" Naomi snapped. "Not only do I have to clean up after you, but the gas could blow this way and blind us as well."

"Sorry," Gilda said. "It was on reflex..."

Before Naomi could shoot back a reply, she heard a rustle behind them.

"Alert! Alert!" Tim yelped. "More hostiles behind you!"

As if on cue, about a dozen figures emerged from the bushes.

They weren't pirates.

"Howdy there, partner!"

A Wild West gunslinger stepped out of the foliage, wearing leather pants, a plaid shirt, and a classic cowboy hat. All his clothing was frayed and stained with dirt. His entire face was missing, revealing a metal skull with camera eyes.

A Roman centurion came out next, followed by a mime, an armless samurai, Attila the Hun, Frankenstein's monster, a lame Pterodactyl dragging itself forward, Albert Einstein with wires coming out of his head, and a multitude of other historical figures. As an added bonus, there was even another Velociraptor.

Not only that, but Naomi heard foreign shouts from a distance. Even more pirates were coming to join the assault.

"I bet Slate's just having a blast," Naomi spat.

***

"Cease-fire!" Geppetto yelled, raising his arm. He and Atlas stood behind their dozen remaining mercenaries. The men stopped firing but stayed alert in case there were any unwelcome surprises.

The whole wall had been reduced to Swiss cheese. They had been watching the Helmet Man from a distance, being more careful in their ambush this time. Geppetto wasn't sure if the wall had been thin enough for Slate to have sensed them. Regardless, the plan seemed to work, so no harm done, except, of course, to Slate and his little friend.

"Out of the way, boys," Geppetto told his men. "Atlas, it's your turn."

The mercenaries stepped aside. Atlas lifted his custom-made weapon and squeezed the trigger. A rocket flew out, hitting the wall point-blank. The explosion ripped apart the concrete, smoke filled the air, and rubble rained down.

"Fire again!" Geppetto yelled at his men.

All mercenaries continued to shoot at the building, firing hundreds of bullets. They were taking no chances with the Helmet Man.

"Let's hope that did him in," Geppetto said, fingering his ears. "Tinnitus ... just what I needed. Okay, men! Let's recover that body! If he twitches, shoot first and ask—"

A flash of light came from inside the building. One of the mercenaries cried out before collapsing. Then another flash came, followed by a third. Two more men fell.

"Impossible!" Geppetto shouted. Slate had been right in the line of fire, and those were armor-piercing bullets. Not even he could have survived that. The mercenaries were becoming anxious. Not only did the smoke impede their vision, but they were also running low on ammo. This slaughter wasn't going as planned.

A silver shape sprinted through the smoke. One mercenary was snatched away. His screams were short-lived. Another man spun around and fired. He hit nothing. The silver shape slammed into the mercenary from behind. Electricity went through him. One by one, the mercs kept falling. Geppetto stayed close to Atlas. The giant himself was scanning the smoky area with his weapon at the ready. Atlas and Geppetto were soon the only ones left, just them and their unseen enemy.

"Where are they?" Geppetto whispered.

Atlas didn't respond, just merely continued to scan the area.

There was a flash to their right. Geppetto yelped. Atlas swung his weapon until it pointed toward the flash and fired a rocket at Slate.

The Helmet Man, who had Thomas on his back, raised his finger like a gunslinger and shot a bolt of energy. It hit the tip of the rocket, which was only ten feet away from its target. The projectile exploded. A wave of flames knocked Slate backward into some bushes. Thomas yelped as Slate landed on top of him, but the boy endured it.

Before the initial shock could wear off, Atlas switched his weapon to machine gun mode and pulled the trigger.

Slate got up at the last second, crouched down, and used Thomas as a human shield. The boy seemed to dance as dozens of armor-piercing bullets slammed into his body.

Atlas stopped firing and gaped instead.

"What the hell?" Geppetto screeched. "He just killed that kid!"

"Don't judge me!" Slate yelled, dropping the limp boy to the ground. "Using children as human shields is an honorable pastime."

Geppetto and Atlas were speechless, but if they were shocked now...

"Slate ... ah ... what was that?" Thomas coughed. He got to his feet, dazed but unharmed, and shook out his clothes. Useless bullets fell out of his pant legs. The rags he wore were covered in holes, barely able to hang on his frame anymore.

"Hold on a second," Geppetto said. The shock wore off. Now he could think. "That kid ... he's bulletproof." He started smiling. "I thought the Gifted were the only ones with superpowers. I guess anything is possible."

"Slate used the boy to shield himself," Atlas said, also coming back to his senses.

"Pay attention!" Slate yelled. He picked up Thomas and chucked him at the murderous duo. Atlas responded by swinging his arm at the incoming boy. Thomas was knocked out of the air and hit the ground with a thud.

"Look out!" Geppetto shouted.

Atlas didn't have time to defend himself. Slate had launched himself at the giant. The silver helmet slammed right into Atlas's gut. Geppetto shrieked and dove to the side.

Both Slate and Atlas flew backward into the abandoned laboratory.

***

With half a smile, Cyphrus took in the island from the top of the dormant volcano. It was too hot to wear a fur coat, so she had to resort to wearing a long sundress, an umbrella in hand. She saw plumes of smoke rising from the jungle canopy. Everyone seemed to be having such fun. But her heavy makeup was starting to run. It was best to hurry.

"Come along," she told her escorts. Two mercenaries followed her. She didn't think they would be much help if she encountered Slate or Repulsa, but it couldn't hurt to have them around should they stumble upon lesser foes.

She walked inside a small man-made cave that led into the volcano. A metal door blocked the way, but she merely put her hand on the electric lock. Within seconds, she heard a clank that told her the door was open.

"Way cool," said one of the mercenaries.

"There's no need for commentary," she snapped.

The mercenary shrugged. "Just complimenting…"

Rolling her eyes, Cyphrus collapsed her umbrella and opened the door. The three of them entered and found themselves staring down a dark hallway.

"Let us go first, ma'am," the other mercenary said. "Our weapons have flashlights on them. It's too dangerous to let you take the lead."

"Nonsense," she told him and touched a dark control panel attached to the wall. The ventilation system came to life, and the fluorescent lights flickered on.

"Hey, I thought you didn't have to touch electronics to use your powers," the first mercenary said.

"Hush up," Cyphrus spat. "Like I would reveal something so personal."

After several minutes of walking down a series of twisting corridors, she found the door she was looking for.

"Check it out," she commanded.

Her two henchmen kicked open the door and did a quick sweep of the room.

"Clear," the second mercenary said.

Cyphrus went inside. Four dusty swivel chairs rested in front of a chrome panel covered in switches. She also noticed a glass monitor. How archaic. This place had been built back before holographic screens had become the norm. Wiping off one of the chairs, Cyphrus planted herself in it and put her hand on the panel. The screen turned on, flickering through images. This went on for half a minute before a loud horn began to blare.

"OVERLOAD OCCURRENCE," a recorded message warned over the intercom. "ALL PERSONNEL MUST EVACUATE THE ISLAND. I REPEAT—"

Cyphrus walked out of the room and headed to the exit. The mercenaries exchanged glances before following their boss like loyal puppies.

"What's going on?" the second mercenary yelled over the blaring alarm as they walked out of the volcano, back to their nearby unicopter.

"As you know, this island was an unfinished theme park!" Cyphrus yelled back. "Not only are there androids here, but the creators of the park were also able to create artificial volcano eruptions."

"You're joking!"

"These eruptions were controlled, of course! They were only meant to let out a bit of lava and puff out some smoke. It would have been a popular tourist attraction. But I just overrode all the fail-safes. Now this dormant volcano can erupt properly!"

Both of her men turned pale.

"Wait," the first mercenary said. "You don't mean—"

"I must ensure that Slate and Repulsa do not leave this island alive, and I must destroy that lab and anything else that can be used to undermine my designs!"

"Ma'am, how long do we have till this volcano blows? We need to get out of here."

"Relax and enjoy the fireworks!" she shouted with a smirk and narrowed eyes. "We've got ten minutes. That's plenty of time for a wrap-up!"

CHAPTER 19

Both titans fell into the rubble that was once the lab's wall. Atlas was the first to get back to his feet. He pointed his weapon at Slate, only to see it kicked out of his hands. Slate got up too and threw a punch. Atlas caught it, but Slate had planned for that.

"Looks like you gotta learn the hard way!" Slate yelled.

Electricity surged into Atlas, causing the colossal man to convulse.

But rather than collapse, he gritted his teeth.

"I learn fast," Atlas growled.

He slammed his fist into Slate's gut. The Helmet Man flew backward, hitting a wall with a nasty thud, and slumped to the floor. Atlas charged, pumping his muscular legs and arms, in an attempt to ram Slate.

Slate rolled out of the way. With a thunderous crash, Atlas plowed straight through the concrete wall. He was now in the examination room, disoriented.

While Atlas was distracted, Slate ran through the large hole that Atlas had left behind and fired lightning. Atlas crouched down and crossed his arms. The bolts hit the giant dead-on, burning his clothes and arms, but his skin immediately began to heal. The burns on his arms were gone within five seconds.

"Whoa, gonna need the heavy artillery," Slate said. His right arm started glowing blue. Atlas didn't wait to see what would happen. He began to charge again.

The Helmet Man pointed his glowing arm at Atlas and fired his beam. At the last second, Atlas moved to the left, dodging the attack. His shoulder was horribly burned, but it quickly regenerated. Slate was so focused on controlling his beam that he couldn't counterattack as Atlas came at him. The large foe knocked Slate's glowing arm to the side, causing the beam to hit the ceiling, blowing a hole through the roof.

Slate stopped firing his beam of energy. Although powerful, it took him a long time to charge his arm up. His beams also lacked the precision of his regular lightning bolts. It was not good for all situations, especially the kind of close combat he was about to take part in.

Atlas threw punches with unnatural speed and strength. No professional boxer was a match for him. Slate blocked most of the punches, but a few slammed into his torso. He cried out. Two of his ribs had broken. The giant tried to backhand him. He deflected the blow with his forearm. Whenever Slate made physical contact with Atlas, he sent a little electricity into him. It didn't make much of a difference, only causing little burns on Atlas's arms that healed in no time at all.

Sweeping his leg, Slate kicked Atlas right in the knee, hoping that would topple the behemoth. It didn't. Instead, Atlas took advantage of the opening and grabbed Slate's neck. He lifted Slate off the floor and smashed him into a nearby desk. The old wood broke into a hundred pieces. Then he swung Slate and pounded him into some file cabinets until they were nothing but metal scrap. Bloody cuts covered Slate, his clothes were ripped, and a good many of his bones were fractured. This wasn't going well. Atlas had the upper hand in terms of strength and endurance. There was no way he could beat this big brute at his own game. Slate had to take advantage of his own strengths. What did he have that Atlas didn't?

"I got the air," Slate groaned.

Atlas either didn't hear him or didn't care. The giant raised Slate's limp body in the air and grabbed a broken piece of metal off the floor. It was dull, but it would do the trick. Atlas prepared to drive it into Slate's heart.

"Adios, amigo!" Slate yelled. "That's French for 'You suck!'"

Before Atlas could stab him or point out his mistake, Slate shot up into the air and crashed through the roof of the laboratory.

He flew straight up, electrical arcs trailing behind him. Atlas still had a grasp around his neck, holding on for dear life. Electricity poured into him as they went up, but he managed to keep his grip, at least for now. They were still flying, almost four hundred feet up. Atlas could see the entire island from here, the green jungle stretched out beneath them, the brown volcano sticking out like a sore thumb. Having lost his makeshift dagger, the giant wrapped his free arm around Slate. Atlas knew he might not survive the fall, even with his regeneration. He would have to force Slate to take him down before finishing the job. Flexing his arm, Atlas got ready to squeeze the Helmet Man until he begged.

Then Slate stopped flying. Panic overtook Atlas.

Slate snickered. "Should've let go, pal."

After a few seconds of hanging in midair, they began to fall. Atlas couldn't help but cry out. But gravity didn't get to have all the fun. Slate accelerated downward. Atlas tightened his arms around Slate, hoping to crush him. In response, the Helmet Man did a sudden spin. Atlas wasn't prepared for this and lost his grip. He flailed his arms and screamed as he plummeted to the ground.

"Don't go yet!" Slate yelled. "There's more!"

The Helmet Man flew down and collided with Atlas. They both went even faster than before. Fifty feet. Thirty feet. Ten feet. Atlas shrieked as they smashed through the roof of the laboratory and into the floor. Nearly every bone in his body shattered.

Slate broke his fall on Atlas, but it still hurt like a mother. Plaster and insulation pelted down on them. Both of them were too hurt to care. They stayed crumpled on the tile floor for a few minutes, each trying to find the strength to move. With an irritated groan, Slate finally got to his knees and punched Atlas right in the face.

"Get up," Slate growled. "I ain't finished yet."

Slate punched Atlas again. And again. And again.

"Quit that or else," a voice warned. "Your helmet may prevent me from working my magic, but I got an ace up my sleeve."

Geppetto kept a fair distance away from Slate and the chunks of ceiling that still rained down every so often. Next to him was Thomas, unharmed. But the boy's eyes were filled with unfathomable fear, for he couldn't move, no matter how hard he tried. It was useless. Geppetto had control of him.

Thomas also held a bottle to his lips.

"You're kidding me?" Slate scoffed. "That kid's a useless hostage. You can't harm him. I should know. I just used him as a fricking human shield."

"The kid does seem resilient," Geppetto said. "But I saw him coughing earlier, which means he isn't completely invulnerable. He can still suffocate. He can probably be poisoned too. All that being considered, I don't think chugging expired chloroform would be good for his health. He's a growing boy, after all."

"Wow, I'm impressed a dingus like you could come up with a plan like that. I guess it really was you who strapped the bombs to those pirates."

"Better believe it. They were unwitting victims. Bulletproof vests are expensive, so those greedy pirates naturally didn't complain too much when I gave them some. You could say they were blown away by my generosity."

"Ha! Good pun! But is it really that easy to blow up people?"

"I must admit, I'm not one for cruelty unless my victim disgusts me enough. I actually didn't want to hurt you or the kid. It's just a job. Those pirates I used, however ... I'm not too sad about them. They lived such useless lives, preying on the weak and scrounging for scraps just to survive. How pathetic."

"Yeah, you may have a point there," Slate said. He decided to change the subject. "We met once before, I think, a long time ago, back in South America when we still worked for the Western Union."

"I don't like to remember those days," Geppetto said, rubbing his neck. "But yeah, I remember you. From what I recall, you were just as annoying then as you are—"

"Boring! Here's my next question: What the hell happened twenty years ago? Some guy called the Mentor shows up, and you just decide to betray the Western Union and join the creep? Seriously, I'm really outta the loop on this one."

"It wasn't the Mentor who saved us. It was Sebastian. He arranged for us to flee and convinced us we would have a better life. I suppose we did, in some respects. It's the reason we followed that loon for so long. As for the Mentor, that's just make-believe."

"What are you saying? The guy's made-up?"

"Yeah, now let me ask you a question. You're looking for your dad, right?"

"How the hell did you know that?"

"Houdini mentioned it before you … you know… So, are you?"

Slate didn't answer at first, remembering his father. Was he even alive? "I'm still at it. No worries. He'll turn up sooner or later."

"Well, I'm not going to say that's a pipe dream too," Geppetto told him. "Maybe a few Keymasters are still alive. You know, I could help you find him."

"Oh, I see now. You're trying to trick me into letting Atlas go. Yeah, fat chance. Cyphrus tried pulling the same crap on me, and I don't buy it for a second."

Atlas gave a small moan, but he just continued to lie there.

Geppetto shrugged. "It was worth a shot. Now enough chitchat. I'm going to get the boy to gulp down some yummy chloroform in five seconds if you don't—"

"Hang on, my boy!" a voice cried from the ceiling.

"What the—!" Geppetto yelled, glancing up as the severed head came flying down with its teeth bared. Slate had left Aristotle on top of a ceiling fan to keep the android safe, but it now proved to be an elaborate yet useful trap.

Aristotle landed on Geppetto's shoulder and sank his fake teeth into his neck. Geppetto squealed. Blood poured from the wound. On reflex, he tried to take control of Aristotle's mind, not realizing that the severed head belonged to an android.

Thomas, meanwhile, collapsed and began to sob, dropping the bottle of chloroform. He was free from the invisible grasp of Geppetto. Never before had he experienced something like that. Some chloroform also spilled on the floor, making him woozy.

Geppetto finally tore away Aristotle and threw the severed head against the wall. Aristotle groaned. A few sparks flew from his neck hole.

Geppetto grimaced, clutching his wounded neck. "You idiots are gonna—"

Slate kicked him in the head before he could finish that sentence. Geppetto slammed into the wall and fell to the floor. His eyes rolled back as stars filled his vision.

The Helmet Man limped over to him. "All right, time to talk. Where's Cyphrus at?"

Geppetto wasn't given an opportunity to answer. Bullets began to rain down around Slate. In one smooth motion, Slate grabbed Thomas and shielded himself with the boy.

"This feels weird!" Thomas yelled as the bullets struck his body, his tears drying up. "It's like hard rain!"

A unicopter hovered above the hole in the roof. The bullets from its mounted gun had torn through the ceiling as though it was paper. One bullet managed to hit Slate in the shoulder, despite Thomas's protection. The Helmet Man cursed as blood dribbled out of him.

Geppetto, not fearing the bullets, ran over to Atlas. The unicopter lowered down a harness. Geppetto had trouble slipping Atlas into the harness but managed to do it within ten seconds. He gave the cord two tugs, and the harness began to retract. Geppetto held on to Atlas's broken body as they were reeled up. Bolts of lightning flew by them. Two hit Atlas in the back, but he merely grunted. Slate kept shooting at them, still holding Thomas up as a human shield with his other hand. His aim was off, however. He had been distracted by a tremor.

"The ground's shaking!" Thomas exclaimed.

"Thanks for telling me the obvious," Slate snapped.

Something exploded in the distance. Sections of ceiling and wall came crashing down. The lab was falling apart. The unicopter stopped firing. Slate growled as it flew away. Geppetto and Atlas had escaped.

"Time to split," Slate said. "We got what we needed."

"Aristotle!" Thomas cried. "He's hurt!"

The severed head had taken three bullets. Bits of hardware and fake skin dotted the floor. What remained of Aristotle's face twitched into a grin.

"Good luck ... my boy..." Aristotle said, spitting sparks. "Enjoy the world beyond this island ... and all its..."

Aristotle's voice turned to a drone. Then it ceased all together.

"Is..." Thomas whimpered. "Is he...?"

"Yeah," Slate said. "He's dead."

Thomas cried silently. Slate sighed, put Thomas on his back, and limped out of the laboratory. As soon as they entered the jungle, half the lab collapsed in on itself. Dust flew everywhere, causing Thomas to choke. It didn't distract him for long. Something caught his eye that made a collapsing building seem pitiful by comparison.

A towering plume of smoke billowed from the top of the volcano, and rivers of lava flowed out. The volcano was now very much active.

"Geez, Cloak really pulled out all the stops on this one," Slate said.

"Oh, no!" Thomas shouted. "The others are in danger!"

"Crap, the androids... Hang on, kid. We'll have to fly."

Thomas tightened his arms around Slate's neck so hard that a normal person wouldn't have been able to breath properly. Slate flew upward like a bird with a broken wing. The beating that Atlas inflicted had taken its toll. Thomas was nervous being this high above the jungle, especially since half of it was on fire now. The lava was making quick progress. At this rate, it would consume the entire island within ten minutes.

"There it is!" Thomas yelled, pointing downward.

Due to the pitch of the slope, the lava had already reached Thomas's house, and the trees surrounding it were ablaze. The two androids, freed from Cyphrus's control, stood on the rooftop. They didn't seem particularly panicked, even if they had every right to be. When Washington spotted Slate and Thomas, he gave them a casual wave.

"Very hot out, isn't it?" Washington yelled at them.

"We've come to save you!" Thomas told them. "Grab Slate! He'll get us out of here."

"Kid, I don't think I can carry much more," Slate said, still bleeding from his bullet wound. "Besides, their circuits will fry if I—"

"No! You can do it! We'll figure something out. Just—"

Washington's hair caught fire. He had the good sense to look perturbed.

"I say, does anyone have an extinguisher handy?" he asked.

"Slate, they're burning!" Thomas screamed.

"It was a mistake to come here," Slate said. "Let's go. It hurts to fly … badly."

"They're burning! They're burning and dying!"

"Sorry you had to learn the hard way, kid…"

"No!" Thomas tried to jump off Slate's back, but the Helmet Man managed to restrain him as if he were wrestling a tuna.

Now Washington was engulfed in flames. His clothes burned. His face melted. He did not scream. He did not shout. He simply stood on the roof with a kind of dignity that Slate hadn't thought a machine was capable of.

The knight unsheathed its dull sword and raised it high.

George Washington saluted as well. "My dear Thomas," he said. "Time to fly the nest."

The roof caved in. The androids fell into the lava.

Thomas screamed for the whole island to hear.

CHAPTER 20

The assault happened so fast that Straper couldn't recall much of what happened. All he remembered was firing his weapon at anything coming at him. The androids had all charged at the same time. Straper shot the Roman soldier and the gunslinger in the head. He then hit the crawling Pterodactyl in the neck. One by one, he took out the machines. These androids were slow, but they had obvious hostile intent.

Naomi, meanwhile, was busy with the pirates lurking in the jungle. The androids were merely serving as a distraction so the pirates could close in. These pirates lacked bulletproof vests, but that didn't make them less bold. Naomi jumped over Gilda's immobile walker that had been her cover and landed in the line of fire. The pirates didn't know why she would do something so foolish, but they shot at her with little complaint.

That was their big mistake. She raised her hand. The bullets stopped in midair, and she repelled them back at her opponents. Many hit the pirates, and a few died instantly. Naomi punched the air. The unseen blows knocked the weapons out of the grasp of three nearby pirates. She twisted her arms, snapping their necks like twigs. She then levitated a log and threw it at a pair of pirates shooting from farther away. They tried to run, but the log slammed into their backs.

Gilda's walker may not have been able to fly or walk, but her cannon still worked. She fired multiple shells into the jungle. They blew down trees and burned away shrubs. Only a few pirates were injured, however; she just wanted to scare them.

The pirates soon had enough and began their retreat. Straper was finishing up shooting the androids. He had just killed the mime robot when he felt a horrible pain in his arm.

"Ah! Get it off! Get it off!"

The Velociraptor had been smart enough to sneak around under the brush. Straper screamed shrilly. Blood flooded from the wound as he tried to yank his injured limb away.

"Hang on!" Naomi yelled. She sent a telekinetic punch at the Velociraptor's skull, crushing it completely. The machine went dead. She pried open the robot's jaw with her mind. Straper pulled his arm out like a wounded coyote escaping a bear trap. Naomi knelt next to him to check the bite, frowning in thought.

"It's not too deep," she determined. She took out a small spray can and applied a growth patch to Straper's arm. It solidified on contact, and Straper stopped screaming. He took several deep breaths, calming himself.

"Ah ... uh ... thanks..."

"No problem," Naomi said.

The ground started to shake.

"What was that?" Gilda asked.

"A tremor, Ms. Gilda," Tim said.

"I know that. What caused it?"

"I can venture a guess," Naomi said. She pointed at a large plume of smoke. A red glow could also be seen in the distance.

"The volcano's erupting!" Gilda yelled.

"Great, just what we needed," Straper said.

"No time to dawdle." Naomi raised her hands and levitated Gilda's walker. "We're almost at the beach. A boat might be there."

Nobody had any better ideas, so they all ran for the shore. The ground shook some more. Trees toppled around them. Flocks of birds took flight.

"Watch yourself!" Naomi shouted. "Keep moving!"

As they kept running, the ominous red glow drew closer. Straper could smell burning wood behind him, which motivated him to run even faster.

They arrived at the sandy shore. Naomi scanned the beach, looking for any sign of a boat. She was just about to admit defeat when Straper spotted hope with his keen eyes.

"Ship!" he shouted, pointing down the shore. Nobody else could see it, but they took his word for it and ran there. Tremors continued to occur with increasing frequency. One almost caused Straper to trip. The red glow was getting brighter, the sky darkened with ash, and the smell of burning wood was overwhelming.

The trio could now see a boat anchored near the shore. It had belonged to the pirates, but they must have forgotten it, or there hadn't been enough pirates left alive to take it. Either way, they were in luck. Naomi was first to reach the boat and gave it a quick examination. The vessel didn't look all that sturdy. It was covered in rust, and there were holes in its hull, the faded paint job being the least of her concerns, but at least it seemed big enough to carry Magenta. Naomi lowered Magenta onto the deck. As soon as the walker was settled, Gilda climbed out of the cockpit and began to tie it down. Naomi floated over the water, also levitating Straper, who yelped, and they both landed on the vessel.

"What about Slate?" Gilda asked.

"He'll be fine," Naomi said. "If anyone can survive a volcano, it's that annoyance."

"Is the island really gonna be destroyed?" Straper asked in a shaky voice.

To answer his question, he saw a sight so awe-inspiring that he had to do a double take to make sure it was real. A flood of lava was crawling toward them. He could only just make it out, but it was coming. Trees ignited. Androids melted. Flaming buildings collapsed. Everything from plants to animals was being devoured by the molten rock.

"We need to leave," Naomi said in a controlled but urgent voice. "Slate can catch up with us later."

"No, he's coming!" Straper yelled.

"We can't wait for him."

"No, I mean I see him coming right now!"

Naomi looked up and saw that the Helmet Man was indeed flying their way.

"That's him!" Gilda exclaimed.

"He has something on his back." Naomi squinted. "What is it?"

"It's a kid!" Straper yelled. "What's a kid doing here?"

"More importantly, how's a kid able to hold on to Slate?" Gilda asked. "He should be getting electrocuted to death right now."

The Helmet Man finally reached them and flopped onto the deck with a grunt.

"My friends!" the boy cried, rolling off Slate. "They're on the island! Please, we have to go back. They're all I have!"

"There are other kids on the island?" Straper asked in horror.

"Just robots," Slate groaned. "Get this boat moving."

"At last, you're reasonable," Naomi huffed, headed for the steering room.

The boat jolted forward, and they motored away from the island at full speed, leaving the inferno behind them. The entire island was ablaze. What was left of the laboratory and the amusement park was incinerated, along with the hovel Thomas had called home.

"We got to go back," Thomas sobbed, tears streaming down his face. "They can't be dead. Take me back! Take me back now!"

Naomi left the control room with the boat on autopilot. She walked up to Thomas and stared down at him. Thomas stopped crying long enough to look up at her. He had never seen a member of the opposite sex in person before. His only experience with women came from a few decaying androids and watching female hosts of kid's television shows. Not knowing how to react, he just looked up at her with a slack face.

Kneeling down, Naomi wrapped her arms around the boy.

Nobody knew what to make of it. In the short time they had known Naomi, the group had never seen her do something like this. Straper shuffled his feet. Gilda looked at Naomi, blinking a few times as if that would clarify the scene.

After getting over the initial shock of touching a female, Thomas began to cry again. It started out as a little snivel, but soon it turned into a cascade of tears. He burrowed his face into Naomi's shoulder and cried his heart out.

This didn't stop for some time. The others looked at the burning island. Now the lava was pouring into the water. Steam rose from the boiling ocean. As the boat went onward, Slate lay on the deck, beaten and drained. His silver helmet reflected the ominous glow from the island.

***

"Who was that boy?" Cyphrus asked, staring out the unicopter's window as the island was scorched clean. If only everything in life was this easy to clean up...

"Sorry, I didn't catch the kid's name when we were getting pummeled," Geppetto said. He was tending to Atlas's wounds. The giant's twisted body was sprawled on a stretcher. His broken bones were healing too fast for them to be set properly. It wasn't a pretty sight.

Cyphrus sighed. "Come now. Surely you overheard something."

"I think we got bigger things to worry about than one bulletproof brat," Geppetto said. "What are we going to do when the Chinese find out about this fiasco?"

"We'll improvise. The Chinese Empire still needs—"

Cyphrus had a thought midsentence. "Geppetto, how old did you say the boy was?"

"That kid again? He was, like, ten or eleven. I don't know."

Cyphrus's thought no longer seemed outlandish. It had become a valid hypothesis. Beads of sweat dotted her forehead. Her makeup started to run. A tremble went through her hands. Geppetto was too preoccupied with Atlas to notice any of these subtle changes. Cyphrus was good at hiding her emotions, though she couldn't help but let some of her rage slip out.

After all these years, that brat was still alive...

***

"You're telling me that this kid is bulletproof?" Gilda asked.

"That's right," Slate said. "He was a great defense."

"You used a ten-year-old boy as a human shield!" Straper yelled. "What the hell, man? How could you do that?"

"Oh, well, first I picked up the kid and put him in front of me. Then I crouched down, and that's about it. Pretty easy, actually."

"Would you be quiet?" Naomi snapped, walking into the ship's kitchen, where Slate stood and the others sat. "I just got our new companion to take a nap. No need to wake him."

It was two hours since they left the island. Slate's numerous wounds and Straper's bitten arm had been tended to, Gilda had begun to repair her damaged walker, and Naomi had put the heartbroken Thomas to bed after he had cried himself to exhaustion.

"That boy had these on him," Naomi said, holding up two small disks. "According to the labels, the disks hold copies of the research data for the mind-control weapon. My goodness, I almost thought our mission was in vain, but thanks to that boy, we might have a fighting chance of stopping Cloak's plans."

"Hey, I gave him those disks!" Slate yelled. "You should be thanking me."

Naomi smiled thinly. "I'd rather not."

"What? What did I do?"

"You used a kid as a human shield," Gilda reminded him. She didn't know what to make of Slate's actions. Maybe Naomi *did* have a valid reason not to like him.

"The kid is bulletproof," Slate said. "Why not use him?"

"You're a fricking moron!" Straper yelled. "Even if he's invincible, he's still just a kid. Just look at him! Who knows where his brain is at?"

"Those scientists must have done something to this child," Naomi said. "I thought the only research done on the island was on the mind-control nanobots, but it seems the scientists may have been engaged in other pursuits. Perhaps Cloak was trying to make more supersoldiers. Imagine, that boy's whole world has been turned inside out. Everything he has ever known is gone. How is he ever going to integrate into society? He lacks social skills and education, and his abnormal abilities make him a complete outcast, if not a target. In all honesty, I'm not sure what we're going to do with him."

Gilda laughed humorlessly. "So, we're going to have a little kid tag along with us? That sounds like a heap of trouble both for him and us."

"We don't even know his name," Straper huffed.

"It's Thomas," Slate said. "Geez, almost as bad a name as Jeffery."

Naomi scrunched her eyebrows. Hadn't she known someone named Thomas? He was about ten years old, so maybe he...

Her eyes bulged. Every inch of her body got goose bumps. No. It wasn't possible. It couldn't be... It couldn't be true.

Slate turned to Naomi. "What's the matter with you? You're acting like you just smelled your own fart."

"A real ladies' man," Straper scoffed.

"What is it?" Gilda asked Naomi. "Did you just figure something out?"

"Ten years old..." Naomi muttered. "Named Thomas... Kidnapped when he was an infant. Yes... There's no doubt. It's *him*."

"I'm not following any of this," Gilda said.

"Join the club," Straper added.

"Ten years ago, a kidnapping occurred in London," Naomi told them, her voice quivering. "It was an infamous case that shocked the world."

Gilda stopped breathing. Her eyes were massive. Even Straper now knew what they were talking about and was agape in astonishment. The only one who wasn't on board was the Helmet Man.

"Hello!" Slate yelled. "I've been living under a rock for twenty years. Literally! Would someone care to explain why you're all so worked up?"

"That boy sleeping a few rooms over was kidnapped ten years ago," Naomi said. "He's the long-lost prince of the United Kingdom."

Straper buried his face in his hands. "And we just found him..."

CHAPTER 21

"That kid's a prince?" Slate asked. "Seriously? He barely looks like a peasant."

"So, not only did Slate use a kid as a human shield, but he also used a British prince as a human shield," Gilda said.

"Oh, man, we really *are* enemies of the West now," Straper moaned.

"Give me a break," Slate said. "I probably wouldn't have used the kid as a shield if I'd known he was royalty."

"*Probably*?" Straper cried.

"Hold on," Gilda said. "We don't know for certain that he's a prince. For all we know, he's just some random kid."

"No, it's him all right," Naomi said, regaining her composure.

"A fricking prince," Straper said. "They never found out who did the kidnapping. Were Cloak and the Gifted really behind it all?"

Naomi lowered her eyes. "I'm afraid so."

"Great, I guess Cloak's also behind the Bermuda Triangle and the Loch Ness Monster."

"What I know of the kidnapping is sketchy at best," Naomi said. "Sebastian kept most of the details from me, but from what I gathered, Cyphrus decided to kidnap the royal baby and kill the queen's husband. I'm not sure why she did this, but Cloak hadn't sanctioned the kidnapping. It was one of the few times I saw Sebastian noticeably irritated. I assumed he had the infant killed, but it seems he found a use for the baby as a test subject."

"He must have experimented on that baby to make it invulnerable," Straper said. "Fricking sicko. Reminds me why we got to take out Cloak."

"Then why did Cloak leave this kid on a deserted island to fend for himself?" Gilda asked.

"I can only speculate," Naomi said. "Sebastian had all the scientists killed five years ago. I believe he did so because he wanted to cover up the existence of the mind-control weapon and was also getting no results from the experiments on Thomas."

"But the experiment must have been a success," Gilda said. "Maybe Cloak thought they killed Thomas, but his invulnerability saved him."

"Yes, and those androids probably found him soon after. Cloak left the androids alone, because they weren't deemed a risk and could be used for security and surveillance, lucky for Thomas. Without those androids, he wouldn't have lasted long."

"Having nothing but TV to teach him and robots for friends must have sucked," Slate said. "But he got over it. Hell, he even flourished."

"But now all his friends are gone," Naomi said. "I can't imagine what he must be going through, the poor child."

A mechanical grinding interrupted the discussion.

"Dude, what was that?" Straper asked.

The grinding was followed by a large bang. The hum of the engine stopped.

Naomi frowned. "Splendid. What a worthless boat we picked up, but what do you expect from dirt-poor pirates? Gilda, you're somewhat of a gearhead."

Gilda smiled, getting up from her chair. "Somewhat? I am a gearhead. I used to help out the mechanic at the Bunker all the time."

"Then get to the engine room and find out what's going on. I'm going to check on our young prince and see if he was woken by the ruckus."

The women left, leaving Slate and Straper alone.

Straper shook his head. "A human shield..."

"All right, quit your whining," Slate said. "I expect that from Gilda and the hottie, but not you. We're supposed to pal around, remember?"

"You mean I'm just supposed to go with whatever you do?"

"Look, you fail to realize that the kid isn't even human. He's a monster, just like me."

"Being invulnerable doesn't make you a monster. What you did does."

"Uh, no. Being a monster means being abnormal. I should know from experience. People judge at a glance and write you off. You thought I was a freak the moment you laid eyes on me. Trust me, that kid will never live a normal life. He's doomed. And what if we somehow turned him normal? He's never experienced pain before. How do you think he'll cope with getting a little scrape or breaking a leg?"

Straper almost felt angry tears come out of his eyes. "It shouldn't be that easy. What you did... What you always do... It shouldn't be *that* easy."

Slate leaned in. "Well, it was."

Before the argument could escalate into a yelling match, Naomi dashed into the room. Her composed demeanor had evaporated.

"The boy's gone," she told them.

"You're kidding," Slate said.

"Look for him," Naomi ordered. "On the double!"

Slate immediately forgot the argument. Straper didn't, but he knew they had a situation on their hands. They left the room with Naomi to begin the search.

The hijacked boat wasn't very big. Most of it was covered in rust and grime, the furniture rotten and old. The cots the pirates had slept on were stained with alcohol and bodily fluids. Cigarette butts and beer bottles littered the hallways. These pirates were about as hygienic as college freshmen. Straper was actually a little disappointed. He had imagined pirates as lovable swashbucklers with talking parrots and buried treasure. The Neutral Zone pirates just seemed like a bunch of dirty hobos.

"Over here!" Slate shouted from the deck.

The others ran over. Slate stood next to Thomas, keeping a respectable distance. Thomas was wearing rank pirate clothes too large for him, but his old rags were even worse, so Naomi had chosen to dress him in the lesser of two evils. Thomas sat cross-legged on the deck. He held a fishing pole that he must have found lying somewhere. A small smile was on his face, but his eyes were still red.

"Where have you been?" Naomi asked.

"Hey, you've never shown me this kind of concern," Slate whined.

"Because you don't deserve it," Naomi said. "Thomas, what are you doing out here? I thought you were taking a nap. If you plan on running off again, please tell us before you do. And especially don't run off with Slate. He's an idiot."

The Helmet Man stomped his foot. "I'm right here, you know!"

"Okay, I'm sorry," Thomas told Naomi. "Hey, I caught one!"

He tugged on his line and pulled a large fish out of the water. It flopped on the deck for a few seconds before Thomas clocked it on the head.

"Whoa, where did you learn how to fish?" Straper asked. "Way cool! That's a neat skill to have. I barely know how to microwave popcorn."

"Thanks," Thomas said, his smile growing. "I saw it on TV, but I never had a fishing pole, just a stick and some twine I found."

"Well, you're very good for being self-taught," Naomi said with a wide grin. "You know, we could have a late lunch. Why don't you catch some more fish so we can make a proper meal? I'm sure there's other food lying around."

"Sure!" Thomas exclaimed. "I'll catch more fish. I promise!"

The group searched the boat for food while Gilda worked on fixing the engine. Straper tore open cupboards, finding only packaged noodles and rotten produce. Naomi, however, found a bundle of fruit that was still edible. Thomas managed to catch several more good-sized fish, all of which were cooked by Naomi after she gutted them. Straper boiled noodles and found some seasoning they could use. The meal was ready in less than an hour. The gang gathered around, ecstatic and hungry.

"This looks good," Thomas said. "Are those real noodles?"

"Yes, you probably haven't eaten many carbohydrates," Naomi said. "I have a feeling you'll enjoy noodles. They're very tasty."

Gilda was the last to join them with motor oil covering her wrists. She was getting close to fixing the old engine, but it would take more time.

They all dug in, leaving no leftovers. Naomi ate the most, operating like an elegant vacuum. While eating, Thomas told them about his adventures on the island, like how he gathered food and weathered stormy nights. It took everyone's thoughts away from fouler things. Gilda forgot about her damaged walker, Straper forgot about his victim, and Thomas managed to somewhat forget about his android friends. All of them ate and forgot.

All except for Slate.

The Helmet Man stood in the corner with crossed arms, away from the others, observing. Slate couldn't eat. He could barely remember what it felt like, how much joy could be taken from a single bite, how a single morsel could brighten one's day. And he couldn't share a meal. He couldn't socialize like the others. Even Naomi seemed to be able to do it. But not him. Not only that, but they seemed to be giving him the cold shoulder as if he weren't even there.

Cyphrus had asked him to join Cloak. What was that about? Cloak wanted him, flaws and all. Not these people, though. Even when he was saving their lives, they still rejected him.

Slate left the room. Nobody noticed his departure.

***

After a two-hour flight, the unicopter landed on Cloak's yacht and Cyphrus exited. Two mercenaries followed, carrying Atlas on a stretcher. Geppetto waddled after them with a bandage on his neck and his face twisted in worry.

But Cyphrus wasn't worried, just annoyed. Slate and Repulsa had gotten the better of her. This was bad. The Chinese emperor had ordered her to kill those fools. If he found out she had failed, it could ruin her plans to marry the monarch. She might even end up in the Traitors' Garden, trapped for life inside one of those wretched statues.

And then there was the prince...

Well, at least the island was destroyed, along with that pesky lab. Curse that Sebastian. It was as if he had left the lab intact just to spite her. In all likelihood he had.

A pale-faced mercenary emerged from inside the yacht. "You have a call."

Cyphrus raised an eyebrow. "Who?"

The mercenary gulped. "Mao Long."

Cyphrus went from looking bored to grinding her teeth. Mao didn't just happen to call right when she arrived. He must be keeping tabs on her. Was one of her mercenaries a spy for the Chinese? Fantastic. She would have to fire them all just to be safe.

"Assist Geppetto," she hissed at the mercenary. "I'll deal with this."

Cyphrus stormed inside the yacht. Why was Mao calling her? It could only mean he had found out that Slate escaped. She entered the communications room and saw the hologram of Mao Long flicker before her. He was wearing a casual red suit and a smug smirk.

"Mao, what a wonderful surprise," Cyphrus said with false friendliness.

"I'm glad to see you're so happy after such an embarrassing debacle," Mao said. "It takes a true simpleton to be happy when they stink of failure. I envy you … almost."

"Have no fear, Prime Minister. The hunt is not over yet. The boat our enemies took originally belonged to pirates under my employ. Naturally, I had the foresight to hide a tracking device on all their vessels. I've now sent six pirate crews to intercept the hijacked boat. They'll ensure there are no survivors."

Mao sighed. "Alas, I wish I could trust your word, but I can't leave you with such an important task. I must handle this myself."

Cyphrus wanted to curse. If Mao managed to kill Slate before she could, the emperor would side with his son, alienating her.

"You can't do that!" she shouted. Cyphrus immediately wished she hadn't shown emotion like that in front of her enemy, but it was too late to take it back. "The Chinese Empire is not allowed to go into the Neutral Zone. The emperor gave me this task, not you."

"The emperor never prohibited me from interfering," Mao said. "As for the Neutral Zone, the treaty says it is only our military that isn't allowed there. So, instead, I have sent an agent of the Black Lotus to put an end to the Helmet Man."

"What are you talking about?"

"I'm talking about Mistress Lotus herself."

The blood in Cyphrus's veins went ice cold. That black sphere... Mao seemed to notice her shocked reaction, for he grinned like a madman.

"You're telling me ... that rumor is true?" Cyphrus whispered.

Mao continued to smile as he ended the transmission.

***

Thomas bounced onto the deck with a boyish grin. Slate leaned on the railing. He appeared to be sulking. The boy stopped next to him.

"You okay?" Thomas asked, his grin fading. "Why weren't you at the party?"

"They needed a break from me," Slate said.

"I thought they were your friends."

"Starting to wonder if they are. Honestly, they just met you, and you've already got their friendship. I keep saving their lives and try to lighten up the mood, and they couldn't care less. No matter what I do, people always keep their distance. Just my dad. Only my dad..."

"But I like you," Thomas said. "You saved me from the volcano. You tried to help my friends." Emotion swelled in his voice at the mention of his former companions, on the verge of tears.

"Stop that," Slate said. "No crying."

Thomas wiped his eyes. "It's not fair. They never did anything wrong."

"Don't worry, kid. I'm on a mission to stop Cloak. Cyphrus and the others can't keep doing as they please. Guess I can't either."

A projectile hit the water near their boat and exploded on impact. Slate and Thomas both stumbled backward but regained their balance.

The others ran up on deck, startled and tense.

"What the hell was that?" Gilda asked.

"I think I have the answer," Naomi said, looking through her binoculars.

About half a mile away, six cruddy-looking ships approached. Scruffy men wearing dirty clothes stood on deck, holding rifles and rocket launchers. They had just shot the rocket and were about to fire one again.

Naomi put away her binoculars. "Cloak must be tracking our ship. How bothersome. Looks like we didn't search the ship thoroughly enough."

"Blown up by a rocket launcher," Straper muttered. "Can our demise at least be a little more original?"

That's when things got original. The water around the pirate ships began to bubble. Large waves smashed into the vessels, rocking them almost to the tipping point. Shouting in fear, the pirates started to shoot at the water.

"What's going on?" Gilda asked.

"It's a sea monster!" Straper cried. "Oh, I take it back! I don't want an original death. Give me pirates any day. At least they won't eat me."

"Sea monster!" Thomas screeched.

"Keep calm," Naomi said. "Straper, you need to stop spreading panic. That's just Captain Young-Bum and his superstitious beliefs talking. There's no such thing as sea—"

A geyser shot up from under one of the enemy vessels. The pirate ship flew a hundred feet into the air before falling back down and smashing into the ocean.

Everyone gaped at this display.

Slate chuckled. "Boy, that sure got me out of my funk."

CHAPTER 22

"We're gonna die!" Straper screamed.

"This is impossible!" Gilda shouted.

All Naomi could do was croak, unable to form words. Thomas kept shrieking as he fell onto his rump.

Naomi snapped out of her trance. "Gilda, fix that engine, *now*!"

Snapping back to reality, Gilda nodded and ran below deck.

"Everyone else, inside!" Naomi ordered. "All except for you, Slate."

"Lady, not even you're hot enough to convince me to fight a sea monster."

"I'm staying here. Are you saying women are braver than men?"

"What? Then I'm staying! I shall protect my sexist ways, even if I must die doing so."

Naomi rolled her eyes.

Thomas and Straper fled inside the boat. Thomas was crying and screaming, grabbing Straper's hand while they ran.

"Are we going to be okay?" he cried.

"Hell no!" Straper screamed. "End of days, brah! End of days!"

"Would you shut up?" Naomi hissed after him.

More bubbles rose, and terrified shouts resonated across the water as the pirates scrambled to move their vessels away. No amount of money offered by Cloak was going to convince them to go up against this insanity.

While the pirates weren't paying attention, one of their crewmates dove into the ocean. Naomi noticed this and frowned. It didn't look like this pirate was abandoning ship, but she was far too preoccupied to deal with it. She pointed her palms at the water and pushed with her mind. The boat began to move away from the bubbling water and the pirates. Until Gilda got the engine fixed, she would have to propel the boat herself.

The water started to swirl near the pirate vessels. It soon turned into a giant whirlpool. Naomi could feel their boat being tugged toward it. She grunted, trying to resist the pull of the current, but despite her efforts, they began to inch toward the swirling water.

"I could use some help!" Naomi screamed at Slate. A vein throbbed on her forehead.

"Do I get a date if I do?" Slate asked.

"Do it, or I'll rip your arms off!"

"Is that a maybe?"

One of the pirate ships was now on the edge of the whirlpool. The men on board screamed. Some jumped out of the boat, trying to save their skins, but they were sucked into the whirlpool. Their ship was swallowed as well, ripped into a hundred pieces. Another pirate vessel soon followed its counterpart to a watery grave. Naomi couldn't help but feel a shiver of fear run up her spine. Whatever was causing this bizarre phenomenon, it wasn't natural.

"We've got to stop it!" she yelled.

Slate shrugged. "Why? Those pirates were trying to kill us. For all we know, that whirlpool is being made by a friendly undersea chum."

"Then why are we being dragged in too?"

"Collateral damage."

Naomi wanted to snap at him again, but she was distracted by a mackerel that had flopped on board. It was followed by several dozen more fish of various species. They thrashed and gasped, and the deck was soon covered in them. Her eyes widened. Something was freaking out the fish, something—

A great white shark flew out of the ocean. With a four-foot-wide mouth, it soared right at Naomi with its teeth bared. She froze in place. It was just too weird, too out of the blue. She couldn't react. She couldn't—

"Take that, tuna!" Slate shouted, punching the shark's face with an electrified fist. Half its teeth were knocked out, and the smoldering corpse fell back into the ocean.

Naomi almost fell from the sheer surprise, but she remained focused on the water. She had to get them as far away from the whirlpool as possible. It had consumed its third pirate vessel.

Out of nowhere, a geyser erupted. The column of water did not collapse, however, remaining erect and imposing. It looked to Naomi as though the ocean was growing a limb as big as an air traffic control tower. The impossible event created waves that almost capsized their vessel. Naomi cried out in exertion as she forced the boat back onto its belly. Sweat poured off her like a waterfall, her teeth clenched.

"Do you still think that thing is friendly?" she seethed.

"Man, you're really judgmental," Slate said.

The column of water hung in the air for a moment before swinging down. It was going to fall right on their boat.

"Hurry, Slate!" Naomi shouted.

Slate charged his arm, giving off a blue glow, then aimed his palm at the incoming water tower and fired a beam. His aim was spot-on. It went right through the column. A good chunk of it turned into steam. The rest of the column collapsed harmlessly into the sea. Right after that, the whirlpool stopped spinning, and the water was calm once again.

If that wasn't enough good news, Naomi felt the boat's engine come to life. It looked like Gilda had managed to fix the piece of junk. The boat moved forward. Straper, who had gone to the control room, was piloting it away from whatever was attacking them, going full throttle.

"Slate, you and I need to distract that thing so the others can escape," Naomi said. She stopped using her powers to propel the boat, letting the engine take over. Her knees shook from exhaustion. She had difficulty just standing up.

"You ain't going anywhere," Slate said. "It's against my code to let a hot woman get in the line of fire. Besides, look at you. Even Straper could beat you in your state."

"My involvement is nonnegotiable," she snapped, steadying herself. "Now let's go."

Naomi flew up, and Slate had no choice but to follow. The remaining two pirate ships were now fleeing. The ocean itself was still and silent.

"Did it run away?" Naomi asked Slate, floating next to the Helmet Man.

In answer to her question, a geyser burst from the ocean's calm surface. Slate and Naomi flew out of the way, the geyser shooting past them. Such a blast could have been fatal if either of them had been directly hit.

"Man, whatever's attacking us is pretty badass," Slate said.

"Stop praising it," Naomi hissed.

The water began to boil again. Shadows stirred beneath the surface. Then a mountain of water two hundred feet tall erupted from the sea. Two thick, liquid arms hung from its sides. They were shapeless but big enough to crush ships. Whatever this thing was, it loomed over Slate and Naomi, the size of a kaiju.

"Quick, take a picture!" Slate yelled. "Wait... I can't see photos anyway!"

The water monster swung one of its large arms, which were each about as long as two railcars. Naomi flew up and Slate dropped down, both avoiding the attack. Slate started charging his arm and pointed it at the creature. He fired his beam. It hit the monster's body. Steam filled the air, but the water creature regenerated itself. It had an endless supply of water at its disposal. A geyser shot out of the monster's chest. Slate dodged to the side, but the water grazed him. He spun around like a top before stopping himself. Angrily, he sent at least thirty lightning bolts at the liquid being. The monster took all the bolts with ease.

Floating above the creature, Naomi threw several punches, compressing the air and sending down invisible attacks. They all hit the water monster but did little damage. Now the creature turned its attention to Naomi. It somehow managed to make itself taller and swung an arm at her. She glided backward, smiling. This was turning out to be an easier fight than she expected. They didn't even need to kill it. All they needed to do was keep the thing distracted long enough for the others to get away. As long as she stayed out of its reach, this sea monster was no threat to her.

Or that was what she thought.

Right when she was feeling smug, a geyser shot out of the monster's arm. She was taken by surprise. It hit her legs, and she spiraled through the air, disoriented and vulnerable. The monster swung again but missed on pure chance.

Slate kept his distance as he tried to figure this creature out. This was a tough foe. Water dampened his powers, so this was literally the worst enemy he could be facing. It couldn't be made entirely out of water, could it? It must have a brain of some sort, something that could be damaged. The Helmet Man couldn't sense through water all that well, but he did detect an object near the center of the monster. It was spherical in shape and about four feet in diameter.

"Hey, Naomi! What the hell is that round thing?"

Naomi got herself reoriented and saw what Slate was talking about. A black ball was floating inside the monster.

"Go get it!" Naomi yelled. "I'll keep the creature busy."

"Great, give me the hard jobs!"

Naomi didn't have time to indulge the Helmet Man with a witty reply. She flew around the creature at breakneck speeds, throwing telekinetic punches. They splashed against the creature's watery surface and managed to irritate it. It tried to hit Naomi with one of its limbs, but she maneuvered out of the way.

With the monster preoccupied, Slate used the chance to formulate a strategy. The only real attack that had any chance of hurting that black ball was his beam, but it had been unable to get through all that water. He would have to get closer to the ball somehow, and he could think of only one way to do it.

Slate growled. "I hate baths."

He flew at top speed at the creature and collided with its liquid body, submerging himself in the salty water. He was thrashed about as the currents beat his body. His powers were almost nullified in water, but he had already charged up his arm for a beam attack. Slate only had one shot. If he failed, it was quite possible he would be dragged to the bottom of the ocean. He could not drown, but the pressure would crush him.

With great care, Slate aimed his palm and fired.

The creature was being generated and controlled by Mistress Lotus, the leader of the Black Lotus. She had given up her body long ago, her brain now encased within a black metal sphere. Mistress Lotus was able to control large bodies of water via a device that made water molecules selectively more cohesive. A face bearing her old likeness was carved on the front of the sphere, but that was all that remained of her former self. She needed no body. Having the power to control the waters was all she needed to serve her emperor.

Mistress Lotus noticed Slate's beam at the last moment and made the currents move her body out of the way. While the beam didn't hit her dead-on, it managed to take a large chunk from her metal form. Mistress Lotus was unable to feel pain anymore, but she did know that she had sustained critical damage. Curse Mao Long and his plots. Although the Black Lotus was obliged to obey the prime minister, she wasn't keen on getting embroiled in a feud between Mao and Cloak. She would have to speak with the emperor about this. With great resentment, Mistress Lotus decided to retreat.

The creature began to collapse back into the ocean. Naomi smiled as she witnessed her opponent running away. Then she noticed that Slate was falling out of the creature's side, unable to fly. She flew down and caught the Helmet Man with two outstretched arms.

"Ugh ... my hero..." Slate groaned.

"Let's not do that again," Naomi said as she flew away from the retreating monster, cradling Slate in her arms. "And if you so much as cop a feel, I'll drop you in the ocean."

"Ah ... decisions, decisions."

***

After ten minutes of frantic boat driving, Straper eased up on the throttle. The danger was gone, but the engine was about to overheat. And his seasickness was returning. Great.

Gilda and Thomas came up from below to join him. They looked haggard, but they also looked unhurt, which was the important thing.

Straper checked the GPS with a withered grin. "Guys, we're almost out of the Neutral Zone. We'll soon be in Western Union territory. Pirate-free waters, baby!"

"And monster-free," Thomas added, still in shock.

"We can't go too far without Slate and Naomi," Gilda said. "I'm going on deck to keep an eye out for them."

"Be careful," Straper said. "We ain't out of the woods yet."

Thomas looked confused. "Woods? Isn't this an ocean?"

Gilda went outside and leaned against the railing. The fish on deck had stopped flopping around. The salty smell of their flesh had already become overpowering. The tropical sun didn't help either. She kicked a sardine away and sighed. For the moment, Gilda was left alone with her thoughts. She wondered about the creature that had just attacked them, but long-standing questions and worries soon occupied her mind. The enigma that was Naomi kept bothering her. What was her story? Gilda only knew that Naomi hated Slate for some unknown reason, was ashamed of her past affiliation with Cloak, and, like Slate, sought to kill Cloak's leader, this so-called Mentor.

Now that Gilda thought about it, she knew nothing of their true enemy. Who was the Mentor? Was Cloak's leader one of the Gifted? Could the Mentor be a Keymaster? Whoever it was, Gilda knew the Mentor had to be taken out if this war with Cloak was ever going to end. The problem was they had no idea where to begin looking. Perhaps Sebastian or Cyphrus knew. Gilda and the others would have to capture one of them first for interrogation. Then they could find and face the Mentor. It was the only way to defeat Cloak. Then she could...

Gilda found herself unable to finish that thought. Then what? She hadn't figured out what would come next in her life. The prospect of a career as a military walker pilot was toast. That much was certain. What about a court-martial? Pruning? Prison? Firing squad?

And yet Gilda found herself with no regrets. She knew Cloak was evil. She knew how Henry had died. She didn't care about having a career. She didn't care about having a love life. No, she definitely didn't care about *that*. A spasm of anger went through her, remembering some of Naomi's taunts and how she flaunted her good looks to drooling idiots like Slate and Straper. Gilda vowed not to be like Naomi. She vowed not to be like—

Something startled her, a dripping figure on the edge of her vision. She spun around to see a pirate staring right at her. He was soaking wet with a weapon clenched in his hand. It flashed too fast to identify, but she did feel it hit her head.

Then it went dark.

Inside the wheelhouse, Straper heard Gilda fall to the deck.

"Hey, you all right out there?" he yelled.

The door burst open, a figure flashing by at impossible speeds. A glint of metal was all Straper saw as Thomas was slashed down, flying backward and slamming into the wall. Straper screamed. His heart felt as if it was about to burst from his chest, but he didn't waste time thinking about what he just saw. All he did was reach for his gun.

He never had the chance to fire. Something knocked the gun out of his hand. Straper didn't even know what had disarmed him until it swung at him a second time.

It was a sword.

Keito Kusanagi slammed his blade into the side of Straper's head.

CHAPTER 23

"I can't believe that thing exists," Naomi said as she and Slate flew high above the ocean. They were both heading in the general direction that Straper had taken the boat. Slate could now fly on his own after drying off a little. While Slate was full of energy, both electrical and bodily, Naomi was near her breaking point. She didn't know how long she could keep flying and was more than a little jealous of Slate's remarkable recovery from his ordeal on the island. He could shake off two broken ribs without a second thought.

"So, what was that water monster?" Slate asked. "Thought I'd ask before forgetting."

"I've only heard stories," Naomi said. "I believe that was a member of the Black Lotus, Mistress Lotus, to be precise. I've heard claims that she can bend the ocean to her will. It seems some legends aren't exaggerated after all."

"Who are these Black Lotus jerks?" Slate asked.

"They're supersoldiers, just like us. When the Western Union made the Gifted, the Chinese Empire secretly made the Black Lotus in retaliation, but unlike the Gifted, the members of the Black Lotus have remained loyal to their creator."

"Hey, wait a sec. If those pirates back there were in cahoots with Cloak, why did this Mistress Lotus attack them too?"

"Either they were caught in the crossfire or there's some kind of power struggle going on between Cloak and the Chinese. Let's hope for the latter, since that would benefit us the most. And let's hope we come across our boat soon. I don't like the idea of leaving the others undefended for so long."

***

Thomas remembered what his android friends had taught him. In this kind of situation, he needed to keep his eyes shut and try not to breathe so loud. They called it "playing dead" without ever explaining to him what death was. Aristotle would have probably given him a long-winded answer if he had asked, but the question had never seemed important until recently.

His hands were tied behind his back to a rusted pipe. All he could recall from the attack was getting hit on the head and smashing into the wall. He wasn't hurt, unlike the others. Gilda and Straper had also been tied up with rope next to him and were currently slumped over with closed eyes. Thomas risked taking a peek and noticed that they were both still breathing. It didn't seem like they were "dead." At least he thought so.

Thomas saw their assailant at the wheel. The swordsman had changed out of his nasty pirate clothes and now only wore black shorts, topless and barefoot. Dozens of red scars covered the man's torso. A sword also hung from his side, clean and sharp. The man had disabled his captives with the dull side of his blade, though Thomas hadn't figured that out. Where were they going? The man hadn't "killed" them, so he wasn't working for Cloak, but Thomas still didn't like him. This man was too cold.

The swordsman reached into a small bag near his feet and took out two canisters and a syringe. He stabbed himself with the syringe and pushed the plunger down before pulling the pins from the two canisters and dropping them on the floor. The canisters released a blue gas that dissipated quickly. Thomas soon felt woozy. Was the gas doing this to him? The swordsman didn't seem sleepy. Did that needle...?

Before Thomas could reach a conclusion, his eyelids fell shut.

***

After almost ten minutes of flying, Naomi landed on their boat, exhausted and disoriented. She needed rest. Not only did she just endure that extensive odyssey on an island filled with robots and pirates, but she had also fought a giant water monster created by an insane emperor. A volcano had almost killed them too. Oh, and they had found the long-lost British prince. Naomi shook her head. She really needed to write all this down.

Slate touched down next to her, stretching. "Man, I'm beat! How about we give each other massages?"

"I'd rather get an appendix removed," she said, trudging up to the boat's wheelhouse to talk with the others, crushing dead fish beneath her feet. When she opened the door, she was surprised to discover no one was manning the wheel. The boat was still moving forward, so the autopilot must be on. Could they just be busy with something else?

Naomi heard a moan from the left. She spun around to see Gilda, Straper, and Thomas all bound and unconscious. Her adrenaline spiked. She went into battle mode and raised her fists. Where was the perpetrator? Who could have—?

Naomi stumbled backward. Her mind became cloudy. The adrenaline in her system wasn't working anymore. So tired... So...

A man pounced out of a nearby doorway. She moved back and threw telekinetic punches, but the man sidestepped, the punches only hitting the wall. He took out his sword and sliced at her. Naomi nearly got gutted five times over. What was going on? Had she been drugged?

Before she could find the answer, a lightning bolt flew past her. The swordsman raised his weapon and blocked the bolt. Naomi finally recognized the assailant. It was the mercenary, Keito Kusanagi, Slate had fought in Tokyo. How did he just block that lightning?

"It's you, the Asian Batman!" Slate cried. "We have unfinished business!"

"Surrender," Keito told him.

"Not a chance!" the Helmet Man yelled. "I'm gonna—ah ... what the...?"

Slate started to wobble. Naomi couldn't believe it. Slate was being drugged as well. He couldn't inhale anything due to his helmet, so there must be something in the air that could go through the skin. This was definitely not good. If Slate was disabled too, this swordsman had a realistic chance of winning.

Keito rushed forward and swung his weapon at Slate. The Helmet Man hopped to the side, the sword almost hitting him on the shoulder. Swinging again, Keito managed to cut Slate's leg, making it bleed a little. He sliced the air some more. Slate only narrowly avoided a severed arm. Naomi tried to focus on Keito in hopes of snapping his neck, but she could barely see straight. She decided to settle for simply raising her hands and pushing forward. The front windshield cracked, and the control panel caved in a little. One of Keito's legs was knocked out from under him as well, but he quickly regained his balance. Naomi swore groggily. Then she lost consciousness and fell to the floor.

However, when Keito had lost his balance, Slate used the opportunity to grab his sword. The sharp blade dug through his gloves and cut into his hand, but Slate held on. He sent a surge of energy into the blade. Sparks flew around them. Keito used both hands to try to free his blade from Slate's grasp. They fought over the sword, tugging and pulling.

A red light began to blink on the sword's handle. Keito seethed. He opened up the handle and took out a cartridge, replacing it with another. The Helmet Man didn't know what Keito was doing but took the opportunity to spin around.

Taken by surprise, Keito kept hold of his sword as he was tugged off his feet. Slate let go, sending Keito flying out the door and over the boat's railing.

The swordsman hit the water hard. Their speeding boat soon left him behind.

Slate couldn't sense if Keito had survived or not, but he didn't really care at the moment. All he did was squeeze his bloody hands and stagger outside. Once he got on deck, the effects of the gas started to wear off. He shook himself until he was alert and went back inside to drag everyone out onto the deck and untie them. After laying their bodies outside among the dead fish, Slate turned off the boat and kicked his friends awake.

"Get up, lazy bones!" Slate yelled. "No time to diddle around!"

Naomi got up, groaning. "Can't say I'm too happy with that wake-up call."

"I dreamed I wasn't here," Straper grumbled.

"What happened?" Gilda asked, brushing a dead anchovy off her chest. "Did one of those pirates knock me out? Did he get anyone else?"

"Yeah, he used a sword on us," Thomas said. "It was scary. Do you guys always have this much fun?"

"Thankfully, no," Naomi said, shaking off her drowsiness. "At least I managed to squeeze in a nap. Keito Kusanagi must have used gas to disorient us, a clever trap."

"He also put something sharp in his arm," Thomas said.

"Probably so he wouldn't be affected by the gas."

"What was he going to do to us?" Straper asked.

"Hand you over to his employers. I don't think he's working for Cloak. He only disguised himself as a pirate in order to get close to us. I saw someone swimming for our boat, but I didn't think it was a major concern. That was a blunder on my part. Forgive me."

"Uh, okay…" Straper said. Everyone else looked a little uncomfortable. Nobody expected Naomi to apologize. It was both humbling and concerning.

Naomi ignored them. She had noticed the disposed cartridge in the wheelhouse.

"What's that on the floor?" she asked.

"It came outta that guy's sword," Slate said.

Not wanting another dose of gas, Naomi pointed her finger at the canister, causing it to levitate out of the wheelhouse. She snatched it from the air and inspected it.

"We'll find out what this is," she said. "Maybe we can figure out how Kusanagi can block Slate's attacks so we can develop a countermeasure."

"You think he's still alive?" Straper asked.

"Possibly, but somebody else could use this technology against us. We need to be prepared."

A welcome sight then appeared: a black submarine was rising up out of the ocean. The water frothed around it.

"We're safe," Straper said. "Finally, a break from this craziness."

"What is that?" Thomas cried, pointing at the sub. "It's awesome!"

"That's a submarine," Naomi said. "It's also our ride out of here."

***

They were inside the submarine several minutes later, abandoning their boat. Captain Young-Bum was waiting for them in the common room. He looked relieved but irritated. He had searched for Slate and the others on his radar when they didn't meet him at the rendezvous point, getting lucky and finding them only a short way off.

"I thought you had died," he told Naomi.

"We managed to avoid any casualties," she said. "And I owe you an apology."

"For what?"

Naomi smiled. "You were right about the sea monsters."

Young-Bum didn't have a good reply to that.

The *Eodum* submerged itself.

"Incognito called earlier," Young-Bum said. "He is anxious to hear how your mission went. Speaking of which, did you accomplish your task?"

Naomi took out the two disks that she found on Thomas. "We managed to find the key to defeating Cloak. I better send this information to Incognito. No need to prolong—"

The submarine shuddered. Everyone almost fell over.

"Swell, what now?" Straper asked.

"I've had just about enough of these surprises," Gilda spat.

A crewman ran into the room. "Sir, a depth charge just went off next to us. Over a dozen large ships have appeared on our radar too. They came out of nowhere."

"Everyone, to the control room!" Young-Bum ordered.

The group followed Young-Bum to the center of the sub. They were led into a dim room filled with computer screens, complicated machinery, and ten crewmen sitting in chairs, scrambling to figure out what was going on.

Another blast shook the ship, rattling everyone.

"Whoever is attacking is not trying to sink us," Young-Bum said. "They are attempting to scare us into submission."

"And it's working!" Straper cried.

"What's happening, Naomi?" Thomas whimpered, grabbing her arm.

She patted his head. "Don't worry. We're going to be all right."

"Sir, one of their ships is sending us a hologram transmission," a crewman said.

"Put them on," Young-Bum growled. "Let us see their petulant faces."

A hologram materialized before them, a blonde woman wearing a blue uniform. Her face held no expression.

"Who are you?" Young-Bum snapped. "Why are you attacking us?"

"My name is Camilla Ryder," the woman said in a monotone. "On behalf of the Western Union, I have called to demand your surrender."

CHAPTER 24

"Surrender, is it?" Naomi spat. "What kind of surrender?"

"Unconditional," Ryder droned.

Naomi knew they didn't stand a chance against over a dozen Western Union warships. The *Eodum* was built for stealth, not combat, and if one of those depth charges managed to hit them, it was all over. Whoever this Ryder was, she had been smart enough to wait until their sub was deep underwater before attacking. This way, neither Slate nor Naomi would be able to resist or fly away. No matter how Naomi looked at it, the Western Union had them trapped.

"How did you find us?" Young-Bum demanded. "The *Eodum's* stealth capabilities are unmatched. Not even the Western Union's most advanced ships can detect us."

"We didn't have to detect you," Ryder said. "You were easily led to where we wanted you to be."

Something clicked inside Naomi's head. "Kusanagi works for you, doesn't he? He was taking us to you. When he failed, you were waiting nearby and saw our sub go under."

"Unfortunately, I was unable to pursue you inside the Neutral Zone," Ryder said. "But because Kusanagi is technically not with the Western Union's military, he was able to enter the zone with impunity and successfully bring you all within my reach."

"We didn't see any ships while we were on the surface," Naomi said. "How were you able to hide in plain sight like that?"

"Our ships were cloaked, rendered completely invisible. They can also become invisible to radar, much like your sub. We only now revealed ourselves so you could see how outnumbered you are."

"Is that why your ships appeared out of nowhere?" Young-Bum asked.

"Correct." Ryder turned to Slate. "I have answered all your questions, so I would like an answer to mine. Do you surrender, yes or no?"

"What if we say no?" Slate asked.

"Then you die."

"Oh, then we surrender."

"Don't decide things without us," Naomi hissed with a false smile.

"I'm with Slate," Straper said. "Let's surrender. For once, he's the voice of reason, as messed up as that sounds. I'd rather be pruned than killed any day. Let's just hand over our intel on Cloak to the Western Union. They can take it from here."

"Ridiculous," Naomi muttered. "The Western Union has never made any real effort to track down Cloak. They'll just continue to protect their own skins."

"Then what do you suggest?" Straper snapped. "Should we let ourselves be blown to bits? I don't think so, lady."

"I'll do whatever Naomi wants me to do!" Thomas yelled.

"Who is this child?" Ryder asked.

"He's the prince of England," Slate said.

"Very well, don't tell me. My superiors do not have much patience, so you need to decide now what your course of action will be."

"We're not surrendering," Gilda told her.

Everyone looked at her as if she had just grown a second head.

"Gilda, don't say such stupid things," Naomi told her. "I decide what we do next."

"Yeah, I don't want to throw my life away," Straper said. "It sucks that we can't fight Cloak anymore, but it's over. It was stupid to think we could make a difference anyway. The Western Union may be controlled by a bunch of turds, but they're still the good guys. And Incognito ain't a good guy. I'm pretty sure of that. We managed to get a lot done. That's the important thing. Cloak's on its last legs."

"Last legs?" Gilda scoffed. "We still haven't even found the Mentor yet."

Ryder glanced at her. "You must be Gilda Plato, the daughter of our top military scientist. How did such a promising cadet ever become brainwashed by Incognito into thinking she was fighting supervillains?"

"Liar!" Gilda cried. "Cloak is real! I saw my best friend's body bleeding out on the floor. I saw the burning bodies of over a hundred cadets littered on the ground like they were trash. I saw an entire casino of people slaughtered for no reason. Do you think I just imagined it all?"

"The Helmet Man is a known terrorist," Ryder said. "You're just remembering things differently. This man you call your comrade is a heartless killer. You betrayed the Western Union and have allied yourself with this terrorist, all for the sake of revenge."

"We stopped Cloak from destroying the Helios Tower, and we saved Japan from getting plunged into war. All you scumbags have done is lie to the world and accuse Slate of crimes that he didn't commit. Yeah, Incognito is a creep, but he's the lesser of two evils here. He's the only one who cares if Cloak is stopped. And honestly, can you blame him for hating the Western Union, the way the military's been treating the natives? You want us to turn ourselves in? You want us to do the right thing? Then maybe you should start setting an example, bitch."

"Incognito seeks the destruction of our entire way of life. You may not have caused direct harm to the Western Union, but by assisting Incognito in his other pursuits, the United Third can now devote more of its resources toward anti-Western activities. No matter how you spin it, Ms. Plato, you have betrayed the free world and all your loved ones."

"Cloak needs to be stopped," Straper said. "This is justice."

"No, what you children are doing is satisfying your need to see another's blood," Ryder said. "You support a madman in his quest so you may do this. That is not justice. That is merely self-gratification. The Western Union, however, is just. We are reordering the world from the chaos caused by the Choke."

Ryder raised her arm high as if holding a beach ball above her head. "As the sword of the Union, I will not hesitate to slay anyone who promotes chaos, putting my own life second to this task. I will serve the West, the one true order, the one true justice."

The passion that came briefly into her voice was the only time anybody had heard an actual person beneath that expressionless exterior. However, it did not last. As Ryder lowered her hand, her voice went back to a drone.

"Not that you care," she said. "Now please, surrender."

"Shut your sexy mouth."

Slate walked up to the hologram and stood taller than he typically did.

"Are you attempting to dress me down as well?" Ryder asked.

"I've had it with your crazy talk," Slate said. "The Western Union doesn't care about justice. All you care about is power. Just like the Chinese Empire. Just like Cloak. You people were willing to torture children so you could win your stupid wars. And now that the cat's outta the bag, the Western Union is scrambling to cover up its crimes."

"The world must be protected. Sacrifices are a necessity."

"Well, if that's what we have to do to survive, we oughta let the world burn." The Helmet Man curled his hands into fists. "I changed my mind... No surrender."

"You're right," Gilda said. "If we don't stop Cloak, nobody will."

Straper shook his head. "Whatever. We've come this far, haven't we?"

"I suppose we have," Naomi said, smiling.

"Well, I am more afraid of Incognito than depth charges," Young-Bum said. "Go ahead. Blow us away. We will fight you to the last breath."

The submarine shook. Everyone thought it was just another depth charge, but Young-Bum seemed more perturbed than before and dashed to a console. It took a moment before he could confirm his worst fear.

"That wasn't a depth charge!" he exclaimed.

"Correct," Ryder said. "That was our special forces clogging your missile launch tubes, preventing any attempted resistance."

"Uh-oh," Slate said.

"You were distracting us this whole time while your goons were blocking our launch tubes," Naomi seethed. "How could I fall for such an obvious trap?"

***

Thirteen Western Union warships circled above the *Eodum*. The largest ship, an aircraft carrier, was where Ryder had decided to set up shop. She stood on the bridge, which was filled with navigation equipment and operators in dark blue uniforms. Next to her was Rear Admiral Bowden, a plump man in his fifties. He leaned forward as he listened to Ryder, intrigued by her conversation with the Helmet Man.

"I ask you to reconsider your options," Ryder said as she looked at a holographic screen that showed the Helmet Man and his friends. "You will have ten minutes to do so. If you refuse to surrender again, we will have no choice but to take hostile action."

She ended her transmission and folded her hands.

"I never thought I'd get to witness the famous Ryder catching her prey," Bowden said. "It seems the stories about you weren't hyperbolic after all."

"Do not underestimate your contributions, Admiral," Ryder said. "The Western Union is made up of many dedicated souls working together to bring order to the world. Without your help, this operation would not have been possible."

Bowden blushed. "Uh … thank you."

"Yeah, don't mess with the West!" Hank Powers jeered. His arm had regrown, but it was still weak. That didn't seem to be an impediment, however, since he was just as arrogant as ever. "What now, boss? I wanted the chance to take on that Helmet freak again and expose him for the phoney he is. Maybe I could—"

"Ladies and gentlemen," a voice said over the loudspeaker. "I was innocently on my way to meet with my subordinates when I spotted your gaudy ships floating about. You clearly don't know how much this irks me."

"Who's on the loudspeaker?" Powers demanded, his thick muscles tensing.

"Sir, there's someone on the bow of the *Emancipation*!" one crewman yelled, pointing out the window.

"Get a close-up of him," Bowden ordered. "I want to know who this joker is."

A holographic screen appeared before them, showing a man standing on the bow of a slender warship. He held a small microphone in one hand.

He grasped a scythe in the other.

"Listen here, Western scum," Incognito said. "Release my peons or be subjugated to swift retaliation. Do not test me."

CHAPTER 25

"That is Incognito," Ryder said, staring at the holographic screen with dull interest. "Make sure the mounted cameras on every ship are recording."

"Already on it," replied a pale-faced soldier at a console.

"You're saying that freak is public enemy number one?" Powers asked. "Well, if it really is him, he just came to the wrong neighborhood."

"Mobilize the snipers!" Bowden ordered. He shook his head. "Just how did that ingrate get on one of our vessels?"

On the decks of several ships, dozens of snipers got into position, their sights on the terrorist mastermind. Incognito stood on the bow of the *Emancipation*. He wore his usual suit and oval mask, relaxed yet somewhat impatient.

"Sir, snipers are in position," a marine told Bowden.

"Blow that sucker's head off," Bowden said. "We'll be rid of the Western Union's greatest enemy forever."

"Wait," Ryder said. "Incognito is no fool. There is more to this than meets the eye. We should play along for now."

"Sorry, Ryder," Bowden said. "But I can't risk letting him escape. If that is Incognito, this is a once-in-a-lifetime opportunity."

All at once, the snipers fired.

But none of them hit their mark.

The bullets went right through Incognito as though he weren't there at all and merely slammed into the deck of the ship.

"He's still standing," Bowden growled. "Fire again!"

"You dare shoot at *me*?" Incognito spat over the loudspeaker.

A horde of armed marines stormed out from the control tower of the *Emancipation* and stopped several yards behind Incognito.

"Put your hands up," one marine ordered. "You got nowhere to run."

"I told you…" Incognito began.

As if he were a ghost, he sank and disappeared into the deck.

"Damn, that must be some kind of hologram," the marine said. "Search—"

"Do not test me," Incognito finished, floating up out of the deck, now behind the marines. They twirled around, gaping at the apparition.

"Open fire!" the marine screamed.

What happened next was insanity. Incognito glided toward the men. They fired, but all of the bullets passed through his form. He swung his blade and stabbed one enemy in the stomach, tore the blade out, and swiped it at another man. Many of the marines stumbled backward, shooting and screaming, but Incognito kept cutting them down. One man tried to punch him. His fist never connected and was chopped off instead. Another man was stabbed in the chest and flung up in the air like a rag doll, his corpse crashing into the water below. The remaining marines tried to retreat. They never got the chance.

"Impossible!" Bowden cried. "He's killing trained marines with a farmer's tool. Quick, deploy the unicopters!"

Four unicopters took off from the ship closest to the *Emancipation*. They flew in a V formation and readied their guns.

Just as they were about to attack, Incognito blasted off into the air. He flew so fast that he reached the unicopters in the blink of an eye. He slammed his scythe into the side of a unicopter and spun around. The aircraft was dragged along behind him, helpless to resist. It collided with another unicopter, and they both exploded in midair. Debris slammed into the blades of the other unicopters, causing them to fall out of the sky and sink into the ocean.

"That's some kind of magic trick!" Powers shouted, shivering all over. "No way can somebody do that. No way!"

Bowden looked like he was about to go into cardiac arrest. "All ships, fire!"

Missiles launched. Artillery guns blasted. But it was all in vain. Incognito dodged the missiles with ease and let the shells pass through his body. He swooped down to a nearby destroyer and slammed his scythe into its side.

He then lifted the ship out of the ocean.

All Powers and Bowden could do was stare with dropped jaws.

Ryder raised an eyebrow.

The fifteen-thousand-ton vessel flew through the air as Incognito towed it behind him, ascending four hundred feet, before taking his scythe out of its side. The giant ship found its weight again and fell. It collided with the destroyer below it, resulting in both vessels crumpling into unrecognizable heaps of twisted metal. The sound was deafening. Bowden covered his ears. A few explosions resulted as well. The entire mess soon caught fire. It was clear none of the crew members on either ship had survived. The two vessels sank.

"Retreat!" Bowden cried. "Get out of here! We can't fight him!"

But it wasn't over. Incognito glided toward an aircraft carrier and stabbed its hull with his scythe. He flipped the carrier over his shoulder, tearing the behemoth ship out of the water. It wouldn't stay out for long. The carrier fell, upside down, dropping on top of a smaller ship. It literally turned its target into a pancake.

Both warships sank into oblivion. The collision produced a monster wave that capsized two other ships, many crewmen tumbling over the guardrails.

In just a few short minutes, half a dozen ships had been taken out by a single foe.

Incognito, however, wasn't done.

He began flying toward the aircraft carrier Ryder was on.

"He's coming!" Bowden squealed. "He's coming to kill us!"

The phantom terrorist phased into the aircraft carrier's control tower and landed on the bridge where Bowden stood. The rear admiral was sobbing beyond control.

"Kill him!" Powers roared, unholstering his service pistol. He and five marines fired their guns at Incognito. They had no effect. Incognito stabbed one marine in the arm, causing him to drop his weapon. He beheaded another with a flick of his scythe. The masked terrorist was quick to cut through all the men and women on the bridge, chopping them up until only Ryder, Bowden, and

Powers were left. Blood pooled on the floor. Dozens of lifeless eyes stared at the ceiling. The smell of gunpowder only increased the feeling of suffocation.

Bowden shook all over. Tears rolled down his face. "Spare me!" he blubbered. "Please, I'll tell you anything... I know so much... Oh, just don't cut me!"

"How revolting," Incognito spat. "Such cowardly behavior will not be rewarded."

He swung his blade at Bowden's chest. The disgraced rear admiral collapsed, blood spewing from his wound. The entire bridge was covered in oozing corpses, but not a drop of blood had stained Incognito's white suit.

Powers fell to his knees in dumb shock. Ryder was standing at attention, looking almost bored. Incognito appeared behind her and put the edge of his scythe to her neck.

"So, you are Incognito," Ryder said, unfazed. "May I ask how you managed to lift up an aircraft carrier with no effort while being unaffected by our weapons?"

"I have no reason to tell you Morlocks any of that," Incognito scoffed. He leaned in and sniffed her neck. "Tell me, why aren't you shriveling up in fear?"

"Because I am not afraid of you. But I do accept realities. It seems we have been beaten. What is it you desire?"

"Call off your dogs. I still have use for the Helmet Man and his lackeys."

"Very well. I shall not interfere in your retreat."

"Don't act as if you have won, shrew. I'll be nearby, so refrain from acting foolish. You wouldn't want more casualties."

He took his blade away from Ryder's throat and sank into the floor, vanishing.

Ryder smoothed out her suit. She touched her neck, and her fingers came back red. The scythe must have nicked her. She took a tissue from her pocket and wiped the blood away with it. From what she could tell, Incognito could make himself intangible, along with anything he came into physical contact with. Whoever this man was, he had abilities that surpassed even those of the Helmet Man.

"Tricks…" Powers whispered. "Nothing but tricks… Illusions… All illusions…"

Ryder handed him a spare tissue.

***

Five hours later, a trio of men gathered in the Oval Office. President Jacob Hynes sat behind the desk, emitting a grim aura. Admiral Redwood and Vice President Powell stood by his side. A holographic screen presented an apocalyptic scene. A man wielding a scythe had just flipped over an aircraft carrier.

After the video was finished, the holographic screen disappeared. Nobody said anything for the longest time until President Hynes broke the silence.

"Powell, is this man one of our rogue supersoldiers?" Hynes asked.

"Absolutely not," Powell said. "None of our subjects were able to do anything like that, not even Slate. If you're thinking about blaming me for this, don't. Ryder was the one leading the mission, barely a week after letting the Japanese prime minister die."

"She did try to avoid a confrontation with Incognito," Redwood noted.

"We told her to keep it discreet. Deploying an armada ain't discreet. As for Bowden, he behaved so disgracefully that we'll have to doctor the recordings so he can die a hero and we can preserve the military's reputation. Just think of the cover story we'll have to come up with. Six ships at the bottom of the ocean. A fortune in damages. Countless military personnel dead. And to top it all off, both Incognito and Slate got away."

"Ryder will be held accountable, as will anyone else responsible for this debacle," Hynes assured.

"The only silver lining is that this incident forced Incognito to tip his hand," Redwood said. "We've never seen him in person before or even knew what he looked like. Now that he's shown himself, we may finally figure out who this villain is."

"But was it worth six ships and thousands of men?" Powell questioned.

Hynes sighed. "Computer, what are the results of the video analysis?"

"Good, Mr. President," a disembodied voice said from hidden speakers.

"Oh, geez, that response was worth billions in funding," Powell scoffed.

"Elaborate, computer," Hynes ordered.

"From his mannerisms, movements, and glimpses of what was underneath his disguise, it is evident that Incognito is of African descent and elderly. His eyes were visible through the holes in his mask, meaning a retinal scan was possible, and we have just received the results. We have a positive match."

Powell looked like he was about to lay an egg. Redwood tightened his hands into fists.

Hynes merely shifted in his seat. "Just tell us, computer."

"He is a former scientist of the Western Union," the computer said. "However, there is no additional information beyond that."

"Not even a name?" Hynes questioned.

"The only files related to him were several vague reports and this symbol."

A holographic image popped up before them, a bloodred key surrounded by an equally bloodred horseshoe. Powell's eyes widened until they seemed to take up half his head. Hynes massaged his pounding temples.

"What's wrong?" Redwood asked.

"The Keymaster Project..." Hynes said.

"The what?"

"The Keymasters were the scientists who created our rogue supersoldiers. The key unlocks Omega, the end to war, the end to our struggles, perhaps even the end to our very evolution. Or so they said."

Redwood had gone pale. "Yes, I understand your concern now."

"Incognito is one of the Keymasters," Powell snarled. "It's him ... that America-hating weasel. He must have made himself into a supersoldier somehow."

"You *know* him?" Redwood exclaimed.

"Powell supervised the Keymaster Project during its final years," Hynes said. "He knew most of the Keymasters personally. He even knew the supersoldiers."

"I thought the supersoldiers killed all those scientists."

"Apparently not." Hynes got up from his chair and turned to face the window, hands behind his back. "Gentlemen, there is only one course of action. We must reveal to the public the truth about Incognito, Cloak, and the Keymaster Project."

"What?" Powell shouted. "That's the stupidest thing I've ever heard! If you do that, you'll destroy this administration, right when we're on the verge of war."

"If we reveal that Incognito used to be employed by the Western Union, it will destroy the United Third. All support for Incognito would disintegrate. He'll be seen as a hypocrite. And if his minions learn about his powers, many of them, especially the ones with deep religious convictions, will call him an abomination. We could destroy one of our greatest enemies if we spin this right. At the same time, we will finally be able to openly pursue Cloak. That would just leave us the Chinese Empire to deal with."

"At least leave out the part about Cloak and the supersoldiers," Powell shot back. "Can't you see we've come too far? Telling the truth now would destroy the Western Union. If you cared about our way of life, you'd know that."

"That's enough," Hynes growled, breaking his normal cool. "I've made my decision. Next month we go public. End of discussion."

Powell's eyes were confused and enraged. He didn't know how to respond. After a moment of tension, the vice president stormed out of the Oval Office.

Hynes let out a breath and dumped himself in his chair. His face went slack, and his belly expanded. A few gray hairs might have even just grown. Redwood couldn't believe it. This great statesman now looked almost as old as the Chinese emperor.

"This is it for me," Hynes said. "My political career is over. I'll be lucky if I don't end up thrown in jail."

"I think only Powell needs to worry about that," Redwood said.

"After the maiden voyage of *Leviathan*, I will begin preparations for our announcement. Let's just pray that Powell doesn't try to pull anything. Just because his father was the president before me doesn't give him the right to behave like a spoiled child. Well, I suppose this is my punishment for sending Eisenhorn on such a cruel errand. I accept it."

"Eisenhorn? What about him?"

"Nothing... Nothing I can do now, anyway."

"Well, sir, if I may say so, I have never been prouder of you than I am now. You're doing the right thing. I'm sure of it."

Hynes smiled ever so slightly. "Let's hope the public feels the same way."

***

Powell thought faking anger was the easiest thing in the world. What was really hard was trying not to burst into laughter. Those fools had no idea how much they misjudged him.

He walked into his office, planting himself on his plush armchair, enjoying his digs while he still had them. Pretty soon, he was going to get an upgrade.

"Sir, Vincent Quinn is here to see you," his secretary said over the intercom.

"Send him in," Powell said.

A trim man with a shaved head entered the room, looking almost as smug as his boss. Quinn used to be with the military police and later the Western Intelligence Service. He had since become Powell's top aide and go-to guy for all clandestine enterprises.

"Here's the report you wanted," Quinn said, handing Powell a folder. "It shows there's a credible risk that *Leviathan* will be attacked during its maiden voyage next week. An agent of ours overheard Prime Minister Mao Long himself talking about it on his private golf course. There's also mention of nanobots that—"

"Does Hynes know?" Powell asked. "Does anyone know?"

Quinn grinned. "Just you and me."

"Good," Powell said. He shoved the report into his paper shredder. The scraps would be burned later, of course.

"Hynes ought to be warned," Powell said, his eyes filled with insane greed.

"But only one of us can be president."

CHAPTER 26

Eisenhorn felt something coarse rub his face. He grumbled and opened his eyes. This fricking sand... Not only did he hate the feel of it, but it also always managed to get between his—

The general gasped. "Sand! What the hell?"

He jumped up, cursing. Where was he? Turning his head, he found himself on an island. It was only about twenty feet in diameter, a perfect circle covered in brilliant white sand. The surrounding sea was pitch-black in color. He shot a look up at the sky and almost fainted. It was a star-filled canopy unlike anything he had ever seen before. Both a spiral galaxy and several celestial bodies with rings hung above him. He also saw a Jupiter-like planet taking up a good fifth of the heavens. But despite the fact that it was a night sky, it was daytime-bright. The general gave himself a quick once-over and found that he was wearing his uniform. No, this wasn't possible... After a string of swears and some stumbling around, Eisenhorn snapped.

"Where am I?" he bellowed at the sky. "Am I dead? Whoever put me here, you better come out!"

Nobody answered.

Eisenhorn ground his teeth. He scanned the horizon. There didn't seem to be any other landmasses within sight, or any boats or people. He was all alone in this surreal environment. He half-expected to come across a melted clock like the ones in that fruity painting. This was all hurting his head.

"If this is the afterlife, it's a pretty crappy place," Eisenhorn mumbled.

"You aren't dead," a voice told him.

Eisenhorn yelped and spun around to see a woman behind him. How did she get there? Did she teleport like that Houdini character?

"Scaring me, eh?" Eisenhorn growled, raising his fists. "You Chinese must be tricking me. Trying to get me to give up military secrets? No way that'll happen."

"I'm not Chinese," the woman said. She was covered in ragged, mismatched clothes that covered her from head to toe. She wore a green long-sleeved shirt, big yellow sneakers, blue mittens, and red shorts over white long johns. A multicolored scarf was wrapped around her neck and head, concealing her face. Anxious eyes peered out.

"Terrorist!" Eisenhorn screeched. He ran right at her. The stranger side-stepped the charging lunatic. He ended up darting past her and tripped, falling flat on his face. The general let out a groan as he lay limp in the sand.

"Please listen," the woman said, rubbing her mittens together. "My name is Klara. In a few moments, someone will try to kill you."

"Terrorist!" Eisenhorn cried, running at the stranger yet again. But Klara dodged with supernatural speed, and Eisenhorn fell on his face for the second time.

"Um ... are you done?" Klara asked. "I'm a friend. Please, trust me. As I said before, a man will try to kill you."

Eisenhorn hopped back to his feet. "I ain't listening to any of your lies, terrorist!"

"I am not a terrorist. Listen, when you wake up, you will find a man about to inject you with a syringe. Do not let him use it on you, or you will perish. Fight off the man and get the syringe. Then hide it, for you will require it later."

"This is a dream?" Eisenhorn asked, reexamining his surroundings.

"Yes, you are still in the Forbidden City, sleeping in your quarters."

"How do you know I'm gonna get whacked? Unless ... you helped plan it! Ha, caught you red-handed, terrorist!"

Klara looked at her mittens, blinking. "My hands aren't red..."

A low rumble shook the minuscule island. Eisenhorn became alert, his eyes darting every which way. This was too much craziness for a man his age.

"You're waking up," Klara said. "Remember to hide the syringe once you get it. Oh ... and please don't die. And *do not* inject yourself until I say so. I cannot stress that enough. Good luck and best wishes."

"Wait, I don't even know who you are!" Eisenhorn shouted.

Klara gave him a brisk salute. "A comrade in arms."

The world went black.

***

Once again, Eisenhorn opened his eyes, greeted by semidarkness. He was lying in a pile of sheets and clothes inside his closet. The bed was too stiff for his tastes. This closet was also the only place where he felt even a little secure in this madhouse.

But not anymore, because a man now stood in the closet doorway. And he held a syringe.

A sudden rush of adrenaline went through Eisenhorn. He ran headfirst into the man. The intruder hadn't expected this and fell backward. The man was unhurt, however, and got back to his feet. But before the man could act again, Eisenhorn kicked his opponent inside the closet and swung the door shut. Eisenhorn leaned against the door, trying to keep the intruder trapped.

"Help, assassin!" Eisenhorn yelled. "Get your imperial asses in here!"

The intruder rammed the door, taking Eisenhorn by surprise and causing him to fall over. The intruder jumped out of the closet and landed on Eisenhorn's chest, knocking the wind out of him. The intruder pinned his arms down with his knees and leaned forward to inject him with the syringe.

"No!" a woman screamed. She charged right at the intruder and knocked him over. Both the woman and the intruder collapsed in a pile of tangled limbs. The syringe fell out of the intruder's hands and rolled under the bed. The intruder tried to shake off the woman, but she resisted with such ferocity that it looked like she might win. Eisenhorn's rattled brain then recognized her. It was Shu, his caretaker. She must have heard him.

The intruder kicked Shu off. She wheezed and grabbed her stomach in pain. The intruder ignored her and decided to attack Eisenhorn again. But instead of going for the syringe under the bed, the man took a twisted dagger from his pocket. Eisenhorn gulped. Getting stabbed with that knife looked like it would hurt, a lot.

The man ran at Eisenhorn. The general got to his feet and put his fists up. When the intruder swung his dagger, Eisenhorn twisted out of the way and punched his opponent in the gut. The intruder staggered back. Eisenhorn then nailed him square in the face. The intruder went down, defeated.

Eisenhorn faintly heard guards yelling. They must be headed to his room to see what all the commotion was about. Too little, too late.

Then he remembered the dream. The mystery woman, Klara, had told him a man was coming to kill him. Her prediction had come true. Eisenhorn had no idea who that woman was, how she got into his dreams, what she wanted, or how she could predict the future. However, it did seem that she was on his side.

What else had that lady said? Right, the syringe. She told him to hide it. Eisenhorn thought that was a good idea. He might need another weapon in case someone else tried to kill him. He had already tried to make a weapon out of a sharpened toothbrush, but it was quickly confiscated. Wherever he hid the syringe, it had to be a very secret place, one the guards wouldn't stumble upon.

Eisenhorn darted underneath his bed. Shu was still lying nearby, curled up in a ball. Eisenhorn didn't have time to comfort her now. He had to act. He felt for the syringe and found it. He hoped his luck would last.

The general had a special place for hiding things he had made after the toothbrush incident. He pulled back the bed and took out a floorboard, revealing a small hole. He put the syringe in there, covered up the hole with the board, and shoved the bed back in place. Shu didn't notice, too distracted by the pain.

The guards came barging in just as Eisenhorn finished putting the bed back. They drew their swords and swept the room. Eisenhorn raised his hands. The guards paid him no mind. Two of them carried Shu away. Three other guards, meanwhile, turned the fallen intruder over on his back. Eisenhorn could now get a good look at his assailant, since one of the guards had lit the gas lamps. The intruder was a middle-aged man wearing servant's robes. The dagger stuck from his chest. He must have accidentally stabbed himself when he tumbled to the floor. He was dead. No question about it. The vacant look in his eyes confirmed it.

Two guards grabbed Eisenhorn and dragged him out of the room.

"Hey, get off, Chinamen!" Eisenhorn barked. "I'm an ambassador! I almost get stabbed to death, and this is how you treat me? What kind of hospitality is this?"

The guards didn't bother giving him an answer as they took him away.

****

"I'm gonna need your help, Wook," Geppetto said.

Wook nodded, doing his best to look humble. He was an overweight Indonesian and one of the pirate captains hired by Cloak. Wook and his crew had retreated when Mistress Lotus attacked, and it was safe to say that Cloak was not happy. Wook felt his mouth go dry. He never should have agreed to work for these maniacs. Most pirates inside the Neutral Zone were content with scavenging the abandoned Indonesian cities for canned food and valuables, but a few were either desperate or foolish enough to engage in mercenary work.

Wook had been a little of both. He had also felt the urge to satisfy his curiosity. Every worthwhile criminal in the world knew about Cloak. Even the West Russian mafia quivered whenever Cloak was mentioned. Now there were rumors that Cloak had some sort of deal with the Chinese. Wook couldn't have helped but be a little enamored. He had longed to meet one of Cloak's elusive leaders and bask in their supernatural presence.

But now he wanted nothing to do with Cloak. He just wanted to go back to scavenging. He never should have accepted this death sentence of a job. He was going to die. He was sure of it. Both he and Geppetto stood in the infirmary on Cloak's yacht. Atlas lay nearby, sprawled over a white bed. The giant wore a look of indescribable pain. Limbs twisted and bent at awkward angles... ribs poking through the skin... the spine misshapen. A bead of sweat rolled down Wook's brow. He avoided looking at Atlas.

"Want to know what happened to my friend?" Geppetto asked.

Wook gulped. "I am ... curious."

"Atlas got into a little brawl with the Helmet Man," Geppetto said, walking over to the other side of the room. "Many of his bones were broken, with lots of internal bleeding."

"But isn't ... isn't your friend able to heal fast?"

"Correct, but Atlas healed *too* fast. You see, if you don't set a bone properly, it could heal wrong. But when Atlas broke his bones, they healed in less than a minute flat, not long enough for them to be set. This is the sad result, a deformed body."

Wook stole a glance at Atlas again and then wished he hadn't.

"Fortunately, there's a solution," Geppetto said. "Normally, one would require extensive surgery where the bones are broken again and then set properly. But Atlas has another option available only to him."

Geppetto opened a cabinet and shuffled through its contents. "Atlas has a unique ability besides speedy regeneration and superstrength. He's also a universal organ acceptor. He can fuse with any other human's organs and make them part of his body. As you can imagine, the whole process is gross as hell."

The pirate captain had a hard time believing or understanding what Geppetto was telling him, but he did manage to ask the most important question of all.

"Then why am I here?" he whispered, barely audible.

Wook's body froze, unable to move. Panic overcame him. His heart pounded like mad. The dwarf had used some kind of magic on him.

"Right, I forgot to tell you," Geppetto said with a false smile. He grasped a bone saw from the cabinet and approached the ensnared pirate. "We need a hefty donation," he went on. "Don't worry. It's for a good cause."

CHAPTER 27

After hours of waiting, Naomi's patience was rewarded when Young-Bum came out of the submarine's infirmary. He looked like he was about to fall over from exhaustion.

"How is he?" Naomi almost yelled as she blocked his way.

Young-Bum wore blue scrubs stained with spots of blood. He rubbed his sunken eyes. All he wanted to do was crawl into bed with a bottle of liquor, but it was clear Naomi wasn't going to leave him alone until she got a full debriefing.

"I do not know," Young-Bum said with a helpless shrug. "My doctor says he has been exposed to radiation for years. Although he has been treating it very well himself, it is only a matter of time until … well … his time runs out."

"What have you done to help him?" Naomi snapped.

Too tired to be intimidated, Young-Bum merely let out a breath and continued. "We have given him medication through an IV, including antibiotics. We also stopped the bleeding, but he lost a lot of blood. Growth patches do not appear to work on him, which may explain why he is in such bad shape to begin with. All in all, we think he will live for now."

Naomi relaxed, the tension leaving her body.

Young-Bum sighed. "But I do not think he will live for much longer. There is no question about it. Whether he will die tomorrow or within a year is anyone's guess."

"That's okay," Naomi said. "He doesn't need very long."

***

Hours prior to the diagnosis, soon after the *Eodum* had escaped the clutches of the Western Union, Naomi left the others in the common room to go meet with her employer.

"Stay here," Naomi told them. "Get some rest. And please don't follow me."

"Hey, what happened?" Straper asked. "First, we were at the mercy of that crazy blonde chick, then all the sudden we're free to go with no strings attached? I may not be the brightest guy around, but even I know this smells fishy."

"He's right," Gilda said. "Something's not right."

"What's going to happen now?" Thomas asked Naomi.

"Sorry, but I don't know much more than you," Naomi said, patting him on the head. Thomas couldn't help but look pleased.

"Hey, quit hogging the chicks!" Slate yelled. "Don't make me lock you in the closet."

Gilda sighed. "Where's child services when you need them?"

"I don't have time for this," Naomi huffed. She left the common room and made it to the back of the sub, where she was to meet Incognito. He was already there waiting for her. Despite the fact that they hadn't surfaced, Incognito had still managed to get on board the *Eodum* with ease. Naomi couldn't help but feel her skin prickle. This man was truly something else, an embodiment of death, a man turned—

Incognito bent over and let out a sickening succession of coughs. His scythe clattered on the floor. The terrorist himself fell on his hands and knees. Blood dripped from his mask, dotting the floor with red.

"No!" Naomi screamed. She ran to Incognito's side and helped him up. He continued to cough. More blood dribbled from his mouth. Naomi felt her gut knot up. She grabbed his arm and helped him walk down the empty hallway.

"You can't die," she seethed. "I still need you."

They entered the infirmary. Nobody else was there. Incognito pushed her away and staggered toward the nearest bed. He collapsed onto it, another fit of coughing overtaking him.

"Get ... a doctor..." he wheezed.

Naomi ran out of the room, locking the door behind her. Nobody needed to see Incognito like this. She dashed to the bridge, where Young-Bum was supervising his quiet crew. Not bothering with subtlety, she grabbed Young-Bum by the collar.

"What are you doing?" he exclaimed.

Naomi didn't have time to explain. She dragged the captain out of the room. The crew did not intervene, knowing what powers she possessed. Naomi led Young-Bum down the hall and shoved him into the infirmary. He was just about to make a formal protest when his eyes settled on the coughing figure lying on the bed.

"Incognito..." Young-Bum said under his breath.

"Save him," Naomi commanded.

"I ... I will get help."

***

Naomi now sat next to Incognito's bed inside the cramped infirmary. His steady breathing and closed eyes told her that he was asleep. His mask was still strapped on. She knew how much he detested taking it off. The terrorist also wore a hospital gown and was covered in a thin blanket. His long ponytail was curled up beside him like a coiled snake. It was incredible that he still had hair despite the long-term radiation exposure. It was the only part of him that had remained unscathed. No wonder he grew it out so long.

After sitting silently for an hour, Naomi spoke to the unconscious man.

"You will not die," she told him. "Not yet. Not until I've had my revenge."

***

Thomas played on the floor, attempting to make a house of cards. He usually only got two levels up before it all tumbled down. After a while, he got bored and looked around for someone to hang out with. Naomi was still in the infirmary, so he decided to approach Gilda and Straper, who were perched on the edge of the couch as the news played in the background.

"You think it was a freak storm?" Straper asked Gilda.

"It'd be awfully convenient if that were true," she said. "But no."

"Maybe there was a negotiation or something."

"They had us cornered. What would they have to gain?"

"Man, do you think they all died because we—?"

"Hush up," she whispered harshly, just noticing Thomas.

Straper turned his head. "Oh ... Hey, Tommy boy. What's up?"

Thomas went rigid. "Nothing, I... Are you all right?"

"Sorry, we're just having a private chat," Gilda said. "Do you mind playing over there?"

"Sure," Thomas mumbled.

Gilda and Straper went back to their hushed conversation. Thomas drifted away from the couch. This now left him only Slate to hang out with. The Helmet Man was leaning against the wall in the corner with his hands up before him. Sparks of electricity danced between his fingers. It was interesting at first, but Thomas soon got tired of watching and scampered over to pester him.

"What are you doing?" he innocently asked.

"Training," Slate said, unusually concentrated. "Go away."

"Oh, can I help?"

Slate stopped generating sparks and lowered his hands. "You can help by going away."

Thomas whimpered and sulked off. Straper noticed this and halted his conversation with Gilda. He gave his head a shake.

"Hang on a minute," he told her.

"Sure." She sighed, turning her eyes back to the news.

Straper let out his own sigh and went over to Slate. "You know, that kid has had it pretty rough. Maybe you should be nicer to him."

Slate scoffed. "I just saw you scare him off. I was actually busy training while you were chatting it up with Gilda and watching TV. What makes you so high and mighty?"

"Human shield, remember?" Straper replied coldly.

"Oh, great. This again. You do realize that he's invincible, right? What was I supposed to do, get shot to death? Both the kid and I would be dead then."

"Doesn't mean you can joke about it."

"Got to blow off steam somehow. You do it too."

Straper couldn't imagine joking about shooting that pirate. Then again, telling a joke or two did help blow off some steam.

"Fine, I ain't a saint either," Straper said. "And maybe we should have invited Thomas to sit down with us. It's just ... that Ryder lady had us cornered. And now we just get off scot-free? What the hell happened? The news isn't saying anything. Did we—?"

Slate took a step toward him. "Whatever happened up there ain't your fault. Remember that. And we're all alive. That's what matters."

Straper took a breath. "Okay, thanks."

Both of them heard Thomas moan to himself where he sat on the floor nearby. Straper could also spot a hint of tears coming from the boy's eyes.

Slate shook his head. "I ain't qualified to take care of a traumatized kid like that. We need to ditch him the first chance we get, for his sake and ours."

"At least try to be friendly," Straper said. He then smirked. "You gotta think about this for a second. Being nice to him is actually a good thing."

"How could being nice to a child possibly be a good thing?"

"Don't you see how attached Naomi is to that kid?" Straper asked. "She has a total soft spot for him. You can use him to get a date with her. Chicks love guys who are good with kids. I don't know why. Something about hormones and maternal instinct."

"Hey, you're right! I gotta treat this prince like a prince and use him to reel in the babes. Yes, my lecherous aspirations shall finally be realized!"

"I can hear you creeps!" Gilda yelled from across the room.

Slate gave Straper a knowing nod. "We'll talk later."

***

Cyphrus felt a little better. Mao Long had failed to catch Slate, the laboratory was destroyed, and Operation Leviathan would soon be underway. The only obstacle left was Slate and Repulsa, but she could deal with them after the operation was over. However, she did plan on sending something special to Union Network. She was sure it would be an extra-good kick in the teeth for Slate.

But what about the bulletproof child Slate had rescued? Was it *him*? Cyphrus didn't want to believe it, but the truth was undeniable. Sebastian... That swine had kept the child alive. Her contempt for both the boy and Sebastian only grew. Cyphrus sighed. She supposed it didn't matter. Why let the little brat worry her?

She stood next to two silver barrels with nozzles on top. All she needed to do was get them on board that new ship, *Leviathan*, perform a few other tasks, and she would soon find herself married to the emperor. With that marriage, she would rule over an empire that covered a good quarter of the world. The Chinese Empire was technologically backward, but it did have resources. The Chinese had invested a fortune into the development of this mind-control weapon, while Cloak had spearheaded the research necessary to develop the nanobots. It was costly just to make a small amount, but the results were impressive enough to warrant such hefty spending. Using the weapon on the Japanese prime minister had merely been a field test. Operation Leviathan was the real goal, the true prize.

A droplet ran down her face. Cyphrus shot a look at the ceiling. Water dripped from the vents. She cursed and checked her makeup with her compact, making sure her scars weren't visible. She knew they could never be gotten rid of. *He* wouldn't let her. She knew *he* would be angry. That wasn't a problem. She could still look pretty. She could still—

She shook her head and snapped her compact shut. That man was dead. She was sure of it. They were dead. All those foul men were dead. The Mentor— no... Sebastian had them all killed. No matter how much she hated Sebastian, she would always be indebted to him for slaying those men, especially him.

Cyphrus took a sizable breath and headed for the infirmary. Geppetto was still tending to Atlas. She had to make sure they were both in top condition. She had fired all the remaining pirates and most of her mercenaries, only keeping a few to guard Sebastian. Atlas and Geppetto were now the only agents left at her disposal to carry out Operation Leviathan. If anything should go wrong with Atlas's procedure...

Cyphrus reached the infirmary. It stank of bleach, yet there were still small red stains on the floor. She scrunched up her nose. Geppetto was never the cleanest, but even he could have done a better job than this.

"Is Atlas almost ready?" she asked, standing outside the door. No way did she want the smell of cleaning products clinging to her for the rest of the day.

"Just about," Geppetto said. He wore latex gloves and a black apron. Next to him was a bed covered in a white sheet.

"Is it a suitable match?" Cyphrus asked. "I don't want to have to get another body."

"See for yourself," Geppetto said. He tore off the sheet from the bed, revealing a hideous sight that made Cyphrus's stomach turn.

Atlas's severed head had been sewn onto Captain Wook's neck. Cyphrus gagged. It was like something out of *Frankenstein*. At least it was sewn on straight.

"Body mass is about right," Geppetto said. "Lots of fat to burn. Should be enough for Atlas to work with."

Cyphrus took another step back from the doorway. "How long will it take?"

"Give it a second," Geppetto said, smacking the body with his tiny hand as though he was starting up a used car.

On cue, the body convulsed. The muscles of the pirate's body tightened. Its limbs fought to flail around, but leather straps restrained the flabby flesh. Pounds of fat burned away in seconds. Its skin turned paler, splotchy at first, and then the new skin color replaced the old one completely. Sickening cracks sounded as the bones started to grow, the arms and legs getting longer by the second. The pathetic muscles bulged out. Old scars were healed. Birthmarks were erased. This grotesque metamorphosis was not for the faint of heart to witness.

The transformation finally stopped. In a minute flat, the body now looked exactly like Atlas's old one. Even the stitches on his neck were gone.

The giant opened his eyes. He sat up, the leather straps breaking. They were unable to contain the power that was Atlas.

All Cyphrus could do was stare in disgust. Atlas had done this three times before, and she herself had witnessed it only once. It was an experience she had hoped never to have again. But she had to see. She had to see that her comrade was revived.

Geppetto walked up to the bed. "Hey, Atlas. How you feeling?"

The colossal man turned to his companion and smiled softly. "Famished."

CHAPTER 28

Athens was chock-full of people. Hotels were booked solid, and tourism activity was at an all-time high. Dozens of TV cameras were broadcasting this historic day around the world. A crowd made up of thousands of patriots and curious onlookers gathered on the beaches and docks, eager to see the launching of the world's largest ship, *Leviathan*.

A platform had been erected on a beach. A hologram projector resting on it created a giant hologram of the Western Union's leader, Jacob Hynes himself. The crowd converged around it. The gargantuan president looked down stoically upon the tiny people.

"Citizens of the Western Union," Hynes boomed. "Today is a grand day, for we launch a ship unlike any other. After years of research and development, we have managed what was only decades ago considered science fiction."

The crowd murmured. They knew this ship was supposed to be impressive, but what made it so spectacular?

Hynes continued. "Athens, the cradle of Western civilization, is a fitting place to begin the next phase of modern warfare. *Leviathan* is already docked offshore. Several other Western Union leaders and I have the privilege of being passengers on this maiden voyage, but you will be able to witness this ship for yourselves and see our enemies tremble before its might. Ladies and gentlemen, I present the pride of our military, *Leviathan*."

The air shimmered on the ocean a mile away. *Leviathan's* cloaking device was turning off. The ship was soon visible to the naked eye. Almost everyone gasped.

Saying *Leviathan* was big would be a blatant understatement. It was monstrous, almost the size of an island. A city block could be put on top of it and still have room for parking. The ship was gray, except for the blue Western

Union logo on both its sides. A boxy control tower was situated near the rear. The flight deck could even accommodate landing aircraft. Nobody could imagine such a vessel being any bigger.

But it was.

"I hope we now have your undivided attention," Hynes said with some satisfaction, though his face was as stern as always. "This is what the people of the West can accomplish if we all focus our will on one end. But you have yet to witness the true potential of *Leviathan*. My loyal citizens, today we fly."

The ship began to warm up its engines. It sounded like the roar of a mighty lion, but there was an electric hum underlying it as well. Columns of steam billowed from the sides of the imposing ship, obscuring *Leviathan* for a moment, but the wind soon blew away the steam, revealing to the world what *Leviathan* was capable of.

Flight.

Leviathan floated hundreds of feet above the ocean. The lower half of the ship looked like a giant bicycle seat, two giant turbine engines attached to each side. On the bottom of the behemoth were black stripes that ran from the bow to the stern. These were repulsion pads, which were normally used to stabilize unicopters. The turbines were for moving forward, to the sides, or backward, while the pads changed altitude and kept the beast in the air.

All across the Western Union, people stared in wonder at the images being broadcasted to them, agape. For centuries, people had dreamed of cities in the sky. Now they were witnessing the first true step toward that dream. Granted, it was a military aircraft, but that was the price of progress, the price of ascension.

"This is the power of the West," Hynes told the awestruck masses. "This power cannot be denied or fought against. Try as our enemies might, they shall not prosper, for this is the true might of the Western Union."

***

After passing over the Parthenon, *Leviathan* rose until it was above cloud level.

The plan was for the ship to tour around Europe, first to Rome, then to Paris, London, Brussels, Berlin, Warsaw, Moscow, and back to Athens to conclude the tour with yet another reveal.

The bridge of *Leviathan* was the size of a small movie theater. Rows of military personnel manned monitors and navigation equipment. President Hynes sat in the commander's chair, which was on a small balcony that gave him a bird's-eye view of the bridge. Other Western Union leaders stood behind him, including the president of West Russia, two British cabinet ministers, the Italian prime minister, and several other foreign dignitaries. Secret Service agents also lurked nearby, but they were relaxed and relatively inattentive. To Hynes's right was Pierre Abel, a balding Frenchman and the captain of *Leviathan*.

"I hope you're impressed with the ship, sir," Abel said.

"I am," Hynes said, though he didn't look it.

"This is truly a magnificent vessel," Abel went on. "With it, we shall swiftly pacify all those extremists. That Incognito and his United Third spring to mind."

Hynes had to agree with that, though he knew this ship hadn't been built solely to intimidate a bunch of terrorists hiding in caves. This was an unspoken message to the Chinese Empire that their aggressive expansion would not be tolerated. They were a red tide that swept across nations, their billion soldiers annihilating all that stood against them, but even their nearly inexhaustible army would think twice before going toe-to-toe with this war machine. Just thinking about it almost made Hynes grin. Almost.

"All nonessential staff, please report to the cargo bay," a female voice announced over the intercom. "The president will address the crew."

"What's this?" Hynes demanded. "I'm not planning anything of the sort. Find out what's going on. Tell them no address will occur."

"Sir, we'll look into it," Abel said. He snapped his fingers at three of his subordinates, who ran away to find out what was going on.

Hynes growled. "This is totally unacceptable."

"Captain, we can't get the intercom working," a crewman told Abel.

"Then fix it," Abel ordered.

"Sir, communications are down!" an officer cried, gaping at her monitor.

"Find out what other systems are nonresponsive," Hynes said.

"Sir, how will we convey orders to the rest of the ship?" Abel asked.

"By hand radio, if necessary."

"Radios don't work well inside *Leviathan*. Neither do cellphones."

"Fine, get the crew to run and convey orders personally. My first order is to make sure the crew remains at their posts. We will also need to send someone via unicopter to inform the ground about our situation."

Abel pointed to a crewman. "Convey those orders!"

The man nodded and ran for the exit, but just as he was about to reach it, the metal door slammed shut. All the other doors leading onto the bridge came down as well, trapping everyone. The Secret Service agents took out their weapons, no longer on standby.

"Hynes, what is happening?" the West Russian president asked.

"Get us out of this bloody deathtrap!" one of the British ministers yelled. The other politicians standing behind Hynes also began to panic.

"Calm down," Hynes said. "There's no need for—"

Everyone on the bridge froze in place. Their muscles refused to obey their commands. Captain Abel started to sweat like mad. Fear welled up inside the frozen politicians who couldn't even lift a finger. Only Hynes was calm enough to notice one of the doors open.

Three individuals walked in. None of them looked like military personnel. One was only a few feet tall, followed by a giant who carried a silver barrel under each arm. The last one to walk in was a woman wearing heavy makeup and a brown fur coat. She smiled as the door closed behind her. The trio took their place smack-dab in the middle of the bridge, the woman standing ahead of the other two.

"Why, hello there!" the woman yelled for the entire bridge to hear. "I am known as Cyphrus. Behind me are Atlas and Geppetto, my loyal colleagues. We represent Cloak and the Chinese Empire. This, ladies and gentlemen, is our revenge."

Hynes would have roared in anger if he could. This was Cloak. These cretins had abandoned the Western Union and used their gifts to harm the innocent. If what that cursed woman said was true about their alliance with the Chinese, then they had also sided with the enemies of freedom. He knew Cloak should have been dealt with long ago, but Powell had convinced him that overt action would only draw unwanted attention. In the end, however, it seemed secrecy had failed to pay off.

"Thanks to our abilities, it was quite easy for us to sneak aboard your flying vessel," Cyphrus said. "The rest of the crew should be arriving in the ballroom right about now. Let's check up on them."

A massive holographic screen appeared, showing the ballroom located near the center of the ship. It had a high ceiling, red carpets, and crystal chandeliers. Crew members wearing gray uniforms were filing into the ballroom, waiting for the presidential address that would never come. Very soon, almost all of *Leviathan's* crew was gathered inside one enclosed space. The people on-screen didn't notice the doors close behind them.

"They're like cattle," Cyphrus said. "I used to be like that. Now I'm a little more evolved. Now I'm the butcher." She snapped her fingers.

The people on-screen, over a hundred in total, fell to the floor, gasping for air like fishes out of water. They were even flopping like fishes, limbs twisting and hands clawing at their throats. Their eyes bulged out of their heads like something you might see in a cartoon. But there was nothing comical about this. No, these people were dying. They had no other option but to breathe in the deadly gas.

"What nasty worms you are," Cyphrus told the frozen people on the bridge with a smirk. "There's a lot of nerve gas on board this ship. No doubt you were going to use this on populated areas. Oh, well, life goes on ... but not for them!"

Nobody moved in the ballroom. The floor was littered with the dead.

It took all of Hynes's willpower to move his lips, but he managed to get out one word.

"Monsters..."

Geppetto shot Cyphrus a look. Nobody had ever managed to resist his control like that before. Cyphrus only shrugged. She walked up the stairs to the balcony where Hynes sat. She stared at him for a moment before grabbing his thick neck.

"You people bred us to be killers," she said, leaning in close to Hynes. "We were tortured beyond imagination. With all your talk of justice and restoring balance to the world, you took ten children and twisted them into something horrid, something that couldn't be loved. You denied us our humanity. For that, you will suffer. But you won't die. No, that'd be too merciful."

She let go of the president's throat and turned to the frightened politicians that stood behind Hynes. They could not have fathomed the hate that coursed through her.

"You will all suffer," Cyphrus told them. "And you will become *my* tools."

Atlas put both barrels down with a sober expression. Geppetto looked almost as ecstatic as Cyphrus but glanced nervously at Atlas for the briefest of moments. The Gifted then put gas masks over their faces.

"Now see our wrath!" Cyphrus cried. "Feel our rage!"

The giant opened the two barrels. Inky gas poured out of the containers, dissipating fast. The gas stopped flowing after a few seconds. Nothing seemed to happen. Atlas looked at Geppetto, who only shrugged. They didn't know what to wait for.

Cyphrus, however, grew even smugger.

Hynes felt a sharp pain go through his head. A small stream of blood rolled out of his nose and down his shirt. An involuntary shiver went through him. The pain began to grow. It grew to the point that it felt like his brain was about to split down the middle. A guttural scream came out of his throat. Geppetto had released his victims from his invisible hold, not that it mattered now. All across the bridge, people fell to their knees and squirmed in their chairs. Cries of unimaginable anguish echoed around the room as blood squirted out of their noses. Their veins on their heads soon became black. The nanobots were literally ripping their minds apart and piecing them back together again into something less than human. They became puppets. They became tools. They became slaves.

The cries stopped. Hynes was the first to stop screaming, as well as the first to stand. One at a time, everyone on the bridge stood up, eyes glazed over. They had no will of their own now, only the will of their masters.

"Yes," Cyphrus cooed. "This is the way things were meant to be. Now you can leave all the thinking to me. I'm sure there are no complaints, right?"

The tools that were once people just stood there, unmoving.

Cyphrus grinned. "Good. When in Rome…"

***

Naomi walked into the common room, noticing that everyone was here. That was good. She needed to speak to them all. After days of suspense, they deserved at least a small explanation as to how they had escaped the Western Union. But just as she was about to speak, Thomas ran up to her, followed by Slate, who urged the young prince along.

Naomi sighed. "What is it?"

"Um… I think you should go out with Slate," Thomas muttered.

"Louder!" Slate snapped.

"He's very handsome and very successful and a good role model!" Thomas yelled.

Naomi rolled her eyes. "Thomas, I don't have time—"

"Say the rest of the lines," Slate told the boy. "Hurry, I still have a chance!"

"No, you don't," Naomi said.

"He also said you're a 'nine out of ten,'" Thomas said with a smile, going drastically off script. "And he's also trying to 'reel in the babes.' What does that mean? Is it like fishing?"

"Don't make me beat you!" Slate hollered, shaking his fist. That was when he noticed the fiery look Naomi was giving him.

"Uh ... nine out of ten is still pretty good."

"Guys, you gotta check this out," Straper said in a panicky tone.

"Yeah, we gotta check it out!" Slate agreed quickly. "No time to waste!"

Exasperated and annoyed, Naomi went over with Slate and Thomas to the holographic TV. A giant flying ship was being shown on-screen.

"Is that *Leviathan*?" Naomi asked.

"Yeah, and it's been hijacked by terrorists," Gilda told her.

"Oh, great," Slate said.

"Who's behind it?" Naomi asked, not taking her eyes off the screen.

"They don't know yet," Straper said. "The whole Western Union is freaking out."

"Ladies and gentlemen," a man announced as the TV continued to show a live feed of *Leviathan*. "This is Jeff Springer reporting. Half an hour ago, authorities received a video containing the terrorists' demands. One of those demands was that the video be aired on all major news channels. Union Network will now show it to you. We must warn you that this video may disturb some viewers. Viewer discretion is strongly advised."

The video began to play. It showed a man standing in front of a black background. He had a deep voice that inspired fear in all who heard it.

"Greetings, Western Union," he said. "I represent the United Third. You may know me as the Helmet Man."

CHAPTER 29

"Hey, Slate's on TV!" Thomas pointed out with glee.

"Yep, that's me all right!" Slate declared. "I'm a star! Naomi, can you honestly still say that I'm not appealing?"

"You're not appealing," Naomi told him. She stared at the screen with calculating intensity. What did this mean? Someone was impersonating Slate, the same someone who was responsible for hijacking *Leviathan*. Could Incognito be behind this? No, she didn't think he would undertake an operation of this scale without telling her. At least she hoped not. But one thing was for sure: whoever was responsible wanted Slate to take the fall.

"For centuries, the West has ravaged the Third World, enslaving and killing the proud inhabitants of these lands," the impostor ranted. He was dressed as Slate, wearing a silver helmet, but his voice was too deep and too serious. Slate talked like a spoiled five-year-old, Naomi thought, not a deadly terrorist fiend. Without a doubt, this man was an impostor.

"We are regaining control of our own future," the impostor said. "No one shall deny us our right to mold our own destinies. This revolting machine that I stand on is a symbol of our enslavement. Now, Westerners, it will be turned on *you*. We have the head of the Western Union and many of your other leaders in our custody. Do not attempt to intervene unless you wish to see them fall to their deaths. You Westerners now only have two choices. The first option is to do nothing. The second option is to give into all our demands. Neither is very appealing to you, I'm sure, but a decision must be made. I would advise the latter."

"This guy's got moxie," Slate said. "But he doesn't have my sense of humor."

"Thank god for small favors," Straper said.

"I heard that!"

"Would you guys shut up?" Gilda snapped.

The impostor continued. "Our demands are numerous but fair. First, all Western military and peacekeeping forces will withdraw from all non-member nations of the Western Union. Next, a trillion dollars will be distributed to the people of the Occupied Territories as restitution for your crimes. Finally, you will cease all efforts to capture Incognito or hinder him and the United Third in any way. All these demands must be formally promised within one day, or else we shall take extreme action."

Straper scoffed. "No way will the government agree to any of that."

"Not unless these hijackers have something up their sleeve," Naomi said.

"To demonstrate our power, the United Third shall utilize the very weapons that the West would have used against us," the impostor said. "*Leviathan* has on it an abundant supply of nerve gas, enough to wipe out a dozen cities. It will *all* be used on European civilians unless the Western Union fulfills our demands."

"That's insane," Gilda said. "Those monsters are going to kill countless people."

"I know many of you won't take this threat seriously," the impostor said. "To show the conviction we have in our beliefs, a demonstration will be necessary. Right now, *Leviathan* is traveling above Rome on its programmed course. Please pay attention to what's about to happen, because if you don't learn this lesson, it will have to be repeated."

***

It was a sunny day in Rome. Everyone had expected severe overcast, but only a few puffy white clouds dotted the sky. Crowds of people had gathered in squares and other public areas, eager to see the flying wonder that was *Leviathan*.

Now they all fled.

A formal evacuation warning had been given to Rome. Thousands of people tried to escape the city, but the roads were clogged at this point. Many climbed over slow-moving cars in a futile attempt to cross the streets. Military unicopters flew in to help evacuate children and high-ranking officials. Some people tried to hang on to the sides of these unicopters, only to fall to their deaths with sickening thumps.

A roaring hum soon became audible over the screams of the mad crowd. When people began to hear it, they all became eerily silent. Soon, the entire city went quiet. Not even a car horn went off. All eyes were focused on the sky, witnessing the massive metal vessel that approached from the horizon.

The crowd then transitioned from dreaded anticipation to all-out panic. Children cried. Fights broke out. People even began to trample over each other.

A canister was launched out of *Leviathan*. It left behind a trail of what appeared to be smoke as it sailed through the air, but it soon became apparent that it wasn't smoke.

It was nerve gas.

The canister landed in the center of the Roman Colosseum. Gas flowed out of the ancient structure and onto the modern streets, which were filled with the frightened faces of the desperate. They ran as fast as they could. But it was useless.

An old man was the first to fall. He grabbed his throat and convulsed on the ground, vomit filling his mouth. A woman fell next to him, unable to breathe. A middle-aged man tried to pull himself out of his car as he asphyxiated, but he only managed to fall on the sidewalk before dying. In less than a minute, over a thousand people were dead. That number would rise to three thousand in another minute and continue to climb. The streets around the Colosseum were soon lined with the bodies of hundreds of civilians.

Leviathan did not change course. It continued toward the City of Light.

***

"This ... this is just too horrendous to describe," Springer said. Images of the carnage were being shown to the world. "We ... we have just been informed that *Leviathan* is currently heading for Paris. An official evacuation order has been given for the entire city. Military leaders are gathering to ... to discuss the next steps following this ... this..."

Naomi turned off the holographic screen.

Straper deflated. "It's the Bunker all over again ... except bigger."

"All those people are..." Gilda whispered. "No ... this is horrible."

"Slate, I'm scared," Thomas whimpered, grabbing Slate. Naomi shot a look at Slate, but he didn't seem to notice her. The Helmet Man just stood there with his arms crossed.

"I see," a new voice said. "This is what they had planned."

Everyone turned to see Incognito standing at the door. He leaned against his scythe, wearing his regular white suit and oval mask. Naomi couldn't help but be impressed. After his ordeal, it was mind-boggling that he could even get dressed by himself.

"Who is this child?" Incognito questioned, gesturing to Thomas. The boy squeaked. He let go of Slate and hid behind Naomi. Gilda and Straper started to sweat. This was the worst situation they could imagine. Thomas was a British prince. If Incognito found out Thomas's true identity, who knew what he might do to him?

"He was an experimental subject of Cloak's," Naomi said, telling a half-truth. "We rescued him from the island."

Gilda and Straper relaxed a little. Thomas was safe, for now.

"You shouldn't be out of bed," Naomi told Incognito, changing the subject.

"Don't tell me how to live my life," Incognito spat. He limped into the room, scrutinizing everyone around him. "I've been watching the news from my bed. That Helmet Man impostor spoke well. I couldn't have written a better threat myself."

"Were you behind this?" Gilda asked with venom.

"Nonsense," Incognito scoffed. "I was busy saving you all from being sunk to the bottom of the ocean. But do not get me wrong. I feel no remorse for those greedy worms who were gassed to death. The only shame is that I wasn't the one to pull the trigger."

"Monster," Gilda growled.

Incognito ignored her. "This was not the work of any terrorist organization. I'll give you one guess as to who's the true culprit."

"Cloak," Naomi said.

"Correct. I cannot think of anyone else with the skills or motivation to pull such a stunt."

"So, you're Incognito," Slate said, approaching him with a cocky stride. "I never actually met you before. You always use others to talk to me. Why is that? You chicken?"

"It's because I don't have time to deal with your impudence," Incognito said. "Although you are a useful tool, you are still insufferable. Why these fools put up with you is something I will never understand."

"Same goes for you," Slate said, standing right in front of Incognito, face-to-face, mask-to-helmet. "I've been putting my ass on the line for you. We all have, yet you're talking to us like we're a bunch of trash."

"Because you *are* trash."

"You son of a—"

"This is why I haven't spoken with you, because you have the manners and intelligence of a lobotomized orangutan."

"And you got the moral compass of a skinhead."

"Do you realize how easy it was to manipulate you? Merely getting a voluptuous woman to order you around and a few weakling munchkins to tag along as leverage has turned you into my puppet. A creature like you never uses his brain. You are a brute, Helmet Man, a tool of colonialism. You are a beast with no goals of his own, no philosophy, no ambition. Your willful ignorance infuriates me. Truly, you are a spawn of the West."

"Your ass is about to get fried."

"Enough of this," Naomi said, putting her arms between the two of them. "We have bigger issues at hand than this macho competition."

"Fine, whatever," Slate spat, backing off.

"I would advise you not to overstep your boundaries," Incognito told Naomi. He turned to the rest of them and continued where he left off. "From what I can tell, Cloak has used its mind-control weapon on Hynes and his cronies. *Leviathan* was the perfect place to do it, since it was isolated, far from any potential witnesses or help."

Gilda almost fell over. "What! If they turned the president into a puppet, along with those other Western Union leaders, who knows what kind of damage they could do?"

"That's the Chinese Empire's objective," Incognito said. "They are planning to sabotage the Western Union from the inside out. Their main foe would be crippled, and they could continue their quest for global domination unhindered."

"All right, that makes sense," Straper said. "But why did they gas all those people? That just seems like overkill."

"He's right," Naomi said. "If they wanted to infect Hynes and the others with the nanobots, why weren't they more secretive about it?"

"It doesn't matter," Incognito said. "All that matters is that they succeed."

The bombshell was dropped. Nobody knew how to respond for several seconds.

"I beg your fricking pardon?" Straper snapped. "You *want* Cloak to win?"

"You're crazy!" Gilda shouted. "What would you possibly get out of that?"

"It's actually quite ingenious," Incognito said. "I always thought that Cloak would use this weapon against the Western Union. I even suspected that they would attack *Leviathan*. Granted, the gassing was somewhat surprising, but I have no objection, so long as they infected Hynes and the others with the nanobots. After a few months, when those Western leaders have had time to cause some damage, I will tell the world about the mind-control weapon and how the Chinese Empire created it for the purpose of trying to topple the Western Union."

"That's why you sent us on those missions. It wasn't to stop Cloak. You just want to use the intel that we got for your own schemes."

"Precisely. Once I reveal the existence of the weapon, as well as how to diagnose if someone has been infected or not, the Western Union will undoubtedly check all their leaders for signs that they are being controlled. When they discover that Hynes and other high-ranking officials are infected, they will be forced to confront the Chinese Empire."

"You're trying to start a war!" Gilda gasped. "You're crazy!"

"They wouldn't really go to war!" Straper cried. "They can't! They both got nukes."

"Animosity often trumps logic," Naomi said. "Besides, there have been many treaties signed between the two superpowers about the rules of engagement. It's quite possible for them to have a war without ever resorting to nuclear arms."

"If the Chinese Empire and the Western Union go to war, it could be the end of everything," Gilda told Incognito. "You can't do this."

"Wrong. I can," Incognito said. "The Western Union will be crippled by Cloak's sabotage. They will also start diverting their military resources to fighting the Chinese. The United Third will take this golden opportunity to rise up and topple the Western hold on our lands. The Third World will rise to power under one banner, one ruler."

"All right, I've heard enough," Slate said. "What's stopping me from electrocuting you till that ponytail catches fire?"

"For one thing, I shall cut you in half. And we are in a submarine. Discharging energy like that would be bad for the sensitive electronics. Wouldn't want to hurt your friends."

"You piece of shit!"

"We won't let this happen," Gilda said. "We're going to keep Cloak from getting what it wants, even if you're against us."

"I'll try not to soil myself in fear," Incognito said. "But this submarine will not surface unless I give the command. You are all trapped here until Cloak is finished poisoning the rats."

"I thought you wanted to stop Cloak!" Gilda shouted.

"*And* I want to stop the Western Union. Stopping Cloak here would not be a fatal blow to them. Until such a time arrives, I will focus on curing humanity of the cancer that is Western civilization. Have no fear. You will soon see things my way."

Incognito limped out of the room, leaving his outraged and helpless subordinates behind, trapped a thousand feet underwater.

CHAPTER 30

"We're stuck here," Gilda said, staring at the ceiling. "And half of Europe is about to be wiped out with nerve gas, not to mention that the head of the Western Union just had his mind rewired by supercriminals."

Straper snorted. "Thanks for cheering up the place."

The group lounged in the common room, where the holographic screen still showed the news channel. No good or bad news had been announced since Rome was gassed. *Leviathan* was still heading for Paris while the Western Union scrambled to find a solution.

"This sucks," Slate said. "I can't stand waiting here."

"What else can we do?" Straper asked. "There's no way off this submarine. Even if there was, we haven't even left the Indian Ocean yet. How are we supposed to get from here to Europe? And how would we attack *Leviathan*? It's a fricking flying fortress!"

"Why can't Slate just fly out of the submarine and fight the bad guys?" Thomas asked.

"Water and electricity don't mix," Slate said. "Geez, learn basic chemistry before contributing to the conversation."

"Maybe *you* should learn what chemistry is first," Gilda told him.

"What do we do, then?" Thomas asked. "Cloak can't get away with this. They destroyed my home and took my friends away. Now they want to make people dead again. Naomi, you can help us. I know you can. You're a good guy, like Slate."

Naomi was leaning against the wall, looking bored, but she had been listening in on the conversation, purposely not adding her input.

"Hey, that's right," Slate said. "Incognito may have grounded us, but I bet Naomi can break us outta here."

"You're right," Gilda said. "She could also arrange for us to get to Europe and even to *Leviathan*. But there are two problems with that. For one, Incognito might kill us all if we do anything to piss him off."

"Boy, that *is* a problem," Straper groaned.

Slate scoffed. "I'm not scared of a guy with a ponytail."

"I say we let the Western Union handle this," Straper said. "It's not our problem. How could we help? If anything, we'd get in the way."

"By the time the Western Union does something, Paris could be a graveyard," Gilda said. "And the government doesn't know about the nanobots or Cloak. Even if we told them, they wouldn't take us seriously, not without those disks, and Incognito has them."

"Besides, those pansies can't fight the Gifted," Slate said. "Only Naomi and I can."

"I thought you were poking holes in this plan?" Straper asked Gilda.

"Don't get me wrong," Gilda said. "I want to help. I'm just being realistic."

"Fine, so what was your second point?"

"That Naomi isn't willing to help us."

"No way!" Slate exclaimed. "She can't say no to me. Right, baby?"

"Wrong," Naomi said. "I won't help you."

"What!" Slate yelled. "You gotta be kidding! After all this tough talk, you're just going to let the enemy walk away?"

"I follow orders," Naomi said. "That's the way the cookie crumbles."

"But you're a good guy," Thomas said. "You have to help us. You just have to."

"I don't have to do anything," Naomi said, staring intensely at the boy. The prince yelped but didn't back away.

Straper laughed. "Whoa, somebody has a temper."

"Shut up!" Naomi spat, raising her hand. Straper's laughter stopped with a choke as an unseen grip squeezed his throat.

"Naomi!" Gilda shouted. She ran forward to try to stop her, but she became weightless, floating a foot above the floor.

"Please, stop!" Thomas yelled, grabbing Naomi's arm. She shot him a look that was half rage, half frenzy. Raising her hand, she was just about to strike him when a gloved hand grabbed her by the shoulder and sent an electric jolt through her.

"That's enough of that now," Slate said. He caught Naomi just as her knees gave out. Straper gasped, falling to his knees, while Gilda managed to land on her feet. Gilda got her wits about her and looked to see Slate throw Naomi over his shoulder.

"Where are you taking her?" Gilda asked, still shaken. Had Naomi just tried to kill them, or had she only acted out of anger? Either way, Gilda didn't want Slate to hurt her. Naomi was a bit snobbish, but for some reason, she had grown on her.

"Don't worry about it," Slate said, full of cheer. "Stay here and make sure nobody broke anything important. This shouldn't take long."

The Helmet Man left and went to an unoccupied bedroom, away from the sub's crewmen and his friends. He dropped Naomi on the bed and stood by the door with his arms crossed. Naomi rubbed her head as she got her senses back in order.

"I was wondering when you'd snap," Slate said. "You put on a good act, but you can't keep that kind of frustration hidden for long."

Naomi's eyes snapped open. She floated to her feet, her fury reignited. "I'm not going to justify myself to filth like you or explain why I obey orders."

"You gotta be kidding, right? Despite my numerous attempts to ease the tension, you've been a real poor sport. You think you're better than me? Is that why you've been treating me like a turd and why you tried to kill me at the Pale Pyramid, when Incognito wanted me alive, by the way? You were okay with disobeying orders then."

"That was different. And of course I'm better than you. You take joy out of murdering others. Then you go looking for trouble, just so you can mur-der some more."

"Hey, I kill bad guys!"

"That's just an excuse. You side yourself with a cause that you could care less about and use it as a pretext to go on a killing spree. That's not justice. That's exploitive."

"And that's why you hate me?"

"Not to mention all the sexual harassment."

"Sorry if I didn't want to miss my one chance at getting a lady friend. I thought you of all people wouldn't think I was a freak. I thought if anyone could look past this goddamn helmet, it'd be another science project. But no. Even the monsters hate me."

"Really? You expect me to take pity on you? All these sob stories are just excuses. Why do you think I left Cloak? It's because if I was ever going to be a better person, I had to get away from them. They're all deluded psychopaths. Do you think I would betray my lifelong comrades only to side with you, someone just like them?"

Slate raised his hands. "Okay, sure. I'll admit that I'm not a good guy. I'll admit that I like killing a bit too much. Hell, I'll even admit that I'm a hypocrite. But you're the same. You act all high and mighty, but how do you explain what just happened in that room? When you weren't able to have things your way, you went berserk."

"What about Thomas? You don't even think he's a human being. That's why you can use him as a shield with no qualms."

"Yeah, well, you think of me exactly the same way."

"You volunteered. Thomas is a child."

"Well, if you're so interested in being a 'better person,' do you really think working for Incognito is the way to go?"

"That—you don't know anything about my situation!"

"Then why exactly are you with Incognito? Who is he? Where's my dad? What happened twenty years ago? What's your motive? What's Cloak after? And for the love of Pete, who the hell is the Mentor?"

What followed was an air of quiet that seemed taboo to be broken, but after a minute of this silence, Naomi deflated, the fight taken out of her.

"He's one of the Keymasters," she said.

Slate sprang to attention. "Who? The Mentor?"

"No, Incognito. He was one of the scientists who created us."

"He's a Keymaster? Then how come I don't remember him?"

"He worked on other projects and wasn't directly involved in raising the Gifted. I never encountered him myself either until four years ago."

"So, where did he get his powers from? I thought you had to be born with them."

"Somehow, he gave himself abilities like we have. He is able to become intangible at will. That man single-handedly destroyed all those Western Union ships that had us trapped before. Without a doubt, he is more powerful than any of the Gifted."

"Even me?" Slate shouted. "How can someone be better than perfect?"

Naomi smiled a little, but it dissipated fast. "He's far from perfect. Every time he uses his gift, it destroys him. His powers are not stable, unlike ours, so he only uses them sparingly. Right now, he's on his deathbed."

"Okay, so why are you working for him? I don't know if you noticed, but he's a real jerk and also a little … uh … politically incorrect."

"Because he's the only one who can help me complete my revenge."

"You mean revenge against Cloak?"

"No," Naomi said, hate lacing her voice again. "I mean revenge against the Mentor. Cloak is just the Mentor's tool. The Mentor is the true enemy that everyone is ignorant of. Cyphrus, Geppetto, and Atlas don't even believe the Mentor exists. Nobody believes in nightmares, but this nightmare is real."

"So, this guy exists? Then where's my dad? If Incognito's a Keymaster, maybe some of the others are still kicking around."

"I honestly don't know, but if my revenge will ever come true, I need to obey Incognito no matter what. His abilities are unmatched. If anybody can defeat the Mentor, it'll be him."

"Now I get it. You're pinning all your hopes on Incognito, but you also wanted to help us. Caught between a rock and a hard place, eh? That's why you went psycho. You were frustrated that you couldn't do anything."

"You're presumptuous. Why would I want to help you?"

"Because you want to do the right thing. Those people on TV were gassed to death, and there'll be more victims unless we stop Cloak ourselves. Incognito is gonna let all those people die. You said you left Cloak because they were monsters. It looks to me like you just switched from serving one evil to another. If you really want to redeem yourself and not just have your stupid revenge, you need to help us stop Cloak."

Naomi lowered her eyes. How could that buffoon be so convincing? Even so, would she throw away everything she had worked for just so she could help this man and his kid friends?

"What about the Mentor?" Naomi asked. "If Incognito decides not to help me, how will the Mentor ever be stopped?"

Slate tilted his head forward, the light glinting off his silver helmet. "Do you even have to ask? I'm gonna murder the bastard myself. I kill bad guys, remember?"

***

On the USS *Liberation*, a hundred miles off the French coast, Fleet Admiral Redwood walked into the briefing room, which had a glass table in the center. A three-dimensional holographic map hovered above the tabletop. Three individuals were looking at the map. One of them was Vice President Powell, his brow creased with worry. Redwood wasn't thrilled to see Powell but was even less thrilled to see the man standing next to him.

"Marker, what are you doing here?" Redwood demanded. "I thought I kicked you off my ship after you assaulted General Eisenhorn."

"He's my guest," Powell said, putting a protective hand on Gerald Marker's shoulder. The secretary of defense's limbs jittered about. There were dark circles under his eyes. Marker had been a wreck ever since his son died. Redwood felt sympathy, but Marker was unstable, having attacked Eisenhorn in the heat of anger.

And yet Marker still had his job, despite clearly not being reliable. Seeing Powell's hand on his shoulder made Redwood realize the truth. Powell controlled Marker, taking advantage of a vulnerable man for personal gain. Was this thug going to be the next leader of the Western Union? From the looks of what was happening on *Leviathan*, it was a strong possibility.

Camilla Ryder also stood near the table. After her encounter with Incognito, she had been put on an unofficial leave of absence, but now she was back, despite the fact she was supposed to be in Washington, DC, for debriefing.

Redwood growled. "Why are you here, Ryder?"

"The Helmet Man is behind this," Ryder said, monotone. "Due to extreme circumstances, I took it upon myself to return. It is my duty to pursue him, after all."

"You're on very thin ice."

Powell smacked the table. "Enough! Let's discuss options. Right now, the president is trapped in a flying fortress full of terrorists. *Leviathan* is also headed for Paris, preparing to wipe out its entire population. The terrorists only gave us one day to consider their demands, and our time is almost up."

Redwood approached Powell. "This nerve gas, why was it on board *Leviathan*? I've received information that you personally had the gas placed on that ship."

"In anticipation of future conflicts. What do you think?"

"And just how much is there?"

"Enough to wipe out a dozen cities," Marker said.

Redwood sighed. "What are we going to do? We sure aren't giving in to their demands. I know that much."

"They do not want their demands fulfilled," Ryder said.

Redwood turned to her. "I beg your pardon?"

"While making his threat, the Helmet Man said that neither choice was very appealing. This was unintentional, but the enemy accidentally revealed their true goal to us. They seek to kill civilians, nothing more. They gave us those demands so they could pretend to be terrorists and hide their motive. Also, that impostor did not sound like the Helmet Man."

"Are you saying the Helmet Man isn't behind this?" Powell asked.

"Possibly," Ryder said. "For sure, there is more to this than mere extortion."

"This might explain why their demands are so unreasonable," Marker said. "But we're still left with the same situation. How are we going to stop *Leviathan*?"

"For reasons unknown, all drones and fighter planes shut down when they come too close to the ship," Ryder said. "Any incoming cruise missiles or explosives dropped from above are destroyed by *Leviathan's* automatic defense systems. Attempts to take control of the ship from the ground have also failed. The only realistic option now is to destroy *Leviathan* from a distance before it reaches Paris."

"We can't destroy it," Redwood said. "The president is on board, not to mention the other Western Union leaders with him."

"There's more at stake than a couple of politicians," Powell said. "Millions of lives are on the line. That's why I've been considering the nuclear option."

"You want to nuke the president over France!"

"Don't make it sound so bad. A nuclear bomb would be detonated above *Leviathan*, out of range of whatever is disturbing our electrical devices. It wouldn't destroy the ship, but the shockwave will definitely knock the sucker out of the air."

Redwood looked at Powell as if he had grown a third eye. "This is insane. Your whole plan rests on the assumption that whatever is interfering with our equipment has a limited range. At least consider sending in a tactical team first."

"No time. That ship is going to be smack-dab over Paris in an hour. Since the president is out of commission, I am officially in charge of the Western Union and its plentiful nuclear arsenal. It's about time we put it to good use."

"You're going to kill President Hynes."

"This ain't China. One man isn't the Union. Hynes of all people knew that."

A young officer ran into the room. "Sir, we have a problem!"

"Looks like it's my problem now," Powell said. "What is it?"

"It's the Helmet Man! He–he's been spotted approaching *Leviathan*!"

CHAPTER 31

Mao Long walked down the hall to his personal quarters, the hunger growing inside him. Lily followed as they made their way through the palace. They would watch from afar as the West was thrown into chaos. Rome had already been attacked, over ten thousand souls meeting their end, and the frenzy was only just beginning.

Yet hunger was not the only feeling in Mao's stomach. There was also a feeling that something was missing, that he had neglected to see an obvious truth.

Then he figured out what it was. It was that delirious Westerner, General Eisenhorn. He had been sent to replace the previous ambassador, who had died under mysterious circumstances, too mysterious for Mao's liking. But what Mao couldn't get his head around was why the Western Union had appointed a fool like Eisenhorn to the position instead of someone well-spoken or level-headed. It was true that ambassadors acted only as hostages of the emperor, another way to control the subservient nations of the empire, while the Western Union only had an ambassador in a futile attempt to keep relations open between the two superpowers.

But that was what bothered Mao. If the Western Union was so invested in avoiding war, why would they send this irritating blowhard as their spokesman? There must be some hidden agenda, something that would warrant such an action.

As Mao arrived at his private quarters, he noticed an unwelcome face waiting for him.

"I see you are retiring early," Xing said. "And I believe a guest is waiting in there for you. Entertainment, perhaps?"

"Don't you have better things to do than harass your elders?" Mao asked.

"No, I am done with my work for today. Oh, I was sorry to hear about how Mistress Lotus failed to kill the Helmet Man. She sustained considerable damage. The emperor was very upset when news of the incident reached him. You best be careful from now on. Even you, my dear prime minister, can only anger the emperor so many times."

Mao took a threatening step toward Xing. "Insolent brat. You dare talk to *me* like that? I am the prime minister and your future emperor. My father won't always be around for you to cower behind, so you best treat me with the respect I deserve."

"Let's just hope your little project with Cloak bears worthwhile fruit. Otherwise, there may be a new heir to the throne."

Xing left Mao to fume, walking down the hall in no hurry. Mao turned to Lily, who merely shrugged back at him. What was she supposed to do? Mao growled as he entered his room. That display of insubordination had been the last straw. Once he was emperor, he would make sure Xing had a special place in the Traitors' Garden.

Two timid servants closed the doors behind Mao Long and Lily. Mao's room was covered in Chinese artwork, rich red carpets, and plush furniture. A table covered in food stood near a wide couch that had two guests sitting on it. One of them was General Eisenhorn, who wore his peaked hat and a green uniform that looked crisp and new. His face was agitated and covered in new wrinkles. Next to him sat Shu, who had placed a calming hand on his shoulder.

"What is *she* doing here?" Mao spat.

Shu was quick to stand upright and bow. "Your Highness, forgive me! I will leave if that is your wish."

"It is not my wish," Mao hissed. "It is my command."

"Get going, old lady!" Lily yelled, grabbing Shu by the bicep.

"Easy there, hussy!" Eisenhorn barked at Lily.

"Please, do not worry," Shu told the general. "Do as they say."

Eisenhorn grumbled but nodded.

As soon as Lily kicked Shu out, Mao began pacing around the couch, examining Eisenhorn with great distaste.

"Do you know who I am?" he asked Eisenhorn.

The general scratched his head. "Yeah, it's Pow Tong or some crazy name."

"My name is Mao Long… And now that I've seen you up close, I am still not certain why you were chosen as the new ambassador. The mystery only deepens when you consider the recent attempt on your life. So, why are you here?"

"You're the one that invited me!"

"I am asking why you are in Beijing," Mao said, suppressing his irritation. "Never mind. You obviously don't know, and it soon won't matter."

"Huh, why's that?"

"Because you will be dead in a few minutes."

"You threatening me?" Eisenhorn snarled, jumping to his feet.

Ignoring him, Mao yelled something in Mandarin. A holographic screen turned on, showing a giant ship floating in the clouds.

"Hey, how come I don't get a TV in my room?" Eisenhorn objected.

"Being prime minister has its privileges," Mao said, pacing around the room. "This is a live satellite feed of *Leviathan*, the Western Union's newest vessel. It recently embarked on its maiden voyage with the president and some of his loyal supporters on board."

"Hynes is on that ship?" Eisenhorn asked.

"Let me finish, you revolting mongrel!" Mao spat. He took a deep breath through his nose, settling himself down. "The Western Union threatens us by building this floating hunk of scrap metal. There is no reason to build something so formidable for combating terrorists and ragtag rebels alone. We could not let this insult go unanswered, so we hired a group of individuals you are well acquainted with to hijack this vessel."

Eisenhorn scrunched up his brow, but he was coming up blank.

Mao turned red. "Cloak! I am talking about Cloak!"

"Those villains!" Eisenhorn exclaimed. "They killed my cadets and Johnson! What are they up to? Answer me!"

"They are—" Mao began but stopped midsentence when he noticed the screen.

"That's weird," Lily said, squinting at the projection. "Something's approaching the ship."

"What is the meaning of this?" Mao demanded. "Those aren't Western Union aircraft. Computer, zoom in on those incoming objects!"

The screen focused on three approaching dots heading for *Leviathan*. One of them was a unicopter and a flying walker.

The other one was the Helmet Man.

Mao ground his teeth. "Yet another buffoon that needs a beating..."

Eisenhorn couldn't help but smirk.

***

"We're almost there," Straper said, glancing out the unicopter's window. "Man, I still can't believe this is happening. This the craziest thing we've done, and that's saying something."

"Well, you best get your head in the game," Naomi said, piloting the unicopter. Straper wore green combat gear while she had on a loose white outfit that looked solely for comfort but in reality let her move her body and channel her powers more effectively. They were inside a two-seated unicopter while Gilda piloted her walker and Slate flew ahead.

It had been an arduous task to go from a thousand feet under the Indian Ocean to five thousand feet above France, but they had done it. Naomi had apologized for assaulting the others and said she would assist them as atonement. The apology was hastily accepted. With the entire group on the same page, they set off on their mission.

The first obstacle was getting out of the submarine. Incognito was resting in the infirmary, so they didn't have to worry about a direct confrontation, but surfacing was not an option. Incognito would clearly notice that, even if he was recovering. However, Naomi still had friends in the criminal underworld from her days with Cloak. She arranged for a small submarine to dock with the *Eodum* and get them to the surface. While waiting for their ride, they made their preparations, getting weapons and gear for the task ahead.

Their biggest remaining problem was Captain Young-Bum. He was loyal to Incognito, but they needed him to allow the smaller sub to dock with the *Eodum*. They all met with him to plead for his assistance.

"I am sorry," Young-Bum said. "But I work for Incognito, not for any of you. Years ago, when the *Eodum* was about to be captured by the Chinese Empire, Incognito saved me and my crew. I could never repay him, but I will try. As well, I am on thin ice with him as it is. One of my former crewmates was responsible for compromising the Japan mission. My refusal to take you into the Neutral Zone did not please him either. One more slipup could mean my life."

"Young-Bum, if you don't help us, millions will die," Naomi said. "Can you honestly sit by and let that happen?"

The captain said nothing, but his eyes betrayed his true feelings.

"You despise the Chinese Empire," Naomi said. "This is all their work. If we let them win, they're only going to get stronger. Please, Captain. We need you. If not for us, do it for those who have suffered under the rule of the empire."

Young-Bum looked shaken and petted his mechanical hand like he would a cat. It took half a minute of deliberation before he made his decision.

"Knock me out," he told them. "If Incognito thinks I helped you, I will be killed for sure. My crew won't interfere with your docking. Just try not to arouse Incognito. Hurry, do it now. Make sure to leave a visible injury too."

Happy to oblige, Slate headbutted him.

After they surfaced in their small escape sub, they met up with a seaplane, which brought them all the way to Sicily. Naomi managed to get her hands on a special stealth unicopter that would get them to *Leviathan*. By that time, the one-day waiting period was almost up. The Western Union had not given in to the demands, so *Leviathan* continued toward Paris.

There were two other major challenges to their endeavor. The first was they had to transport Gilda's walker, which was still damaged from its battle on Blast from the Past Island. Both the sub and the seaplane were able to take the massive walker with them. It was tricky to get it off the *Eodum* without alerting Incognito, but Naomi's telekinesis made it possible. During their flight, Gilda finished her repairs to Magenta. It was soon ready to roll.

The final problem, however, was even more troublesome.

"What do you mean I can't come?" Thomas yelled.

"Calm down," Naomi said. "This is for your own good. You can't handle a fight like this. You may be physically invulnerable, but you could be emotionally scarred for life if we took you. It's bad enough what you had to go through already."

"No, they killed my friends! Please, let me help. I've got nothing left."

Gilda's heart went out to the kid. He was just like she'd been when Henry died at the Bunker. Straper also felt bad for him, but they all knew they couldn't take him along. He would only slow them down.

"We'll figure out your future later," Naomi said. "For now, you will wait for us at a safe house in Sicily. I'm not sure what Incognito might do if we left you here on the sub."

"We should also decide how to deal with Incognito when we get back," Gilda said. "You know, if we come back ... or even want to come back."

The color drained from Straper's face. "Oh, man ... Don't remind me."

Thomas ran up to the Helmet Man. "Slate, I could be your shield! Just like before! You want me to come, don't you?"

Naomi shot Slate a look. They had already agreed beforehand what had to happen.

"Sorry, kid," Slate said. "You can't go with us, but there's no need to worry. I won't lose to the likes of Cyphrus. You can count on me."

Thomas pouted, but he nodded.

Now the group found themselves approaching *Leviathan*. They would land on the flight deck and make their way to the bridge. It would then be a matter of seizing control of the ship and defeating the Gifted on board.

"Naomi, I have a question," Gilda said over the radio. "If Cyphrus can control tech, why did we bother bringing Magenta with us? Won't she just control it as well?"

"She didn't do it when we were on the Blast from the Past Island," Naomi said. "My guess is Cyphrus can only control electronics either by direct contact or if they have a receiver of some sort. Your walker and this unicopter have their radios on isolated systems, so we're fine. Just don't come into contact with her. The ones you should really worry about are Geppetto and Atlas, but Slate and I can handle them."

"Everyone, hostiles are approaching!" Tim warned.

Straper and Naomi looked out the back of the unicopter. Two fighter jets were trailing behind them, ready to blow them out of the sky.

"Is it Cloak?" Gilda asked.

"No, it's the military," Naomi said. "Seems we get to fight the Western Union too."

CHAPTER 32

"Ready to engage, sir," the pilot crackled over the radio.

Redwood stared at the holographic screen. "All right, fire when—"

"Hang on a minute," Powell said. "We should hold off on killing the Helmet Man and his Merry Men for now."

"Didn't you say we were short on time?" Redwood snapped.

"Sir, this is our chance to kill the Helmet Man!" Marker cried. "We can't keep letting him get away. Not after all he has done."

Powell shot Marker a sideways glance. Its iciness was apparent.

Marker sweated. "I ... I just don't understand your thought process ... sir."

"Neither do I," Redwood said. "Explain yourself, Powell."

"The Helmet Man obviously isn't behind the hijacking," Powell told the briefing room. "He must be here to stop the real culprits. You agree, Ryder?"

"It certainly fits the profile of the Helmet Man," she said. "He is an interventionist by nature. It spawns from his impulsivity and self-righteousness."

"A dangerous combination," Redwood muttered. "But what are you saying, Powell? Are we going to let them board *Leviathan* without any resistance? What if the Helmet Man aggravates the hijackers further?"

"The terrorists already seem as aggravated as they're going to be," Powell said. "Besides, we've seen what the Helmet Man can do. If he can't stop the hijackers, I doubt anyone else can. And once he does our dirty work for us and is about to drop from exhaustion, we'll swoop in and finally capture him. It's a win-win for the Western Union."

"But what if the Helmet Man isn't able to stop the attack?"

"Like I said, we have the nuclear option."

***

The fighter jets closed in, easily keeping up with their prey.

"What are we gonna do?" Straper yelled. "There's no way our unicopter can withstand one of their missiles!"

"Gilda and Slate could lead them away from us and take them out," Naomi said, glancing out the window behind her. "I'll protect the unicopter and—"

Almost lazily, the fighter jets turned around and flew away.

"Hey, are we getting off easy for once?" Straper asked. "This must be a trick."

"It could very well be," Naomi said. "But we don't want to pick a fight. Let's just leave them alone and focus on the task at hand."

Now *Leviathan* was in full view. The massive ship took up a good portion of the sky. They were in awe at how something so large could float like that, but their awe was soon replaced with panic.

Leviathan had just launched dozens of missiles at them.

"Ah, evasive action!" Straper cried.

Naomi needed no encouragement. She expertly flew the unicopter in jerky and unpredictable patterns. Slate shot bolts from his pointed fingers and destroyed all the missiles. Gilda also helped, shooting her own missiles at the launchers on *Leviathan*. The sky was soon littered with explosions. Fire swirled around them. *Leviathan's* mounted guns fired. Slate and Gilda easily dodged the bullets, but they weren't the intended targets.

Naomi swerved the unicopter around a midair explosion. The turbulence constantly rocked the aircraft, but that did not keep her from sensing the incoming barrage of bullets. She raised her hand and stopped them with her mind. The bullets halted momentarily, only to fall to the ground far below, but more and more, thousands upon thousands, kept coming with increasing frequency. Finally, one got past her and managed to hit their rotor. The unicopter jerked sideways. Naomi fought for control.

"We're losing lift," she said as she continued to block incoming bullets. "We got to land. I'll try getting us on deck."

"Hey, we've got more problems!" Straper yelled, pointing up ahead.

At least fifteen unicopters were taking off from *Leviathan's* flight deck.

Multiple drone fighter jets also launched, all of them coming for the kill.

"Cyphrus must be controlling them," Naomi said.

"You guys better get going," Gilda said over the radio. "I'll distract them for you."

"You sure?" Straper asked.

"No, but you need to stop Cyphrus before she kills anyone else. We're going to be over Paris soon. We can't waste any more time."

"Good luck," Naomi said.

"Yeah, we'll be rooting for you," Straper added.

Magenta flew to their right and raised one of its cannon arms. It sent a shrapnel shell at a group of unicopters. One unicopter was hit dead-on and was destroyed instantly. Two others were so badly damaged that they dropped out of the sky. They were over farmland now, so Gilda could reasonably assume that no civilians had gotten hurt below.

Most of the unicopters and drone jets now went after Gilda, who flew her walker far away from *Leviathan*. Four unicopters, however, went after Naomi and Straper. Slate fired lightning bolts at them, frying their electronics. As the foes dropped, Naomi made her final approach to *Leviathan*. However, they were flying too low.

"We're going to crash!" Straper cried. "Pull up, pull up!"

Naomi didn't take the time to explain her next course of action. She let go of the controls, crossed her arms, and concentrated with all her might. The unicopter began to rise as she willed it higher. Straper squeezed his eyes shut.

"Come on..." Naomi muttered. "Just a couple more feet..."

They made it with only half a foot to spare. The unicopter landed roughly on the flight deck. Sparks flew as it skidded on its belly. The seat belts dug into their flesh. The unicopter came to a stop after a few seconds. Naomi gasped, lowering her arms in relief. Straper hyperventilated as he slowly opened his eyes.

"Let's ... get out ... of this unicopter..." Naomi panted. "We're sitting ducks here."

They jumped out of their downed unicopter. Straper took his rifle and handgun, while Naomi brought out gas masks and handed him one.

"Put this on," she told him. "We might encounter nerve gas or nanobots, so don't take this mask off, understand?"

Straper nodded and put it on. "Yeah, no problem, Nomi."

"Please never call me that again."

He adjusted the mask's strap. "Why not? Sounds better."

"Because I'm not a child, and why don't we call you Kevin?"

"Only my douche parents called me that. Besides, Straper is cooler."

"Barely!" Slate shouted as he landed on the flight deck. "Boy, great warm-up! Now it's time for the real workout. Hey, where's my gas mask?"

Naomi sighed. "You don't breathe, remember?"

Slate laughed obnoxiously. "Oh, yeah. Suckers!"

A missile flew at them. Reacting fast, Slate and Naomi jumped back, Naomi pushing Straper back with her powers. The missile struck their crashed unicopter and blew it up. Slate turned and shot a bolt of lightning. It hit the automatic missile launcher that was still intact. The launcher shorted out, down for good.

"You were sloppy," Naomi said, staring daggers at Slate.

"Hey, you didn't do much better. You got knocked out of the air in five seconds flat. At least I can defend myself."

"All right, enough. We don't have much time. Let's head to the bridge."

"Guys, over there!" Straper yelled, pointing at the flaming unicopter.

They all turned to see a figure emerge from the wreckage. It staggered through the fire, undeterred by the heat. When the figure emerged in plain view, irritation immediately began to boil within Naomi.

Thomas smiled nervously. "Hi, everybody... Guess I got found out."

"What are you doing here?" Naomi demanded. Her eyes were practically red with rage, but her face was still as stone. "Why aren't you at the safe house?"

"Ah ... I snuck aboard," Thomas said. "I had to hunt animals while living on the island, so I'm pretty sneaky when I need to be."

"Clearly, you are. Why would you choose to do something so reckless?

This is no place for a child. You had plenty of food and a television at that safe house. I even hired men to watch over the place. You should have stayed there."

"I can't let you guys go alone!" he snapped. Naomi actually took a step back. She didn't expect that kind of anger from such an innocent boy.

"No avoiding it now," Slate said. "He's officially part of the team."

"You're *glad* he's here?" Naomi exclaimed. "Maybe you snuck him aboard!"

"He didn't!" Thomas cried. "It was all me, honest!"

"Honesty is the last thing I expect from you," Naomi spat. "Whatever. We don't have time for arguing. Millions of lives are at stake."

"But what are we going to do with this kid?" Straper asked.

"Slate can watch after him," Naomi said in a detached tone, putting her mask on. "If the little prince wants to be a human shield, who am I to stop him?"

She tossed Thomas a gas mask. The boy caught it and was quick to put it on.

"Let's go," Naomi said. "Slate, you and Thomas take the lead. I'll take the rear."

"Yeah, first wave!" Slate yelled. "My favorite job!"

The Helmet Man grabbed Thomas by the hand and pulled him along. They all ran to the large control tower near the stern of *Leviathan*. Naomi knocked down a door leading inside with a telekinetic push. After entering, they ran down the barren hallways of the ship, coming across a corpse once in a while. The bodies belonged to military personnel who had all died of gunshot wounds. Some of them were self-inflicted, obviously Geppetto's work. Nobody said a word about the bodies, but Thomas tensed up every time they came across one.

They went down two levels, following the signs that directed them to the bridge. Naomi noticed security cameras zooming in on them. Cyphrus must know where they are, so why wasn't anyone coming after them yet? Were they being drawn deeper inside the ship so that the enemy could surround them?

"We're getting close to the bridge," Naomi told them as they ran. "We'll most likely find Cyphrus and the other Gifted there. Slate and I will take them on. You two will—"

A metal door abruptly fell from the ceiling. Naomi rolled backward to avoid getting crushed. The door sealed shut, separating her from the rest of the group. Naomi got up on her feet and cursed. She was just about to knock it down when her limbs seized up. Her legs then began to move on their own. She turned around and started dancing like a ballerina, her head snapping backward. Fear overtook her mind. This feeling was unlike anything she had ever experienced, but she had a good idea of its cause.

"Beautiful," Geppetto mused. "Simply beautiful."

With his hands behind his back, Geppetto walked toward Naomi as she danced. Atlas trailed behind him with an automatic rifle, looking sullen yet alert. Naomi tried to gulp, but her throat wouldn't let her. It was clear that she had been outmaneuvered.

"I never thought you would betray us, Repulsa," Geppetto said. "Then again, I never thought I would betray Sebastian."

***

As the metal door sealed shut behind Slate and the others, another door just ahead of them also came down.

"Move your fannies!" Slate shouted.

They all dashed forward, barely making it as they passed beneath the second metal door. It slammed shut. Two solid barriers now separated them from Naomi.

"We have to go back!" Thomas told Slate. "Naomi needs us!"

Slate rubbed the back of his neck. "Those doors look awfully thick. Don't think I can break through them very quickly. We need to find that Cyphrus chick. Naomi can meet up with us later. Relax, she'll be fine."

"What if she isn't?" Thomas questioned. "She could need our help. Use your beam!"

"You see? This is why she didn't want you here. This mission is too important to go back for just one person, even if that person is super hot. I can't risk using a beam inside the ship either. I might end up killing us all. We gotta leave her behind for now."

"All right ... But will we go back for her?"

"Obviously! You know how much work I've put into trying to woo her?"

Gunfire interrupted the conversation. Everyone ducked down. Bullets struck the door behind them. Six men in gray uniforms were shooting at them from the far end of the hallway. It was obvious they weren't looking to take any prisoners.

"Stay behind me!" Slate shouted to Straper. He picked up Thomas by the back of his neck and stood up, using the boy as a shield.

"Again?" Straper cried. "You can't be fricking serious!"

"You want to take the lead?" Slate snapped. "Thought not. Now let's move!"

More bullets came. Slate crouched low behind Thomas. The young prince jerked around as the deadly projectiles slammed into him, but the Helmet Man held on tight to his shield.

"Whoa, this feels weird!" Thomas yelled over the gunfire.

"You're getting shot!" Straper screamed. "Of course it feels weird!"

"I'm ramming these guys!" Slate told Straper. "Follow me!"

The Helmet Man sprinted toward the gunmen, holding Thomas out in front of him. Straper followed with his head low. The gunmen didn't know what to do, so they just kept firing, hoping to hit the charging enemy in the leg.

But they didn't. Slate plowed right into three gunmen, knocking them over. One of the gunmen that hadn't fallen tried to shoot at Slate, but Straper shot the guy's arm before he had the chance. The gunmen didn't react as his arm flopped to the side. Slate finished the job by zapping the man's chest with a bolt.

Another gunman shot at Straper, who rolled out of the way in time. Slate slammed his elbow into the gunman's head, sending electricity into his skull. The man fell with a thud. The sixth gunman fired at Slate. The Helmet Man blocked his bullets with Thomas's body and struck this gunman with lightning as well.

The three men that had been knocked over were getting back up. Slate didn't hesitate to shoot one guy in the head with lightning. The second man fumbled with his gun and aimed, but Slate bashed Thomas into the man, also shocking him just to be safe.

The last man had lost his gun when he was knocked over, so, instead, he jumped up and threw a punch, eyes red and veins black. Slate moved to the side. The punch sailed past him. The man's fist hit the wall instead. A demonic cry escaped his lips as he swung his arm again. The possessed man managed to knock Slate over, but before the man could attack, two gunshots went off. The man stumbled forward and collapsed.

Straper held his smoking handgun, breathing deeply.

"Whew, nice shot, kid," Slate said, getting to his feet. "I was starting to think you didn't have it in you, what with how you've been nagging me."

"No, I have it in me," Straper said, lowering his gun. "Anyway, that thing isn't human anymore. Those nanobots made sure of that."

Thomas stood up next to Slate, shaking his head clear. "I'm okay. Let's go!"

They jogged the rest of the way, not encountering any more enemies. When they reached their destination, they noticed the metal doors leading to the bridge were wide open.

"Do we just go in?" Straper asked.

"Me first," Slate told him. The Helmet Man ran onto the bridge. His other two companions followed behind. They entered only to find a giant room filled with empty chairs and unmanned navigation equipment.

"Where is everyone?" Straper asked. "Are we late for the party?"

"Welcome aboard, gentlemen," a twisted female voice greeted them.

Straper and Thomas stopped moving as if someone had pressed the pause button. Fear was clearly visible in their eyes. Straper took out his handgun and pointed it at his own head in a suicidal gesture. His lips unconsciously trembled.

"Best not move, Slate," Cyphrus said, standing on a balcony above them. "Or you'll suddenly find yourself with one less friend."

Slate groaned. "Ah, crap."

"Although I am surprised you have *any* friends, what with that odd head-gear of yours."

"Says the lady who looks like she's about to skin a bunch of Dalmatians."

Cyphrus snickered and settled herself in the commander's chair. She turned to Thomas. "Hello, boy. It's been a long time, hasn't it? I know you don't remember me, but I most certainly remember you. After all, it's not every day you kidnap a prince."

CHAPTER 33

The battle was short. Even so, Gilda should have remembered something about it.

But she didn't. She was on autopilot, adrenaline pumping through her. There was no thought, only reflex and instinct. The aircraft pursuing her were fast, but Magenta was faster, ducking and dodging, missiles zooming past. Bullets pinned against her walker's armor but did little to no damage. At first, it was hard to deal with all this stimulation, but she soon found a state of mind that allowed her to operate at maximum efficiency, blocking everything else out.

She didn't just dodge, however. She also attacked. Her walker spun around as it flew upward, missiles and shells of all kinds launching out of Magenta's arms. Almost all of them hit their mark. The enemies' movements were predictable. Not that they weren't dangerous. It was just that they lacked spontaneity. Machines just weren't capable of imagination. That was why human pilots were still often used for aircraft and walkers.

One at a time, Gilda blasted her enemies out of the sky. Flaming metal carcasses fell and hit the ground thousands of feet below. Tim helped her lock on targets, but it was ultimately her who decided if they should fire or not. She first just fired at anything that Tim selected for her, but her ammo soon started to run out, so she became more careful about what she shot down. Planes were hit. Unicopters exploded. Drones crashed into each other. It was madness. It was exhilarating.

"Ms. Gilda, you have just run out of missiles," Tim said. "All you have left is bullets and some nonlethal weaponry."

Gilda didn't answer him as she flew toward the remaining aircraft. Magenta punched one unicopter, crushing its fuselage, and spun one of its thin legs into another unicopter. They were smashed to pieces. Smoke and debris filled the air. The remaining fighter jets circled around Gilda, unable to detect Magenta through all that heat and smoke. The machines decided to wait for the smoke to clear, for their ammo was running low too. They would wait for Gilda to make the first move.

And she did.

Nets flew out of the smoke, taking the drones by surprise. Each jet got at least one wrapped around it. One jet became so tangled that it went down. The rest of them tried to shake off the nets, doing barrel rolls and other fancy maneuvers.

Gilda launched her walker out of the smoke. Magenta smashed one jet in half with a swinging arm and kicked another. It wasn't long before the last enemy aircraft was destroyed.

"That was incredible, Gilda!" Tim exclaimed. "Only experienced pilots have ever pulled off maneuvers like that. Most excellent!"

"Thanks," Gilda said, bringing herself back to reality. She seemed dazed, almost as if waking up. What an odd feeling...

Her console began to beep. An urgent siren then went off.

Gilda bristled. "What's that?"

"Ms. Gilda, I'm detecting radiation," Tim said. "It's coming from those two Western Union jets that were following us earlier."

Gilda remembered how those jets had stopped following them for no apparent reason. According to the radar, they seemed to be circling around back to *Leviathan*.

"How come we're only now sensing it?" Gilda asked.

"They must be prepping their missiles," Tim said. "Oh, dear. This is not good."

Gilda's mouth fell open. It all became clear to her.

Leviathan was about to be nuked, Slate and everyone else along with it.

***

"Hold the phone," Slate said, pointing at Cyphrus. "So, you really did kidnap Thomas when he was a baby. What the hell was that for?"

Cyphrus looked down on Slate with a sneer. "I'll be happy to explain, but you must first fully understand your predicament before we continue."

A group of armed men stepped onto the bridge. President Hynes and Captain Abel were among them. The others wore either gray uniforms or suits. What they all had in common were their blank expressions. These were the victims of the nanobots. Their free will was gone, replaced by unquestioning obedience. The shells that used to be humans surrounded Slate and aimed their weapons at him.

Naomi walked into the room soon after, her gas mask off, followed by Geppetto and Atlas. Geppetto wore a sly smirk from knowing he was in complete control. Atlas pointed his weapon at Naomi's back.

Straper still held a gun to his own head, Geppetto able to will him to pull the trigger at any time. Thomas also stood there, frozen and scared. The only time the two of them moved was to take their masks off.

"As you can see, all your friends are being held hostage," Cyphrus told Slate. "If not for that helmet of yours, Geppetto would already have ensnared you with his powers, which is why we are forced to take such elaborate measures."

"Then why wait?" Slate asked. "Just kill me and be done with it."

Cyphrus smiled. "Cloak is weak. Almost all the Gifted are either dead or out of commission. What you see here is the last of us. Cloak's resources are dwindling as well. Fellow criminal and terrorist organizations along with other clients have given us a wide berth ever since the Helios Tower incident, not to mention that many of our employees are also dead. In all honesty, Slate, you really did a number on us."

"So, this is a last gasp of a dying power? Great, so what do you need me for? While we're at it, why is Mentor chasing me?"

"The Mentor isn't real, remember?"

"All right, forget it. Let's go back to what we were talking about earlier. You admitted to kidnapping the kid, right?"

"Correct. Geppetto, release the boy."

Geppetto shot her a look. "You sure about that?"

"I am. He may be invulnerable, but he is still only a child."

Rolling his eyes discreetly, Geppetto released the prince. Thomas gasped and fell to his knees. He clenched his fists and let out a small whimper.

"Quit mewling," Cyphrus spat. "Ask me anything, boy. I am the reason you were trapped on that island all your natural life. Is crying on the floor all you're going to do?"

Thomas calmed himself, took a breath, and got onto his feet. Fear was written on his face, but he faced Cyphrus without backing down.

"Why did you hurt my friends?" the prince demanded.

"Because they were inconsequential," Cyphrus said. "Why don't you ask me something that matters, or is your imagination that limited?"

"It does matter, you witch!"

"They were androids. It's foolish to have an attachment to them."

Thomas trembled with raw anger. "Naomi told me what you did. You stole me from my mum… You killed my dad…"

"You don't even remember your parents. Quit feigning outrage."

"Better watch your mouth," Slate said. "I don't care if you're a woman. I'll smack the shit outta you. Now spill it. Why'd you kidnap this kid? What did he ever do to you?"

Cyphrus sighed. It didn't seem like she would answer at first, but then she got up from her chair and started pacing around the balcony. She did this for about a minute before speaking.

"Our lives were misery," she said. "No parents … no love … tortured daily … forced to kill… That was our childhood. After we escaped the Keymasters, our situation hardly improved. At least the military fed us and kept us clothed. But for a time, we had to use our powers to act like petty thieves, and we kept on killing. It wasn't until years later that we became the glorious criminal organization that is, or was, Cloak.

"Ten years ago, Cloak was starting to take off, but most of the money we made went to Sebastian so he could fund his secret projects. We barely had enough to spend on ourselves. Crumbs... I always had to settle for crumbs.

"Then one day, after returning from a mission, blood staining my hands, I saw a crowd move like sheep toward a park. I followed, curious to see what had entranced them, but what I found... I saw the British royal family. They were waving to the stupid masses, clown-like grins plastered on their faces. In the queen's hands was a little infant who everyone fawned over, who everybody cared for, who everybody loved."

Now Cyphrus was pacing around her chair like mad, a look of demented anguish strewn over her face. Her eyeliner ran down her powdered face, but she just kept pacing.

"You, it was you!" she shrieked at Thomas. "You had love! You had wealth! But what did I have? Nothing! What made you so special? What made you so excellent? Were you truly better than me, or was it yet another swindle?"

"If you wanted revenge, why didn't you kill the kid?" Slate asked.

"I wanted to show him off first ... let the other Gifted get a good look at him ... let them know we can fight back ... But only Houdini and Ember found it amusing. And Sebastian ... he had the gall to tell me that I had stepped out of line, that I had endangered Cloak and the rest of the Gifted. He chastised me, that slime ... him of all people."

She turned to Thomas again. "To add insult to injury, Sebastian kept you alive, giving you powers that you don't even appreciate. Nanobots were injected into you, reforming your flesh down to the molecular level. Your skin is natural Kevlar, your bones are stronger than steel, and you take it all for granted. Spoiled brat! Western trash! All you filthy termites need to be exterminated. It is my destiny to do so. It is my privilege!"

"Is *that* your reason for kidnapping a baby?" Slate asked. An unusual coldness had appeared in his voice. Thomas almost jumped back. He had never expected a tone so ominous from Slate, the epitome of foolishness.

"Do I need any other reason?" Cyphrus asked. "That boy was the pride of the Western Union. I took that pride away. Incognito may be my enemy, but he and I share the same hatred of the West. And you should too. You should hate them for what they did to you, for what they did to all of us."

Slate turned to Geppetto and Atlas. Both of them looked dispirited.

"Is all that true?" Slate asked. "Was life really worse after I went away?"

"More than you can imagine," Geppetto said, trying not to look at Cyphrus.

"And do you really think that's an excuse to gas entire cities?"

Geppetto seemed to wake up. Atlas became alert as well.

"What are you talking about?" Geppetto asked.

"Don't play dumb," Slate snapped. "Give me a real answer. I have the right to be pissed. She framed the attack on me, ruining my already bad name."

"What is he talking about?" Geppetto asked. "Cyphrus, what did you do?"

She shot Geppetto a look that almost sent a chill through him.

"I killed ten thousand people," she said without a hint of regret. "Paris is next, followed by London, followed by—"

"But why?" Atlas growled in a low tone. "This is too extreme."

"In order to wed the emperor, I had to get him a wedding gift the likes of which he's never seen. The emperor is a sadist. He hates the West with all his heart. Corrupting their leaders is one thing, but exterminating millions of vermin is a whole new level of pleasure."

"You're out of your mind!" Geppetto yelled. "You're just like Sebastian! I didn't get rid of one crazy leader just to get another. We're professionals! Has everyone forgotten that?"

"Do you really care about the scum down there? They were the ones who let the Western Union come into power. They are the ones responsible for what happened to us. They are the benefactors of violence, of imperialism, of oppression, of our misery. It's their fault. Let them taste their own medicine."

"But now you're no better than them!"

"How can you say that? We're all we have! Do you think I want to become an empress solely for myself? We'll live in luxury for the rest of our lives. This is it, the end to our struggle! No more will we be manipulated. No more will we obey the Western Union, mad scientists, or our so-called Mentor. We're safe! We're free!"

Cyphrus pointed to Slate, her eyes unfocused and agitated. "And you, Helmet Man! You can join us too! These people surrounding you aren't your friends. They despise you! They hate you! They use you! All we have is each other. That's the true reason I never killed Sebastian, because he's one of us. And so are you. You can join us! Come, Slate! Abandon these frauds so we can at last take what is ours, together!"

Nobody uttered a word. Thomas stared at Cyphrus. His own anger and outrage were ebbing. That lady's story... Was that her life? It didn't even sound like a life. How could he hate someone so ... broken?

The Helmet Man started to clap. "I finally understand. Oh, man... I finally understand."

Cyphrus lowered her pointing arm. Her left eye twitched.

"I always knew we were monsters," Slate told her. "But man, I'm realizing just how messed up we really are. I kill people and brush it off with some joke. I used a kid like a tool, treated him like a soldier, because all my life, that's how I was treated. I never thought it was wrong. I still don't, to tell you the truth."

Thomas kept quiet, staring at Slate with intense focus.

"Look at us," Slate said. "I've killed more people than I can count, and I barely feel any regret. Hell, I like it sometimes. You just killed ten thousand people with no remorse. Maybe it was the Western Union who put us on this track, but we chose to stay on it."

"Then what makes you better than me?" Cyphrus spat. "What could possibly give you the moral high ground over me?"

"Because of my friends. They keep me in line and tell me when I'm wrong. They don't hide their feelings when they disagree with me. And they definitely don't always laugh at my jokes. I can tell you that for a fact."

Geppetto and Atlas looked at each other. Cyphrus merely scoffed.

"That's the thing," Slate told them. "I don't want friends like you. All the Gifted do is tell each other sob stories to justify acting like psychos. That's why Naomi left Cloak. That's why I'll never join, because you don't want to get better. You just want an excuse."

Cyphrus didn't respond for several seconds, only looking down at Slate from on high. After a minute of this, she gave a small smirk. She walked down from the balcony and approached Slate until she was right in front of him.

"You know what? I don't want friends like you either." She reached into her fur coat and produced two syringes, each filled with black fluid. "Killing you would be a waste. I don't know if these nanobots are effective on the Gifted or not. Our genetic makeup is much more different from that of normal humans, but I have a feeling it will work. Both you and Repulsa shall become my servants. We will be together, whether you like it or not."

"Do you really expect me to stand here and get injected with that crap?"

"If you move, they die."

"But if I don't move, you'll just kill them afterward. Might as well go out with a flash!"

The Helmet Man threw his hand up. Geppetto flew backward, smashing into the wall with a sickening crack. He slumped to the floor, unconscious. Naomi and Straper found themselves free from Geppetto's clutches.

The first thing they did with their freedom was shut their eyes.

A bright burst of electricity came out of Slate's hand. Everyone who didn't have their eyes covered was temporarily blinded. The blank-faced minions had their red eyes nearly burnt out. Atlas grunted. Cyphrus squealed.

Slate and the others, meanwhile, used the opportunity to strike.

The fight was on.

CHAPTER 34

Slate raising his hand was the signal.

They all knew to close their eyes if he did that. They also knew they needed Geppetto out of commission. What Geppetto failed to realize was that Naomi could still use her telekinesis even if she was unable to move, although it was harder to control. All she managed to do was knock him backward, but it had been enough. Now they were free and ready to rumble.

After Slate blinded his enemies, he shot bolts from both hands, taking eight people out in five seconds flat. Naomi also attacked, snapping the necks of six opponents. Even Straper helped by shooting three gunmen in the chest.

Atlas was stunned for a moment but then turned his gun on Slate. Before the hulk could shoot, lightning hit him, burning half his face. Atlas dropped his weapon and roared in pain.

Two of the human puppets managed to make a stand. One was the former Captain Abel. He fired his gun at Straper, who rolled out of the way, barely dodging. He lifted his rifle and shot Abel right in the head, putting the captain to rest.

The other puppet who fought back was President Hynes. The man was a former soldier, and a good one at that. He was already dangerous without the added strength that the nanobots gave him. Now he was almost as strong as Atlas.

Hynes lunged at Slate. The Helmet Man moved to the side and managed not to get tackled. Slate shot a bolt, but Hynes ducked just in time, grabbed a gun from the floor, and fired it. The bullet merely bounced off Slate's helmet. The Helmet Man roundhouse-kicked the gun out of the president's hand.

But Hynes wasn't finished. He raised a fist and threw it with all his might. Slate ducked, the blow never making contact. The Helmet Man swung his own fist and struck the side of Hynes's skull. Hynes's head spun around. Teeth flew out. His neck snapped like a twig, and the president hit the floor, dead as a dodo.

The entire room was soon still. Cyphrus and Atlas had escaped during the chaos, taking the unconscious Geppetto with them. Only Slate and his friends remained.

"Dude, you just killed the president," Straper said with amazement and horror.

"Oh, do I get a prize for that?" Slate asked.

"All right, enough," Naomi said. "Slate and I are going after Cyphrus and the others. If she isn't stopped, we'll never get *Leviathan* under our control, and Paris will be history. I'll attempt to coerce Cyphrus into stopping the ship for us. Straper, you stay here with Thomas and watch over the bridge. We might need you here if something goes wrong."

Straper nodded. "Will do."

"Good luck, Slate," Thomas said. "You're a hero, no matter what anyone else says."

"Shucks, thanks, kid," Slate replied. "Hope you guys don't die."

With that short farewell, the Helmet Man and Naomi sprinted away.

***

Atlas trudged behind Cyphrus, who moved at a much more frantic pace. The giant carried the unconscious Geppetto with one arm, his other arm injured. One of the bullets fired by Captain Abel had accidentally hit Atlas in his left palm and broke several bones. They had healed all wrong, and his hand now looked like a deformed fin.

"This can't be happening," Cyphrus seethed. "Now I know how Houdini felt as his entire world crumbled around him."

"Cyphrus, it's time to retreat," Atlas said. "We have failed."

"We need to complete our mission. I must become empress. Even if we escaped, the Chinese would hunt us down for the rest of our lives."

"Enough is enough. You were right. We need each other. But Slate was also right. I cannot be a true friend if I continue to blindly follow you around."

Cyphrus stopped in her tracks and turned her eyes toward him. "Are ... are you betraying me? No, not you too! You're all I have left!"

"You still have me ... for now. But if you don't listen to my advice, you will lose me. Don't allow that to happen. Please."

Atlas was so busy talking to Cyphrus that he didn't notice her stabbing two needles into his useless arm until it was too late.

"What are you—?" Atlas began, but he stopped talking as blood began to flow from his nose. The giant fell to his knees, dropped Geppetto on the floor, and grabbed his head in agony. The veins on his head turned black. His eyes became bloodshot. Foam bubbled forth from his mouth. A roar escaped his lips as his mind was ripped apart.

Cyphrus stared at the transformation of her friend. At first, she couldn't believe what she had done, but then a laugh escaped her throat. "Now you can't leave me. You were going to betray me, run away, and join Slate on his little adventures. But I stopped you! Yes, for your own good!"

A group of gunmen approached from behind. They wore blank expressions. These mind-controlled crewmen had been sweeping *Leviathan* for any remaining survivors.

Now they had other plans.

Cyphrus laughed. "Yes, you're here! Good, go kill the Helmet Man and his lackeys. Atlas will lead you. Go! Kill them all!"

The gunmen looked at each other for a moment before nodding.

They pointed their guns at Cyphrus.

"What ... no ... you can't do this..." Cyphrus whispered.

Atlas rose behind her, eyes red, all compassion gone. There was only a puppet now.

And Cyphrus wasn't pulling the strings anymore.

"I command you to stop!" Cyphrus ordered, but it sounded more like begging. "I made you! I made you my puppets! Stop! You have to stop!"

The gunmen pulled their triggers.

A metal door came down between her and them just in time. Cyphrus heard the bullets hit the metal and shrieked at the sound. How could this happen? How could everything deteriorate so fast? Was it the nanobots? Could she control them? No, she needed direct contact, and they were already ingested. The damage was done. She had run out of allies.

Atlas punched his fist through the door and grabbed her by the coat. Cyphrus shrieked again, but she managed to slip out of her coat. Picking up Geppetto, she scrambled away down the hall. She willed more doors to close behind her as she heard Atlas rip apart the first metal door with his bare hands. Escape! She had to escape!

No ... she couldn't. Not yet. She might not have Hynes or the other politicians anymore, but she still had *Leviathan*. Maybe the emperor might show lenience if she managed to gas a few more cities. She just needed to kill everyone on board first.

"I'm ... not ... done ... yet..." she panted.

***

"So, that's your plan," Eisenhorn growled. "You Chinamen plan to brainwash Hynes, my comrade, as well as those other politicians. That way you can sabotage the Western Union and continue your plans for global domination without any trouble. Talk about ridiculous. Sounds like something cartoon supervillains would do."

"Do not act so horrified," Mao said, oddly calm. "The Western Union would have done the same if they had obtained the nanomachines first."

Eisenhorn had just heard the prime minister go on for some time about Operation Leviathan. Mao had been angry at first, but now he was behaving a little too chill for Eisenhorn's liking. At least angry people were more predictable. Lily, meanwhile, sat on a chair across from Eisenhorn with a playful smirk.

"Maybe the Western Union would have done the same," Eisenhorn said. "But we don't gas entire cities just for giggles, unlike you depraved imperialists."

"That was not planned for," Mao said as he paced around his luxurious apartment. "You see, one of Cloak's Gifted, a woman named Cyphrus, if you could call her a woman, proposed to marry my dear father."

"What, that's crazy!"

"At least we agree on that," Mao said, walking up to a red cabinet. "Of course, the emperor doesn't just marry anyone. His wives must have something of great value to offer him. Beauty, wealth, political influence—"

"What does your creepy girlfriend offer you?" Eisenhorn questioned, pointing at Lily.

Mao scowled. "Do not say such foulness. She's my bodyguard, as well as my half-sister."

"All Black Lotus agents are children of emperor and Mistress Lotus," Lily explained in fractured English. "It what make us so loyal."

"That explains a few things," Eisenhorn grumbled.

"Cyphrus wished to marry the emperor," Mao said, now rummaging through his cabinet. "But she was getting old, was leading a dying organization, and had already failed the emperor once, so she offered her last remaining gift: entertainment."

"Gassing millions to death ain't entertainment!"

"I must admit, my father has strange tastes in terms of comedy," Mao said, still looking through his cabinet. "Of course, I couldn't let that Western wench steal the throne away from me. That is why I reprogrammed the nanomachines. We were the ones who manufactured the weapon and paid for everything. Cloak merely supplied the recipe. So now, at the point when the mission has either succeeded or failed, the mind-controlled subjects will do away with Cyphrus and those other two supersoldiers."

"Slate and his friends will stop you," Eisenhorn said. "If not him, then the Western Union will find out about this scheme of yours."

Ignoring the general, Mao took something out of the cabinet and closed it.

He snapped his fingers at Lily. She plugged her ears and hummed to herself.

"She does not need to hear this," Mao said. "Now, you are most certainly wondering why I brought you here. You see, I have a ... hobby of sorts."

He held a golf club in his hand, a heavy driver stained with blood.

"I hate my father," Mao said. "He is deranged, pathetic, decrepit, and weak. This is the same man who fed my mother to dogs in front of me after discovering she had a second lover. He is beloved by all his subjects, but I can barely stomach the sight of him. And yet I also envy him in a way. I want to be him. I want to live like him, with no morals, no equals. I want to become so powerful that never again would I need to care for anything or anyone. I could float away. I could float away to Heaven..."

Eisenhorn didn't say anything, not liking where this was going.

"I cannot kill my father, for obvious reasons," the prime minister said, swinging his club. "All I can do is bide my time until he perishes of natural causes, but that doesn't satisfy my immediate urge to ascend, to take the place of my repellent father, which is why I must resort to other means."

Mao approached Eisenhorn. The prime minister's face was still, not a trace of emotion visible. Lily continued to hum and plug her ears, but she kept her eyes on Mao, eager for the violence yet to come.

"You're not the first," Mao told Eisenhorn. "You're my fifty-second. All of you were just like my father. Deluded, old, clinging to past glory ... I never had a Westerner before, though. It will be interesting."

"Now hold on here," Eisenhorn said, raising his quivering hands. "I'm an ambassador ... remember? You can't just kill me."

"We will soon wage war on the West," Mao went on. "Will we succeed in world domination? Unlikely, but we will most certainly succeed in taking the rest of Asia and the Pacific Islands. The West shall die a slow death, decaying until it becomes nothing but a memory. The time for the Chinese is now, and I will lead them into the glorious future."

Mao swung his club down. Eisenhorn rolled out of the way, the driver hitting the couch instead. The general snatched up a stone statue of a dragon, planning to use it as a weapon. No way would he become another victim of this serial killer.

But right as Eisenhorn was about to fight back, Lily appeared out of nowhere and jabbed him in the arm. He cried out and dropped the statue. The general kicked her in the leg, but he might as well have been kicking a lamppost. He grimaced at the pain.

"What are you made out of, woman?" he cried.

Lily laughed and backhanded him. The general spun through the air and fell on the couch. He tasted blood. This woman was not normal. She was too fast, too hard, too resilient. Whoever she was, Eisenhorn could now see why Mao had made her his bodyguard.

Eisenhorn got on his feet. Lily giggled. A thin sword extended out of her palm, literally growing out of her flesh. She had somehow hidden it inside her body. No blood was visible. Eisenhorn stared at the sword and gagged. This woman was definitely not normal.

"Black Lotus agents also cyborgs," Lily said with a hungry grin, her snakelike eyes sizing up Eisenhorn. "Let's dance, old man!"

She swung her blade, almost cutting Eisenhorn in half, but the general had vaulted over the couch. Lily only managed to slice the cushions open. She shrieked in amusement.

"Lily, he's mine!" Mao ordered in Mandarin. "Just disable him!"

Lily jumped over the couch with little effort and landed behind Eisenhorn. The general had no time to react as she cut his Achilles tendon, causing his right foot to give way. Eisenhorn cried in pain and went down on his hands and knees. His blood soaked into the carpet. Lily kicked him in the gut. He fell on his side and coughed.

"He disabled, all right." Lily giggled, the sword retracting into her hand. Not even a scratch was visible on her palm. The general, despite his pain, had to stare. How could the Chinese make cyborgs when they didn't even have light bulbs?

"What a foolish old man..." Mao breathed, wearing no expression as he approached Eisenhorn. "Just like my foolish old father. There are just too many foolish old men. It's up to me to kill them all. Yes ... embrace your death. Failures deserve nothing more..."

Mao raised his club.

CHAPTER 35

The evacuation of Paris was more orderly than the one in Rome. Even so, Rome had been only a demonstration. Now the terrorists were planning a more massive assault, and nobody wanted to be around to witness it.

The streets were congested, filled with every wheeled vehicle that the city had to offer, from delivery trucks to more agile bikes. Soldiers handed out disposable gas masks to civilians, but they soon ran out. Boats on the Seine ferried people away. All the vessels were at maximum capacity. Most of downtown had been evacuated, but there were still three hundred thousand people within the city limits.

And *Leviathan* was only twenty minutes away.

*****

Slate and Naomi sprinted down the halls. Neither ran out of stamina. A small trail of blood left behind by Atlas made it easy for them to track their enemy. As they ran, Naomi crushed ventilation shafts and yanked out wires from walls.

"Vandalism seems a bit beneath you," Slate said.

"I'm making sure Cyphrus can't pump nerve gas through the halls or into the bridge," Naomi said. "She's bound to try anything at this point in order to win."

Bullets flew at them, almost hitting Slate, but he dove out of the way. Naomi saw a group of gunmen firing at them from an adjoining corridor. More bullets came. She diverted them before forcing a metal door to come down and crush the men. The puppets made no noise as they drowned to death in their own blood.

"Whoa, gruesome," Slate muttered. "Crap, behind you!"

Naomi spun around. A redheaded giant stood at the other end of the hallway.

"Atlas..." she said under her breath. "Seems he wants a fight."

"Great, I still feel sore from the last time I fought this guy," Slate said.

"No, you need to go after Cyphrus. Atlas is mine."

"You're gonna take on that freak alone? I could barely beat the guy by myself."

"That's because you aren't half as clever as I am. Get going. We don't have time to argue."

Slate shrugged. "All right, just try to leave a pretty corpse."

The Helmet Man bolted away. Naomi turned to stare at Atlas, who stared back. She raised her hands slowly. Atlas cracked his knuckles, his eyes redder than an albino's.

Naomi scowled. "Atlas ... what did Cyphrus do to you?"

Atlas didn't respond. All he did was charge.

***

Cyphrus made it to the flight deck. Harsh wind welcomed her. She shivered, wishing she still had her fur coat. It took a minute to jog across the endless flight deck until she reached the center. She went to her knees and placed her hand on the metal surface.

A rumble went through the flight deck as it opened up.

A blue walker rose from beneath.

Cyphrus strained to grin, but she grinned, nonetheless. With shaky legs, she climbed into the walker. A few beads of sweat ran down her face. She swore to herself, worrying about her makeup as she situated herself in her seat. The cockpit door closed behind her. Cyphrus took a moment to collect herself. She had found a security office to put Geppetto in while he was still unconscious. He ought to be safe there for the time being.

For now, Cyphrus had to worry about herself and killing her foes. She placed a hand on the console. The walker was picking up signals from two jets flying high above her. They felt awfully suspicious, so she probed their computers to see what their mission was. When she discovered what those jets had planned, she almost had a heart attack.

They were going to nuke *Leviathan*.

Cyphrus calmed herself. She had anticipated that the Western Union would get this desperate, so she used her power to connect with the jets and fed them new instructions. By the time she was done, Cyphrus almost wanted to snicker.

Those jets wouldn't be up in the sky for long.

***

A lone passenger sat in one of the two jets. It was on autopilot, so the passenger did nothing except flex his fingers in anticipation. The military had waited patiently for the Helmet Man to stop the attack himself, but they had wasted all the time they could spare. *Leviathan* was getting dangerously close to Paris. They had to nuke the vessel. It didn't hurt knowing that one of the Western Union's most wanted terrorists was on board.

"Missile launch in sixty seconds," the computer said.

The jet then began to go up.

"Missile launch cancelled," the computer said.

The passenger leaned forward, frowning. The jet was behaving oddly. The Western Union thought that staying far away from *Leviathan* would protect the jets from being hacked. Now it seemed that assumption was dead wrong.

The other jet also flew upward at a steep angle. The passenger saw that there were no more clouds at this altitude, the sky getting darker.

The passenger realized what was happening. The jets were going to keep going up until their engines froze over. The passenger cursed. He pushed the emergency ejection button, but it did not respond. His vision became blurry. He would have to use the manual eject. Just as he was about to pass out, he pulled the lever to his right.

The seat ejected, launching the passenger out just in time. The parachute was soon deployed. He could see that the engines of the jets had frozen over. The jets stopped their ascension and hung in midair for a moment before plummeting back to earth. He briefly thought that the nukes could accidentally go off when the jets crashed, but numerous fail-safes and safety protocols would prevent a nuclear detonation. Nonetheless, it seemed the jets had failed to stop *Leviathan*.

Now it was up to him.

***

"The jets are down?" Redwood yelled. "Impossible!"

"This is definitely upsetting," Ryder said, not sounding upset.

Anxious murmurs filled the briefing room. Powell took control of the situation by putting his thick fingers into his mouth and whistling.

"This is unacceptable!" he yelled. "How soon can we get more jets up there?"

"Fifteen minutes," an officer told him.

"Paris will be exterminated by then!" Gerald Marker cried, looking faint. "Can't we nuke them from a ground site?"

"*Leviathan* would be too close to Paris by the time the warheads arrive," Redwood said. "The fallout would do even worse damage than the nerve gas."

"Then what else can we do?"

"I believe I have a solution," Ryder said.

Redwood shot her a look. "You do?"

"Yes, my agent is ready. He will stop *Leviathan*. It is the only option left available to us."

Admiral Redwood turned to Powell. The vice president nodded.

"Very well," Redwood told Ryder. "Be smart about this, Ryder. No unnecessary risks. Millions of lives are in your hands."

"Understood," Ryder said. "I will not fail."

***

Naomi fled down the halls, using her powers to close the metal doors behind her. It was an attempt to impede Atlas that proved futile. Without slowing, Atlas ran right through one of the doors she had just closed. It had easily been an inch thick. The giant dashed after her, the veins on his head pumping black blood. There was no way she could fight him with brute strength alone. She needed an advantage. Fighting in these hallways would get her killed. She saw signs that directed her to a ballroom. That sounded like a place where she could make a stand.

But Atlas was catching up to her. She stopped running and now flew horizontally down the halls. Up ahead, she saw two large doors that led into the ballroom. She glided through them and slammed them shut with her mind. She almost gasped when she saw dozens of bodies lying on the ballroom floor. They were former crewmen of *Leviathan*. The nerve gas had been vented out of the room, so at least that wouldn't kill her. Naomi didn't have time to feel revolted or saddened. She had a battle to fight. She hid behind a trolley full of dishes. She couldn't stay here forever, but it might give her the element of surprise.

Atlas smashed through the doors, leaving a large hole in his wake. Pieces of metal stuck from his flesh, but he pulled them out, skin and muscle healing. Naomi resisted the impulse to vomit and instead planned how to proceed.

The red-haired giant lumbered over to the right. He didn't even seem to be looking for her. Naomi now noticed that one of his hands was missing. He must have removed it because it was too badly damaged.

Atlas saw a fire axe hanging on a nearby wall and snatched it up. He then walked over to the nearest corpse and grabbed its arm. Naomi looked away, squeamish, as Atlas removed the body's hand. He took the severed hand and pressed it against his stump. A nasty sucking sound was produced as the hand fused onto his arm.

Naomi couldn't believe it. That was some trick. But now she had an opportunity to attack. Looking up at the ceiling, she noticed a fancy chandelier hanging above Atlas. She focused her mind on the light fixture and yanked on it. With a crack, the chandelier came loose and plummeted down. Atlas barely had time to look up before the chandelier struck him and pinned him to the floor.

This was her chance. Naomi ran from behind the trolley and went for the kill.

But Atlas threw the chandelier at her. Naomi raised her hands and stopped the object in midair. It floated there for a second before she dropped it. He hadn't been disabled after all. Naomi swore as the giant charged at her. Atlas threw a punch, but she ducked before it could land. He swung again, also missing, and then again, with the same result. Naomi sent invisible blows into her opponent's torso, but Atlas wasn't damaged. He swung a massive leg at her. She floated over it and dropped back down.

Grunting, Atlas ran at her, throwing countless punches. His blows were so fast and powerful that even one direct hit might kill her. Despite the impressive performance, Naomi dodged them all with expert ease. Atlas might have strength, but she had agility.

Naomi sighed. This dance was getting old. She jumped up and flew to the nearest exit. Atlas followed her, his legs muscles bulging.

She glided into a hallway and made a sharp turn to the right. Atlas pursued her, not even breathing hard. He skidded to a stop, for Naomi was in his sights. Not only that, but it was clear that she had nowhere else to go. The hallway she stood in appeared to be a dead end. Atlas crouched down and got ready to charge.

"Atlas, we were comrades once," Naomi said. "If you're still in there, know that you were the best of us. You only stayed with Cloak because of Geppetto. I wish I were half as loyal as you. I truly do. And now you are nothing but a mindless beast. Please, forgive me."

Atlas sprinted forward to flatten Naomi, but she floated up at the last second, pressing herself against the ceiling. Atlas ran under her at full speed.

Naomi let out a sad sigh. It was over. Despite what Atlas thought, the hallway wasn't a dead end. It had an emergency exit.

She unlocked it with her mind.

Atlas had no time to change direction. The door swung open with him running right at it. Air blew out of the ship, blowing Atlas out as well. He clawed for a handhold and managed to grab the door handle. Another force was also pulling him out, however, something even stronger than gravity or the changing air pressure. One of the giant turbines that propelled *Leviathan* was sucking him in. But he was stronger. He began to pull himself into the ship.

"Don't prolong the inevitable," Naomi said. She focused on his wrist and broke it.

Atlas's grip loosened. The handle slipped out of his hand. The turbine sucked him in.

In Atlas's last moments, for the briefest of seconds, the nanobots in his head were unable to combat his regenerative powers. Memories resurfaced. Individuality returned. He was himself again, if only for an instant. He thought of Geppetto. He thought of his wasted life. Why did they stay with Cloak? Was it just all they knew? Was the Mentor's grasp that irresistible? Or were they just the most insidious kind of evil, the kind of evil that believes it is good?

No answer came to Atlas as he was sucked into the turbine.

Only pain.

***

The Helmet Man emerged onto the flight deck. The wind howled as *Leviathan* continued its flight toward Paris. A shudder went through the ship, causing Slate to briefly lose his balance. Smoke billowed from one of the turbines as it died. *Leviathan* only needed one of its gargantuan turbines to move, however. He considered disabling the second one, but he knew he couldn't leave Cyphrus alone, and *Leviathan's* weapons would still be operational. Stopping her meant stopping *Leviathan*.

Slate clenched his fists. He walked out to the middle of the vast flight deck. The remains of their unicopter were still there, but that didn't interest him in the slightest.

"Where are you, ya crazy dame?" Slate yelled. "You've caused me a lot of trouble. It's time to face the music, once and for all!"

Sensing movement behind him, the Helmet Man rolled out of the way. A blue foe sliced the flight deck with a blade of some sort. It left a clean gash in the metal. If he hadn't rolled away in time, he would have been cut in half.

"That's some nice hardware you go there," Slate said, getting back on his feet. "But be careful with that sword. You could poke an eye out with that baby."

Cyphrus did not respond to his ramblings. The blue walker touched down on the flight deck. Two large wings folded inward into the bulky frame of the mecha. Tinted windows obscured Cyphrus from view. The white symbol of the Western Union was painted on the walker's front, its boldness almost tacky.

But what grabbed Slate's attention was the ten-foot-long sword. It extended out of the walker's right arm and vibrated at a high frequency, reminding him of a buzz saw. The vibrations likely helped the sword slice through resilient materials, but the blade's thickness and weight alone seemed substantial enough to do major damage. Slate was definitely glad not to have been sliced by that.

"I am the weakest of the Gifted," Cyphrus said from the walker's loudspeaker in a frank but hissing tone. "My powers are only useful whenever there are electronics around. Even Geppetto can defend himself better than me. After all, people are far more commonplace than fancy walkers like these."

"Thought Magenta was the only flying walker."

Cyphrus giggled with a hint of nervousness. "Yes, President Hynes must have been eager for the end of *Leviathan's* tour so he could show it off, the Western Union's first flying walker ... Sapphire. You didn't think that Plato girl would get to have the only one forever, did you? I'm so glad. Now I have one too, except it's better. Ironic how her famous father created this superior version. Do you think he'll find out his own creation killed her?"

"That piece of crap won't kill her."

"Oh, but it will. This walker has thicker armor and is invisible to detection. I was planning to use it as my escape vehicle after the mission was complete, but now I have to get my sword dirty with your filthy blood."

"Please, you couldn't even nick me with the element of surprise."

"You wretch... You don't know what you cost me. Now I have to—"

Slate turned his head. "Eh? What's that over there?"

Cyphrus turned her walker and saw what had captured Slate's interest. A man had parachuted down in an ejector seat and landed on the flight deck of *Leviathan*. He now unbuckled himself and stood to face his enemy.

"No..." Cyphrus murmured. "It can't be..."

"Aw, hell," Slate groaned, sounding exhausted. "Why won't you die?"

Keito Kusanagi drew his sword.

CHAPTER 36

Straper squeezed his rifle impatiently. He had no idea what would transpire in the next hour. It would be either euphoric triumph or immense disaster. For now, he was forced to wait. Despite having minimal experience in the tech world, Straper had tried to make use of his time by attempting to access *Leviathan's* mainframe, but he was locked out from even basic functions that required no password or retinal identification. Cyphrus must have had something to do with it, he realized before deciding to give up. Now he could only squeeze his rifle as he sat hunched over in a swivel chair. Thomas observed his nervous tic with mild interest.

"Is it hard?" Thomas asked while sitting cross-legged on the floor.

Straper turned to him. "What are you talking about?"

Thomas looked at him. "Killing."

Straper stopped squeezing his rifle.

"Slate and Naomi do it so easily," Thomas said, sounding even younger than he was. "I can't imagine doing something so…"

"Permanent."

"Yeah, peppermint."

Straper smiled. "No, *permanent*. It means lasting forever."

"Oh," Thomas said, smiling back.

"To be honest, I've only killed one person besides these brainwashed guys. It was one of those pirates that attacked us on your island."

"Was it easy?" Thomas asked.

Straper let out a breath. He rubbed his forehead. "Yeah … it was. That's what scares me so much."

"It does?" Thomas whispered.

"The only thing scarier is not being useful, being a deadweight. Gilda has her walker. I got my rifle." Straper scoffed. "If I'm gonna carry it around, I need to use it, right?"

"I guess."

"Yeah, need to use it more…"

A large bang echoed throughout the bridge.

"What was that?" Thomas yelped.

"Something banged on one of the doors," Straper said, raising his rifle. "At least Naomi sealed the room before she left."

"I hope it holds," Thomas said.

Another bang sounded. This time, however, the door caved in a little.

Straper gulped. "Don't jinx it, man."

"They can't get through those big doors," Thomas said. "They can't…"

A white flash erupted from the main door. Thomas screamed and scrambled backward. The flash died immediately, having melted a hole in the door. Now a red eye peered through the hole, followed by a screech that made both their skins crawl.

"Ah, you jinxed it!" Straper cried.

***

Naomi burst through the door and stepped onto the flight deck. Her ordeal with Atlas had been tough, but her victory had given her confidence. She was prepared for anything.

Except what she found before her.

Slate, Keito Kusanagi, and a blue walker with a sword were having a three-way standoff. Naomi only took a moment to be flabbergasted, realizing that Cyphrus must be in the walker, before moving to help out Slate. No way could he fight both Cyphrus and Keito.

"How ironic, Cyphrus!" Naomi yelled in a playful tone as she strolled forward. "You despise the Western Union but are forced to use their toys."

Cyphrus swore from inside Sapphire. Not only did she have to kill Slate, but she could also end up fighting Repulsa *and* the world's deadliest mercenary at the same time. She could only be so confident in her walker.

Keito unhooked his parachute from his back. His fingers tightened around the handle of his blade as he scrutinized the Helmet Man from afar.

Naomi joined Slate. Both of them took fighting stances.

"Slate, may I ask you a question?" Naomi asked.

"Bad time for questions, isn't it?"

"I just want to know something. It's about what you said on the bridge to Cyphrus. You talked about how your friends were your salvation. Tell me, was that true?"

Slate chuckled. "Nope."

Naomi tried to suppress a smile but failed. "You're a real character. If we manage to survive this, perhaps I will go on that date with you."

"Oh, sweet! What changed your mind?"

"The fact that you're not as deluded as I thought."

Cyphrus licked her lips. Her mind rushed to think of a solution. If she made the wrong move, this could turn into a free-for-all with her in the middle.

"Sapphire, zoom in on that man!"

The image on the holographic screen magnified until Keito's face could be seen in detail. His piercing eyes made Cyphrus gulp involuntarily, but she also felt the weight lift off her chest ever so slightly when she caught a glimpse of the wireless earbud he wore.

"You work for that Ryder woman, don't you?" Cyphrus muttered. "In that case..."

Outside the walker, Naomi noticed Keito move a few inches closer.

"So, how do we get out of this one?" Slate asked her.

"I have an idea," Naomi whispered. She turned to the swordsman. "Keito, I know you're here to stop the hijacking! Well, the woman inside that walker is the one behind the attacks. The Helmet Man was framed. This woman is one of the Gifted and is using her powers to control *Leviathan* as we speak. If we stop her, we can save Paris!"

Keito made no move either way.

"Don't think he believes you," Slate muttered.

"Can't blame him," Naomi said. "The stakes are too high to make a mistake."

With time limited, the swordsman was about to make a decision before a voice spoke to him through his earbud.

"Kusanagi, are you on board *Leviathan*?"

Keito perked up, hearing his master. "Yes," he murmured.

"Kusanagi, you must kill the Helmet Man," Cyphrus said in Ryder's voice. "We are remote-operating the walker from the ground and will use it to deal with the woman."

"And *Leviathan*?"

"Our computers are almost finished hacking into its mainframe. Now, quickly..."

The swordsman gave a small nod.

Then he attacked.

And so did Cyphrus. Naomi ducked as Sapphire's sword swiped at her. It left a deep gash in the flight deck. Naomi punched the air, but the invisible attacks struck the metal armor with dull thuds. They didn't even make a dent. The walker fired bullets from its left arm, Cyphrus grinning as she willed the gun to go off. She didn't need to use the controls, not when her powers allowed her to directly interface with the machine.

"Like a glove..." she hissed.

The bullets were too fast for Naomi to stop with her mind. Instead, she dove to the right as they ripped through the deck. The sword swiped at her again, creating a gust of wind that nearly knocked her over. As she got reoriented, Sapphire raised its foot. Naomi rolled to the side right before it stomped down. The boom made her ears ring. Grimacing, she flew upward, throwing invisible blows behind her. Again, the thuds did little to deter Sapphire. Its wings snapped open. The walker soared after Naomi with its sword extended.

"Give up now, Repulsa, and I'll be sure to kill you fast," Cyphrus said to herself.

Down on the flight deck, Keito swung his sword at the Helmet Man, nearly beheading him. Slate shot bolts at him. Keito blocked them all with his sword. Slate kept shooting. Keito kept blocking. The sword was practically a blur. Keito kicked the deck, the repulsion pads on his feet activating. They propelled him twenty feet into the air. Slate fired a beam. The swordsman, however, kicked the air and flew to the left, avoiding the attack.

Keito landed on the deck in front of Slate. He wore a small grin.

"You have skill," Keito said. "This is truly a challenge."

Slate snickered. "Man, I actually liked it more when you didn't talk."

The two warriors continued their brawl.

***

Gilda flew her walker at top speed, hoping to catch up to *Leviathan*. Those enemy aircraft had kept her preoccupied for quite some time. Now she needed to help the others.

"What happened to those jets?" Gilda asked. "Did they decide not to nuke *Leviathan*?"

"It appears they crashed," Tim said.

That was both good and bad news. Slate and the others were safe, but *Leviathan* was still in the air. Gilda prayed that it wasn't too late to stop the nerve gas.

The massive ship soon came into view. As she approached, she began to make out shapes speeding around. One of them was shooting lightning at a quick-moving target hopping through the air. That was Slate, Gilda thought. Whom was he fighting? Then she remembered the swordsman who had attacked them in the Neutral Zone. Was it the same man?

Getting closer, she caught a glimpse of another pair fighting. A woman was flying upward. A blue object with a massive sword flew after her. It took Gilda a moment to recognize the blue shape for what it was.

"It's a walker!" Gilda shouted. "And it's after Naomi!"

"A flying walker?" Tim yelled. "No, it's taking my thunder away!"

"Who cares about that? We have to stop it."

"But Ms. Gilda, you have no missiles."

The blue walker made an abrupt turn. It no longer pursued Naomi.

It was headed for Magenta instead.

The blue walker fired dozens of missiles from its back. Their flight paths twisted through the air, their vapor trails doing the same, before they headed toward Magenta. Gilda cursed and flew away at top speed. The missiles stayed on her trail, despite her maneuvers. In fact, they were gaining on her.

"Tim, fire the flares!"

Ten bright flares shot out of Magenta's backside. Six missiles exploded as they hit them, but the others merely swerved around the fiery bloom and continued the chase.

"Hang on, Tim," Gilda said. "We're gonna have to try something stupid. Scan to see whether there is anyone in *Leviathan's* control tower."

Tim took only a second to complete the task. "No one is inside the control tower, Ms. Gil—wait, are you going to—?"

Gilda gunned Magenta straight for the control tower. Tim wailed as they were just about to hit it, only for Gilda to pull the walker up at the last minute.

But the missiles couldn't pull off the maneuver. They struck the control tower and detonated, blowing out windows and melting steel, the structure collapsing into a flaming heap. Even inside her walker, Gilda could almost feel the heat on her skin.

"Ms. Gilda, to the left!" Tim yelled.

Sapphire shot out of the smoke with its sword raised. Gilda dropped Magenta just in time, the blade sailing right above the cockpit. Magenta threw a punch, but Sapphire hovered backward and swung its sword down. Gilda continued to maneuver her walker away from the slices, aware of how fragile Magenta's wings were, but none of her counterblows could connect. Sapphire was just too fast. Gilda cursed as she tried to decipher its next moves.

"There!" she shouted, making Magenta throw a kick that struck Sapphire's side. Cyphrus grunted as she was shaken in her seat.

"Damn brat," she spat. "But here's a little surprise for you."

Gilda felt a shudder go through her walker's left leg.

"Tim, what was that?"

Her autopilot did not reply. Swearing, she looked out her window and saw a small black disk on Magenta's left leg, the one that had kicked Sapphire. It took a moment for Gilda to recognize the device as a transmitter that could be used to download malware into an enemy vehicle. Magenta had powerful firewalls, but if Cyphrus…

Gilda swore again. "Tim, can you—?"

Magenta abruptly turned to the right. Gilda gasped. The walker had done that on its own. She fought the controls, but they were locked in place.

"Tim, Magenta isn't responding!" Gilda screamed, helpless as her walker did a complete one-eighty. It now faced Naomi, who had been waiting nearby for a moment to intervene.

"I spot the enemy!" Tim shrieked, his voice taking a manic tone. "We're out of ammo. I'll proceed with physical assault!"

Magenta darted at Naomi, swinging one of its fists. Naomi flew out of the way, but she was almost nailed by the walker's leg. Another fist flew at Naomi. This one barely missed her shoulder. Gilda tried to regain control of her rogue walker. It continued to ignore her.

"Tim, Cyphrus is controlling you!" Gilda yelled. "Don't fall for her tricks. You're hurting friends, not enemies!"

"Oh, Ms. Gilda, I'm so sorry!" Tim cried. "I know how much you hate oxygen. Next time I'll remember! Why don't I remove that pesky particle for you right now?"

The vents started to hiss. To Gilda, it sounded like an anvil being dropped.

"No!" she shouted. "Tim, I need oxygen to live!"

Tim laughed. "Then why do you hate it so much, Ms. Gilda?"

***

Another hand reached through the door, fingers feeling for something to grab hold of. Straper shot the hand with his rifle. It pulled back, deterred for the moment.

"We can't keep back these bad boys for long," Straper said. "Crap, if only that computer worked, I could save the day."

The computer then made an unwelcome announcement.

"Tear gas dispersal in five minutes."

"That sounds bad," Thomas said.

"It is bad," Straper said. "But we've got time. Let's hope they—"

A gun barrel poked out of the hole in the door and fired continuously. Straper took cover. Thomas didn't know what to do, getting hit harmlessly with a few stray bullets.

An aerial view of the outside world could be seen on a holographic screen at a work terminal. The clouds had given away to a view that sucked the hope right out of the room. Despite the gunfire, Straper saw it from the corner of his eye. He poked his head up to confirm beyond a reasonable doubt what he had just seen.

The City of Light was visible in all its glory on the screen, *Leviathan* hovering thousands of feet above the world-famous metropolis. Straper knew from one glance that this was Paris, since the Eiffel Tower was in plain sight. Countless people would soon be gasping for air as the nerve gas took effect.

And they only had five minutes left.

CHAPTER 37

Naomi now had two attackers.

First, she had to deal with Cyphrus, whose walker darted back and forth, attempting to slice her in half. And now she also had Magenta fighting her. Worse still, she couldn't help but notice the city beneath them. Paris. They were here. Time was almost up.

The walkers weren't taking turns either. Magenta and Sapphire came at Naomi simultaneously from opposite sides. Naomi couldn't go full-out on Magenta, since Gilda was trapped inside, adding to the challenge. At least both walkers were out of missiles.

The only solution was to focus on attacking Sapphire. If Naomi took out Cyphrus, her control over Magenta would be broken, and the fight would be over.

Naomi jetted away, flying close to *Leviathan*. She tore off large chunks of the hull with her mind and threw them in the general direction of her pursuers. Cyphrus dropped Sapphire down to evade the debris. The walker even cut a sheet of metal into pieces with its sword, more out of anger than self-preservation. Magenta, however, didn't even bother dodging, letting the debris slam into it. Naomi winced. She had to be more careful not to hurt Gilda. Cyphrus had no qualms about playing dirty.

Naomi dove. She went fast, but Magenta and Sapphire had no trouble keeping up. Naomi was now flying beneath *Leviathan*, its bottom covered with repulsion pads. It made her queasy thinking about the gigantic ship that floated right above her head. The fact that it obscured most of the sky also didn't help.

Magenta descended, breaking off its pursuit as it kept far below the ship's bottom, while Sapphire did the same, even slowing down. Naomi looked back and frowned. What was Cyphrus planning? It didn't seem to make any sense.

Then she heard a humming sound above her. Terror gripped her heart. She had put two and two together, getting an obvious but frightening answer.

She dropped down, moving as fast as possible, but it was too late.

The repulsion pads were about to discharge.

The pads that kept *Leviathan* afloat increased their output, pushing the air downward. The air slammed into Naomi and almost cracked her skull like a walnut. She saw stars. Her body went limp. She began to fall toward earth.

Sapphire snatched her up from the air with one of its hands. Mumbling gibberish with her eyes half-closed, Naomi offered no resistance as the walker tightened its grip around her. Cyphrus watched her captive with amusement through the walker's window.

"I want you to truly understand your failure before you perish," Cyphrus said. "You will watch Paris die from above, helpless to intervene. Then, after I torture you for information, this walker will rip you in half."

***

It took all of Gilda's effort to stay awake. Things were happening outside. Naomi and the blue walker fighting… Magenta throwing punches… The lack of oxygen made it hard to focus. She would soon pass out. Then she would suffocate.

Gilda was barely aware of Magenta landing on the flight deck. Sapphire also landed nearby with its cockpit door open. Cyphrus peered out from within. It seemed she wanted to enjoy her victory with her own eyes.

"Only a few more minutes," Cyphrus said with a crooked sneer. Most of her makeup had come off too. There was something on her face, Gilda noticed with blurry vision. Scars or something. But it didn't matter. Not now.

"I will accumulate all!" Cyphrus ranted, raising her hands. "Nobody will stop my ascension to power. It's mine! All of it mine! You're all fools for thinking otherwise. I will become the empress of China! I will slay the Helmet Man! I will destroy the West!"

Something stirred in Gilda. Her eyes snapped open and darted around the cockpit, looking for a solution. There had to be a way to get out of this. Her eyes focused on a small box attached to the side of the cockpit. Before she could black out, she took her arms out of the control sleeves, opened the box, and grabbed the contents.

Next, she eyed the lever near her right. She didn't think Cyphrus had control over it, but it would have been dangerous for obvious reasons if she had pulled it before. Moving sluggishly, Gilda wrapped her hands around the lever.

Cyphrus snickered. "Now, Repulsa, it's finally time to ask the question that's been nagging me for some time. Why *did* you betray Cloak?"

In one swift movement, Gilda pulled the lever.

The cockpit door flew off Magenta and smashed onto the deck of *Leviathan*. Sapphire nearly fell over as the door clipped its side. As Cyphrus cried out and Sapphire regained its balance, Gilda took a large breath of fresh air. Her mind immediately sharpened. Taking off the cockpit door midflight would have been a great way to invite falling out, but that was no longer a concern now that Magenta had landed.

Raising her hand, she aimed the flare gun that she had gotten out of the box and pulled the trigger.

Cyphrus had no time to close Sapphire's cockpit. The flare struck her right in the face. She screamed, toppling out of Sapphire and crashing to the flight deck, clawing at her face. Cries of anguish escaped her throat as she thrashed about.

At the same moment, Naomi snapped back to her senses. She focused her mind on the giant metal hand restraining her and pried it open. She slipped out from its grip, landed on her feet, and pointed her hand at Cyphrus. Sapphire made a move for Naomi, but Cyphrus raised her arm with frightened eyes.

"Stop!" she told the walker. Naomi could easily cave her head in at any time. Cyphrus had no choice but to give up.

Sapphire stopped moving. Cyphrus scowled as anger boiled within her.

"It's over," Naomi said. "Your sick plans have fallen apart."

"You..."

"There's no way you could ever have succeeded. You flew too close to the sun, Cyphrus. That's what gets people like you every time."

Cyphrus shrieked. Her limbs thrashed about as if she were having a temper tantrum. The burns on her face glowed red enough to do justice to her rage.

"Why?" she cried. "Why did you betray us? You think you're better than us, better than me? You left us! You traitor! You deserter!"

"Call off the attack. While you're at it, put my friend's walker back to normal."

Cyphrus glared at Naomi, trying to figure out a way out of this situation, but came up empty. There was only one thing she could do. Seething, she placed her hand on the flight deck and sent a signal telling *Leviathan* to stop the attack.

"Attack aborted," the computer announced over the intercom, echoing throughout the ship. Naomi wiped the sweat from her brow.

Cyphrus then crawled toward the walker and put her hand on one of its feet. Magenta seemed to relax, no longer a threatening presence.

Naomi approached Cyphrus and examined her fallen foe up close.

"You asked me why I betrayed Cloak," Naomi said solemnly. "It's true that I want to become better and redeem myself, but I'm also doing this..."

She leaned down, her face inches away from Cyphrus's.

"For my mother."

Something took hold of Naomi right after she spoke, and she was unable to move. Against her own volition, she stood straight with her arms tight to the side. Gilda also found herself frozen, a wave of fear going through her. It was obvious who the culprit was.

"You killed Atlas!" Geppetto hissed. He pointed a handgun at Naomi's chest. He was hunched over, still hurting from being slammed into the wall. He stood far away from Naomi so he couldn't be knocked over with her powers like last time.

"Geppetto, kill them!" Cyphrus spewed. "Do it now!"

"You killed him too," Geppetto spat at Cyphrus. "After I woke up, I saw the security tapes. You injected Atlas with those nanobots, your own comrade."

Cyphrus gritted her teeth. Tears of frustration streamed from her eyes. She never should have given him access to the ship's computer. It should have just been her and her alone.

Geppetto pointed his gun at Cyphrus. "You're all going to die! Atlas was like a brother to me, the only one who made me feel like I mattered. Nobody takes that away from me. You hear me? Nobody!"

Before Geppetto could even consider pulling the trigger, one of Magenta's arms swung around and hit him from behind. He flew forward and hit the deck with a thud, knocked unconscious for the second time today. Naomi and Gilda found themselves free of Geppetto. They calmed their pounding hearts and got their heads back in the game.

"Oh, I'm so sorry for before!" Tim cried. "Please, Ms. Gilda! Forgive me!"

Gilda smiled. "All right, sheesh. I think you made up for it just now."

Cyphrus tried to take advantage of this distraction by slipping away, but before she could, a steel cable came to life and wrapped around her. She squealed.

"Can't kill you just yet," Naomi said, a hand raised as she tightened the cable with her mind. "I have to make sure you really did stop the attack. If *Leviathan* so much as launches one canister of nerve gas, I'll snap your neck myself."

Cyphrus wriggled on the deck like a worm. "Filthy little tart! You were always an insolent child, Repulsa!"

Naomi sighed. "Sisterly love..."

"Hey, I hear something," Gilda said.

Naomi raised her head. She heard it too. It sounded like an alarm of some sort.

"What did you do?" she asked Cyphrus. "Need I break a few bones?"

Cyphrus turned pale. "This isn't my doing! I'm as ignorant as you."

"Then find out what it is, and no funny business."

Cyphrus scowled. Touching the deck with her cheek, she closed her eyes, connecting with *Leviathan*'s computers once more. It was difficult for a normal person to conceptualize how her mind processed all that data. For Cyphrus, the information just seemed to fall in place.

"Well?" Naomi snapped.

"Give me a moment! The computers are behaving frantically. It's hard enough deciphering all this without you—" Cyphrus paused. Her face went slack. "What ... that can't be! Don't tell me they're not functioning anymore?"

"What's not functioning?"

"We–we need to get off *Leviathan*! Right now!"

***

"Attack aborted," the computer repeated.

Straper would have kissed the holographic screen if it had been tangible. Too bad he was still being shot at. He did manage, however, to access the security camera feed as the bullets flew overhead, since Cyphrus no longer impeded his efforts.

The screen displayed an image of three men holding automatic weapons. The remaining brainwashed crewmen were all trying to break into the bridge and seize control of *Leviathan*. A gun still fired at them from the hole in the door. Even worse, the enemies kept ramming their bodies with unnatural finesse against the door, making visible progress as the metal bent inward. Straper figured he had five minutes at most before those freaks broke through.

Red strobe lights began to go off above their heads, accompanied by a blaring horn.

"Fantastic, what now?" Straper asked, shooting at the door again. One of the bullets managed to go through the hole and hit the enemy shooter in the arm. The gunfire stopped, and the barrel poking out the door disappeared. On the screen, Straper saw one of the men move back from the door, replaced by another with an even bigger gun.

"Attention. Sudden discharge has shorted out forty percent of pads," the computer said. "*Leviathan* is unable to maintain lift. Descent is imminent. I repeat, descent is imminent."

"What does that mean?" Thomas asked.

The entire ship shuddered, followed by an unnerving decrease in a humming noise that they had all gotten used to.

This was followed by the sensation of falling.

Straper gripped the console near him. Sweat poured off his face.

"It means we're gonna crash..."

CHAPTER 38

"We're going to *crash*?" Thomas exclaimed.

Straper wasn't able to comfort him, still taking cover behind a row of consoles, taking potshots at the door in an effort to keep the enemy back. It wasn't working, but he had nothing else to try, and he also had to deal with the ever-increasing feeling that he was falling. *Leviathan's* unexpected descent was getting noticeably faster.

"Do something, Straper!" Thomas yelled, grabbing his jacket. "You're smart! You can fly this big ship, can't you?"

Straper shook his head, doing his best to keep his cool. "Even if Cyphrus isn't controlling the ship anymore, I don't think I can!"

"Try anyway!" Thomas cried. "Please, no one else is here!"

The barrel sticking out of the door started to hiss. Straper's face went pale as he recognized the weapon.

"Flamethrower!" he yelled at Thomas. "Get back!"

Fire spurted out the barrel, bright orange and deadly hot. Its reach was so long that it almost licked Straper's boots. He scurried backward, out of the flame's reach for now. Sensing the smoke, the sprinklers went off, drenching them. A few computers spat sparks. Paris grew in size on the holographic screen. *Leviathan* was barely a thousand feet above it now.

"I think I gotta get to the master control station," Straper said. "That's where you steer the thing, but it's on the balcony in front of the commander's chair."

"Hurry, Straper!" Thomas yelled, his hair dripping.

Straper shot another look at the balcony. The stairs were the only way to get to it, but the stream of flame coming from the flamethrower was blocking it. His ears popped, which reminded him how desperate their situation was.

Then he had a thought. It shamed him immediately, made him realize his hypocrisy, but it was the only idea that had a chance in hell.

"Kid, block the door!" Straper paused. "I mean, if you aren't able to—"

Before he could finish his sentence, Thomas dashed toward the door. He raised his hands, screaming as he ran into the inferno.

"Wait!" Straper cried. "I didn't mean it!"

The prince, however, kept running. His clothes caught fire, but no harm came to him. Straper's horror turned into amazement. The kid truly was invincible.

Thomas made his way to the door. He used his body to cover the hole, blocking the flame. The fire curled around the prince, trying to eat through him, but it was no use. He wasn't budging anytime soon.

Straper knew this was his chance. Leaving his rifle behind, he sprinted for the stairs, passing Thomas. He made it to the stairs and climbed up until he reached the balcony. Straper sat in the commander's chair and started typing on the holographic keyboard in front of him. He could feel himself becoming more weightless by the second.

"Computer, start the autopilot!" Straper yelled.

"Autopilot damaged due to shortage," the computer said.

Straper looked at the sprinklers and growled. "Damn, what else is there?"

A steering column rose out of the floor. Straper's jaw dropped. Two handles folded out from the control column, emphasizing the point.

"I'm gonna have to steer this thing..." Straper told himself.

Leviathan lurched downward, freefalling for a moment. Straper almost fell out of his chair, but he grabbed the armrests before he could. The ship slowed its fall some. The blood rushed to Straper's head, making him lightheaded.

"Hurry!" Thomas yelled from below. "We're falling faster!"

Not dawdling any longer, Straper grabbed the handles, a holographic screen of the outside world appearing before him. At least not all of *Leviathan's* repulsion pads were broken. More than half still worked, but not enough to slow their descent. If they hit the ground, it wouldn't be pretty. This ship was the size of a city block and had nerve gas on board. Crashing would mean killing a lot of people. Straper had to find a way to slow *Leviathan* down or at least crash it where it wouldn't do so much damage.

"Computer, get the repulsion pads that still work to … uh … discharge when we're … ah … fifty feet above the ground," Straper said.

"Doing so would destroy all hovering capabilities," the computer warned.

"I know, you piece of crap! Just do it."

Straper turned the steering column and felt *Leviathan* lurch to the right. This thing didn't turn on a dime, but he did have limited control.

Down below, Thomas kept his body in front of the door, but the flames had stopped. As an added bonus, the sprinklers stopped too.

Straper took a quick look and felt like clapping. "At last, some good luck!"

A large hand came out the hole and grabbed Thomas's arm.

"Help!" he cried, trying to pull himself free.

Straper scowled but knew he couldn't leave his seat. Instead, he took out his handgun, aimed carefully, and fired. He managed to shoot the appendage over twenty feet away from his high vantage point. The hand retracted, letting go of Thomas, who sprinted away and took cover behind a console.

Leviathan went into another brief free fall for a second. Straper's heart almost jumped out of his throat. He didn't know what to do. Where should he land this gigantic ship? His eyes scanned the holographic screen as he took in the layout of Paris. He needed to find somewhere deserted for *Leviathan* to break its fall.

His eyes settled on a good candidate.

The Seine, the sizable river that ran right through Paris, was the best possible place to land. It was practically a water runway. Straper didn't know if the river was wide enough for this monstrous vessel. He didn't even know the river's name. But now wasn't the time to be picky.

"Buckle in, kid!" Straper shouted to Thomas, taking his own advice as he strapped himself into the commander's chair. Thomas did the same with a workstation chair, which was bolted to the floor before a console. Straper changed *Leviathan's* course, steering it to the right. He wanted to line himself up with the river.

"Object in flight path," the computer said. "I repeat, object in flight path. Recommend immediate course change."

Straper shot a look at the screen and tried not to smack himself in the face. How could the cameras not see the wrought-iron structure blocking their way until now?

Leviathan was going to hit the Eiffel Tower.

"Fricking France!" Straper screamed as he turned the wheel hard, willing the flying hunk of junk to go around the tower. They were already turning pretty tightly, but now Straper had the steering column twisted as far right as it would go. On the screen, the tower went out of view. For a brief moment, Straper relaxed. Had they made it?

Leviathan jolted to the side, shaking everyone. Straper grimaced and fought to stabilize the ship again. After a long second of uncertainty, he got *Leviathan* back under control. The ship settled down, as did Straper's heart. He glanced at the screen and saw the rearview image. The top of the Eiffel Tower was taken off, leaving only a jagged stump with girders jutting out every which way. Straper winced at the sight. He hoped nobody had been in it, but he pushed the thought out of his head.

"Straper!" Thomas screamed. "There's something coming through the door again!"

Straper looked at the door. What could be worse than a flamethrower?

Oh, a rocket launcher. Much worse.

But there was nothing he could do about it. Straper could only hope those brainwashed attackers would take their time. He got *Leviathan* in line with the river. Straper tensed up, bracing for impact.

Straper felt the ship slow down. The repulsion pads had just performed their last discharge. He could now make out the old buildings and monuments lining the river. He quickly prayed that everyone had been evacuated.

Now they were right above the water. This was going to be a snug fit. Straper had no doubt they would be skimming the banks of the river.

Straper started to scream. Thomas did the same as he clutched his armrests. *Leviathan* hit the water.

***

The Helmet Man had to get off.

After they had smashed into the Eiffel Tower, he had flown away from Keito at top speeds, abandoning the fight with the swordsman.

"My cue to skedaddle!" Slate shouted.

Keito, however, followed him, kicking the air so he flew upward. Glancing down, Keito witnessed as *Leviathan* made a rough landing in the Seine.

But this changed nothing. The duel would continue.

Keito increased his speed and continued his pursuit of the Helmet Man.

***

Magenta hovered above the City of Light. Gilda sat in the pilot seat, witnessing the carnage that *Leviathan* left behind, while Naomi floated next to the hovering walker. They had made a difficult decision. They had decided to abandon ship, hoping that the others would take care of themselves. There was no way they could have gone to the bridge and back in time. Both of them looked at the scene below, silent and fearful.

Leviathan plowed through the river. Waves smashed against the stone banks and even flooded into the streets of Paris. The ship also rammed through multiple bridges. Chunks of rock crashed onto the flight deck. *Leviathan* also crushed the abandoned boats that had been left in the river during the evacuation. Nothing in its way remained intact. It left behind a massive trench filled with water, an ugly scar that desecrated the vibrant city.

"My dream…" Cyphrus said. "My dream… I was supposed to become the empress of China… I was supposed to have my revenge… Now it's… now it's…"

"Hush up," Naomi said, levitating Cyphrus and Geppetto next to her. She had taken them with her in case *Leviathan's* crash happened to be a part of some plot, but judging by Cyphrus's reaction, it seemed her lack of involvement was genuine. Not even an actress like Cyphrus could fake that kind of dejection.

Gilda couldn't believe any of it. What made it worse was the fact that Straper and Thomas were on board that crashing ship, being shaken until they couldn't take it anymore. All she could do was grit her teeth and pray they would live.

***

Straper focused on steering as best as he could, but it was a nearly impossible task. He was being thrown to and fro, the seat belt digging into his flesh. A wretched screeching filled their ears, made by *Leviathan* scraping against the stone banks and the riverbed. Thomas squeezed his eyes shut. They were jostled whenever *Leviathan* hit a bridge. Straper felt like he broke a rib every time the straps dug into him.

Meanwhile, the rocket launcher went off, but the brainwashed victims had flown backward when they crashed, taking the rocket launcher with them. It was no longer aiming through the hole. The rocket hit the floor instead and exploded in a bright burst of heat and shrapnel. All the puppet crewmen died, consumed by the explosion. A pillar of fire erupted from the hole in the door and went upward, almost scorching Straper alive, but he was too busy spewing out a stream of curses and obscenities to notice.

The last remaining turbine was in full reverse, attempting to slow the ship. It did little good at first but soon started to have a noticeable effect against the massive ship's momentum. *Leviathan* was slowing down. Straper and Thomas soon ceased their screaming. Thomas opened his eyes, his heart slowing. The screeching faded away. Sparks stopped flying. *Leviathan* made one last lurch forward. Then it ceased moving altogether.

After the traumatic ordeal, the ship had come to a complete stop.

A few seconds of complete quiet went by.

Then Straper began to laugh. "Okay, forget what I said earlier. I'm *totally* pulling my weight around here."

***

"It stopped," Naomi said with relief.

Gilda felt her muscles melt into jelly. It didn't seem as if the main body of *Leviathan* had been that badly damaged. Straper and Thomas were most likely safe.

"What now?" she asked Naomi. "Do we rescue the others?"

Naomi was about to answer when a rush of air knocked her aside. Sapphire soared past her, snatching up Cyphrus and Geppetto. Gilda cursed. The walker must have flown off just before *Leviathan* crashed and circled around to rescue its master.

"Let's go after her, Tim," Gilda said.

"Don't bother," Naomi said. "She's no danger to us anymore."

"What? She killed thousands! We can't let her go."

"*Leviathan* is down in an evacuated part of the city. It couldn't properly disperse the nerve gas now even if ordered to. Cyphrus won't risk continuing the attack either. She doesn't want us going after her, and I don't want to corner a rabid dog. Besides, we need to go help the others and get out of here before the Western Union shows up."

"But if we let her go, she might try something like this again."

"I wouldn't worry about that," Naomi said, watching as the blue walker disappeared into the horizon. "After all, the Chinese Empire does not forgive."

***

"We're almost there, Ms. Ryder," the pilot said. "Are you sure about this? The nerve gas could still leak out at any time."

"The threat is over," Ryder said. She stared out the unicopter window with blank eyes and her hands folded in her lap. "All that is left is to deal with the Helmet Man."

The pilot chuckled. "Well, if there's someone for the job, it's you, Ms. Ryder."

Camilla Ryder did not respond to the compliment. She only stared out the window, absorbing the destruction below, taking in the wreckage and smoke of Paris. She imagined all the bodies that could have been lying there. Even so, plenty of ruin remained. Blood did not run down the streets, but mayhem still prevailed.

The Helmet Man had caused this. Ryder knew this to be an absolute truth. That reckless beast would trample over everything in his way. It was in his nature. It was his destiny. Ryder knew this to be an absolute truth as well.

Her heart began to pound. She grabbed her chest.

"Please hurry," she told the pilot. "I need to ... land."

CHAPTER 39

Slate didn't like being on the defensive.

He liked being the first to strike. It made things that much easier for him because he was able to finish fights faster. Average people didn't stand a chance against him.

But Keito wasn't average.

And he had just made Slate go on the defensive.

Keito swung his sword. The Helmet Man caught it before it could slice off his head, careful of the sharp edge. Both of them hung in the air for a moment, a hundred feet over Paris.

"No way I'm gonna die above this fruity city," Slate told himself. Sparks came off him. He began to pour all his energy into the blade. He had been waiting for Keito's sword to become fully charged. When they had fought in the Neutral Zone, a cartridge had been ejected by Keito's sword. Naomi had taken it in hopes of figuring out what its purpose was. Later, on the sub, she figured out the cartridge's function. In the process, she also found out how Keito was able to block Slate's bolts.

The cartridge inside the sword's hilt was filled with positively charged material. Slate's energy was attracted to it. However, the cartridge would stop being positively charged after absorbing enough electrons, becoming useless. The backup cartridge would only last a short period, giving the swordsman just enough time to change out the primary cartridge. Keito most likely got this technology from the Western Union in an effort to level the playing field.

For the entire fight, Slate had been waiting until Keito needed to change out his cartridge. Now he had a firm hold of the sword and wasn't planning on letting go until it was filled to the brim with his energy. Then he would take Keito out.

The swordsman, however, had other plans. He pointed his legs at Slate and kicked forward, the pads on his feet sending a shockwave into Slate's gut. The Helmet Man curled up in pain, but he didn't release his grip on the sword. Instead, he flew down toward the ground. Keito was also dragged along. Shaking off the surprise, Keito twisted around, causing both of them to spiral out of control as they fell. Keito shifted his weight, putting Slate between himself and the ground. He was going to make Slate break his fall.

But the Helmet Man pointed his feet at the ground. A blue glow surrounded his legs, arcs of energy flying off them. A beam of energy shot out of his feet. It was unfocused and erratic, but it slowed their descent.

"I'm a footsie grandmaster!" Slate declared.

A red light began to blink on Keito's sword handle. He glanced at it and yanked his sword back. Slate lost his grip on it, despite his best efforts, and cursed.

Both of them landed on the ground in front of a large glass pyramid surrounded by three smaller pyramids. Slate and Keito didn't know it, but they were in front of the Louvre, the world-famous museum that contained some of the finest artwork ever created.

Keito had his back to the glass pyramid as he fiddled around with his sword handle and took out the cartridge. Slate knew this was an opening. He fired a beam. It hit the pyramid, exploding it into a thousand sharp pieces. Shards of glass rained down over the courtyard. Some of them bounced off Slate's helmet.

"All right, where'd you go, jackass?" Slate growled, stomping over to the shattered pyramid, searching for any sign of the swordsman. Keito had disappeared. But where to?

The sword swiped at Slate, grazing his arm. Slate groaned as his blood dribbled to the ground. Keito was in even worse shape. His flight suit was torn to shreds, and small cuts covered his body. One big shard was even lodged in his shoulder.

Keito didn't seem to notice or care. He just attacked again. The sword moved too fast for the naked eye to see, but Slate sensed every stroke, ducking and jumping out of the way. The Helmet Man soon had his back to the broken pyramid. There was a gaping hole in the ground where the pyramid once stood. It led inside the museum.

Slate decided he would try to lose Keito in the building and jumped down the hole. He landed on a tiled floor covered in broken glass and found himself in an immense lobby, which was currently vacant due to the evacuation order, as was most of central Paris. Keito jumped in after him. Slate sighed at the swordsman's persistence and flew for the nearest hallway, entering the Louvre. Keito followed close behind, keeping up by using his repulsion pads to accelerate. The floor cracked wherever he kicked, leaving a trail of small craters in his wake.

They went up a couple floors until reaching a level where numerous paintings hung. Many of these works of art were hundreds of years old. The museum staff had rushed to clear the museum of its most priceless pieces, such as the *Mona Lisa,* and secure those they couldn't take, but the military had forced them to leave before the task could be completed.

It was a mistake they would pay for dearly.

"Hey, found some ammo!" Slate grabbed a few paintings as he flew by and hurled them at Keito, hoping it would slow the swordsman.

It didn't. Keito swung his sword and knocked the paintings out of his way, slicing some in half. One after the other, he managed to cut through a dozen masterpieces.

"Whoa, no respect for art!" Slate yelled.

Flashes and blurs were all any normal observer would make of the fight that followed. Slate and Keito danced through the hallways, blocking and striking at each other. They made it to a large window, which Keito broke with the back of his sword. They jumped out of the museum and landed in the courtyard below. Slate kept shooting and Keito kept swinging as they exited the museum grounds and entered the city. Lightning struck abandoned cars. Beams annihilated storefronts. The Helmet Man flew up, shooting downward. In response, Keito bounded up after him with his repulsion pads.

And so it continued. They lost all sense of time. Swords swinging, helmet blocking, beams shooting... It all seemed so fast, yet so deliberate. Neither stopped fighting until they found themselves on top of a massive stone arch, the Arc de Triomphe. Far away, unicopters were approaching, heading for the crash site of *Leviathan*.

Slate and Keito faced each other, both near their limit. Keito was visibly panting. Slate slouched, unsteady on his feet. This fight would be over soon. They both knew that. What they didn't know was who would come out on top.

"You just won't give up," Slate said. "This is stupid."

"No, this is struggle," Keito told him. "We both wish to see how far we can go, how much we can take, how much we can grow. Do you wish to give that up?"

"Good point. How could I say no?"

The Helmet Man lunged at Keito. The swordsman raised his weapon, determined to stab Slate in the neck. Instead, it skidded off Slate's helmet, not even leaving a scratch. Slate wrapped his arms around Keito, and both of them tumbled off the Arc de Triomphe. As they spun through the air, Slate unleashed his energy into Keito's torso.

The two of them hit the concrete, bones breaking in the process.

Slate now lay on the ground with his arms splayed out. Blood leaked from his wounds. The Helmet Man didn't move for an entire minute. Then he got on his feet and staggered toward Keito. The swordsman's fingers twitched. He was unable to move. He knew for sure the Helmet Man was coming in for the kill.

Slate stood over his defeated opponent, chuckling. "Is this how you plan to grow?" he asked with amused agony.

Keito was still breathing, but it was becoming irregular, his eyes unfocused. "I ... I thought ... losing ... would be ... unbearable..."

Keito passed out. His heart stopped beating.

The Helmet Man turned away, planning to fly out of there.

But something kept him back. Not something physical. It was a feeling. He turned toward Keito again. Again, he considered leaving, but the feeling just wouldn't stop.

Slate grumbled. He pointed downward. A bolt came out of his finger and hit Keito's chest. The swordsman started coughing, the bolt restarting his heart. Keito was alive, but he was in no condition to fight anytime soon.

"Don't feel like killing you," Slate said. "You're just doing your job, and you didn't kill my sidekicks when you had the chance. I also want to see how much you'll have grown the next time we fight. Who knows? By then, maybe I'll have grown a bit too."

A blob struck Slate on the arm. He jumped in surprise. The blob was deep violet in color and stuck to him like chewing gum on a shoe.

"Ah, get this stuff off me!" Slate cried, shaking his arm. He sent electricity into the blob, but it didn't even singe the sticky substance. Where had that come from? If he hadn't been so injured, he likely would have sensed the shooter already.

Another blob hit him in the leg. Knocked off-balance, Slate fell flat on the pavement and was now stuck to the concrete. More blobs came at him. Two hit his remaining limbs, while another struck his neck. The blobs didn't stop coming until he was rendered completely immobile. These blobs also prevented Slate from using his electricity, insulating the Helmet Man. It was futile to struggle. He was pinned.

Camilla Ryder approached the scene with a tubelike gun in her hands. She had shot the blobs at Slate from a distance while he was busy talking to Keito. No emotion showed on her face as she knelt beside the Helmet Man. She examined him with empty eyes.

Slate tried to shrug, the blobs restraining him. "What? What did I do?"

"I never thought I'd get this close to you," she said. "This is ... this is..."

She pressed her face right against Slate's head, stuck out her tongue, and licked the smooth surface of his silver helmet.

Slate stopped struggling. "What the ... oh ... oh, my! You're moving a little fast. Maybe we should slow down!" But his tone suggested otherwise.

Ryder curled up on the ground next to him. Her eyes quivered.

"You…" she whispered. "You make me feel…"

Unicopters landed nearby. Armed soldiers poured out of them.

"Secure the area!" one soldier shouted. Another soldier ran up to Ryder but came to a halt when he saw her expression, or lack thereof.

"Uh … ma'am, are you okay?" the soldier asked.

Ryder was in the fetal position. "You … make me feel…"

***

Mao raised his club.

But he never had the chance to bring it down on Eisenhorn's head. A bullet ripped through the prime minister's shoulder. Mao squealed. His club hit the floor. The general stared at the club, relief flowing through him, knowing that driver had almost caved in his head.

Mao staggered backward, falling on his rear, gasping. Over a dozen guards came bursting through the door of his apartment. They all held automatic weapons.

But they weren't aimed at the general.

They were aimed at Mao.

"What is the meaning of this?" Mao demanded, covering his bullet wound with a shaky hand. His face was already pale from the blood loss.

"Allow me to elaborate," Chao Xing said. He strolled into the room, smiling. A giant black ball rolled next to him. It seemed Mistress Lotus had also decided to gloat.

"Xing…" Mao hissed. "You dare act against *me*? You dare harm the heir to the imperial throne? Your prime minister? Your next emperor?"

Xing ignored Mao and knelt beside Eisenhorn.

"About time you showed up," Eisenhorn said. "What took you?"

"Sorry, but it took more time than expected to get confirmation," Xing said.

"What are you blathering about?" Mao spat.

Xing stood back up, smoothing out the wrinkles in his suit. "Oh, nothing…

General Eisenhorn merely assisted us in thwarting an enemy of the emperor."

Eisenhorn chuckled. He reached into his shirt and ripped out a wire.

Mao's eyes widened.

"Electronics aren't allowed," the forsaken prince whispered.

"An exception was made," Mistress Lotus boomed. "I almost died in the Neutral Zone over your petty squabble with Cloak. Now I find this..."

"How dare you talk back to me, creature! A brain in a jar has no right to judge me."

"How shameful," Xing said. "You insulted our emperor and even claimed to kill men who look like him for amusement. Truly depraved, Prime Minister. No one is allowed to commit such offenses, not even you."

The guards grabbed Mao's arms and lifted him up.

"Xing, you deceiver!" Mao screamed. "My father will not forgive you!"

"Oh, but the emperor has already overheard your conversation with Eisenhorn," Xing said. "He is very displeased."

"He won't be fooled!" Mao shouted as he was being dragged away. "I am the son of the emperor. You can't do this to me. Lily, stop them! I command you!"

"My daughter no longer works for you," Mistress Lotus said. "You have abused the power of the Black Lotus for the last time."

Lily, who hadn't said a word during the entire ordeal, merely shrugged.

"You cannot do this to me!" Mao shrieked, on the verge of hysteria.

"Don't worry," Xing said. "You'll have plenty of time to think about what you've done in the Traitors' Garden."

Any remaining color left Mao's face. "No... No... Not that... Please, not that!" He struggled against the guards' grips. "Forgiveness! I demand forgiveness!"

Xing tsked. "Oh, Mao... Have you forgotten our motto already?"

The guards took their prisoner from the room. Mao Long refused to stop shrieking.

After they left, Eisenhorn sat upright and rubbed his head. "I did what you wanted, and I got my keister handed to me because of it. Shu better not be in trouble, right?"

"Her failure to protect you from the assassin will be forgiven," Xing told him.

"How thoughtful," the general snorted.

"Although you may not care, you managed to remove a dangerous man from a position of power. I thank you. The empire and the world will be better off for it."

"Yeah, whatever." Then something clicked in his head.

Klara...

"I want my old room back too," Eisenhorn demanded.

Xing nodded. "I will see what I can do."

Eisenhorn nodded. If all went well, he could get his hands on that syringe hidden in his room, just as Klara told him to. Why shouldn't he? He owed and trusted her.

Even so, he wondered what would happen if he did inject himself.

***

Straper and Thomas each took a deep breath as they stepped onto *Leviathan's* flight deck. They had made it. They were free. And it tasted good.

Magenta and Naomi landed close by. Everyone gathered, relief flooding through them. Naomi embraced Thomas, who returned the favor. Straper nodded toward Magenta with a grin. Gilda smiled back and gave him a salute. They were all here and safe.

Except for one...

"Where's Slate?" Naomi asked.

"I think he ditched the ship," Gilda said over her walker's intercom. "Keito must be giving him a harder time than we thought, but I'm sure he's fine. He is Slate, after all."

"So, what now?" Straper asked. "Do we vamoose?"

Naomi smiled. "You better believe it."

"Freeze!" a voice shouted.

Dozens of soldiers surrounded them. They wore green uniforms and aimed their weapons at the group. Unicopters hovered above and walkers lined the shores.

A large yellow walker was also on the flight deck.

"Got you punks cornered!" Hank Powers yelled. "You kids and your hot nanny thought you could get away with that attack on Rome, did ya?"

Straper shook his head. "We're trapped. Not good."

Thomas ran up to Naomi and grabbed her leg. Naomi and Gilda stayed silent, both trying to figure out how to escape this situation.

"By the authority of the Western Union and the French government, you're under arrest," Powers said. "You in the walker, get out now! The rest of you get on your hands and knees. Any tricks and we'll blow you away."

"No tricks," a cold voice said. "But there are certainties."

Incognito floated out of *Leviathan's* deck. He was in his usual getup and held a scythe. Everyone looked as though they had seen a ghost. They might as well have.

"Not you again!" Powers cried. "Damn, I've got the worst luck!"

"And with certainty I know this," Incognito said. "You will not catch us."

"Everyone, grab him!" Naomi shouted.

The soldiers were too stunned to stop them. Magenta rolled over next to Incognito while Naomi and the others grabbed Incognito like he was a lifeline.

"And I also know this," Incognito finished. "The West *will* fall."

"Stop right there!" Powers yelled, raising his cannon.

But it was too late. Incognito touched Magenta and phased into the deck again. The others all sank with him, becoming ghosts themselves. The soldiers did not know how to respond. Only Powers reacted in any overt way.

"Running away a second time, I see! A phoney, that's what you are! Nothing but parlor tricks. You took one look at this walker and shriveled up in fear. Phoney!"

The other soldiers weren't so celebratory. They had once again let the world's most wanted terrorist escape.

But at least they caught the Helmet Man.

CHAPTER 40

Cyphrus didn't know how long they had flown, but it felt like at least an hour. They were no longer above Paris. Endless green fields sprawled out below them. She shifted anxiously in her cockpit seat as she kept her eyes on the walker's sensors for enemy aircraft. The Western Union hadn't caught them yet, since Sapphire was invisible to radar, but Cyphrus had no idea how long this luck would hold out, especially given her recent track record.

Geppetto stirred in her arms, still unconscious. Cyphrus didn't know what she was going to do with him, but he was all she had left. Tears ran down her face. She had failed. There was nothing left but to wallow in despair. The Chinese would hunt her down. Once they caught her, they would vivisect her and put her organs in separate jars like the ancient Egyptians did to their pharaohs, forcing her to watch as they did. This was not wild speculation. The emperor was known for doing this to those who—

Cyphrus cried out. Her limbs had seized up.

Geppetto's eyes snapped open. "*You...*"

With no will of her own, she slammed a pedal with her foot. Sapphire did a sudden nosedive, still several hundred feet above the ground.

"Stop it!" Cyphrus screamed. "You'll kill us!"

"Good."

The walker pulled up just as it reached the ground, but they crashed, none-theless. The cockpit window smashed into a thousand fragments. Geppetto flew from Cyphrus's arms and out of the walker. He rolled across the grass until coming to a stop. His ears rang for a moment before he worked up the strength to stand on his own. Blood dripped from his forehead. His shoulder throbbed. Geppetto got up and saw that Sapphire had crashed several yards away. Smoke rose from its crushed body. A few sparks spat out. He limped to the front of the walker, only to see Cyphrus's limp body hanging out of the cockpit. Her neck was twisted at an unnatural angle that made Geppetto wince, despite his loathing.

"Ah!" she cried. "I ... I ... I can't move!"

"Well, I ain't using my powers right now. Looks like you're crippled."

"I can't move my legs! Geppetto, help me!"

"Cry me a river," he spat, taking a switchblade from his coat pocket.

A choking sound came from her throat, followed by another sob.

"Maybe you could have gotten fixed up," Geppetto said, moving toward her. "Medical technology these days is fantastic. But you killed Atlas. That's something I will *never* forgive. Selfish hag... You really do only care about yourself."

"No!" Cyphrus cried. "We can still be happy!"

"We could have, but that ship sailed the moment you stuck those needles in Atlas."

"Spare me, Geppetto! Oh, please! Not you too!"

Geppetto was now next to her. He raised his knife. Cyphrus cringed. She had only one chance. Her limbs might not work, but her powers did. Maybe Sapphire could still crush Geppetto with its arm. Maybe she could—

A dart hit Geppetto's neck. He pulled it out with minimal interest. Then his eyes fluttered as he collapsed for the third time that day.

Cyphrus screamed. She tried willing Sapphire to move. It shuddered before spitting out more sparks and moving no more. Another dart came, this one burrowing into her own neck. She tried to shake it off, but the drugs had already taken effect. She felt herself slip into unconsciousness. Her misery faded into one bad dream.

Minutes later, a truck rolled up next to them. Poppy, the Black Lotus agent, stepped out. He poked at his victims with a rifle to see if they were awake. They weren't. He surveyed the scene to make sure he hadn't missed anything. It was a needless precaution. His misshapen eyes were cybernetic implants, better than any human's. Nothing escaped his sight.

He opened the back of his truck and threw in his two captives. He also put IVs in their arms to make sure they stayed asleep and tied them up for added measure. He injected Geppetto with even more drugs. This was to ensure that Geppetto, should he somehow wake, wouldn't have enough focus to use his powers.

After closing the truck, Poppy got in and drove off, headed for a nearby harbor where a stealth ship waited. From there, he would make the long journey back to China.

"Be sure to make these foreign devils suffer, Father," he muttered to himself in Mandarin. "It is the only talent you still possess..."

****

"I was beginning to doubt you," Redwood said. "But you and your team managed to save millions. You also avenged Hynes and the thousands who perished in Rome."

"Keito Kusanagi was the one who stopped the attack," Ryder said. "He's recovering in the infirmary now. He sustained those injuries for the sake of the Western Union. I believe he deserves better than to have his achievements overlooked."

"Well ... the government thinks otherwise. People want to see a blonde warrior save the day, not an Asian man, especially considering our tense relations with the Chinese Empire. Can't say I'm too happy about it myself. But you're a hero now, Ryder. That means photo ops and interviews, which also means you got to smile."

"Then this will be my most difficult mission yet."

Redwood chuckled. Then he stopped, his own smile fading.

"Ryder..." he began. "When the soldiers found you ... ah ... you appeared to be crying on the ground next to the Helmet Man. I'm ... not sure what happened, but I would feel better if you had a psych evaluation and went on leave for a while."

"I refuse."

"That's not a request."

"Let the hero do as she wishes," Powell said, walking into the hangar. His personal crony, Vincent Quinn, trailed behind him with a smirk.

"Sir, it's not safe in here," Redwood said, raising his hands. He may not have liked Powell, but with the president dead, he needed to be kept safe. "Please, leave now."

"Why? It looks like he's contained. In fact, I want a moment alone with the prisoner. Everyone except Quinn leaves."

"Sir, I must insist on more adequate precautions."

"Get lost. Don't make me ask again."

Redwood frowned. He left the room, followed by Camilla Ryder.

Once the doors closed, Powell began to laugh.

"It's been some time, Helmet Man."

Slate didn't respond. He just hung from his restraints, limp and unresponsive. There were two beach-ball-sized gray spheres covering his hands, which were connected to the ceiling by tethers. Any time he tried to charge up, the energy was diverted through the spheres and up the cords. Another tether tied his feet to the floor, preventing him from swinging around. He was naked except for some baggy shorts and his silver helmet.

Powell patiently waited for a response. The Helmet Man remained silent. For a second, Powell thought Slate might be dead, but then he heard a constipated voice.

"You got fat," Slate said. "And bald too. Seriously, do some crunches in the morning. You're one step away from a heart attack."

"Mind your manners," Quinn said, reaching for his gun.

"Easy there," Powell told his subordinate. "Let the baby have his bottle. It's the last one he's going to get for a long time."

Slate raised his head. "So, you're the vice president now? You came a long way from babysitting a bunch of super-kids."

"I would have been president a long time ago if it weren't for all the trouble you brats have caused me. One of you goes on a rampage, the others revolt and create a criminal organization, and then you and that Incognito team up to become terrorists. Thank the Almighty you freaks won South America for us, or I'd be out of a job."

Slate started fake crying. "Boohoo, get over it! You were always a greedy turd. That clearly hasn't changed over the years. Someone like you would make a lousy president."

"I beg to differ."

"So, are you just here to rub in your victory?"

"Yes, that's why I'm here. This is the price you pay for siding with that scythe-wielding loony, but I also came here to thank you."

"You're welcome."

"You killed Hynes for me. That's something I can never repay."

"You could start by letting me go."

"I didn't say I *wanted* to repay you. I knew letting you on *Leviathan* was a good idea. Because of you and Cloak, Hynes is dead and I'm on my way to becoming president. Of course, I helped a little."

Slate seemed much more alert after this revelation. "Wait, you *helped* Cloak?"

"After my spies discovered the plot, I managed to cover Cloak's tracks," Powell said, grinning like the Cheshire Cat. "Then I had nerve gas put on board to make sure the military shot *Leviathan* out of the sky. I didn't think Cloak would use the gas. Oh, well… Life goes on, though not for those people in Athens."

"Thousands are dead."

Powell shrugged. "That's not my problem. They should have run faster."

"When I bust outta here, I'm gonna smack you to next July."

"*If* you bust out of here. You will be of much use to me until then. A lot of valuable research was destroyed when you supersoldiers ran amok. Studying you will be of great help to the Western Union. Maybe we can even use you to take down Incognito."

Powell waved goodbye and started walking out of the room, followed by

Quinn.

"Powell, get back here," Slate growled. "We ain't finished."

Powell looked back at Slate with a gleam in his eyes. "That's President Powell to you."

***

"Get out of my way!" Gerald Marker cried, trying to push through the guards.

"Sir, we can't let you pass," one guard told him.

"It'll just be for a second! Please, let me through!"

"Hold on there, gentlemen," Powell said, walking down the hall with Quinn.

The guards stiffened. "Sir, Secretary Marker has been trying to get past us for some time. We were tempted to remove him."

"Relax, I'll handle this," Powell said. He stopped beside Marker and put his arm around the man's shoulders. "Hey, Gerald, let's talk somewhere else. I'm sure we can address whatever grievances are eating you up."

Marker was hesitant to leave, but Powell wouldn't have it any other way, pushing him gently yet firmly down the hallway.

A few minutes later, Marker found himself inside one of the USS *Liberation's* sparse equipment rooms. Powell stood in front of him while Quinn guarded the door.

"Gerald, what's happening?" Powell asked, putting his hands on Marker's shoulders. The secretary of defense was a mess. His hair was tangled and greasy, his suit was wrinkled and dirty, and his face had gone pale, with dark circles under his eyes. Marker was also shivering, almost vibrating, from sheer anxiety.

Marker gulped. "Powell..."

"Call me Harold," Powell said, smiling like a caring father.

"Harold..." Marker whispered, tears dripping from his eyes. He reached into his jacket and held something out to Powell.

It was a gun.

"The ... the Helmet Man ... I ... I want to kill him... He killed my son..."

"I know."

"You helped me get revenge before," Marker said, dropping his gun to the floor as his hands went limp. "You got me in contact with that assassin so we could kill Eisenhorn. But it didn't work. Eisenhorn is still alive. But the Helmet Man is here. If you could just give me a moment with him, I could shoot him ... in the chest. I don't care if I go to jail... I promise I won't say anything about you."

"Shush now," Powell said, embracing Marker. "I understand."

Marker was sobbing now. He buried his head in Powell's shoulder.

Powell's expression grew dark. "Yes, I understand all too well."

Before Marker could reply, Powell grabbed the secretary's head and snapped his neck.

The body slumped to the floor. Growling, Powell kicked it.

"Idiot! You almost ruined everything."

Powell took a deep breath, regaining control. It had to be done. Marker had left him with no choice. Not only had he tried to kill the golden goose, but Eisenhorn was almost injected with the trigger when he needed to be stabbed to death. Powell had given Marker specific instructions, and still he managed to foul the job up. If that syringe had been used...

"Quinn, get some rope," Powell ordered as his lackey slipped into the closet. "We'll make it look like the poor man hung himself. He had such a guilty conscience, what with him trying to kill General Eisenhorn."

"Sir, I've been meaning to ask something," Quinn said, unfazed by Powell's actions.

"Shoot."

"It's about Eisenhorn. Why did you convince Marker to try to kill him, and why did Hynes even send Eisenhorn to China in the first place?"

Powell had to laugh. "Hynes wanted to avoid war at all costs, but the Chinese Empire is not what you would call reasonable, so Eisenhorn was sent as a last resort. Should the Western Union fail to make peace with the Chinese, we would use Eisenhorn to kill the emperor and everyone else in the Forbidden City. Of course, we had to 'dismiss' the previous ambassador before we could replace him with Eisenhorn."

"Oh? How could Eisenhorn possibly destroy the Forbidden City?"

Pointing at his own temple, Powell made an exploding sound with his mouth. "Because Eisenhorn has a bomb in his head," he said. "The man who tried to assassinate him was the trigger man. When the time came, he would inject Eisenhorn with a substance that would set off the bomb and destroy everything within a one-mile radius. Obviously, the trigger man had no idea he would be blowing himself up. Only a few people were aware of all the details of this operation. Not even Redwood or the other military leaders knew."

"Hynes used his own comrade as a suicide bomber," Quinn mused. "Guess that explains why Eisenhorn wasn't pruned after the Helios Tower incident. Probably didn't want to set the sucker off by accident. But why this crazy plan?"

"The president was desperate. Although Eisenhorn isn't dead, the trigger man is. We can safely assume the bomb in Eisenhorn's head won't be used anytime soon."

"Hold on. I don't understand your motivation. If you killed Eisenhorn, it would only make war with the Chinese more inevitable."

Powell gave him a look that was not quite sane. "Exactly."

CHAPTER 41

Powell kept his face somber as he stood on the podium. The imposing flag of the Western Union waved behind him, the US Capitol Building acting as backdrop. Thousands of citizens waited in anticipation for him to begin his speech. Lines of cameras focused on Powell's face. This was his inauguration. This was his ascension.

"Citizens of the Union, I greet you all! I wish this were a happy day, but I cannot lie—it is not. President Hynes, along with ten thousand other people, lost his life in the attack recently perpetrated by the United Third. We also lost more than seven thousand military personnel in an act of sabotage near the Neutral Zone. Again, we believe the United Third to be responsible for this incident."

The crowd was silent, far too silent for its size. A few bowed their heads in respect, but most were transfixed by Powell. Across the Western Union, millions, if not billions were watching, mesmerized by his words.

"But after further investigation, we have determined that the United Third was not acting alone in carrying out these atrocities."

For dramatic effect, Powell paused a moment before continuing.

"We believe that the Chinese Empire is secretly funding the United Third in order to cause instability throughout the Western Union."

Almost the entire crowd gasped. Everywhere around the world, the news spread like a contagion. The enemies of freedom were working together to topple all that was right. How could it come to this?

"I was deeply shocked to hear this news," Powell said, pretending to wipe away a tear. "We always knew the Chinese were unpredictable, but never this ... coldhearted."

Powell slammed the podium with his hand.

"Well, I've had it!" he bellowed. "We've tried the route of peace, but Emperor Long and his cretinous lackeys have refused to see reason. Now they have struck us, hurt us, and made us fear for our very survival. Do you wish to cower under the bed as their billion-man army marches forward until this red horde engulfs the world in war and turmoil?"

The crowd murmured. They didn't like the idea one bit.

"I for one will not let that insidious madman and his imperial rodents swarm over our lands and consume everything within sight!"

A few in the crowd began to nod, while others shouted, "He's right!"

"That is why, in my first act as the president of the United States of America and head of the Western Union, I declare war on the Chinese Empire!"

The crowd went berserk, raising their fists in outrage. They had lost their leader. Their sense of safety was gone. They wanted answers. They wanted justice.

And Powell would give it to them.

Several people in the crowd pointed to the sky. A blue walker hovered above for a brief moment before descending and landing behind Powell. A sword extended from its hand and pointed toward the horizon. Sapphire had been recovered and repaired just in time for this declaration. Twenty gray walkers drove up and lined up in a row behind Sapphire. The formation was complete. The grandeur of the display entranced everyone.

"We've managed to take down the Helmet Man," Powell said, not even acknowledging the walkers behind him. "Incognito will be beaten next, followed by Emperor Long and anyone else who stands against us. Rome may have fallen, but the West will rise!"

The crowd exploded, punching their fists in the air, chanting the Western Union anthem. The noise was deafening. The gray walkers fired blanks as Sapphire continued to hold its sword high. The crowd cheered harder. Powell, like a sponge, soaked up their cries. The collective submission of his people only fed his ego. He had a stern yet noble look on his face. It took all his self-control not to grin.

It's finally happened, he thought.

World War III had begun.

***

"World War III," Straper said, hoping that saying it out loud would help him cope.

It didn't.

Gilda, Naomi, Straper, and Thomas all sat in a small room with stone walls and wooden chairs, waiting for the axe to come down. Thomas sniffled, but he made no real noise beyond that. Gilda fidgeted in her chair. Straper sometimes talked to himself. Naomi only sat there, contemplating what the future held.

They hadn't left this cramped space since their ordeal on *Leviathan*. They had been given food and water, and there was a small bathroom in the corner. They were also given pills to counteract the radiation poisoning they got when traveling with Incognito, although nausea was the least of their problems.

The room was deep underground, within the same catacombs that housed the United Third's headquarters, near where Gilda and Straper had trained for months. They had just received word that the new president had declared war on the Chinese Empire. Nobody knew how to react, mostly because they were preoccupied with two other horrid realities.

First, Slate had been captured. Without a doubt, the Helmet Man was the center of their group and a reliable source of strength. Gilda felt empty knowing that Slate was being held in some Western Union prison, likely being tortured.

The second horrid reality was Incognito.

The door opened. Everyone jumped.

A voice spoke.

"*Swine...*"

Incognito entered, and the door closed behind him. The blade of his scythe glinted in the dim light. His eyes weren't focused on anything in particular, but they did glisten with malevolence as he paced around their chairs.

Thomas began to cry, covering his face with his hands. Straper was shivering so hard that he almost fell out of his chair. Sweat poured off Gilda as she gripped the seat of her chair until the wood cracked. Naomi, with large and frightened eyes, couldn't look away from Incognito. Gilda knew from Naomi's expression that their lives were hanging by a thread. They had angered Incognito. They had disobeyed him. They had ruined his plans. And, perhaps the greatest of all their trespasses, they had made a fool of him.

"After dissecting the corpses of Hynes and the others, the Western Union has managed to create a vaccine against the nanobots," Incognito said, his scythe swinging right past Straper, who whimpered but didn't dare move. "The war has already begun, thanks to you fools. I wished to start this global conflict at the time of my own choosing. Alas, my plans must now be put into effect faster than anticipated, and to rub salt in the wound, Slate has been captured. Yes, things are looking bleak indeed."

Incognito stopped pacing and turned to the others. His stare penetrated them.

"As punishment for your failure, I will let Slate rot in jail for one year."

Almost everyone had the same reaction, which was to gape.

Gilda, however, did not respond that way. "You can't do that!" she screamed, forgetting her fear. "He's our friend. You need him. The Western Union will only get more powerful if they study him. Do you want that?"

"That is a risk I'm willing to take," Incognito said.

"We can't let them have Slate! I'll rescue him on my own if I have to."

Incognito seemed to vanish, but he had actually moved faster than the speed of sound. He appeared before Gilda. Before she could gasp in surprise, he backhanded her. She fell off her chair and hit the floor. Blood dripped from her mouth. Straper and Thomas both jumped up to try to help her, but Naomi raised her hands, stopping them. If they intervened, they would only incur Incognito's wrath too.

"I've had it with your tongue," Incognito spat, putting the cold blade of his scythe to Gilda's throat. "Perhaps I should remove it."

"Stop it," a new voice interrupted. "You've made your point."

Incognito froze and snapped his head toward the door. A man with a scraggly beard and light brown skin had entered the room. He was elderly but also in good shape. He wore jeans, a Hawaiian shirt, and ratty-looking sandals.

Gilda, still on the floor, turned to see who had come to her rescue.

"Who ... who are you?" she asked.

The old man chuckled. "Forgive me. My name is Oscar Radcliffe. Like Incognito, I used to be a Keymaster."

Gilda's breath stopped in her throat. Incognito's eyes narrowed. Everyone else was still putting two and two together.

"You mean..." Gilda whispered.

"That's right," Oscar said. "I'm Slate's father."

***

The tea had gone cold over an hour ago, but Katelyn scarcely noticed. Over the years, the queen's hair had turned gray, the lines in her face deepened, and the sorrow in her heart grew. She now sat in an armchair in a dimly lit study. Rarely did she venture outside anymore. She had long ago lost the drive to do much of anything. Food had lost all taste, music no longer raised her spirits, and she avoided engaging in conversation with anyone.

It had all begun with the loss of her family.

As she sat in her chair, a vacant expression etched on her face, her eyes wandered over to the table next to her. She then noticed something was out of place. Reaching over, she picked up a small note she hadn't seen until now.

It read, "Keep quiet. Tell no one."

Katelyn turned to the table again, where she found a metal ball the size of an orange. She recognized it. It was a portable hologram projector, an advanced model by the looks of it.

The queen reached over and picked up the projector. She thought about summoning her guards, but a compulsion caused her to do otherwise.

Katelyn pressed the small button on top of the ball and dropped it.

The projector floated in midair, glowing bright. An image started to flicker around the ball until it became a solid projection of a person.

It was a young boy.

"Hello!" the boy greeted her. "I know we have never met before, but Naomi told me to do this because it'd be nice. Sorry that I can't meet you in person. At least you can see me this way. I still don't know how all this holo-stuff works, but it's pretty amazing. I forgot to say, my name is Thomas. Naomi said that I'm your son."

Katelyn almost fainted.

"I just want to tell you that I'm all right," the boy said. "You can't tell anybody that I'm alive, though, okay? I've got a boss now, and if he found out that I'm a prince, he might ... uh ... kill me? Sorry, I don't know much about all this death stuff either."

Tears began welling in Katelyn's eyes. Was this some kind of cruel joke? No, it couldn't be. He looked too much like her late husband to be a fake.

"I don't know if I'll ever get to see you for real," Thomas said. "Naomi said maybe someday, after our boss is dead. But don't worry about me. I have friends. They're all really nice. Well, except for Slate, but he's pretty funny. Oh, but he's not here anymore. Don't worry. We'll rescue him. I can't say much else, because I'd be in big trouble. Okay, I'm running out of time, so I'll just say that I really want to meet you one day, and I wish I could have met my dad. I heard he died trying to save me. Please, don't be sad. I'm sure you are a great mom. I just hope I get to see you in person. Okay, bye!"

The projection turned off. The ball dropped to the floor.

And so did Katelyn. She picked up the projector and cradled it in her arms. Her son was alive. He was alive all along. She still had family. She wasn't alone...

Today was truly the best day of Katelyn's life.

EPILOGUE

The moon stared down at Cyphrus.

That was the first thing she saw as she woke from her drug-induced slumber. The moon. It chilled her to the bone. The next thing she saw was a statue. It looked so familiar...

Her eyes snapped open. Her grogginess evaporated in an instant. Now it was all too obvious where she was.

The Forbidden City.

Two guards in red uniforms dragged her by the arms. She had been stripped naked and could not move her body. Gazing up, she saw the palace that housed the emperor. The guards were taking her through the Traitors' Garden. As they reached the last row of the statues, she saw one that looked newer than the others. Gagging on her fear, she could not help but recognize the resemblance.

It had the face of Mao Long.

The prince was trapped in there, deprived of all sensory input, barely kept alive by the tubes that ran inside the statue and into his orifices. Cyphrus could make out an audible scream coming from within the statue and almost puked. Would this be her fate as well? She would rather die. At least death was clean.

"Let me go!" she screamed. "I am to marry the emperor! I am your future monarch! You dare handle me this way?"

From the corner of her eye, she noticed Lily leaning next to a doorway. The cyborg gave her a sadistic wink before laughing herself silly.

"So long, old lady!"

Cyphrus screamed even harder. Her captors didn't bother quieting her down. With blank faces, they merely dragged her to the throne room.

When they finally dropped her before the throne, Cyphrus was literally sobbing until she shook, coughing on her own tears. Next to her was Geppetto.

He had also been stripped and was still on the drugs that impeded his concentration, preventing him from using his powers or even having an intelligible conversation. Geppetto looked beaten, his head lowered in shame, his small body wrinkled like a prune. Cyphrus bit her lip. How could they fall so low?

They weren't alone, however.

"So, how did the mission go?" Sebastian asked with a grin. "Not too well, I assume."

Anger overtook Cyphrus. He was in no position to be mocking her. Sebastian was a prisoner, just like her. The Chinese must have somehow found their yacht and captured him. He had also been stripped, now wearing nothing but chains and a blindfold concealing his eyes. However, despite his humiliating state, his petulant grin remained.

"No speaking unless you are spoken to," Xing said. The hairless man stood next to the throne. Imperial guards lined the walls and stood in front of the doors. There were almost five dozen of them, all armed with swords and machine guns. Cyphrus wondered in desperation if she could use her powers but realized the futility of it. This palace was devoid of technology.

Emperor Jin Long himself was planted on his throne, looking and smelling worse than ever. His mad eyes scrutinized the Gifted before him.

After a full minute of quiet, the emperor threw up some words.

"You have failed," Xing translated. "Not only that, but now we are at war far sooner than any of us ever predicted. Perhaps the greatest loss is that the Western Union has already managed to obtain a vaccine against the nanobots and given it to all their leaders. The weapon is worthless now. The emperor, in his infinite kindness, gave Cloak a second chance to redeem itself after its failure in Japan, but his kindness was wasted on fools."

Xing now stared at Cyphrus. "What punishment should we give you? The emperor believes we shouldn't send you to the Traitors' Garden."

Cyphrus sighed, her makeup almost gone from all the sweat and tears of shame. Now both her scars and nakedness were plain to the men before her. But it didn't matter. Not anymore. She had lost. There was no point. But perhaps she could die quickly.

"No," Xing said. "He wants your end to be much more painful."

Cyphrus gulped. Geppetto only shivered.

Sebastian, however, just laughed.

Xing and the emperor didn't react. The guards, unlike them, stiffened and pointed their weapons at Sebastian.

Sebastian got to his feet. The chains that had been restraining him clattered to the floor. He brushed the invisible dust off his bare shoulders, still smiling.

"I didn't think I'd get to meet the emperor so fast," he said. "Most convenient. Everything hasn't exactly gone according to plan, but I can work with it."

"Arrogant words," Xing said. "What makes you so confident?"

"Oh, no, you got me all wrong," Sebastian said. "I'm absolutely helpless right now. Killing me would be an easy chore. All I'm doing is waiting."

The emperor examined Sebastian but didn't feel the least bit threatened. He raised his bony hand. The guards readied their guns, prepared to blow Sebastian away.

"Waiting?" Xing asked. "What are you waiting for?"

Laughing even louder now, Sebastian raised his arms before him.

"Why, for the Mentor!"

The throne room doors blew inward. Yellow light streamed through the doorway. The guards reeled back. Xing jumped in front of the emperor. Not waiting for orders, the guards shot at the light, hoping to quench it.

They could not. Beams of light erupted from the illuminated doorway, burning through the torsos of four guards. With smoking holes in their chests, the men collapsed.

While the guards were preoccupied, Xing whipped out a small handgun from inside his jacket. Before he could use it, Sebastian ran at him, knocked the gun out of his hand, and kicked him in the head. Xing fell and lost consciousness.

Cyphrus, still lying at the foot of the throne, strained to see what was happening, but she could only see the harsh light. There were gunshots and screams. Geppetto spun around. His heart stopped dead when he gazed toward the doorway. The blood drained from his face. Small shivers rattled his body. He tried to scream, but only a whimper came out. He fell to his side, unable to comprehend the monstrosity that approached them.

The emperor was becoming agitated. He squirmed in his chair and commanded his servants to come to his aid. This was the first time in decades that he had felt fear, a true primal urge to flee. He started coughing as he tried to rise out of his throne but only managed to fall out of his seat of power and tumble to the floor.

Sobbing, Cyphrus didn't notice that the gunshots had stopped.

So had the screams.

Fifty bodies lay behind her, many riddled with cauterized holes. The light dimmed. There was something emerging, something coming into the throne room.

Once again, Sebastian began to laugh. "This is it!" he cried. "Bear witness to my Mentor's Temple!"

Cyphrus was inconsolable. All the events of her life swept through her thoughts, tearing apart any bit of sanity left. Everything she had ever experienced, ever done, or ever stood for was corrupt, worthless, nothing. She had nothing now.

No... No, she had something.

She had her Mentor.

Her tears stopped running down her cheeks. Something was behind her. A cloak.

The black material tickled the nape of her neck. There was a symbol stitched in red.

It was the Omega.

She could feel where the blade had cut her so long ago. The same symbol had been etched into her face nine times, disfiguring her. All the makeup in the world could not cover the truth now, the insanity that stood behind her, that bloodred horseshoe on the cloak.

The cloak sheathed a being of incomprehensible malice. It grabbed her by her hair and pulled Cyphrus to her knees. She had no more tears, just the inescapable reality, the one that had suffocated her ever since she was born.

A gurgling laugh escaped the emperor's lips. He dragged his decrepit form across the floor, drawn to the hate.

"Men..." he wheezed. "Men..."

Sebastian continued to laugh, but it now held a hint of helplessness, as though he could be consumed by the inferno at any moment.

Temple grabbed Cyphrus's throat. Intense heat radiated off his hand. Gazing up, Cyphrus had one last revelation.

"The Mentor..." she said. "The Mentor ... is real..."

Light burned through her neck. Blood gurgled from the wound. Her bare arms spread as though she was trying to fly away. But she did not want to escape this. This was the only way. This was the way she was meant to die. This was the way her suffering would end.

When Cyphrus gave her final shake, Temple dropped the corpse.

"Mentor..." the emperor wheezed, coughing and laughing so hard that blood came out of his mouth. "Mentor ... Mentor ... Mentor!"

Emperor Jin Long grasped Temple's foot, giggling out of control. Sebastian fell to his hands and knees, sobbing with joy as his amusement turned into mania.

Temple reached down and dipped three of his fingers into the blood that had begun to pool around the naked cadaver. He then marked himself with his red fingers, streaks of blood blemishing his silver helmet.